The Death
of William Posters

The
Death
of
William
Posters

ALAN SILLITOE

New York: Alfred·A·Knopf
1965

L. C. catalog card number: 65–18751

THIS IS A BORZOI BOOK,

PUBLISHED BY ALFRED A. KNOPF, INC.

FIRST AMERICAN EDITION

Part One

I

ALL AFTERNOON Frank Dawley walked across the Lincolnshire uplands. Grey cloud corrugated the sky and deadened the sound of his feet on the metalled road. His mind had changed with the landscape since leaving Nottingham, surprising him at times by its breadth. A dog-wind snapped at the back of his head. The country was bleak, hilly and monotonous, and he had no reason for walking along that particular stretch of narrow road.

Journeying was cheap. The sale of his car had enriched him by four hundred pounds which he had split and spun out at ten a week for himself and ten for Nancy – rather than be shoe-horned into another job. He left his suitcase at his sister's and set off with a small rucksack, walking, or hitching rides along whatever road suited him. Sometimes he would wait for a lift and, seeing a car coming from the opposite direction, would walk across and thumb that, set off north before south, east instead of west, all decisions meaningless now that he had made the great one of his life. One leg took him from Reading to Manchester, with a TV producer in a jungle-green Jaguar, which Frank also drove and so got him there in half the time by steering through the night, after a beano dinner at some typical English pub with Spanish waiters – coffee, brandy and a skittle-shaped cigar to follow, which this TV bloke said would go on expenses, so drink up and let's blow town, he added, trying to imitate Frank's life. Blinded with drink; Frank wasn't, so let him sleep in the back while he, glad to be at the wheel after a fortnight on foot, took them steadily north through wind and drizzle, the radio playing softly the Fly-by-night Favourites for nomad boozers. He felt light and free, so quick moving and empty of all responsibility and the black care of a working life that he expected a flashing light to flag him down, a copper's voice on the beam-end of it barking for his passport and licence and laughing in his face that it was too good to last. But even his passport was in order, the first official document he had ever voluntarily applied for, on whim six months ago, for no reason but just in case, as important a secret to keep from his wife as if he'd got another woman to warm the other cold half of his life. It was a blue book, new and empty of foreign stamps, the first book in his life he had bought which wasn't a paperback, and he didn't begrudge the price of twenty-five bob, but merely wondered what impulse had forced him to buy its so far useless bulk.

When tired of lifts he wandered along lanes and minor roads, revelled in the smell of fields subsiding under dew and mist, the drift and tread of dead leaves, the steaming semi-circle of cows staring him out as he sat a few minutes on some gate to eat bread and meat.

A limpid watery sun shone through, livened the grass, and waterdrops fell from branches as if melted like wax by the faint warmth. He walked on, only memories taking over the space of dominant sensual impressions. This made him look as if walking somewhere, though there was no objective in his mind. There was too much to slake off as yet. He was just

10

above middle height, with grey eyes, and darkish hair that gave a sallow and tough appearance to his face. A fairly high forehead when he thought to brush his hair back denoted intelligence, though not the assurance of using it properly every time it was called for. A short white fishbone scar had stayed above the left eye after a pop bottle burst there as a kid. It was the face in which a smile would be giving too much away, betraying the deadpan working-man exterior consciously maintained. Stern, it was fenced up to stop things coming in and going out, often with little success due to an exuberance over which he had little control.

Walking along black midnight roads, off the main trunks where cars were scarcer, ready to tramp all night and like it, the wound of his separation from Nancy reopened. He had often considered packing up his life with her but never imagined it would be on a Saturday afternoon. Such a day made it more sure and permanent. If you walk out on Wednesday you are back by Friday. If you pack up on Friday you walk into work on Monday like a zombie and clock in, going home in the evening for your tea as if nothing has happened. If you leave on Tuesday it's only a joke, a bit of bluff, but in the cool dead hour of Saturday afternoon it's almost like cheating it's so serious.

Walking up the path, he had turned in towards the back door, and thanked God no one was at home. There were so many baby and doll prams thrown by the step that it looked like a bloody cripples' guild. The five-year rage that had led to this had deserted him; yet it had left him so cool at last that his purpose was inflexible – so inflexible that he distrusted it. Even his heart wasn't beating faster than normal.

Apart from the good clothes on his back he was surprised at how few he had. They hardly filled the case, and two were bulging when he first came. All the less to carry away, he saw. I'll get rid of the car and travel light, nothing I can't

11

pick up in my own two hands. He looked along his row of books: *Camp on Blood Island, Schweik, Sons and Lovers, War of the Worlds, Dr Zhivago* – to pick out the best, books he had read and enjoyed but finally didn't trust. *Lady Chatterley's Lover* should have been there, but he'd thrown it on the fire in anger and disappointment.

Under the bookshelf was a pile of all-sort records. He was going to look through them but didn't because he'd leave the gram for the kids. The paperbacks looked derelict, forlorn in his bedroom where he wouldn't sleep any more, possibly the only things in it that would draw his thoughts there now and again. It was easy to shed leaves out of a thriller from way back. Held over the fireplace, its guts fluttered down, loose enough to make a fair body of flame when he put his lighter to it. Unwilling to see the flame fold up its yellow wings and die in this cold cage of a grate, he split another volume, tearing pages quickly to keep the fire on the upreach, his hands warming at the work and heat, hardly aware of what they were doing. Satisfied when all were burning, he closed his suitcase, and turned to carry it downstairs.

'Where the hell do you think you've been all night?' Nancy wanted to know, standing in the doorway. His eyes stung from the paper smoke, lips hot and dry. It was hard to answer, but he'd lose no time over it once they moved from the head of the stairs. Her tone changed to one of solicitude for herself, the kids, for him, on seeing his case: 'Where are you going, then?'

'Let's go down,' he said, moving by and soon half way to the living-room. She called after him: 'What have you been burning?' A picture swamped her, of him tearing up their wedding photos, snapshot albums of outings with the kids, marriage certificate maybe, papers and souvenirs that had held them together by more than flesh. 'What did you do that for?' she cried, following him. 'You didn't need to do that.'

12

He stood in the hallway. 'I didn't burn anything of yours, or ours. I can't put up with things any longer. I've got to go.'

She stood also, still in her coat, her pale face unable to show the thousand expressions crowding behind its façade like corroding moons. They looked at each other. Instinct told him to run, but he was somehow unable to move as long as she was without speech. 'I don't understand it,' she said. 'Honest. I don't understand. I knew this would happen though, when you didn't come home last night. Why did you make me wait all day before I was sure?'

'I got back as soon as I could.' Their voices were as closely matched by the twin tones of brevity and desperation as their bodies had often been in the timing and rhythms of love-making. He thought of himself making love to her – on a long summer afternoon when the kids had been packed off to her sister's, and even when there had been no kids – but such memories were dead, nothing left. 'Where are you going?' she asked, not out of curiosity, but to keep him longer in the house. It was as if they were talking on the edge of a thousand foot cliff in a gale. She was afraid of the emptiness he'd leave, and he was afraid of the emptiness he would fall into. 'Don't cry,' he said.

'I asked where you were going,' she snapped.

'What difference does it make? I don't know.'

'Well, I've got to know. I'll want money from you every week. You don't think I'm going into a factory to keep *your* kids, do you?'

'I'll see you're not short.'

'You're always ready with the money, I will say that. Money cures everything, don't it?'

'What do you want me to do? Chop off my legs and leave 'em behind? If it's finished it's finished. Or maybe it's only me that's finished. I'm twenty-seven and I feel like sixty.'

'I don't know what you mean. I don't think you do, either.'

'Maybe not. I'm off just the same.'

'I hope you enjoy it.'

They stood like two armless people under the short claymore sentences chopping across each other, dry, painful and cutting deep. 'I suppose you've been fed up with me, as well, lately,' he said.

'I was fed up with you five years ago. But I'm not like you. I thought: "We're married, and as far as I'm concerned, that's that. This ain't what I thought it would be like at all, not what the stories and magazines or my own mind led me to believe, anyway, but here it is, this is life." That's what I thought, and it didn't take me long to get to it.'

'I can just hear your mother saying that. "You made your bed, now lie on it." It must have made her happy to say it. But I'm not going to be the one to lie for good on the bed you've made. Nor on the one I've made, either. It's finished, I tell you.'

'Don't keep saying it, then. And don't call my mother. She's not here to answer back. It's a good job for you as well, or you wouldn't be getting off so light. She helped us a lot when she was alive.'

'I'm not getting off anything at all. I wouldn't even bother to argue with her if she was here. I can never argue with people I hate. I just want to get away from them.'

She laughed, and he felt bitter because it stunned the fact that he really wanted to explain things. They stood, unable to walk back from each other, attracted and held like two magnets in a field of iron filings. Their thoughts struggled towards unity of expression, but found it as difficult as if buried deep under a mass of twisted metal, pinned hard, stultified and killed as soon as the desire for release became known. They had lived together too long to produce explanations that either would in any case believe.

14

He picked up his case and opened the door, walked out of the house for good, a departure so quick that he later reflected that it must have left her with an appalling undying bitterness. He went along the path, a lighter tread than when he came in from work every evening. The gate slucked, instead of the backdoor rattling. His footsteps got quieter, instead of him walking gruffly across the kitchen to hang his grease-stained cap, mac and knapsack on the hook, before swilling his face at the sink and sitting down to tea and kidnoise.

He stood, leaned on a gate, head down and roaring like a muzzled bull before the shambles. It was a black road, with no moon to help, no stars to goad him on. If his legs hadn't suddenly and for no reason gone on strike against walking, the wound would not have burst. Immobility was still his death. It wasn't that he had regrets, wanted to go back and wallow again in the bitter salt and honeycomb; but he was roaring at blind solitude surrounding him, at a hermit-like future pulling him in and boding little for his own good. He wondered how long he could go on living through various days and black nights before being drawn into the pit of another job, bed, and life even more null and commonplace than the one that he didn't yet know in any respectable language why he had left.

Autumn was no time for travel, certainly, hitch-hike, pushbike and footslog, but he was cursed by the St Vitus zig-zags – and who looked at a calendar before running from a long and painful suffocation? He'd intended making his way slowly around the country, but free transport winged him beyond this speed. His skill at driving often shortened each lift in time, and his gift talk also made a long drive shrivel, the road a spinning discarded umbilical cord lost in bad weather between green fields and sunken crossroads. England was tiny, he'd always known that, but the proof of it in getting from one side to the other in a day gave him the delirium trembles and the kennel-mania shackle-fits. In a fortnight he'd been up to the Lake District, dipped into Cornwall, bounced against Wales, and sped over the flat ditch-crossed Fens between Spalding and Wisbech; hypnotized on the beach near Grimbsy by long shimmering febrile blue-black waves speeding at even pace up the immense zone of sand – each one following the other as if to get out of reach of the deep sea where they might drown. Dogger Bank and the Rhumba-Humber, a North Sea cloud spat in his eye and drove him over on the ferry to Hull, as if 'Bill Posters will be prosecuted' were written on every blade of grass and white sea wave and he was William himself on the run even beyond cities.

All through the twelve years of his factory days and the years of his marriage he had brooded and built up the Bill Posters legend, endowing the slovenly Bill with the typical mentality of the workman-underdog, the put-upon dreg whose spiritual attributes he had been soaked and bombarded with all through his school, home and working life. Frank had fought them off, being like him in no single way at all. Yet the Bill Posters ethos hung around him like a piteous and dying dog and, being so hard to throw off (he sometimes wondered whether this would ever be possible until he kicked the bucket himself) made life more deep and harrowing for him. It was difficult to get rid of him precisely because his sympathies were in the right place, and because the conditions that made Bill Posters still persisted. In some big way Bill Posters had also been responsible for his exploding out of life so far, leaving wife, home, job, kids and Nottingham's fair city where he had been born bred and spiritually nullified. Yet it wasn't so easy, and on buses and foot he was often cast back into those barren streets to dwell upon the predicament of that man who had a firm place still in his heart.

Poor Bill Posters. Everywhere he was threatened with prosecution. The alarm had been raised for him. The whole
16

country, it seemed, was after him, had been for years in fact, certainly for as long as Frank could remember. He must know no rest, for they were still out to get him, painting his name big and square at every corner, and threatening prosecution. What had he done? Frank had always asked, and nobody would ever say, so it was bound to have been something serious and shameful. He had never seen Bill Posters, but pictured Bill as if he'd known him well, almost like a cousin; saw him as he'd seen him even as a kid of six just learning to decipher those words of menace, as a fairly tall thin man of twenty-seven, thin faced and wearing a threadbare unbuttonable jacket as he hurried, looking from left to right, along the street and round a corner – dodging his everlasting evertrailing prosecutors. Bill was always in a hurry, travelling furtively, travelling light, an unwrapped piece of bread in his jacket pocket which he sometimes munched at as he went along. Sometimes not as much as that to keep him going, maybe only the smell of an oil rag and even that was rancid.

But the great and marvellous thing was that they never got him! Bill had been on the run from birth and was more than a match for his persecutors. They could write his name on every street corner, but they'd never catch Bill – hurrying always one street ahead of them, or perhaps even behind, for he was clever and must have his moments of triumph as, from behind a newsagent's shutter (the sublime light of underprivilege spreading a smile over his good-natured and cunning face) he watches them painting his name big on some massive wasteground wall: BILL POSTERS WILL BE PROSECUTED – just wanting to burst out laughing yet too smart to give himself away.

He feels a lot as he watches his name being spread out in public. Bill Posters has been infamous in these streets for generations, bandit Posters, as well known or maybe scorned and scoffed at as Robin Hood, justly celebrated in that hundred verse 'Ballad of Bill Posters' recited for generations in

17

Nottingham streets and pubs. There's been a long line of William Posters, a family of mellow lineage always hoved-up in some slum cellar of Nottingham Streets. His existence explains many puzzles. Who was General Ludd? None other than the shadowy William Posters, stockinger, leading on his gallant companies of Nottingham lads to smash all that machinery. In any case didn't Lord Byron make a stirring speech in the House of Lords about a certain William Posters sentenced to death in his absence for urging a crowd to resist the yeomanry? Who set fire to Nottingham Castle during the Chartist riots? Later, who spat in Lord Roberts' face when he led the victory parade in Nottingham after the Boer War? Who looted those shops in the General Strike? No one has ever proved it, but the ballad sings of it, and historians may make notes for future conjectures. To those who don't think much about the present upholder of the Posters race he is half-forgotten, invisible, or completely ignored, but those wags and sparks whose hearts he lodges in sustain that image, keep his furtive ever-enduring figure alive as it flits at dusk or dawn down slum streets from one harbouring district to another. The fact that he is never caught indicates the vast population of his friends, and the one sure sign that he is never taken off by the cops is that his name is always being painted afresh on some wall or other. His enemies, though, are equally numerous, and it is even harder to say exactly who they are than his friends. Everyone knows Bill Posters is one of us, and everybody knows that his enemies belong to the people whose emissaries come with pots of paint and describe the fact, legally on some chosen wall, that Bill Posters is going to be prosecuted. Why are they so persistently out to get Bill Posters once and for all, to nail both name and man to the flagpole of that arse-rag, the Union Jack? To write so publicly and often the fact of Bill's impending prosecution must mean that they had mountains of evidence against him. All of it was false, of course.

18

Maybe if he hadn't been persecuted, Frank thought, he'd have turned out a different man, been a bloke like me who'd got a job at a factory and worked every week for fifteen quid or so. He might have been a good worker for the union and, who knows, in time become a big official – Sir William Posters 'today went to confer with Beeching, Ford, Robens and Nuffield with regard to the General Strike called for to-morrow by his caucus of unions. According to the *D. Worker* Sir William maintained that he wanted a minimum wage of twenty pounds a week for all workers, as well as a communist government of six hundred and forty deputies to be chosen by him and sent to the House of Commons. Great cheers from all the workers'.

'Don't call me Sir William, lads. I shit on the Sir. Call me Bill – Bill Posters as I was born and bred.' Comrade Posters, party boss, in his cloth cap and big topcoat as he inspects blast furnaces and power stations. 'Good old Bill. We've got what we want now.' Until an aeroplane flying over one day, skywrites high up in the blue: 'No you haven't. BILL POSTERS WILL BE PROSECUTED.'

Mostly the people who gave Frank lifts were happy to do so. One man was not, and said, when they were well into the wolds beyond Louth: 'Don't you sometimes feel ashamed, to be begging lifts like this?'

There'd been no smile when the man stopped to pick him up, nothing but a slit-mouth asking where he wanted to go. He wore a belted mac, and cap, was pale at the face and kept his steel-blue eyes angled towards the road. 'To get where I'm going,' Frank replied, 'it would be cheaper by bus. I only hitch-hike to give miserable bastards like you a break from yourself. Stop this car and put me down.'

The man smiled. 'Well, now look here, I didn't mean to be offensive, you know. I asked a question because I don't see much point in sitting quiet for the next ten miles.'

'If you don't pull up I'll grab that wheel and swing you into the ditch as well.'

The car stopped quickly. He reached for his pack and got out, not a word said, happy to have weight again on his moving legs. He gave lifts to hundreds of people, even those who didn't look as if they wanted one. On the last day before leaving, anything to get out of town, warm sunshine dazzling through the spotless windscreen, he sped along a straight, narrow lane that ran two flat miles across open wasteground, had a yen to take his car off and crash the fence, subside into the ditch and grind up onto wider spaces. But what was beyond them except what he could see now? – the Trent, the power-station and, over the river, hills forming a hazy blackening cloudbank?

Driving towards a rooftop sea of newly built houses increased his worm-eaten discontent. Fields and woods bordered the sluggish river, a live, cloud-reflecting limb held under by a smart new bridge. Beyond the estate he turned to the main road, and, seeing a soldier and kitbag planted hopefully for a lift, drew up to find out where to. 'Loughborough, sir,' came the obliging answer.

'Sling your sack in,' Frank said, opening a packet of twenty, fresh and newly shining like Alfonso's teeth: 'Fag?' He was about twenty – short haircut and come-to-bed eyes for a female ape – sallow-faced and ill at ease as he drew the door to. 'Slam it, mate, or you'll roll out, then you won't be worth much as a soldier.'

'I'm in a good regiment,' the soldier said, stammering slightly. Frank lit up before driving off. 'On leave?'

'Yes, sir.'

'Don't call me sir. It makes my ulcers jump. Call me Frank. I might have a car, but I'm still one of the mob.' Deep angry creases formed on the soldier's forehead, as if he wondered: 'Who does he think he is, telling me not to call him sir?'

'How long you got?' – a few bob a day, and kept on call with nothing to do but read Flash Gordon comics.

'Seven days, sir. I'm a bit fed up. I'm married, and don't see much of my wife. This is the first bit of leave I've had in months.' Frank pitied him, stepped on the accelerator to get him back sooner to his hearthrug pie. 'You know what you ought to do?'

'What, mate – Frank?'

'Pack it in. I'll drive you down to London if you like. Fix you up at my house with a suit of civvies, and you'd never get caught. I'll take your wife down at the same time. It's no good being in khaki and having to jump out of your dreams every time some bloke with two pips on his bony shoulders opens his plumby mouth. I know. Was in myself once.'

'I couldn't.' The soldier hesitated, still with a slight stammer, as if obliged to consider it seriously for the privilege of his lift. 'I'm due out soon. There's no point. Anyway, did you desert, then?'

'No,' he answered, unperturbed, 'there was no one to help me. I was too stupid in those days' – and went on talking as they sped along, making a short journey of it, plying the soldier and himself with cigarettes and hoping to brainwash him into saying: 'All right, mate, stop the car, I'll desert now' – though it's hard to brainwash someone with no brains. Not that Frank was serious; he was playing a game, knew it when a startling question was etched on the emptiness of his own mind, saying that since he was telling this young man to run away from his khaki troubles, why didn't he pluck up guts enough to light off himself, sell his car, buy a rucksack and bike, and just fade out into the blue-and-green? He smiled: it was impossible to do anything while thinking about it.

The built-up area fell like red flakes around them. The youth seemed happier. 'Where's your camp?' Frank asked. 'Is it easy to get into the armoury from outside?'

21

'I suppose so,' he stammered. 'It's right near a wood on the edge of Harby camp. The doors are locked in case anybody tries to get in without a pass.'

Frank laughed. 'Wirecutters and a hairgrip. When you're on guard next send me a telegram and we'll clean it out together. Draw me a map of the camp, will you?' – passed him pencil and paper.

The youth's face became rounded, his eyes and mouth open. 'Do you mean it?' He was glum, set in a grim mould of discontent and fear, which made two of them.

'Don't worry,' Frank said, 'I'm not serious.' Passing a disused railway station, he climbed the smooth tarmac up a hump bridge, and the speed of his fast-cruising car dropped them into an airpocket on the other side.

Ashamed to be begging lifts! I'm learning more in two weeks than twelve years in factories and living with Nancy. I couldn't get this from a paperback. The blue wolds drew him in, treeless heights rolling and dominant. He struck off the main road after making his exit from the car, cut along a minor route marked red and thinly on his map as the veins in somebody's bloodshot eye. No woods or villages, just onward rolling fields, the smell of dead rose bay and the lonely farm every mile or two. At the moment he felt more at home on this paved lane where no traffic passed than he had on the A road further back. Black and white cattle, huge and sleek, were dedicated to a slow contemplative chewing of grass, contrasted to his own troubled mind as he spared a glance for them and walked on.

Sunday and distant bells muffled the cold air. A mile ahead and dropping two hundred feet was a village still locked in afternoon sleep and stillness. Peace was rampant out of town and factory, obtruding, obvious and disturbing, and it wouldn't let you be. The other day he was at Wainfleet about five in the afternoon – and thought he'd nip along a lane and get to the sea, have a paddle before dark. He reached the sand but water was nowhere to be seen, then walked miles, it seemed, out over the hard sand, jumping ruts and channels in places. It was flat, dead flat, and no matter how far he walked and how much he looked across this sand he couldn't see a ripple of the sea. It began to darken so that he couldn't see the land either – it was so flat – and somehow in the distance he could hear water shuffling around like an old man in carpet slippers, looking for the light switch in a dark room. But he couldn't see anything so came back to the proper coast. Near it was an old pillbox, a machine-gun post he supposed from the war, so he went inside and slept the night. Waking up next morning the sea was almost lapping at the door. He stripped off and swam for half an hour, then got dressed and went back to the main road, where he ate some breakfast at a pub, food well-needed because he hadn't slept well in that pillbox. It was cold, and he had rough dreams.

The first house set by itself on the far outskirts belonged to the district nurse so the plaque said. A red Mini was posted outside, and the sight of it made him wonder for a moment, in his biassed state against all four-wheeled friends, whether he should call there at all, or whether it wouldn't be better to walk on to the next house. But he knocked at the door.

'Yes?'

He felt he should say: 'My wife's labour's started. Can you come and see her through? I've been expecting it for a week – she's that much overdue'; but he said:

'Would you give me a drink of water, please?'

2

THERE WAS nothing she liked better than, on a long, free, wild winter's evening, to shut all doors and curtains in the living-room, heap up the fire with coal, and sit down with a book. It was the best distraction from her nurse's life, a deep and final escape for a few hours from the insistent and necessary calling of the outside world. She was old enough to appreciate this solitude, after a child and twelve years of married life, yet young enough to let her book fall and reflect on what had brought her to it, and to realize faintly that this work and solitude was not to be the end of her life.

Vile weather was held at bay, its thumping sea-like roar muffled by walls and comfort. Outside it was wet and violent, the world a boxing-ring for ebony shapeless cloud. Inside there was warmth and clarity, light, good furniture and food. As a woman she respected it, knew its rarity and value. The hours had no end. The end of them was out of sight. They had no frontiers – until the phone pulled her back into the world again, sent her out to birth, death or pain, which was easy to handle since it was no longer her own. So there was always this possible disturbance to cut into thoughts or reading, and the elements growling beyond the walls were always audible enough to eat at the basis of her reasons for being there.

On this Sunday even fine weather, open curtains and in-streaming light from the blue sky didn't save her from the encroaching habit of reflection. Since she had left her husband and gone back to nursing he had made good progress in the advertising firm he worked for. She still received an occasional letter from him, saying he wanted her back – an unfortunate phrase which implied that she had once belonged to him. When she left him he hadn't run off to the woman he was having an affair with – which might have embellished their break-up with some slight yet elevating aura of tragedy; he had gone to his psychoanalyst and spent another year pouring out the soul he had never been able to pour out to her. He imagined, in his suffering, that she must be suffering too, but her pain had died before leaving him, so that when she went away there was never any possibility of her 'going back'. It wasn't possible to go back in life; it might often appear nice and cosy and comfortable, but it would mean a perilous defeat, an annihilation of her true growth, a rejection of the world that she had, after immense expenditure of spirit, come face to face with at last. Even in her lonely Lincolnshire cottage, with the spite-wind of the wolds sealing her in with apprehension and self-questioning, she knew this – that she was out on her own, independent, useful, set at last in the vanguard of her life.

Keith, now in middle age, had told how his mother gave him three choices for a career: either the church, the army, or advertising – and he chose the latter because it was considered something new. Pat thought him dead, hollow, and self-centred, but couldn't deny that he was good at his job. In that, he was forthright and decisive – so she gathered from parties given and gone to – but with her he was never able to

25

make up his mind about anything, threw all decisions onto her. He wouldn't say: 'I'm taking you to the Mozart concert tonight,' but: 'Would you like to go to the concert?' so that she had to wonder whether or not he'd like to go before answering (and deciding) whether or not she'd like to. It was the same in all things, even to the buying of cuff-links or a new tie. The only thing he could decide on without her was a new car. She put it down to a terror of life, and a form of togetherness that she was glad to be away from.

Keith had said in his last letter that he would come up to visit her one day, talk to her (plead, she noted), but she knew he would never have the courage to do so unless she sent a definite word of goodwill. This she could never do, because one's life grew hard and settled after decisions had been acted on at a certain age. The anguished turbulent twenties had played themselves out to the bitter end, though she had at one time seen herself putting up with it for good, queening it forever over their small house near Notting Hill Gate that grew tinier with her discontent.

In her early twenties love had been the most important factor, and no good had come of it because it hadn't been the most important thing to her husband. It was only now that she realised how little love he had been able to give her, both physically and from his spirit. He had wanted to give her all the love in the world (much as if it were a collection of Boy Scout honours and Sunday school prizes), great amounts of it (to recall one of his phrases), to smother her with far more love than she really needed. This was all very fine and well, she recalled, except that he hadn't as much to give as he thought he had. The power of his emotions was so great that it held back the considerate speeches that should have been made; and whereas he saw it as a sign of the overpowering love within him – which it may have been – it only served to prevent him transferring this love to someone else. It was a deadlock that nothing could cure. The only chance was if she

26

called off the fight and left him. Hadn't he indicated once in a quarrel that he had so much love to give, and that it was her fault that he couldn't give it to her, that maybe one day he would find someone with whom a sharing of his great and beneficial love would be perfectly natural and easy? Her unwillingness or inability to accept his love was killing him. After leaving, she suspected that this great untransferable passion he had raved about was really no more than self-love. Perhaps she was unjust in thinking this and, being able to use more intelligent and realistic terms nowadays, knew that maybe her side of it also needed explaining.

The end had been a nightmare, a violent festering wound finally causing death to the body politic of their married life. In the final weeks he had threatened to kill her, then to kill himself – in that order. The house had been a battlefield. He went off to Manchester for a three-day conference, and she knew that he wanted her to take this as an opportunity for going away, of leaving him in peace and sanity. She could, of course, have been mistaken, but she also had wanted to use these seventy-two hours to arrange her retreat from that bleak Labradorian coast of a wrecked and rotten marriage.

Now, in her isolation, she couldn't understand how it had taken twelve years to find out that it wasn't going to work. But the twenties of one's life were like that: painful and slow, to which one tried continually to adjust against the most impossible odds. It was no use brooding on it, for that would merely show that they still had power over you, and such a thing was humiliating to a woman like Pat in her early thirties.

She hadn't thought about it much before. What was the point? It was no use easing the plaster off a sore place until the wound had healed, and she admitted that hers hadn't yet, though it was well on the way since she could reflect on it without getting back to the pain and dread. But to expose it to the fresh air of anybody else's gaze would be both useless

27

and uninteresting. She was very conscious of being now in her thirties, of having crossed certain chaotic miserable territories and landed on a sounder shore. It was no less hard and perilous, but things were seen more clearly than before. She felt more confident now, saw that some mishaps could even be avoided, armed as she was with this new foresight and intelligence. As the twenties had been ruined by love – or her preconceptions about it – so her thirties would be made by work. She grew to believe that work was the most important thing in one's life. It was the rails, the mainstay, the only valid reason for being alive. Without embarrassment she remembered her parents stating exactly this, and she had scornfully denied it, calling them cynical, materialistic, Victorian, but now she knew they were in some way right. The difference was that her idea of work was not theirs. After twelve years of marriage to an advertising copywriter, she saw it clearly. His work to her parents was honest because it was greatly rewarding. Her work – to her – was better because it was rewarding in another way. She didn't want to explain it further than that; but even that was far enough for her to accept the maxim that work was the only thing worth living for. As for love, well, that would either come or it would not.

There was no doubt though that lately she had been getting into a solitary state from which she could only emerge as an old maid with a cat on her shoulder. She couldn't have set herself up in a more remote place. There wasn't much friendship for her in this village. People were cheerful when their noses weren't pressed to the soil by hard seasons, and talked to you often enough, but you were expected to do all the listening. The ordinary people respected her as the nurse, told of their simple and significant troubles, but from a distance that she could never cross. The so-called 'gentry' didn't consider her worth knowing beyond the 'Good morning, how are you?' stage. As a nurse they all imagined she was someone who didn't need ordinary human contact, and thought that her job gave her more than she could want. All she had to look forward to were the holiday visits of her eleven-year-old son, but even these were shared with her husband, and didn't exactly fill her with the intimate and interesting conversation she had gone without all the rest of the year. Still, it was true that she did not rationalize this as solitude, and she did not complain about it now, either. She could not dislike the two years she had so far spent alone, partly because she might have to do so for a very long time, and also from a real and gentle feeling for solitude remembered from the time when she was without it. Since leaving her husband she had a way of liking whatever state her new life led her into. This was an advantage for her wellbeing, but she also saw that it was not so good to glory in such a state of mind, since certain deadnesses of perception and a limitation of experience also went with it. Such a thing was to be expected, but that too would change. After all, not only could you not have everything, but as far as she was concerned it was often true that the less you had the more might be in store for you later. This was a parsimonious, puritanical, yet unpredictable state of mind, at the mercy of any strong outlandish circumstance that came unexpectedly from beyond the outer limits of such prickly defences.

3

'OF COURSE,' she said, 'come in a moment.'

It was a plainbricked four-roomed cottage and, when he entered, a steep flight of stairs faced him. One door to the right led into a parlour, that to the left, a dining-room. 'Leave your pack by the stairs.' He dropped it and followed her into the dining-room. On the table was a tea tray, and she took another blue-ringed beaker from the shelf: 'Sit down and have some tea. That is, unless you're determined on water.' She was tall, had ginger hair and flowerblue eyes, thin lips that smiled back at him. Her frock had a cardigan over it, and she wore stockings and houseshoes. He put her at over thirty, but then, he thought, I've never seen a young midwife. 'You look as if you've walked a long way,' she said.

He faced her across the table, slid down the sweet scald of the big cup. 'From Spilsby.' It had been the longest footslog so far, his eyes fried and feet sore, his body feeling dustcaked and sweatbound. He offered her a cigarette.

'Thank you,' she said. The silence won over the birds,

backed up by heavy cloud shadows approaching road and hedgerows, and the humping softloamed fields beyond the window. A car went by, leaving a heavier silence. 'It's rare for someone to stop at my door and ask for a drink of water – unless it's children in the summer.'

'It's rare for me to get tea when I ask for it. I'm on my way to Lincoln.'

'Why Lincoln?' She spoke well, smoked as if she smoked a lot, and seemed always about to laugh at him, which he sensed and was amused at.

'To get to Sheffield. I'm just tramping around the country.'

'You don't look like a tramp. When I opened the door just now I thought you were an ordinary young man from the village to see about some carpenter's work I want doing.' He had that sort of build – yet now he didn't seem like that to her at all. Maybe that's what put that bastard's back up who thought I was begging his lift, he thought. He didn't know what I looked like, out on the road with rucksack, but dressed in smart enough jacket and trousers, travelling in heavy and well-polished shoes, a short haircut, and a tie on. If I'd snivelled and was clobbered up like a tramp, that would have been O.K., but it worried him that he couldn't place me – private, corporal, sergeant. He thought back again to giving the soldier a lift. After dropping him at a house in Lough-borough he had headed north, the day opening wider as his car drove into it, black trees and green hills of the Trent hemming around the curving road. Summer was poleaxed: the sapjuice smell of wild flowers and dead wheat soaked in sun was giving place to spent grass and barren trees. September was playing it cool, and the first subtle change of season rolled a desperate message up from the turning tyres, whispering it was time to light out to the unlit far-and-wides felt to exist with such potency only by a man more than fed-up to the teeth.

A policeman was flagging him to a halt by a barrier of

black cars and cycle-cops, plainclothes men and brasshats talking together as if the word had gone out to get Bertrand Russell. He slowed down and a black cyclop swung towards him: jackboots crunching, helmet unstrung above a red, vacant face, in truth the timid Midlands visage of a man who should have been serving behind the Co-op counter, joshing with the women in some collier's town. He stood by the car window and Frank twisted the ignition off, tempted to let the wheel roll over his boot and end his days in prison. 'A man's got out of Upton Asylon, and he's dangerous. You haven't given anybody a lift today, have you? He's a young feller of nineteen. Got out early this morning. Wearing a soldier's uniform, and stutters a bit.'

Frank lifted his face, hand on chin as if truly thinking, yet instinctively answering: 'I didn't see anybody.'

He was waved on. It must have been that soldier I picked up. Maybe tonight he'll be raping little girls or coshing an old couple for their pension books. Perhaps I said I hadn't seen him because it would have kept me back from a drink for an hour while they checked my answers. I suppose it's no good, though, not to be bothered, but in most things that's how they like you to be, to watch the telly or have a few drinks and not be bothered, because if I was bothered I wouldn't put up with the death camp I'm living in. So they've got to be satisfied when I can't be bothered to help them to capture some poor soldier who has jumped the looneybin. I couldn't be bothered to tell the police where that soldier was because I couldn't be bothered to be bothered. But they'll get him because thousands of others can be bothered to be bothered, but maybe this dangerous soldier will get his hands on the throat of some fleshhead who can be bothered to be bothered and drop him dead in some dark corner, because those who can be bothered to be bothered are bothered about the wrong things and never bother to get bothered about things that really matter.

32

Still, it worried him that he hadn't told them where he'd driven that soldier to in Loughborough, and now so long afterwards it seemed much more a crime, that in his lunacy of the last day he had committeed without thought, worrying him more and deeper even than his departure from wife and kids.

He looked around the room, at the writing desk, bookcase loaded, mirror above the fireplace. 'It's good furniture you've got.'

'It belonged to my mother. I brought it up from Surrey, and some of it came from auction rooms around here. What else do you want to know?'

He played along with her light-hearted mockery, unused to the idea of eating in such silence. 'I didn't think you came from the north. How did you end up in Lincolnshire?'

'I hope I don't end up anywhere. By marriage I lived in London, and by appointment I got this job here. It's a hard one, but I like it. Have another cup?'

'I will. You've set me off, with such good tea' – and again she gave a smile as if to say: 'I might have taken you in out of the goodness of my heart, but you don't have to say anything nice for it. I'm in charge here.' She laughed at these thoughts: wrinkles beginning around the eyes, but her skin was white and smooth. The dress was buttoned to her neck, and the cardigan didn't hide completely the small swell of her breasts. 'I'd better be on my way,' he said. 'Knock a few more miles back.'

'I don't imagine you'll get to Lincoln tonight.'

'It doesn't matter. I'll sleep somewhere snug. I'm glad of the healthy life for a while. It's not too cold yet, and a barn will do me.'

'Why are you on the run?' she asked. 'I'm curious.'

That makes two of us, he thought. 'I'd had enough of married life. It was getting to be like that play on in London.

33

"The Rat Trap" – now in its fifth year. It kept going along, dead as a doornail, and then, all in the space of a day I'd decided everything, packed in and left, as if those five years were only a sizzling fuse leading to a load of dynamite that suddenly exploded.' All in a day, and the shell-shock was rippling. Out in his fast car he'd had nowhere to go, except home to say it was all finished. He was on the main road after the soldier's lift, doing ninety and dashing around like a tomcat after its own bollocks, tart wild and pub crazy after a stretch of high-fidelity that he'd stood so long because he was temporarily dead, thinking: 'I go round in circles, as if in some past time I've had a terrible crash, and the more I drive in circles the more I'm bleeding to death. I don't feel this bleeding to death because it's slow and painless (almost as if it's happening to another man and I'm not even looking on, but am reading about it in a letter from a friend hundreds of miles away) but I know it's happening because my eyes get tired and I'm fed up to my spinal marrow, while the old rich marrow I remember is withering and turning black inside me. But perhaps it isn't completely bad, because if I thought it was I'd flick this steering wheel enough to hit that fence or pillar box and flake myself to a scrap of cold meat under the soil and greenwood tree. Maybe you can get better from it, because I can't have lost enough blood if I could get in with that woman last night and hump into bed with her. And perhaps I've still got blood in me if I feel it running out of me.'

A paraffin upright stood in the corner, warming the room, perpetuating the smell of tea just made and drunk. Someone walked along the road, whistling. A van drummed by. 'It's quiet here,' he said.

'I don't notice it usually, but when I do, I like it.'

'I've never been in a house so quiet. I worked in a factory where you can't even hear yourself shout. I had a wife and two kids, and a house where you couldn't even hear yourself think above the news being read, or someone yapping about Homo or Wazz.'

'That's modern life,' she said. 'Would you rather work in a field?'

'That ain't why I'm on the run. I don't mind noise at work – though I notice you haven't got a television set.' Out of the factory his face had changed, away from Nottingham and the pubs. It wasn't that his expression had lost self-assurance or his body its confident walk, but his actions were slower, his smile more uncertain. It made him look older, as if thought preceded even the movement of his hands bringing the cigarette up to his mouth, as if his smile or frown was backed by an unfathomable depth of reasoning. 'Maybe I'm on the run to find out why I'm on the run,' he grinned, feeling foolish at making such a twisted statement.

'Perhaps that's why everybody goes on the run,' she said. 'I think you're probably right.' He was surprised and flattered that she took it seriously. She was fascinated at flashes of complexity in a mind she had imagined as too simple to take seriously. So far, he could only see the mechanics of how he'd gone on the run, rather than the cause. She had used the phrase, and he wondered if the time would come when it no longer applied, when he would be going to, and not away from, something. He'd got back to Nottingham, after so much driving around, and felt like using his feet. He parked his car up a side street off Alfreton Road, and the sky was less blue, white clouds hanging around the chimney stacks of Radford Baths. He yearned to let his legs walk, maybe carry him where a car could never go.

Narrow, winding and mildewed, he'd lived in these streets once upon a long time ago, and hovering odours made different air to that in the windswept well-spread estates. He'd hardly noticed such change in the oblivious one-track of getting married. It was amazing how quickly he'd fallen in, but years had gone by before clarifying his vision of it.

35

After the landmarks of birth, school, work you get more handy with the girls. Then at eighteen you're called up, and so look forward to getting out. While you had something ahead of you it was fine. When you got out you went after the women, earned your money and drank your fill. This went on for a couple of years, then there was nothing left, just a fifty mile wall dead in front, starting from your shining shoes and going, as far as you could see, right up to the sky. At the feel of it you stepped up the wild life, went mad for a month or two, spinning around like a bluebottle with a dose of Flit, and people thought you weren't half a hell of a lad. Then you stopped, because even though the thick grey wall had gone and the sky was spring-blue again, you felt that the wall was still there, but inside you, which was worse because it really did mean that life was finished. You brooded for a month, and people thought you'd turned thoughtful and worried because you'd got some young woman into trouble, but you hadn't. It was only your black ever-surviving heart getting you used to seeing a way out that you'd have whistled at in scorn only a few months before. Then your eyes opened, or you thought they did, and in this wall you saw a hole at the bottom, surrounded by rubble and dust as if you'd used the handgrenade of your life so far to blast that hole just big enough to crawl through. So you got married, and it all looked rosy on the other side. The fact that a penny bun didn't cost tuppence any more, but four-and-eleven with threepence off was almost a pleasure to put up with. You loved in bed and comfort night after night and thought what have I been missing all these years?

The marriage was a light-hearted get-together at the Registry Office, standing to repeat after that sanctimonious corpse-head in glasses to honour and obey until the atom bomb parts us. And there was I larking around and pretending I had to be dragged in screaming by my mates because one of the other blokes had got her up the spout and not me,

36

whereas nobody had at all and she was as pure as virgin snow I don't think. Nancy smiled as if nothing was happening. Her mother tut-tutted and didn't know where to put her face because she thought she meant it – and maybe half of me did, but things quietened down and ten minutes later I was under a snowstorm of paper wanting to get my hands on a St Bernard mongrel with a keg of well-bred brandy around its neck. To everybody's disappointment I was icicle-sober that night.

Nancy must have come from a long line of bad cooks, because after a week at Cleethorpes she put a plate of tinned steak, tinned celery and baked beans before him, fortified by several slices of Miracle Bread, so named, he supposed, because it was a miracle it didn't kill you. Ever the gentleman, he tackled it as best he could, able to joke about living off love until the month was out.

They lived with Nancy's mother, and her cooking was worse. Even the meat tasted like cabbage, and there was nothing he could do but push it aside like a spoiled kid. Mrs Stathern thought her cooking the best for miles around and this made him hate her as well, because he couldn't stand up and say he was going down the road for an egg and chips. If she'd known it wasn't so good he might even have eaten some of it – in a joking light-hearted way while waiting for the stomach cramps. All he could do was thank God for a canteen dinner and get Nancy to fry some beans and bacon in the evening, a concoction that got monotonous day after day, but at least it was difficult to spoil, and such repetition eventually turned her into the best cowboy breakfast cooker in the whole of Aspley.

Those early months dreamed themselves by. Food wasn't as important as his thoughts for some reason now made it, for there was house and home to buy and pay for week by week, and the first kid to wait for month by month and his machine to work at day by day. He couldn't understand why it had gone on so long. Was it because of the violent blindoe times he'd made for himself before feeling that wall in front of him? In effect, he'd never left the wall, after having crawled through the shell hole with such relief. Instead of in front, the sheer face had stayed a few feet at his back, and now, lately, it had drawn a circle around him, stifling his life, so that he had to get out or choke to death.

'The thing about this country,' he said to her, 'is that there's nowhere to go. You just keep going round in circles. Have you read *Dr Zhivago*? No? It gives you a marvellous idea of what it's like living in a big country. Spaces thousands of miles wide and long. I'd like to be in a big country. He goes from Moscow to Siberia. When the train is held up by snow everybody gets out and digs. And when he wants to go back to Moscow, he walks. I don't know how many thousand miles it was, but he didn't say: "Oh, I can't go because the trains aren't running." He just walks! He found out why he went on the run after he'd been on the run long enough. You know why it was? I'm just finding out myself as I talk about it: he went on the run because life was too much for him.'

'Do you know then why you're on the run?' she smiled.

He thought, his face hard. 'Ah! I do though, if you want to know. It's because life's too little for me.'

'It's the same thing. He couldn't face life because it was too much. You can't face it because it's too little. Neither of you can face life.'

'You put it neat,' he said, rueful over his shattered epigram.

'I'm not a nurse for nothing. I've been in nursing for fifteen years, on and off. It makes you hard and wise, if you know how to take it.'

'It'll be dark soon, so I must be on my way.'

'I have some sherry, nothing harder, would you like a drop for the road?'

'Yes. Are all those books yours?'

'Mostly novels. Some I've never even glanced at. They're part of the furniture.' The cardigan sleeve was drawn up almost to the elbow, showing freckles on her fair skin. He looked directly at her eyes, and she smiled before turning. 'What I've always wanted to do,' he said, 'is do nothing for a year except read books, and learn something.'

'I don't think you'd learn much, necessarily, but you might enjoy it.'

'You're bound to learn something if you don't know anything.' He finished the sherry, sweet water, cold and griping after the tea. 'There's a drop left,' she said, 'so you might as well finish it. I can't see you getting drunk on it.' It was darkening outside, and she stood to switch on the light. 'If you're not in a desperate hurry to get where you're going I have a spare room upstairs. It's only a camp bed, but you'll find it comfortable. Better than a hedgebottom, though it's up to you.'

He hesitated, as if unable to believe the offer. She laughed, open and frank about it. 'I'm not trying to pick you up. You look as if I might be.'

'I didn't think that. I'll stay then. When you're on the run you're always ready to stop running – like a rabbit.'

'You seem well up on the philosophy of escape.'

'I've never walked so long. Nor thought so much. Walking has turned out to be even more monotonous than standing at my machine at work. But the thoughts are better.' She asked why he had left his wife, but his fullblooded, earnest, airtight reasons had melted. He felt foolish trying to explain something that had taken a lifetime to overwhelm him.

She drew the curtains across: 'I don't want your reasons if you can't give them. I've done so many things I still can't give reasons for. I had a fiancé once, when I was nineteen. He lived in Portsmouth and I lived in Guildford. I found out one day that I was pregnant, and on the same day I had a telegram from his mother to say he had been drowned.'

39

He was caught by the infectious remembering of her voice: 'That was terrible. Where's the baby then?'

'I took steps to remove it, but I got married very soon afterwards, and had a baby within a year. I could act on my decisions quickly in those days, and they always proved to be right. He's a boy of eleven now, very bright. He comes home for holidays, and to everyone here my husband is dead – though I left him in London two years ago. You'll sleep in Kevin's bed while you're here. My name's Pat Shipley, since we've been talking so long.'

He made the exchange. 'Will you come out with me, and have a drink, or supper? We could go to Louth, or some place.'

'Let's have no tit-for-tat, as they say around here. But I thought you were broke, walking to Sheffield?'

'I wouldn't do this if I was – walking, and hitching lifts when I feel like it. If I'd got no money I'd stay put until I had.' She declined, and he would rather stay where he was as well, the oil stove warm and the room closed off in the vast country silence. He wondered what sort of woman she was, whether she would or wouldn't, wanted or didn't want, whether she was a posh tease taking a rest from it, or a sex-starved isolated nurse who worked so hard she'd had neither time nor opportunity in the last year and wouldn't squeal if he made a grab for her before she grabbed him. Not that she was all that much to look at. Nancy would make ten of her, but then, she was dead on him and this Pat wasn't. He looked at her through the clarity of silence: a rather round plainish face, if it weren't for her eyes and long ponytail of red hair. He'd never been with a gingernut before, but the hearsay on them was they were red hot. Not that I'll touch a hair of her red head, though I'd like to.

'I'll fry some sausages soon. I have tomatoes and bread, eggs and bacon.'

'It's too good of you.'

40

'I feel like being good – now and again. It's my job. Haven't you seen the advertisements for nurses.'

'Well, they are a bit daft,' he said, 'that's true.'

'They're more accurate than you think, though.'

'Do you like your job?'

'I'm too busy doing it to know.'

'Don't you find it lonely?' He saw her as called out all hours of the day and night, coming back between long, life-saving watches to an empty house – paraffin stove out, cupboard empty, even the cat gone from the backdoor, gloom and rain spattering the windows, looking around and wondering what to do now that she had a few hours off. Maybe she'd put the light on, hatch a fire in that parlour he'd glimpsed, find some tinned food and boil it, make tea, sit down to a book after letting in the cat that had found its way back to the door and mewed for her. He was right, she thought. That's my life: lonely, hardworking, yet happy if there is such a thing. 'I'm not lonely,' she said. 'I like being by myself. I see lots of people on my rounds.'

'Sick people,' he said. 'Is that enough?'

She spoke in a soft comforting way, yet he felt the edge of nervousness on it. It seemed strange to him that she was a midwife, yet it was possible to imagine her firm and soothing at critical moments of illness or childbirth. 'Not only sick people. What I prize more than anything else in the world is independence. My father was a police inspector and still is, I won't say where – and as a girl I was bullied and disciplined in the most awful stupid way. At school it was worse, and the first time I thought to get out of it I became a probationer nurse, out of the frying pan into the furnace. But it all led to this job, so I don't regret it now. I suppose when you know why you left your wife you'll go back to her?'

'I'll never do that. I haven't only burned my boats and smashed my bridges, but I've burned my heart as well. There's no going back for me.'

41

'You say it as calmly as if you meant it. It's frightening.'

'Yet maybe I'm like a bloody moth near a flame, spinning around so close to Nottingham that I'll have to wrench myself further away to stop going back there to see how things are. I feel the kids pulling at me more than anything.'

'Come on,' she said, 'we'll see what there is to eat.' It was a spacious kitchen built onto the back of the house, and he leaned against the fridge while she cleared up. He hadn't expected to see such desolation. It wasn't as if she hadn't time to get things straight before a call came to say that Mrs Robinson's leg was bothering her again – but it was cluttered with the stains and refuse of weeks. The sink was heaped with pots – tea rims turned green on the inside of cups, porridge mouldy, knives black when she took them out of the water. It's a damp place, he thought. The smallest of the four stove burners glowed red. Hot water splashed over her words: 'I always leave that one burning, day and night. It doesn't cost so much, and it keeps the kitchen warm. I can get coffee quickly without waiting for the stove to warm up.'

Foreseeing a long job he stored away yesterday's groceries in the larder. 'The place is a mess,' she said. 'But don't bother to help. This is woman's work.'

'It's work,' he said. The shelves had no room – about six boxes of various breakfast cereal took up space, some empty enough to discard. Jars of different jam, wrapped cut bread with a few stale slices left, sauces, mustards, various pastes. He'd never seen such a lavish and squalid larder, and threw half out. She didn't object: 'You get careless, living alone. I've been meaning to clear it for days, but it's hard enough keeping my work up. Everybody seems to get ill in autumn and spring – when the seasons change.' She plugged in an electric kettle, turned on a burner of the large stove.

'You fixed up a fine kitchen,' he said.

'Now that it's clean. I'm still paying for it. It's not only the workers who get trapped by H.P.'

42

'No,' he said, 'but there are so many of them that it's them that keeps it going.' He made a fire in the parlour, looked around the small heavily carpeted room. Bookshelves padded every possible piece of wall, and he skimmed their titles – medical, history, books about Lincolnshire, poetry, and books on other books. How did I land in this smart educated place, he thought wryly, supping with the village midwife? He looked through a pile of records, kneeling on the floor to get at them. They were mostly chamber music, old seventy-eights, heaped around a small portable windup. 'I like class-ical stuff,' he said, when she came in with the tray. 'Beethoven, and – who was it wrote the Planets?'

'Holst.'

'Somebody got me Mars and Jupiter for my birthday once. I played them so loud that a bloke next door threatened to duff me if I didn't keep it quieter. I told him to try it, but he backed down and said he'd get the police. I lost interest in it though because Jupiter was what we used to sing at school and I didn't like it at all. Mars made me laugh, and I used to act the zombie to it for my kids. But it's a rotten piece be-cause it reminded me of the Germans smashing everything at war. So one day I snapped the record and threw it out.'

She put sausages and tomatoes on his plate: 'A pity they're only the sawdust type, but that's the worst of work-ing in these outback villages.'

'I don't think I know anyone,' he remarked, 'who likes the work they do. There's always something wrong with it.' He was a quick, orderly eater, as if the food on his plate were a fortified area to be reduced by knife, fork, and mopping-up bread. His manner of speaking annoyed her, of connecting her spoken thoughts too outlandishly to some hook in his own mind. He was a passer-by she'd given shelter to, a foot-loose working-man from whom, at moments, she wanted the same tone of deference that she'd grown to expect from the grateful Lincolnshire villagers roundabout. 'People who work

43

at jobs they don't like are too stupid, unintelligent, and cowardly to break the rut they're in and get work that they would like.'

'If everybody changed the job they didn't like I'd be at the pit face and you'd be roadsweeping.' She'd set the meal as if the idea of eating had no appeal for her, but now she ate as if hungry at the sight of someone else loading it back before her. 'Everyone does the job they're fit for. The natural order of things works pretty well. Eat some bread and cheese.'

'Thanks. We'll talk about that when there's a natural order of things. Most of my mates wanted an easier job, less hours, more pay, naturally. But it wasn't really work they hated, don't think that. They didn't all want to be doctors or clerks, either. Maybe they just didn't like working in oil and noise, and then going home at night to a plate of sawdust sausages and cardboard beans, and two hours at the flicker-box with advertisements telling them that those sausages and beans burning their guts are the best food in the country. I don't suppose they knew what they wanted in most cases – except maybe not to be treated like cretins.'

She went out, returned with a pot of coffee and a jug of hot milk: 'Anything but work, that's what you mean. Strike, go slow, or work to rule, seems the order of the day. Why is it, I wonder?'

He cut bread and cheese. 'Now you're being unjust. It was to vary the treadmill. But as well as that there was a collective wish to change the way things are run, so that they'll have the power of running things. If that happened it wouldn't be a treadmill any more. They wouldn't strike. They'd be too busy. And too interested in running it.'

'That's being idealistic.'

'I know it is, but not too much.'

'I think you're speaking for yourself,' she said. 'You're more knowing and intelligent than the rest. Not only that, but you speak of it in the past tense, I noticed.'

44

'I haven't thought much about the factory since leaving it, that's true, because I suppose there's so much else to think about, soak in. But maybe what I soak in is still connected to the factory that I don't think about. It still separates me from the world in any case, the fact that I've been in one. Whether it's on my mind or not. How many of the others have you met besides me, come to think of it?'

Her face relaxed, and she laughed.

'I thought so.'

'What would you say if I went on strike, a nurse?'

'I'd condemn you. You've no right to go on strike. You sell your knowledge and art, a workman sells his labour. That's the big difference. Oh, don't think I haven't thought about it. If I had a vocation I wouldn't have the right to strike, either. But you must concede it to the others. I didn't know I was so hungry – and talkative. Travelling makes me eat more, though I feel thinner than when I was at work. I don't eat as much as some people. I once knew a man who ate so much he had a blackout. Then he died. I think it was his liver. Some people never know when to stop.'

'That's a story you made up,' she said, pouring his coffee.

'I know. They're all true enough. I think them up when I'm walking.' They sat by the fire. She suspected he was trying to charm her, but was disturbed more by her suspicion than by the fact that it might be justified. He obviously didn't think about what he said, she decided. 'This is a comfortable house,' he remarked, 'I'm enjoying tonight.'

'So am I,' she admitted, 'in a strange way.'

'That countryside was getting me down. It's too green. The road's hard and the sky's too grey. I favour a warm room and the supper I've just had.' To spoil it, his feet ached for the walking they'd do tomorrow. He couldn't thumb any more lifts, as if the man's accusation of begging free transport had broken one part of his spirit, only to have strengthened another that had just become visible to him. 'It's hard to

45

imagine you're not getting lonely though, on these nights.'

She was glad of his curiosity. It comforted her, since it was too rare these days. Yet it was also too brusque and offhand, not only that he might not be sincere in it, but that he might be forgetting that they had only just met, and that such curiosity was premature. Still, she had asked him in – for a cup of tea – and in spite of its short time ago she felt no shyness in talking, mainly because she was only talking out of herself, on the understanding that he would be gone in the morning. In any case, he seemed amiable, almost interesting, though somewhat more remote than a person often is when you stop them in the street to ask a direction.

Relaxed and comfortable by the fire, another part of him was out on the wide spaces of the road, blinded by sky and distance. 'I haven't always lived alone,' she said. 'I was married twelve years, until I split up a while ago, to a typical middle-class Englishman, an advertising copywriter – someone who sat in an office all day in Holborn thinking up slogans that would sell soap powders or a correspondence course in bricklaying.'

Her phrases gave way to a ticking clock, a noise which made the silence deeper than itself. 'You chose him,' Frank said.

'I made a mistake.'

'So did he. So did I. It's a marvel to me how many people make mistakes.'

'You have a sense of humour. But I was tired of the useless life I was leading. It got so that I didn't need him and he didn't need me. He was a sort of father to Kevin, but even that didn't weigh when I decided to leave. Being a housewife in London with a charwoman and an au pair wasn't enough. I was a trained nurse, and was needed in a village like this, by ordinary people who want some sort of looking after. I think everybody should do useful work. I hate idleness or pretence.'

'So do I.'

46

'Tell me about your work. I've never met anyone who worked in a factory, not to talk to.'

'In what way? I'm what they used to call a mechanic, but I was beginning to see further than the end of my nose. I was also what the gaffers called "a bit of a troublemaker", but for years they were baffled by me because I was also a good worker. I could set anybody's tools and take their machine apart as well as the chargehand, and I had many hints that if I stopped being such a keen member of the union, life would be easier for me as far as getting on went. But I saw too much injustice to accept that. I knew which side of the fence I stood on, and still do. I made many others see it as well. They had a favourite trick at our firm of starting on the coloured blokes when they wanted to reduce work rates, but I got the whole shop out once over this, a stoppage they didn't forget because they had to give in over it. People think factory life is a bed of roses, but it needn't be as bad as the gaffers make it. I loved the work – though I didn't realize how much till now. But I can't go back to it, not for a good while.'

'You'll go back to it,' she said, 'like I had to come back to this work after so long away.' She liked people of integrity, but wasn't sure that she liked his brand of it, so foreign to all the things she had been brought up to believe.

'What do you do on these long nights?' he asked. 'I didn't see any dance halls on my way into the village.'

'I keep a journal when I can. I read, listen to music, make dresses sometimes, knit. I'll show you where you're to sleep.'

The stairs were steep, straight up, and narrow, and he followed a few steps behind. The long cardigan gave her figure a squarish, rather old-fashioned look, though the shape of her legs and the unmistakable sway above them redeemed her femininity. When she stopped on the tiny landing, there was some hesitation in her face. He was tempted to put out his arms, kiss her if she responded. But they had been talking too long which, for the moment, killed him with hesitation.

47

She pointed to the bedroom opening to the right: 'Go in, and I'll get you some blankets. There's only one sheet, so you'll have to double it.'

A camp bed lay under the window, and in one corner a tank of four goldfish on a table. It had been the kid's room; shelf of books, a football, boxing gloves, crayons and paint tin, whistles and dinky toys jumbled into a tea chest. The walls were whitewashed – the first time he'd seen it used for other than ceilings – and it made the small cottage bedroom look bigger than it was. 'A nurse in the next village is standing in for me,' she said, dropping his blankets, 'so I'm off for the next three days. Which means that I'm not getting up till nine in the morning, so you can just let yourself out early. Slam the door behind to make sure it locks.'

'I can't thank you enough. I was done-for when I knocked at your door.'

'You looked it,' she smiled. 'I must say. I expect you're tired now, as well.' They shook hands. 'If I don't see you, good luck.' Then she went out, closing the door.

That was quick, he thought. She couldn't get out fast enough. As if I might jump her here by the fish tank, and me on my last legs at that, though I've knee-trembled on no legs at all before now. It was hard to tell whether she wanted me to or not. It was hard to tell whether I wanted to as well. And on that, he was sleeping.

4

IT WAS half past six and still dark, and a driving, wind-crazed rain rattled the windows. Gutters and drainpipes shuttled it musically across the garden path and Frank listened to its stream of consciousness from the warmth of his camp bed, hoping it might stop before he set out towards Lincoln. His first thought on waking was always, nowadays: 'Where am I?' The less comfortable his night's lodging, the quicker came the answer. The space between oblivion and full consciousness was always disturbing, a basalt twilit vacuity, such a depth of neutrality that it was alien and torment to him. In factory days there was no space between deep sleep and dressing, and this new zone had crept into his experience since leaving them.

He stood on the landing. Outside, rain scattered its pellets across shining slates and the heavy blackening evergreen of autumn. No sound came from the nurse's room and, shoes in hand, he stepped softly down stairs that creaked, vibrating so strongly into every room that he expected her door to flick open.

The kitchen was cold, in spite of the single burner left

glowing, so he switched on others and set a kettle to boil, washed dishes from the previous night to the futile dizzying beat of Light Programme light music coming from an eye-level radio. An s o s message before the news requested Mr Albert Handley, last heard of at Skegness in 1943, to please ring Leicester Infirmary where his mother Mrs Clara Handley was dangerously ill. The dragnet was out for some poor bastard who lit off nearly twenty years ago, and even if he wanted to ignore this message he couldn't because his mates at work this morning would say: 'Hey, Bert Handley, is that you the wireless meant? Hard luck about your poor mam. When are you going? There's a train at eleven-five.' And maybe poor Albert will spit on his luck, or change his job, or hotfoot it back to his mam's, just to see her out as a good son should. Which only goes to show how you can never be left alone.

A loud fry-up drowned the news. He sat to breakfast at the kitchen table, hoping the sky would run out of rain and let him walk dry-shod over the wolds. An hour had slid by since opening his eyes, and at this speed he wouldn't be leaving till four o'clock. Newspapers flapped through the letterbox. He lit a cigarette, put up his feet to read. The *Mirror* and the *Times*. Out of curiosity he looked at the *Times* first: adverts on the front page, and most of the back ones full of stock exchange and company reports. A property firm made a profit of seventeen million, and a woman had lost her dog.

Eight o'clock. The kettle on again. Her larder was well stocked with the essentials of life. It didn't seem right to leave without saying good-bye and thank you after she'd picked him up off the doorstep half dead from exposure and crippled feet, nursed him back to life even though he was a stranger. What a legend! Talking so much last night, it seemed as if he'd known her for years, even though he hadn't been to bed with her. She was handsome as well as generous, an unbeat-

50

able combination which only came to him forcefully on the
point of leaving.

He opened the back door and slopped out tea leaves. Daylight and rain showed a garden ending at a meadow, a clump
of trees on the rise of it like a secret meeting of amateurish
burglars whispering to decide which house to do tonight. The
garden was dug over in patches, other parts gone to bush and
speckled weedgrass, a few dead potato heads overlapping
what remained of a path. A good plot – with a few months'
loving care, strong arm and boot. He remembered his night in
the hut on Harry's allotment before leaving Nottingham.
The soil and damp smell was the same. But then, at that time,
there had still been the scent of stubbled wheat and fallen
poppy heads, potato tops, snapped runner beans and updug
soil, vanishing scents of a receding summer that barely penetrated his rubbed-out brain as he zig-zagged towards the
hut.

He had wakened to Harry's spade rhythmically shifting
soil outside. There was no one else he could visit after his
good-bye to Nancy, so he'd left his car at Bobber's Mill,
drunk half the whisky neat between switching off the
ignition and opening the door, then cut across the maze of
gardens towards Harry's. He let himself in with the spare key
under the waterbarrel, sat on a stool and finished off the
whisky, then slid to the floor.

He had twelve eyes in his face all trying to look into one
another and, when succeeding, only meeting twelve more
staring back into each fragmentation, and then into his heart
calling him a bloody fool like the opening mouths of ten
million goldfish. He pulled a hand to his face, sensing he
could put his head in the crook of his arm and crush it like a
walnut. Nothing remained but the fleshless knot of his headache, a fizzled-out brain. He stood up to find a cigarette, but
fell down again, head thumping painlessly against the floor, a
rubber ball dropped by somebody else.

51

Harry said: 'I see you've had a drink or two?' A fist came from Frank's guts: that's the way to talk! Harry the railway shunter out of contact with the acid and battery world; or was it just sarcasm? He was too far in to tell. Harry lit a paraffin lamp, stepping around as if Frank were a normal feature of the hut floor, some garden novelty such as a little boy pissing in a fish tank taken in out of the rain. Frank lay waiting until the anchoring ropes of earth and moon un-knotted themselves from his head. He watched Harry pump a primus, and promise tea, while all he could do was tap his ankle and croak: 'Water!' when he bent down to hear what he wanted.

'It'll make you sick,' Harry said. 'Tea'll be O.K. – if you drink it slow.'

'Water!' Frank said, as if covered in sand. Someone rammed a javelin into his mouth. It stretched from throat to belly and burned like prime acid. He wanted to cough or be sick, jettison it from him, but was unable to make the effort, and in any case if he did all his life's guts would go with it. He was sure of that, waited for his own heat to melt the metal of the javelin, so that he could dare to move again and one day stand up. When he tried, the earth spun in and blacked him out.

'This is no joke,' Harry said. 'You might not be at death's door, but you're at the bloody side-entrance if you ask me. Was anybody mixing your booze?'

'Give me some water.'

'You'll get some as soon as this kettle boils, so hold on.' He closed the hut door and sat on a stool looking down at his guest. 'You can take an aspro as well, and have something to eat. There ain't much I ain't got in this hut. Home from home. Ida's been on her holidays this last week, and I slept here a couple of times, so you're lucky we're well provided for. I've got some sardines and a chunk of bacon on that shelf, and some yesterday's bread.'

52

Frank's eyes were closed; the words 'bacon' and 'sardines' made him retch, but it stopped at that, though ever-ready Harry pushed a piece of sacking at his head: 'Use that if you've got to.'

The clean aromatic smell of hot tea came to him, worse than the idea of oil-dripping sardines, though still the javelin stayed lodged in his body when another set of spasms jerked up from his stomach. 'That's what drink does,' Harry handed him a cup of tea, 'fills you full of bile. You ought to keep off it. Want summat to eat?'

'Ay, give me a deathcake – and a cup o' quick poison while you're at it.' He groaned, rolled away from the white heat of the flaring lamp. 'You been in a fight?' Harry wanted to know.

'Only with myself. I'm still in it.'

'Now you're being funny.'

'Do you ever think about the future, Harry?'

'Eh? Get this.'

'Water. I'm drowning in lung fluid and stomach piss but I'm thirsty as if I've worked a week in soot-dust. My breath's a blowlamp.' He tried to light a cigarette, choked, and lay back down, felt, in spite of feeling weak, sick and near death's outward fires, as if his interior had been renewed after destruction, and the experience of scorched guts and humiliated stomach had somehow rejuvenated his heart and soul. Never before had so much happened in one day, and the thought made him laugh.

A sip of tea set him talking, relieved that his mouth liked the heat of the liquid. Maybe I'm coming back to life. A pan on the fire was frying bacon for a row of breadslices, and after a day's gardening the smell of it was pleasant to Harry: 'Of course I do think about the future. Even at my age. I suppose you're too young to bother with it,' he grinned.

'You're wrong. I'm full of it, the future, it's on my mind all the time. Maybe it's because I don't know that there's going

53

to be any future. You remember that last crisis? Planes were going over day and night and I used to watch their vapour trails from the factory roof – all loaded to the gills with hydrogen bombs ready to go off any minute towards Russia. I felt my nerve going as I saw what might come – a complete deathfire burning everybody. But I'm strong, too bloody strong, and I just went back to my machine. "What's the use?" I thought to myself. But I wondered why everybody was dead at a time when they should be alive. And I thought: maybe it's because everybody's talking about it on the telly and reading all about it in the papers, and while this goes on they think it's a game and can't happen. You don't have a bleeding future while you've got the telly on, and that's a fact. I feel I'll go looney though if I don't get on the move. I'd like to walk ten miles every day for ten years. I feel as if I'm being strangled. This country's too little for me – you can walk to any coast in a week – a bit of eagle-crap dropped out of the sky. I look at all the people round me who have boxed their future up in the telly, and it makes me sicker than that whisky I slung down. The wide open spaces would frighten any dead bastard who didn't like other people. That's what the telly does anyway, teaches you to despise your fellow man. There's nothing left to believe in in this country, nothing left, not a thing.'

'Careful,' Harry said. 'That's because you've got nothing to believe in yourself.'

'You may be right. I'll have to find it then. There's nothing in this country that can help me do it and that's a fact. There's a spirit of rottenness and tightness in it.'

'You can't condemn a whole country.'

'I don't. I never wanted a country to believe in, either. I'm out of a factory. A machine will do me. I was just talking about the feeling. I feel like an ant on a gramophone record that can't get off.' He was sitting up, legs spread along the floor, having eaten his way through a bacon sandwich and drunk the mug of tea. Harry had said little, let him rave on, let the fire in his eyes burn undiminished, glowing as if he'd put back a bottle of paraffin instead of whisky. A hard wind kept up a continual bumping against the hut, as if a huge dog running blind across the gardens stumbled at the hut it could never learn to see: 'You can talk, but the world will go its own way.'

'As long as I go mine. That's all I feel fit for now.' He felt good for even less, but couldn't admit it to Harry: head full of stones, legs dead, body paralysed and yet to be woken up from, as if the whisky had killed him, stopped his heart so that he had actually wandered around in the black limitless emptiness of unearthly death in the hour before Harry found him; travelled among star-sparks of half life on his way back into his eyes and brain, toes and stone-cold bollocks, hands and shoulders that, thanks to the bacon and blind talk, and after so long, were getting blood through them again.

Harry spread more slices in the pan. 'It's all right you blabbing about England being rotten, but it's better than some places I could name, for all its faults.'

'That don't say it can't be better though. It won't last much longer.'

He laughed, and turned the bacon over. 'It'll last me out.'

'Enjoy it then, while you can.'

'I'm not enjoying it. I'm too bloody busy living to let things get my goat the way you do.'

'There's some as can do both,' Frank reminded him.

'And there's some as can't help but do both,' Harry said, 'and delight in it' – turning the rashers over for a final crispness. The hut air was close and heavy with breathsteam, fagsmoke and the top heavy odour of burning fat, a total blend suggesting warmth and protection from the outside world. It was comfortable, even though Frank's enduring prostration on the hard boards wore his bones away and ached into his muscles. It was inside, away from the vile attack of problems,

55

and here the only problem was in talk, and to catch into talk the numerous problematic thoughts that came into his head – before they spun away and lost themselves maybe in the sort of protected atmosphere he'd stumbled into, where no real problem could get at any other problem. His head dizzied at such spinning arrows. He wanted to get up and go outside, lean against the hut, push and strain until the whole ricketty fabric, Harry included, fell into a heap. But he wasn't even strong enough for that after so much drink. I'm waking up in a way I've never wakened up before; or maybe the whisky's scorched the jungle from my brain and left only a few steel bolts and rods that I can find my way through at last. Unless it'll only feel like that until the last drop of whisky's all pissed out and I get into my old leaf-bag skin again.

He reached for another sandwich, while Harry set the kettle on the primus in a self-indulgent excuse to keep the blue flame comforting the vitals of the hut. 'Death means nothing to me,' Frank said to him, 'because my future has been taken away. Yet I can't live without a future, Harry. There's got to be something, but when the whole world can go up in five minutes, what is there? There's not even a chance of crawling back into the swamps and living off fish and snakes. There's nothing at all, because the future doesn't mean anything. But to me it's got to. I've got to rip something out of it. So am I supposed to make a future out of this world that's already taken it away? People are better off without a future, tamer, docile. No, I've got to figure one out for myself, which means I'm on my own, even when I don't want to be.'

He ate, and relaxed. It felt like a truce in life – a white handkerchief slowly ripping in the outside wind. Harry often came here and had this truce with himself, yet he was the one who at work said life was a long continuous battle from cunt to coffin. The wind jumped, caught the hut beam end on, shook but didn't budge it. I don't want to go out into that

56

wind. It's dark outside, and cold. I want to stay where the bacon's frying and the lamp's lit. That wind can never bash the hut flat, but it might crash me down if I go out into it. But what's the use of talking? My mind's made up to go out into it whether I go out into it or not.

He shut the back door quietly so as not to wake Pat, felt like an island, drifting away from the continent of his life, almost as if he'd been pushed off by it like some lifeboat no longer needed. The twenty-seven years of it, three times nine, seemed to be receding from the isolated point at which he found himself. He felt more cut-off from life than even when walking the lonely hedgebound roads an hour before dusk. It was a weird feeling, limboed in some Lincolnshire cottage, feet on the table and drinking tea, radio piping softly.

He had to leave, yet without knowing why, as if there were slow-moving springs in his legs over which he had re-linquished control, months ago, before he had even thought about blowing up the bridges of his life. He stood to re-set his pack, wrote on a note-pad: 'Dear Pat, thanks for everything, Frank.' She'd had quite a life compared to his: fiancé drowned, married life to an advertising nob, nursing on and off, and God knows what else. Mine's been tame, stuck in one place, factory, house, pub, same pals, brands of ale, glorying in a pushbike and then a car, dull when you think of some people. With all her books and records she's a better educated person, and they're the people who move and live exciting lives. Things happen to you, the more you know, the more you think.

Rain had stopped brewing itself into the derelict garden. The brimming waterbutt became still, reflecting the sky growing lighter above the hillock, and clouds as if ready to get a move on at last. He walked along the path, smelling the fresh damp air, soddened grass and the distant whiff of rotting tree bark; sedge underfoot was clean and heavy after the night of saturation. Wind jumped the trees, flicked the outer edge of emptying twigs left and right. In Nottingham the streets would be on the move, main roads flooding well, yet there was a sense of movement around this silent garden which he was beginning to understand.

He stepped back into the kitchen, meaning to get his pack and go. Pat stood by the table, having glanced at his scrawled note. She wore a long dark-blue dressing-gown, her face pale from sleep, hair falling loose. His entrance made her jump: 'I thought you were already off' – not meaning to sound so brusque.

She was more relaxed, lines on her face, a smile less bright, less stern and sure of herself than she seemed last night. Straight out of sleep, a recent battleground of dreams, she wasn't yet accustomed to daytime and the presence of this man she had given shelter to. He made her feel as if she was in a strange place, a home not her own that she had woken up in out of a dream. Her senses were overdrawn, exposed, isolated from what surrounded her. She wanted him to vanish, then to stay. There was something pleasurable in the power facing her, so that she distrusted it but could not retreat. Some people, he thought, get up after a night's sleep; other people recover from it, and you can see it on their faces – as it was on hers. He stood close: 'Not yet. I made myself comfortable for breakfast.'

His hands were on her elbows, moved up her back. 'Stop it,' she said. 'What are you doing?'

The answer was a massive rockface, a cauterization of all social feeling, a force that no will or protest could stop. He pulled her to him, face against the side of her neck. 'This' – kissing her warm smooth skin, feeling her body slowly pressing. Her head drew back, eyes closed. 'No, leave me, for God's sake.'

Her lips were hard, opening so that her teeth were against his, and neither could speak. She forced herself away, saying anything that would preserve her from him until the right moment; whenever that would be. 'Not now. Stay though, if you like. I have to dress and go to the stores in the village.'

He sat in the parlour reading a book to the background of the Clarinet Concerto and a coal fire scorching his ankles, finding it pleasant the way she took the fact of their morning kisses so coolly, being accustomed to this as a time of snap and quarrel, a canyon separating you from the woman you'd just been funny with. But she acted as if they'd done nothing, or as if they'd been courting a year already. Nevertheless Pat found it strange the way he seemed at home so soon, took to a book and Mozart as if he'd been familiar with both all his life. Maybe this was what he'd craved since leaving his wife: a new home, though he'd never admit it. 'I don't know what I'll do with myself while you're shopping,' he joked. 'I can't wait till you get back.'

'Read a book,' she said, busy with a shopping list. 'Put a record on.'

And he hardly noticed her return: 'What are you reading?'

He looked at the cover: '*The Naked Lunch*. I thought it was a dirty book, with the word naked in the title.'

'I can't tell when you're being serious,' she said.

'What do you mean?' Indignant tone confusing her even more, though she didn't show it. He was many moves ahead in being familiar with her, and she envied his uncomplicated social ease when she didn't resent it. 'Where did you get this sort of book?'

'In Paris, last year.'

'You've been to Paris?'

'You sound impressed. Only on holiday.'

'I'd like to travel one day. I can tell it's a good book though from the writing. I hope they banned it. It'll make the bloke who wrote it a lot of money. I reckon they should ban

59

every book that comes out so that more people would read.'

She laughed, taking off her coat. 'Would you like coffee?'

'Aye, one for the road,' standing up to kiss her.

'Careful,' she said. 'You'll get me drummed out of the village. I'm supposed to be a pillar of the community: irreproachable, but invisible as long as I'm alone.'

'Let's go upstairs then,' he said, 'so that we won't be seen. It's lucky there is an upstairs. If there's two things in the world I can't stand it's twin beds and bungalows. If somebody left me a bungalow in their will I'd put a double bed on the roof and saw a hole in the ceiling, so that we could go upstairs when we wanted it.' His hands roamed at her waist and hips, and any moment he expected a swingback from her – as he might have got from Nancy even after years of marriage. But she turned by the top step, forced his arms around her; 'I love it when you do that.'

'I'm not shy,' he said, unable to recognize her unassailable self-possession of last night.

Neither was she; undressing, she asked if he had anything: 'You know, precautions and all that.' He'd never seen a woman get stripped so quickly, yet without hurrying, in a casual and graceful way. It was all off before he could get a good look in and enjoy it – no fumbling with hooks and buttons that crazed him well before glimpsing the real thing. Having regarded it as inevitable, and lacking the patience not to make it so, it was partly shyness that made her undress so quickly. Now that she mentioned it, he hadn't got any: 'I started out with a gross, but somebody picked my pocket in a pub the other night. Everywhere was shut yesterday.'

'I'll cope then,' she said. What's the use being a nurse, he thought, if she can't? The room was white-washed, brilliant, bare pictureless walls showing the flesh dazzle of her body plain before him. The curtains were closed and electric light on, so that it might have been two in the morning, and this seemed like the limit of sloth to him, real sin compared to the fact that he was about to make love to someone a complete stranger now that she was naked. She seemed taller, with long legs and well-shaped thighs, a tapering waist not noticed when clothed. There were faint stretch marks on her stomach from having the baby all those years ago, but her muscles were flat and the navel distinct, while her breasts were small and round, purple-ringed at the nipples. His hands went over them, shaking at the soft velvet touch as if he'd never made love before. Her arms pressed around his neck. I'll shoot my bolt before I get there if I go on like this, so out of practice, and nervous as if I was fourteen.

He lay by her side, and they were content to kiss tenderly. The silence of the house and the day outside made him think they were in the sky, or the smack centre of a millpond ocean. How was it possible for such quiet to be in the world? Her eyes closed, and he knew she was waiting, that the time had come. But he didn't want to move. He couldn't shift. For some reason, for the first time in his life, the will wasn't in him at the crucial moment. Her kisses grew harder, blinder, and the more they increased the less was he able to follow. 'Come on,' she said, 'come on, love.'

But he couldn't. Or, in the deepest layers of himself, he would not. Unable to satisfy such scalding lust, they lay for some time: 'Are you nervous of me?' she said at last. He sat up. 'I shouldn't think so. I've never been nervous of anybody like that in my life.'

'Maybe you don't love me,' she smiled.

'Love?' he said. That had never bothered him before.

'Some people can't do it unless they're in love, been seeing each other for a while first.'

'I hadn't thought of that.' Any reason gave him heart, though it was so unique and stunning he could hardly feel ashamed. Yet beneath all this, a subdued rage was ebbing away: 'I think I'll be off' – standing to get dressed.

'Why are you in such a hurry?'

'I stopped yesterday for a drink of water. I can't swallow the tap as well.'

She frowned, drew on her dressing-gown. 'That would sound like folk wisdom to some. To me it sounds like the cold shoulder, as they say.'

'Well, we'll see. I was meaning to give that garden of yours a dig over when it stops raining. When was it last done?'

'I can't remember. I've been too busy to bother.'

'It's heavy for you, that sort of work. A man should do it.' He went downstairs in his socks, put on his shoes by the still burning fire. 'What was that woodwork you wanted done?' he called out to the kitchen.

She laughed: 'I thought I'd have a couple of shelves above the stove. There's nowhere to put things.'

He went to look. 'I'll get some brackets and plugs. Are there any tools?'

'Under the stairs. I had the wood cut last week, thinking I might try it myself, but I don't suppose I really wanted to.' She peeled potatoes, dropped them into the pot – cooking without an apron, which was something new to him, better in that she didn't hide the goodness of herself in the paraphernalia of domesticity. He stood close behind, kissed her neck, and held his hands over her breasts.

There was less formality about it than the deliberation of walking upstairs and going into the bedroom, and stripping as if to a drill, an exhibition as if performed before all the generations of the world to prove that you were with them in their unconscious battle for survival against the ravages of nature. She turned and lay her face in his shoulder. His hands were below her waist, body pressing stiffly but without urgency. He walked her into the sitting-room. There were no fires of impotence this time; his madness was controlled, hard at the loins, and the hundreds of miles journeying during which he had almost forgotten the need for love had only made him forget it in order to overwhelm him now with an unexpected force and sweetness he'd never known before.

They lay on the floor, clothes hardly disturbed, crying out together as if they had been burnt.

5

THE VILLAGE, when he explored the
roundabouts of it, was set in a horseshoe of the wolds.
After a few weeks he seemed never to have been anything
but a countryman, as if much of William Posters had, for
what it was worth, been excised from his backbone. Walking
alone through the bracken-earth of the autumn woods on a
long, purposeless, satisfying stroll (while Pat was out in her
red Mini on some errand of mercy) he could watch for
pheasants, squirrels, or the erratic flip among upper branches
of birds tough enough not to go south at the first chill breath
of October damp.

He was surprised at how much life there still was. Two
squirrels in the middle of a lane fixed each other, until his
appearance sped them apart. One, with a handsome grey tail
and upright back, had a small red disc for an eye, after fighting the rival which had already made off. The other eye must
have been uninjured, for the squirrel flitted among a confusion of trees and bushes without tearing its hide.

Apart from mistily remembered bus-rides as a child, the
only times he had seen the country was from his car-screen,

stopping now and again to eat sandwiches with the window open, or dashing across fifty yards of greensward to gulp down pints in some sheltering pub. Now he not only lived in it, but spoke about gardens and poaching with men in the Keaner's Head when he sometimes called there. Words like covert, lodge, hill, grange, flew from him – and only a month ago he had been at his machine, driving a car, in bed with Nancy, bawling at the kids. Yet in those days the dominant feeling was that of not living his proper and allotted life, of being ennmeshed in a totally wrong sort of existence no matter how plain and real it was said to be. The present life at least was too new to give any such feeling.

Even so, his mind was at all points of the cardiac compass, unsettled and drifting. Out of the wood, he walked along an open lane, beet fields on either side. A Land Rover was coming and he stepped aside for it. A lean-faced man of about fifty called: 'Where are you going?'

Frank looked at the grey, non-penetrating eyes, and said nothing. The man spoke: 'This is a private road. If you go any further you're liable to be shot at by one of my keepers. I'd turn back if I were you.' His head withdrew, quicker than any argument that could follow, and the car rumbled towards a distant farmhouse.

He mentioned it to Pat. 'It must have been Waller,' she said. 'He's not really so bad. He farms all the land down by Panton Moor, and owns the woods near Clayby. He breeds pheasants by the hundred, and his friends come up from London to shoot. He's rich, one of a shipping family in Hull, and doesn't get on with people around here though – the people at the Hall I mean. He's one of the better ones, believe it or not. His children are great friends of Kevin's. Waller lent him a pony last summer.'

'He still sounded a right bastard to me,' Frank said, thinking that maybe William Posters wasn't dead after all, not by a long way. 'He's no right to have land that nobody else can

65

walk on.' Old Bill Posters of course would never have been caught, would have smelt the set-up and gone through gorse and pheasant farms in his usual sly way, so that even the watchdogs wouldn't have stirred, and he'd have come out with a cockbird in every pocket and a hangdog daisy in his buttonhole.

They sat at the evening meal: grilled steak and salad, bread and cheese. Lights were on, blinds drawn, and the fire humped red. 'You see,' she continued, 'he gets a bit jumpy because people sometimes come in their cars from Scunthorpe and Grimsby, scare his pheasants and anything else that moves.'

'I was on a peaceful stroll. Next time I won't be.' She saw him eating too well to be as angry as he made out. The walk must have seen to that. 'If he'd known you were staying here he might not have been so brusque. He thought you were a stranger.'

'Ah' he smiled. 'You mean he smelt fifteen years of overalls on my back! The Lincolnshire wind hasn't got rid of it yet. You've only got to stray a bit off a lane in England and you find a notice stuck in front of you saying trespassers will be prosecuted.'

'You'll just have to ignore them, if you feel like it.'

'But it's still no good that you've got to.'

'If you feel free, you are free.'

'That's the mentality of a slave. You've got to know that you *are* free.' They were strangers still, and the hardest for her to bear were the long silences. Frank didn't mind them, for they were his, and he could sit for an hour or through a meal without being embarrassed that neither spoke. He was unconscious of the silence until its meaning came to him, in a reminder of past noises that he was trying to forget. In the old days Nancy had always brought up the fact that something was wrong with their lives when the kids were crying, and he couldn't stand crying kids, especially a baby – though

66

he'd willingly agreed to himself that something indeed was rotten in their lives. He'd grown to put up with a lot since the first was born, of course, but the soulless noise of a crying baby lit up the dark spaces of emptiness within him, hammered in the roof to prove that no matter what vast emptiness was there at the moment, it would go on expanding into limitlessness if he didn't flee from it. With such a noise and all its meaning it was a case of every man for himself, to run out and find something of substance with which to fill this vacuum lit by the cry of a baby. He didn't follow his instinct and light off, but his reaction to it had at least pointed out that something was wrong.

Well, he had got over that, and didn't know what reminded him of it so strongly, stuck in front of the fire with the village midwife who was now his mistress. A man's manhood was tested by crying children and he had weathered it, or maybe only thought he had since it came back to him now with the force of an experience more agonizing than at the actual time. Why should he be noting his own rebirth by the memory of their birth, and grieving more for their loss than that of his wife?

Pat knew that he was only silent to her, and that in him were plenty of words that spoke loudly for himself, but because he never shared them she worried that one fine morning he would just get up and go, or that she would find the house empty on coming back from a call one rain-smoaked afternoon. But perhaps one day these huge silences would melt into oceans of talk, to prove their growing regard for each other.

The fire blazed, in the wrong place, he thought, hardening himself to think so. It should be in me, instead of the damp ash I feel. She came back from the kitchen, and her face, utterly on its own and cut off from him, had nevertheless a beauty and dignity that he thought she might not even be aware of. He laid his hand on her wrist, squeezed it so that the veins met and hurt, held on as if the long hard grip were more necessary than the hour of unspoken words, a spiritual refuelling whose lifeline no words could latch into place.

She felt something good in his touch, a desperate healing of interrupted blood-flow, a contact between them that no words were at the back of – and that maybe joined both their wounds. He seemed to forget that she was there at all, as if, after the original impulse to touch her, he had lost all feeling for her consciousness close to his which had to be respected. This she did not like, drew her hand away, went off to the living-room and sat there with her thoughts – until he came in and greeted her with some pun or flippancy as if they'd not seen each other all day.

She asked about his parents, what sort of family he came from. 'Your ancestors, for example.'

'I ain't got any,' he smiled. Growing easier with her, homelier phrases occasionally tumbled through into his speech. 'I don't believe in ancestors. One grandfather was a foundry worker; the other a collier – as far as I remember the old man saying. Maybe we don't go back any further than that. There's no Adam and Eve in our sort of family.' It was almost possible to believe him – his face momentarily bleak during the repose after his statement.

She wondered how much he thought of his wife and children, sensed that when he gripped her in a blind unspoken manner it was to hold back despair rather than prove undying love. She sympathized, yet disliked these moods that claimed him from her. When she had left her husband it needed countless solitary months before she could look at another man and think of love. But Frank had been away only a month so must still be neck-deep in the vat of it – and she refused to think that such upheavals were different for men, that they were more predatory, amorous, foot-loose and dominating (or whatever they liked to call it) than women. Maybe his love for this wife (or whatever he liked to call that,

68

too) had been dug so deeply in after six years that the felled tree-roots still ached at contact with air and sky.

Frank complicated her existence, yet she was sure enough of herself not to refuse the first taste of love since leaving Keith. There had been no courtship with him on the morning he was supposed to leave, but neither of them needed the long sweet agonizing preliminaries that were essential for the naïve and inexperienced – or the idle and sensual. In these few weeks they had grown used to loving each other, love beginning from the middle of the fire and moving outwards to all its subtleties, delicacies and considerations from there. There was a liking between them; as between grown people who could never go back lightly on it.

He could know nothing of all this, she thought. Space and violence had been his lot, which wasn't much to say for the world, but there had been more depth and contact in it. Now they were equals, which is to say that there was no depth yet for either of them, who shared the same house. But she reflected, intelligent and realistic, that they shared it at the moment anyway, for who could be sure when he would leave? To her the concept of love was based on a strong, honest, mutual exchange of feelings, and in this sense it was still impossible to think of the word love with regard to him. Maybe time was still to alter all that, though in spite of his gruffness, halfcocked jokes, occasional clumsiness, he was a comforting person to have in the house, to talk to, to have love from when they went to bed at night (sometimes when she came in from rounds that had dragged on all night).

Her basic views were the same as before Frank had turned up. She liked the idea that he had stayed, like his loud unself-conscious concern for her, his tenderness in bed. Before, the solitary house seemed to die, to turn into a meaningless untidy shell whenever she shut the door behind her for a day's visits; and returning to it, it hadn't been so easy to get the breath of life going again. In fact it had become harder and harder, though she was resilient and self-possessed enough not to have admitted it to herself until now, when it didn't matter. Things were different with a man in the house. Despite his long solitary walks a fire was always heaped up on the living-room grate, the radio just switched off, books put back on the shelves. If she thought to set a record on the wind-up gramophone, she didn't need to work the handle or change the needle before it would go.

Her thoughts couldn't much dwell on how he had come into the house. She must have been in some strange trance-like state, a dream almost, as Frank knocked at the door, and when she woke up, they were living together. It seemed like heresy to ripple the process of it by brute recollection – though at other times she felt ashamed that it had happened at all.

She knew little about Frank, though such a lack didn't stop her liking him. Abiding by her natural talent for scrupulous honesty, she could like him for what he did rather than for what he was. Afraid of drawing too favourable conclusions, she could not let what he did act as a pointer to what he might become. Once bitten, shy forever. In that way, if there was a let down it would be gradual and not from very far up. If their love prospered and she really fell for him then that would be even more of a surprise and ten times as pleasant.

Frank went to the pub now and again, had his pint before closing time, and came back – more for the walk, he said, than the drink. One cold and starlit night he set out earlier. Pat had left the house at six on call, and he wasn't at home when she returned at nine. She made a meal and ate by herself. The ten o'clock news was disturbed by the phone. 'Hello?' she answered. 'Nurse Shipley.'

Button B was pressed. 'Love? This is Frank.'

She smiled into the phone, surprised at her happiness: 'Where are you?'

'In the village.' In spite of his closeness she thought the

phone or line must be faulty. 'But I'm blind drunk, so I thought I'd let you know. Then you won't be shocked. I'm on my way back, but go to bed. Don't see me. I'll be O.K. I feel marvellous, but I'll see you tomorrow.'

Even before the phone went dead she was laughing, her head back, happier than when she had first heard his voice a few minutes ago. She sat in the armchair, feeling as if she had just been told some hilarious story while still young enough not to have experience and age spoil it for her. The black years fell away, as if she were sixteen again and sensing the possibility of easier and freer days than those of puberty, waiting for a shattering experience that would release her from it.

She had no thought of going to bed and cutting off her day as he had wanted. This strange recall of youth and happiness was more mature than the actual one which had had the storms of her twenties before it. There were no storms before her now (she was so much a woman and sure of herself) and she was more capable of enjoying it because she knew what it meant without wanting to know the cause of it.

She looked around the living-room : decorated and set out with all the taste that remained from her marriage. She had scoured auction sales in the market towns, collecting furniture, books, lamps, odds-and-ends to achieve the harmony and comfort of a spiritual base. The house was her own – except for small mortgage payments each month. Twelve hundred pounds seemed paltry when set by the stature she now felt. The first payment and necessary modernization had taken her last penny. It was a venture, to accumulate all this, for who knew when she would have to give it up and go elsewhere? No one ever knew that, but if her life had taught her anything it had been to live where she was, to the maximum that could be achieved, and not to think about what she would be doing in a year so much as how she wanted to live at the moment. On reaching a new job, a new place, one must set down roots as if one were going to stay there forever. She had done this, and the fact of it was part of the present happiness that overwhelmed her.

She decided to put out all lights so that when he came in he'd think she was in bed. There wasn't long to wait – which she was glad of, darkness not being a good cloak for the way she was feeling. His key turned, and she stifled her laughs as he bumped over the threshold.

It was hard to get much sense out of his words, but she felt his relief at thinking himself alone: 'Blindoe,' he kept saying. 'Hate anybody to see me blindoe. Gutterdrunk. Where is she? Snoozing in a warm bed. What a night. A pint of mild and a double rum. A double rum and a pint of mild. The roundabout, as I explained; wouldn't serve me. Well, I said, I'll serve myself. Then he did. Didn't want trouble. Neither did I. I wanted a drink.'

He was falling through the living-room. Hands, unable to get bearings, scooped a book off the table, went by her face. 'Noise, noise – I'll wake the goldfish. I'm in the bloody wrong room. Get upstairs, Frank.' She thought it no joke at all, wondered how she could break it.

His hand touched her, and she laughed again, still at the same pitch of happiness. 'I knew you were there because I'd seen you,' he said. 'Put the light on now, love. Only dead people sit in the dark, and I hate the darkness.'

'You were so funny,' she cried.

He blinked at the flooding light. 'I'm sure I was. I suppose that's your idea of a joke. Well, it's better than snatching the chair from under me, I suppose.' He pulled her out of the chair, dead sure and strong now back in the presence of her. The darkness had been grey and gridded, impenetrable. She spoke between his kisses: 'You sit down, and I'll make us some coffee.'

'Don't bother. I'm done for until morning.' She had left him, was already plugging in the kettle, opening bread tin and cheese dish. He lay in the chair she had sat in, head back, feeling like a survivor on the rim of an explosion – thumped and thrown, drowsy and happy because it seemed that the earth, having spared him, was his friend. He wondered: What am I doing here? This can't be my home. I was never meant to land up here. But maybe I was. You end up where you were never meant to end up. He wondered what Nottingham looked like from the air, but fell like a stoned and frozen bird back near the middle of it. Recollections were never hazy: even half drunk they were sharp and concise in the meaning splayed out to him. I was meant to leave, and that's true. On the Saturday morning of his departure, back from his car ride in the country when he'd given the soldier-lunatic a lift, he parked it and set off on foot down Boden Street, midday chips already steaming in their homely bins, a coalman coming back with his empty lorry, black-faced assistant resting his arse on the scales. The last few years had bored him to death and distraction. He'd even tried following his father's advice and joining a working man's club, but that was worse than sitting at home with the telly smashing one tab, and kids bruising the other with their screams and squabbles as he tried to get the guts out of some book or other. No politics, lads, and no religion. Just drink your pints and sling your darts, heads down for Bingo and look alive to win a fiver at the end. When you're off sick we'll look after you, lad, give you a bit of club money, like, and a seaside booze-up once a year. But no religion, no politics. Don't think. Heads down. You're all free as long as you do as you're told. Legs eleven, bed and breakfast, key of the door. Heads down and look in, sink in that pound of treacle. On its own: number one; the messages fell sharp and fast.

One street funnelled him into space, a view across rubble that a few months ago had been a populous ghetto of back-to-backs and narrow streets. He lit a fag, to shock absorb the sight of all these acres cleared of people, smashed down and dragged to bits. It wasn't unpleasant, this stalingrad of peace, and he'd heard that a start was one day to be made on this triangle of three main roads now with heart and guts scooped out.

He walked into space, few paces taking him across a clearly marked street plan on which as a kid each moss-dewed corner and double-entry had seemed miles from each other, different nations and tribal zones locking their arteries in handshakes of tumultuous life. You could still see the sockets from which lamp-posts had been tugged out like old dandelions and stacked ready for transport to the melters. He thought of going home immediately to Nancy, swinging on his heels this minute. But he rejected the impulse, unwilling to go back there like a bat into hell. Streets in all directions had been clawed and grabbed and hammered down, scooped up, bucketted, piled, sorted and carted off. Where had the people gone? Moved onto new estates, all decisions made for them, whereas he also wanted to uproot himself but must make his own moves, create something positive from the irritating mists of discontent – a freedom which he thanked and cursed at.

He crossed towards real streets, hoping to find a pub. But these streets too were down for demolition, nearly all empty. One or two still had people living in them, isolated houses encased in ruin and desolation. It must have been strange to live there, waiting for the dark ceremonious smash before the dawning of some new house nearer to fresh air and fields. Two up and two down, they were finished after eighty years of life. Many had doors and windows off, smashed in destructive joy by kids, and Frank walked into one, the living-room piled with planks and bedticks, shattered glass and slates, bricks and the heaped throw-outs of family living. He looked over the panels of a half ripped-off door, towards sombre backyards of taps and lavatories. From the fireplace a large rat blinked – though didn't move. 'Robert the Rat,' he said aloud,

74

'your number's up. They're coming for you.' The half brick flew from his hand, but the rat clawed a way up the chimney, unharmed.

On the next street corner was a pub called The Rising Sun, which he thought at first to be untenanted, but a few Saturday morning people had already gathered there when he pushed his way through to the bar. It was a clean, cheerful sort of pub, customers mostly elderly. He unclipped a pound: 'Pint of mild, mate' – his call overloud since he wasn't used to being served straight away. He also wasn't a regular at this dying beacon among the ruins, and all the stares of the old men were on him. He leaned against the bar and stared back, thinking: 'Christ, am I going to be like that in twenty years? Not if I know it. But maybe I don't know it. Not much I don't.' They turned from his thoughtless eyes, back to low talk and dominoes, the comfortable vacancy of a half empty glass. He put his drink down after one medium sip.

In over ten years he had formulated certain rules about drinking beer. For example, he wouldn't drink bad beer, and to cut down the chances of this he would never be the first at the bar for a drink when the pub opened its doors, wily enough to let some other get that hop-spit-and-a-sawdust down his unsuspecting gizzard. He often left a pint, walked out after one swallow if it tasted the slightest bit off-centre. Too many pals, himself included at one far-off time ago, had come to work on Monday suffering more from a couple of pints than some men did from a sling-down of forty. You couldn't be too careful. And this fancy bottled beer they were always trying to shove at you had more heartburn in it than any of the draught stuff. As far as beer in tins was concerned, excuse me while I commit suicide – no, don't wait, just turn your back. But the worst of all, bottled or not, was warm beer, and that's what this pint of mild was that had just been dished up.

He invited the publican over. 'This ale's rotten. It's warm,'

75

he told him. Everyone stopped what they were doing, and stared again, that concentrated stare kept by the old or finished for a member of the encroaching young, or a plain enemy with the expression of friend on his face. He slid it towards him : 'It's rotten. Taste it. Warm as Monday's suds.'

'You must be mistaken,' the publican said. 'My beer's never rotten.'

'Taste this, then.'

'I have, friend, I taste every barrel before it's put on.'

'A young 'un like that don't know what ale is,' an old man called, while the others chuckled comfortably.

'Still,' Frank said to the publican, surprised at the tense atmosphere over a matter nearly always rectified in willing silence, and quickly. 'Still, whether you tasted it or not, that ale's rotten, and so would my guts be if I drunk it. Warm ale once gave me the colic for a week.'

The publican's face grew redder. 'That's about the tenth time you've called my ale rotten. It ain't rotten.'

'It's warm though, and that's the same to me. So how about changing it?'

'I'll do no such thing.' He smacked one-and-six down on the counter. 'Clear out.'

'You soon know where you stand in this place. I expect it'll be flat on its face next week.' He took the pint jar, slow, mechanical, absent minded almost, a black feast for all staring eyes, including the publican's, and emptied its ale onto the floor: 'I don't drink warm suds,' he said. 'You should have changed it.'

Frank realized that he, in any case, ought not to have splashed out the beer with such deliberation, ought simply to have left it and walked out – or maybe knocked it accidentally with his elbow while turning from the counter. 'Get the police,' a voice called above the muttering cauldron of advice.

'Set into him,' someone else cried. 'He don't belong here.'

He walked unmolested as far as the door. On his way there

he observed a good fire going in a side parlour, horse brasses above every shelf, regulation dartboard on the wall, coloured prints of horse races in black-bead frames, as well as the usual sick, dog, children, blind and ex-soldier collection boxes along the bar. The publican caught him by the arm. 'Come back, you bleeder.' Grey eyes, pupil and retina, glazed into one unseeing pint-sized point, were beamed onto him. The publican thought Frank was drunk, even though he seemed to carry it rather well. 'You're coming back. I want your name.'

Frank's hand was on the door. People closed around to make themselves part of a climax. He looked at the publican's concerned, determined face that hadn't bargained for trouble this Saturday morning: he wore a blazer with an air force wing badge on his lapel, and a Marks and Spencer's old school tie of black and red pattern. 'Come and clean it up.'

'Ar, that's right,' ran the chorus, 'that's just.'

Frank wanted to hit the man for suggesting he was the sort that would wipe up some mess, especially one that he had made. A bastard like that had never done a real day's work in his life, he thought, as his fist stamped into him, causing a startled cry as the publican fell into the not so old man who had called out: 'Ar, that's right. That's just.'

He was back in the street of empty houses, running along it and holding his fist, shoes crunching over smashed slates, kicking against half bricks and rotting woodlumps. The publican's gang weren't far behind, and he expected nothing less than lynching if they caught up. At great speed he ran into the same house, along the hallway and back into the living-room. By the fireplace he trod on the startled rat before it had time to shift, but it had scattered up the soot-banks and into the chimney before the publican's boots squashed all life from it.

Frank, in the backyard, heaved himself to the roofs of a dozen insecure half-gutted lavatories, his egress fixed now into the next street. A brick parapet divided the sloping roof

77

of one set of lavatories from the slates of the next, and Frank stood precariously astride this high ridge – a ridge so rotten that he could bend down now and again to lift up a brick from it, or even a piece of one, to threaten his attackers – since they too had access to bricks and were now industriously prising them loose for a short-range stoning.

He was perched eight or nine feet above, and at his first shot they scattered. Frank had had enough, was ready to make his retreat towards Hartley Road and back to his parked car. But the world swayed, as if he were about to faint, to roll down limp at the feet of the exulting posse.

A brick caught him weakly on the shoulder. He hurled two, clearing the space of backyards. The earth swayed again, his shoes moving slightly on the slates, several bricks cascading from the parapet between his legs. Are any of them bastards pushing at the walls? No, they couldn't, otherwise he would have seen them. He stood under the clear sky, fighting for his balance, a horse on all fours, then straight and uneasy, ready at any second or footweave to use his hands again. He hurled his last brick through a window that still had glass, and at the force of his swinging arms the whole line of lavatories swayed like a slate-blue wave of the mid-ocean sea. His attackers drew back terrified into the house, as if running for their lives from some huge towering scar-faced monster high in the sky behind that Frank could not see.

He heard them falling over each other (trod on that poor bloody rat again) scrambling back through the house to the comparative safety of the street as if the whole district might crumble, only too glad to go laughing in to their snug pub at the poetic justice of that young bogger up to his neck in ruins and bruises.

When the collapse began under his feet, Frank slid pell-mell down the slates and onto hard asphalt of another backyard. The lavatories collapsed as if dynamited, like a bit of war from a silent film of long ago, ending in a mass cave-in of bricks and splintering wood, a rising grey stench of bug-ridden slatedust settling over the lot as he made his way out of it, back towards the car, and hoping the same fate would be soon in store for the pub from which he had been so discourteously thrown.

She came back with a laden tray, set it on a low table somehow missed on his crazy zig-zag across the room. He was drunk no longer, yet she needed to shake him as if he were, back into the immediate environs of love and care at the heart of Lincolnshire: 'If you want to drink and not suffer you should eat a slice of bread first, with butter half an inch thick. Or drink a glass of water between each glass of whisky – or whatever it is you drink.'

He waved his hand. 'What's the use getting drunk if you prepare for it in such a scientific way?' Pills and Alka Seltzer were on the tray. 'Knowing so much would stop me enjoying it.'

'If knowing stopped you enjoying life, then you wouldn't be much of a person. Come on, love, eat. Drink.'

His eyes were fully open. 'Would you marry me?'

She looked, all laughter gone. 'As far as I'm concerned, we are married. Why do you ask?'

'I suppose we are. You don't need to answer. I'm in love for the first time in my life.' He found it impossible to say why he loved her, had been so busy in his life that she was the first woman he had thought to ask this question about, frightened into it because early on in his stay he would sometimes wake up in the morning and be unable for a few moments to think of her name. Such a thing proved how completely she had altered his life, and you could only be in love with a woman who had done that to you. She had become a midwife indeed, getting him out into some new lit-up world still beyond the touch of his hand and brain to reach.

6

🌿

FURROW-LINES refused to break as he walked over them. Frost made the earth hard as steel, coated the ridges that bent the arches of his feet. A copse on the opposite hill was bare, sky visible through upright posts. A dead bird seemed a piece of hoar-shaded soil until he was right up to it. There was no wind: winter had brought a biting lacquer of frost that numbed his face and half-closed his eyes. At two in the afternoon the land was silent, all doors locked against it.

He had walked since morning in a great circle, down the valley-path and across the old railway, cutting over the speckled leprous surface of a frozen stream and heading between coverts to Market Stainton. With a cold pint in him he trekked over Dog Hill, took the sloping track through fields that met the houses of High Benniworth. His eyes had sharpened and, as winter gripped, more life was evident. The faintest impress of rabbit feet vanished into a spinney. Magpies argued on a dung heap just inside a farm gate; dogs and cocks called in tune with vertical smoke going out of the chimney – life in spite of all doors closed. By Warren Hilltop, where the sun reflected shadows on the green-white landscape, a spring poured from a hedge bottom. Gulls screamed upwards – often seen no matter how bitter the weather, and always reminding him that the sea was close, only fifteen miles east of his crunching feet, a flaking, slow, raw-heaving sea of frost and desolation. Winter was in the earth like King Arthur's sword, waiting for a hand of resolution to heave it out and set off over land and sea. He smiled at such a flamboyant impossible image, knowing he was fixed in Lincolnshire for a long time with the sort of love he had on his hands.

In drunkenness he had spoken the truth, saying he was in love for the first time. He reminded Pat next morning that he had said this, and neither had she forgotten the night that his words had branded. Understanding of them had matured, and his drunkenness subsided by the time they got to bed. He was surprised that she hadn't resented his coming back in such a state. He'd mistrusted her amusement at it, having expected, when phoning in advance, a retort to stay out until he was sober. Not a bit of it. She took it well. Maybe she was not as rigid as he'd often thought. She even seemed more relaxed, as if flattered at the possibility that for the first time he had revealed part of his real self to her. They drew closer together in spirit. She hadn't even bothered to ask why he'd got drunk. Not that he knew, either, though maybe it had been so that this understanding could be reached between them. Things sometimes worked that way, though he could never imagine her admitting it, and in any case he would never get drunk again.

They talked about Kevin, who was to come up in a week from boarding school, and stay for Christmas. 'How are you going to explain me?' he asked.

'I'm not. I'll simply tell him.'

'Isn't he a bit young?'

'You don't think I could lie, do you? He's eleven. He's old

81

enough to know.' They drove to Lincoln, Frank at the wheel, taking it slowly on frosty bends. Kevin had caught the express from St Pancras, then the diesel from Nottingham. It drew quietly into the long platform on time, half empty so that Frank thought it a train still to go out before the one waited for came in. He expected all trains to arrive crowded, people packed by the windows ready to disembark. Right from the beginning of childhood, railways had been life lines to him, the double attraction later on of machines travelling. A train rushing under a bridge and through a station was a serious and romantic sight, mystical and full of power over a person's life. He had rarely taken a train, rather bus or car, because to do so would be committing himself in a way he felt hardly ready for.

They walked along the platform. Pat wore a heavy camel coat and fur boots: Frank a thick sweater under his mackintosh, and ordinary shoes. Kevin already had his case down, stood by it till he saw them. Expecting his mother alone, it took some time to recognize her. She embraced him: 'Hello, darling' – and asked about his trip down.

He was a tall, dark haired boy of eleven, had the same shape and colour eyes as his mother, though lacking their clarity. His features were similar, slightly darker, and his presence seemed more poised and careful regarding the different worlds he moved in, as if much of Pat's one-time and far-off assurance had passed early to him – though the seeds of something like her present conflict and uncertainty loomed in his eyes. 'I was looking out of the window all the way,' he said, 'watching things. Then in Nottingham I had a pie and some coffee.' He glanced up.

'I want you to meet Frank,' she said. 'He's living with mummy now.'

'Hello,' Kevin said, not, as Frank observed, batting an eyelid. They walked out to the car. Frank fastened his case on the luggage rack. Pat embraced her son again. 'Don't you

82

think he's handsome?' Frank agreed, but wondered why the boy wasn't shy of so much fuss. He sorted out the various combinations regarding their journey back. Should Pat drive and the boy sit in front with her? Or should he take the wheel, and the two of them sit together in the back? What about her driving, and Frank sitting beside her, with the boy behind? Which would be best for the wellbeing of their time together? They couldn't all sit in the front, and that was a fact – which was the worst of these mini cars. He laughed, to find himself blessed with so much consideration, only to wonder what the hell it mattered. Well, things do matter, he decided, pulling forward the front seat so that Pat and Kevin could get behind. But halfway to the village Kevin had to sit in front because he felt car sick.

For the first days he was taciturn, studious, and went only once to visit Waller's farm. Frank talked to him, spellbound him with facts and possibilities of the various machines he'd worked, discussed motor cars, and natural history which he had taken an interest in through Pat's books and on his walks.

The sensual monotony of their existence was broken. Kevin sat at the table for meals, and when he wasn't telling his mother about school he either ate silently, or looked at a book while slowly dealing with food on his plate. Pat didn't mind him reading at meals, and on this point Frank wondered whether she was spoiling him, or allowing so much freedom simply because it was good for her. Frank had the sense to treat him as another man which, in intellect if not experience, he often seemed to be. 'I'm glad you're here,' Pat said, after Kevin had gone to bed. 'Before, I think he used to be lonely, with me out on my calls so much of the time.'

'He seems a good lad,' he remarked. 'I can't make much of him, but then, you never can at that age.'

'I often don't like the idea of him being bandied about from one part of the country to another, yet it's best, as things are, that he's away at school.' Seeing how she treated him at home, he realized that she must have worried about him a great deal when he wasn't there, though she had kept it well concealed during the long autumn weeks.

On his ramblings he had noticed a small plantation of firs in an isolated hump of land beyond Panton Hall – trees that were part of the estate. He set out with a trowel, circled and undermined the roots until the slender trunk sloped into his arms and he could pull it clear. Steering a return course through the backbone of the night, head bent and breathing evenly under the coarse weight of the tree, he felt happy at having made off with a piece of greenery that had sprouted from the earth, land which he considered belonged to him, but was denied by circumstances or sham legislation. He felt nothing like a thief except in the caution of his getaway, and hoped the tree would be missed in the morning – likely, since he'd all but trodden a fence down to get at it. As for being tracked, he'd walked the half mile of a nearby road, and turned across fields from there. Low cloud held back stars and moon, and no one else was out on the broad earth. The frost had broken, loam softening underfoot, a smell of soil and bracken cutting his nostrils as he breached a hedge. It seemed as if the year had doubled on its heels to bring autumn back.

He sat down to smoke in the Lincolnshire blackness, his tree a piece of plunder towards which freedom had led him. The roots of it smelled of sap and stored-up frost, comforting soil and crushed fir-needles, the fruitful odours of a life snapped out of its accustomed earth and rut. He thought of Nancy and the children, not with shame or anguish, simply saw them for a moment in front of his eyes. Memories made him uneasy, helped him over the long stretches of field bearing his tree, but he wanted to be further away from them, felt as if tied by the ankle and barely hovering beyond the darkness of their confines – whereas a thousand miles might make him feel as if the whole complex recollection had been worth abandoning.

They were surprised to see him pulling the tree through the back door. 'Here's a good-looking conifer for the Christmas pot.'

'What a robust specimen,' Kevin exclaimed. Pat came in from cleaning the kitchen, and asked with a cold glance: 'Where did you get it?'

He weighed up her disapproval, and said for Kevin's sake: 'Panton village. I met a man in a pub last week and told him to put one by for me. I paid ten bob for it. Cost a pound in Lincoln.'

He trimmed it, and Kevin helped him gather soil and fix it in a large earthen pot – which they stood in a corner of the dining-room because Pat hinted strongly that it would spoil the furnished perfection of the lounge.

When Kevin was in bed she demanded: 'Well, where *did* you get it?'

'I dug it up. You don't think I'd buy a thing like this when there are so many around?'

'No, I don't. But don't bring anything else that's stolen into this house. And don't tell Kevin where you got it. Not that he doesn't suspect already.'

The tree framed him, two trees, his own foliage gone deep within. She would certainly never see it, only the mirror of his grey eyes beating back her inquisition. It was the sort of strength she hated in a man, features as if they had been set for generations, fixed like stone that had somehow learned to move. 'Kevin's got a head on his shoulders,' he said, amused that she should control her anger and not come right out with it.

'It's a good job he has, otherwise he might mention the tree to someone who'll hear that one is missing from Panton Hall – to Waller, for example. You still have your city ways: they only have to miss a pound of apples around here and it's

85

the talk for weeks. Next time, have a head on *your* shoulders and don't rely on Kevin having one. I want him to be honest, as well as intelligent.'

How could you argue with a woman who was worrying about her kid? Especially when he'd tried to do them a favour. There was no love for him that night.

But on other nights during the holiday their love was more silently rapturous. Her son was in the room across the landing, and this was all he could put it down to. She folded Frank with her warm arms and slender legs, slept naked with him, in spite of the winter, which she had not done before. Her face changed for love in the moments before the light went out, softened in the frame of her outspread reddening hair. He kissed her lips, and flower-blue eyes that wouldn't close until he touched the light switch. The strong love, the unique tenderness felt when looking at her, compounded itself when he thought back to her anger, seeing how his love had drawn her out of it, and even without him knowing had transformed them both. They had to be quieter with someone else in the house, and maybe this gave their love that slow-motion, secretive bitter-sweet ritual under quilt and blankets that sent through them such all-flooding passion. Unable to cry out with pleasure they bore it within themselves, touched by its sensual echoes long after the first violent spasms, until they were still and separated, pulled down by some irresistible force into an enclosed boat of sleep and left to drift in blackening dreamlessness.

Such intensities subdued them during the days that followed. Waking up, Frank felt he had been wrenched by a claw-hammer out of a week's sleep. But he was downstairs before Pat, often while it was still dark. A lorry had dropped off a load of trunks, and he'd set up the horse by the back door, got to work in the bleak air with jacket loose, drawing back the teeth that he'd filed one by one to sharpness so that his rhythm caused streaks of sawdust to mark the asphalt, and created a log-pile by the kitchen wall. At eight he filled the house with a smell of bacon, took breakfast up. They talked, and he watched her put on her clothes as if, he thought, they belonged to someone else, looking at each item as if she'd never seen it before, examining it for cleanliness rather than colour or style. 'You were up early.'

'I felt like it. I always do after the sort of love we did last night. It turns me into a new man.'

'I'm glad of that,' she laughed. Sometimes when the phone snapped her out of bed she dressed in a few minutes, ruthlessly. He hated the noise of it, had used one rarely enough in his life to know he would never sound otherwise than a hungover aborigine when forced to listen and make words at it. Her self-possession when called to it at certain moments never stopped surprising, and, in a way, pleasing him.

She pulled on her long woollen underwear, and fastened her brassiere – something which he considered her breasts could well live without. Occasionally she left it off, and he would kiss her from behind, his hands roaming the nakedness under her sweater. 'I thought I'd get the bus today into Louth,' he said. 'Buy some things we need.'

'Take Kevin if you would.'

'I was going to. You know, love, I've been wondering if it wouldn't be better for him to live here all the year round.'

'I've thought about it, too. But I'm not sure he's not better off at school. He's settled there now, and likes it. Apart from that, his father wants him at school, and I'm afraid he has the final say. You see, I was the guilty woman who abandoned my husband and child.'

'Well,' he said, with a hollow laugh, 'you can always rely on a society of equals taking it out on the women.' He thought she was making this up as an excuse, on the assumption that if they all settled happily together he'd go off one day and leave them high and dry, murder their bloody happiness. She must have had a few knocks in her life if she

87

imagines that. He couldn't tell her all this, but he put his arms around her. 'I'm with you for good, love, you know that, don't you?'

'I know you are.'

'Don't smile. It means you're not sure.'

'If I didn't smile I'd be lying.' Her lips hardened, ends pointing downward, a sign of boiling sands beneath. 'What do you want me to say?'

'I want to believe that you feel sure about me,' he answered, standing by the window, his back to her.

'That's up to you then, as well.'

'I know.' He turned, and she was already dressed: a heavy brown sweater, skirt, thick stockings and shoes. 'You think I don't know it? But it seems easier for me to feel sure.'

'We'll have to wait and see whether it does.'

He felt as if an axe had chipped through to the ashes in his stomach. Her eyes rounded, but she wasn't smiling: 'That shouldn't have sounded as hard as it did.'

'I'm able to wait and see whether it does, whether you're sure of me.'

'I love you,' she said. 'Isn't that enough?'

He turned on her: 'That's the trouble. We love each other. It's too easy to say. Maybe we only think we do, which would be better as far as I'm concerned, because there'd be some hope for us of a real love then. There's too much missing still. In the last few months I've had my guts ripped out and put back again. After last night I can't stand to look at anything. I can't think at all.'

Tears were falling: 'What are you trying to do to me? To get from me?'

It was an effort to stay calm, and embrace her: 'It's what I want to give you,' he whispered. 'We're trying to make something here.'

She grew quiet and they went downstairs.

The days were short, occasional sun. Frost would have been

88

better, for mostly it rained out of low cloud that swirled as mist along rolling tops of the hills. Bare hedges and trees were laden with it, and the garden was waterlogged, spreading a heavy permeating smell of rain and soil and soaked wood. It was an odour Frank liked: every sight and tang of the countryside emphasized his complete limb-rip from the past, stamped his isolation from it even more than living with Pat. He stood at the end of the garden; watching far-off house-roofs wilting under rain.

One morning they stayed late in bed, a rare happening, and Kevin tapped at the door with a tray of breakfast he'd made. 'Just a moment,' Pat answered, reaching for a night-dress. Frank got into pyjamas, and all three ate a relaxed easy breakfast in the room.

After lunch, shadows drew in, leavened by silence. Frank kept lights burning all day, closed the blinds before night had time to thicken. Pat hated the winter. It made her work a double burden, depressed her with its dragging timelessness. Kevin was sent to bed at ten, so they sat in the lounge reading, a logfire scorching the small room, hissing and spitting as sap rolled into the flame.

One morning early they went for a walk. It was a winter's day, the blue dazzling snowless heart of winter in high Lincolnshire. Kevin had stayed at the cottage and tuned in to French lessons on a set of records his father had found one year at the Portobello market. It was winter only because it was cold, air chipping like invisible scraps of steel at the dead flesh of the face. They stepped quickly along the southward lane, through fields of frosty grass, as if they were going somewhere. 'I hate to stay still,' Frank said. 'There's no work on days like this so I feel good to be walking.'

She grasped his hand, as if they had much to say to each other, but which her vanity had decided was unnecessary: 'It's a change to get away from the house and be alone like this.' They climbed the sloping hillside of loam, a hard hour's walk, edging slowly towards the top line that separated them from the touching sky.

The crest was gradual, shaved off, but suddenly there was nothing between them and the deep mist of the sky. The only sound that the world gave was that of their breathing. Up here, there was nothing else. They stood still: animals were underground, birds dead or far away, no roads, people, houses, nothing to make noise. Such uplands were a world on their own, not high, but isolated by the North Sea, the Fens and marshes, the Humber, and the subtle snakiness of the grey Trent that needed wide lowlands to breed and flood in to the west. Hamlets were half lost in frosty air. The rim of blue haze on the horizon was the pink of spring flowers, campion petals, premonitions of cuckoo spit and primroses, soft grass and tadpoles. The land was a whitened waste, copses and woods like dropped hoods set down to cover something special until spring, isolated farms and cottages hard to see but for minute darkenings of chimney-smoke. The hard breath of their climb subsided, until it could only be heard to each separated self; then they became aware of it, and it decreased again until they were as silent as the bitter unobtrusive air touching hands and faces.

Unwanted words were spelt like a lit-up newsflash across the inside of his eyes: 'Now what do we do?' The noise of his own life had been taken away, and the sound of all others, too. A pool in one of the fields had turned to ice, as if molten lead had been poured into a hollow and left to set, unbreakable, fixed forever even through summer. He was immobilized by lack of sound.

To break it he said, releasing her hand: 'Let's go down,' and their feet moved with comforting heaviness over the frost as she took his hand and obeyed.

7

IN FOUR MONTHS he hadn't seen a film. At the pub, he drank in a private room to get out of the death-ray of television. Once a week he made tracks there, had a pint, watched by those who speculated on his long sojourn at Nurse Shipley's house.

He offered to take her to Louth or Lincoln for an evening, but she said: 'When I want you to, I'll let you know. If you want to go, just do so. You know that I'm all right here.' He too liked the peace and isolation – while often wondering how someone like Pat could stand so much of it since she'd already done a couple of years.

He had cleaned out all he considered to be the good books of her library, and looked forward to the huge shiny-sided van drawing up outside the house to lend them more. 'I'm happy here,' he said, 'lapping up these books like a cat lapping up milk' – so that she wondered whether he were here for any other purpose than that. Still, in a discreet, offhand way, she advised him what to read, careful not to praise any book but merely putting it in his way by such phrases as: 'This one isn't bad' or 'You might like this one.'

He had an irresistible yen to fill his shattered mind, to separate himself from the world, and yet have something to talk about with Pat. He secretly wanted to catch up with her in all she had read, felt that such continual reading was altering the basic mechanism of his senses in a way that reading had never done for Pat. For her, books were an accepted part of life, even to the reading of them, whereas they had been something rare and foreign to him, seen in other peoples houses as part of the furniture – a showing-off part, at that. He had detested books at school as symbols of torment, employed only to prove in public what he had always known about himself in private – that he was dead ignorant. He assumed readily that Pat's books must be good because he didn't feel uneducated or foolish while reading them. Having tackled so few in the last ten years made them so much easier to absorb now.

They weren't the sort that taught electricity, plumbing, engineering or gardening, but they widened the world beyond the range of his eyes and softened the hitherto hard limits of his perceptions. Reading Homer or Sophocles, he couldn't scorn the idea of gods or God if he wanted to enjoy and get any good out of them. This wasn't easy. The many Greek names in a single book of the Odyssey bothered him, but Pat had a dictionary, so that he reduced his natural strong hankering to know what happened next, and actually enjoyed looking up every name until, towards the end, he had a rough idea who and what they meant, soon recognized them as clearly as he once had the names of players of his favourite rugby teams. He looked up words in the English dictionary, then lost his shyness at seeming half literate, and asked Pat what they meant to save himself the trouble of moving from the fire to the bookshelf. He'd previously bought or borrowed books to read about war or sex, but now he got pleasure from a story taking in neither. Or he found that if a book was well-written about love or war then it gave more satisfaction than a paperback half a notch above comic books. He'd liked *Tom Jones*, struggled through the peace parts of *War and Peace*, read *Tess* and *Jude*. One day he said: 'I suppose a lot of those people gassed by the Germans had read good books like these.'

'Of course. Many of them must have,' she answered.

'Those German bastards,' he retorted, and went on reading in the savage light of illumination.

Kevin was seen off from the crowded platform at Lincoln. Frank had been indifferent to his visit at first, only wondering what effect it would have on him and Pat, realizing finally that in a curious way it had enriched them. Frank had grown used to him, and by the time he left they'd become so attached to each other that Kevin had promised to write. 'I'm glad you go on so well,' Pat said on their way back from the station. 'I was worried, naturally.'

'Naturally,' Frank said. 'But why didn't you tell me you were, though, instead of letting it drop only now?'

'What's the point? It would have been useless to let you know I was worried before he came.'

'We could have talked about it,' he said. 'Talk is the staff of life. You don't think I'd have taken it the wrong way, do you? I've come to the conclusion people don't talk enough. There's not enough talk. The powerlines are cut when a person hasn't anything to tell or say. I don't believe in the strong silent type – he might be strong, but he's dead. I've met enough of them to know this, looking back on it. I prided myself on being one, once. But talk is blood. It's a bandage as well. You're a nurse: you should know. You wrap it around your wounds and don't bleed to death.'

They drew in for petrol. 'Honestly, I didn't see the point of mentioning it.'

He said, when they were on the road again: 'If you didn't, why do you mention it now that he's gone back and the issue's over?'

93

'You say you think people should talk more. So do I. Which doesn't mean only you, either. I suppose your ideal is really somebody who didn't talk at all except to say "yes master" and "no master" to all that *you* had to say.'

'If I didn't want you to talk, the only way would be not to talk myself.' It was pointless to bicker, as useless as the frost-bitten sunshy road in front. 'Anyway, I hate arguments while I'm driving. You know: careless talk costs lives. But I'm sorry Kevin's gone. We'd got used to having him.' He saw she was upset, about to weep. 'Don't worry, love. He'll be back soon.'

While still in bed at Pat's warm side he sensed that more snow had drifted down, felt the cold presence of it beyond drawn curtains and shut windows, pressing thick over wolds and fields. Like a magnet it drew him out, silently to gather his clothes and tread naked to the kitchen where he dressed and saw by the clock that it was barely half past six.

Eighteen inches of snow had fallen during the night, drifted against gates and fences up to double that depth. He looked across the garden, at sprout tops like deformed mushrooms humped above milkwhite snow. It was a silent, low-clouded dawn, steely and lifeless, without colour. A shiver started at the roots of hm, shook its way out. Winter seemed to go on for ever. The quiet countryside was more savage when at the mercy of snow than were hard paved streets in the city that put an invincible layer of paving between you and the rich worms. He'd slung his hook at the wrong time, landed himself first in the rainy season, now in the ice-age.

A path would need clearing to the road – though on first wielding the spade he didn't know why, since no one would get up that route awhile to set down milk or newspapers. Still, a path looked good: if a ghost on skis passed by he would see from the sunken snowpath looped around half the house that someone lived there who was alive in it. The radio called this the worst winter for many a year, and no one could say it was lying.

Dawn had not yet churned its full shoulder above the bleak land. It was half dark, half day, day surfacing after being half-drowned by final blackness. But it had fought its way out, a rebirth of the day in hard uncompromising silence. Not a twig cracked, not a lip of wind, not one muffled paw in the settled snow. Even his spade was soundless, slicing layers of snow up and on to long mounds on either side. A silver light shone from the open kitchen door, and when the kettle signalled its boiling guts his path was already by the house-wall and nearing the lane. The whistle was subdued by zero air, by frostbite hovering over the newly created path, sounded like a whistle found in a Christmas cracker rather than its usual full-blooded shriek that dominated the tiny cottage until Pat could stand it no longer and snapped it off. The path, he thought, before turning to do so, will need cutting even further than the village if she gets called out today – which is bound to happen. Yet, strange to him, she'd hardly been summoned in the last week, beyond routine visits to the usual aging sick. 'Snow is healthy,' she explained, 'but just wait for the thaw!' Which was a fact: he loved the not-too-bitter silences of snow, the thick covering of whiteness and the hard digging needed to clear it. The ruthlessness when fighting it filled his heart to think of all that nature might still throw against him. He relished the shut-in evenings that seemed rich with life, more than he'd ever known; and if this wasn't much, then it brought him back to life, which was everything.

No papers this morning. He heard the news headlines and flicked up the switch. It was a day to start with a breakfast, spread rashers on the grill and run the opener round a tin of tomatoes, crack eggs into a pan. It was an enjoyable life: a pleasant loneliness filled in trying to bridge the here-and-now with Pat to his old life with Nancy, in which the gorge of

95

chaos was wide and deep. But the effort annoyed him, because it was too early to throw out the bridge, spring the camber and tighten the hawsers. Better to look back on it over much land and time, when the gaping earth wound of now would be a mere slit to step back over. Living with Pat he felt a contentment more enjoyable because he sensed its precariousness in that they hadn't been visited by any sort of fatal quarrel. He and Nancy went at it like cat and dog, but here, maybe they were too absorbed to argue yet. And perhaps it wasn't true that quarrelling was proof of love, for it was marvellous that they didn't, apart from occasional sour looks of a too-early morning.

He cleared away breakfast and hatched a fire. There was a smell of tea, the subtle combined residues of tea made or about to be, a pleasant herbal odour joining generations of people and memories that persisted when the windows of summer were thrown open, went even beyond the drastic cleansing of renovation when Pat first came. Drawing back the curtains, thick flakes were drifting zig-zag in a hypnotic slow-motion down the outside windowpanes. It seemed strange, a snowfall in early morning. He'd always fixed the prevailing time for it as being towards dusk or during darkness. There was no telling where the base of the clouds began: the sky was particles of white, lapping slowly through the livid scar-blue of a day not yet wakened. In spite of the fire, he rubbed his hands: it was an ashen desolate marvellous window, but had to be turned from. Nothing would get through, not mail, milk, newspapers nor breadwagon – only perhaps the phone would ring for help from the village or beyond. He would have to dress up in compass and gumboots and brave the blizzard for provisions. Not that they needed much, for he'd taken care that they were well-stocked for such an undistinguished calamity, but he'd maybe slog it to the village just for the battle against piling snow.

He took orange juice and tea up the steep stairs. She lay

with pillows heaped behind, and a book in front, wore a heavy cream woollen bedjacket rolled slightly at the sleeves, showing her white wrists. 'I heard you making the fire. I think before that I was wakened by the sound of snow coming down. It's funny how it wakes you.'

'I thought you'd be still deep in it,' he said.

'No. A day like this is like the end of the world, so you've got to be awake.'

'It's the beginning, more like.' He sat on the bed-end. 'Unless you get called out, we'll be locked in all day.'

'Not a hope,' she laughed, pushing strands of hair back over her shoulder. 'I'm usually looking at people in bed. It's good to be resting for a change.'

'I should be in with you,' he joked. 'But I like to look at you. It's a bit of a change, anyhow. Maybe I'm getting old, or older. I feel more alive than when I was in Nottingham. It's funny, that. It's not so many months ago, either, but it seems years. A family kills you; it kills everybody, I think, the way it drags your spirit down unnecessarily.'

'That's the only way to live.'

'It needn't be. There must be a better way. If there isn't I'd cut my throat. In China they reckon there is, but not here. Go on reading if you like. I'll go down and throw something in the pan.'

'No, sit here for a bit. You're always so restless. The air's muffled with so much snow around, as if I've gone a bit deaf. It's good to talk when it's so quiet: words mean something. You know, you don't have such an accent in your speech as you did when you first came. It must be my influence!'

'I'll be giving out the news on the BBC if I'm not careful. "Here is the news, and this is William Posters reading it. An atom bomb got lobbed on London this morning, so will everybody with a sore throat please report to Nurse Shipley on their way north through Lincolnshire?" I can see that, right enough.'

97

'You don't take anyone or anything seriously.'

'It was your joke,' he said. 'I do though, inside myself. But outwardly I'm cool, dead cool.'

'If you're so cool, you want to be careful the fire isn't out.'

'No danger of that. If I'm cool it's because I'm burning up. I haven't got guts but a firegrate full of prime pit dust that you get no flame from but can toast bread at.'

She looked at him sitting there, smoking a cigarette, out of his depth, and not knowing where he belonged – a strong aura clinging to him that made her think she would one day wake up and find him gone. She couldn't imagine the house without him. Or she could, in which case she couldn't imagine staying in it, feeling that both she and it would collapse if something impelled him to leave as unexpectedly as he'd come. There was always a danger of it, but he would deny it in a blind rage if she mentioned it. So she never would, and maybe in this way it wouldn't mystically lodge in his brain, and he would stay for as long as always turned out to be. He was downstairs, and came back with tea and fried eggs.

'It's stopped snowing. It's freezing over where I cleared away. I wish I knew how to skate or ski, then I'd get to the village in no time for whatever we want.'

She smiled: 'There's nothing we need. The pantry's full.'

'And the fire's burning a treat. Even if you come down in your shimmy you won't feel the cold. I've never known a house so warm in winter.'

'As long as the taps don't freeze.'

'I'll melt snow.'

'I can ski,' she said. 'I went to Switzerland the year before last.'

'Where are they?' looking around as if they might be in the bedroom.

98

'I don't have any, rented some when I got there.'

'You've been around,' he said. 'I wouldn't mind travelling a bit, out of this country. I never used to think about it. Maybe it's reading books that set me going, and talking to somebody who's travelled.'

'I wouldn't say I've travelled,' she said, a little too quickly.

'Now you're showing off,' he laughed. 'Maybe we'll go one fine year, who knows? Hump our bags to Spain or Italy. I'd like to do that. I knew a bloke in our factory, about my age but single who set off to travel round the world. He saved up, and planned it for years, said he'd work when money ran out. I looked on him as a real adventurer, someone to envy. We had a party for him before he went, and it was even in the paper about him. I was sad to see him go, yet bucked at the idea of what he was doing. Six weeks later, he was back. He'd been through France, got as far as Barcelona I think. I was disappointed, almost didn't want to know him. If I go away I'd want to do better than that. Don't you ever get fed-up in this village?'

She shook the pillow, put it back under her shoulder: 'Who doesn't get tired of the place they live in?'

'I mean bone-tired, right from the guts?'

She smiled. 'You want me to say I do, don't you?'

'I want you to say what you think.'

'You're a smug bastard. As if anybody ever says what they think. It's always what somebody else thinks – in a different form. You just want me to say "Yes, I'm thoroughly tired of it, so let's go away, this minute, tomorrow" – just because you want to disappear. Why don't you come right out with it?'

'Well, it doesn't mean that much. I only feel like that because I'm in a snowbound cottage with the only woman I've ever really loved. I can't be happier, so I think of the wide open spaces open to us.'

'Open to "me", you mean. If you had any love in you

99

you'd keep such thoughts to yourself. The first sign of love is when you think about the person you love, and apply the thought to her before turning it to yourself. As it is, you just torment me.'

'If that's the way it makes you feel, forget I spoke. I don't believe in that sort of self-sacrifice.'

'I can't forget. You can't undo things just like that. If you want to go, go.'

'Excuse me while I get my skis and foodbag.'

'Why do you turn everything into a joke? You have no respect for people. Nothing is serious to you.'

'Listen,' he said, 'I'm shooting my mouth off. I love you. I like being here. But I'm alive. I talk because my arms and legs move.'

'You think so? You talk, to show me your wounds.'

'I've got less wounds than most people. I can wound more than most people, as well. Anyway, I didn't say anything about going. What did I say? I forget. I can never remember what I said five minutes before. Five years, maybe.'

'You said we should go away together.'

'Is that all? Well that's not much. Why are we fighting over that?'

'I suppose it's because I want to go too. But I can't.'

'Forget it,' he said. 'I don't want to go, either.'

'You said you were fed-up with the village.'

'Let it drop.'

'That's what you said.'

'Forget it, love.'

'You say something, and then you say forget it, because the damage's already done. If you're really tired of living here, you must go. But don't destroy everything bit by bit before you do. I won't allow it. I have to stay, so leave something intact.'

His hand touched her shoulder, feeling its shape under the jacket and nightdress, a reminder of better hours than this.

100

'You're making a wrong sort of picture. It's not true to our life here.'

'It is. You want it to be.'

'Make up your mind. I've already made more out of my life in the last three months, than in ten years before that. You know why? Because I met you. Since then everything's changed, my whole mind. I feel as if my eyes are a different colour.'

This did the opposite of calm her: she couldn't bear the responsibility for it: 'It's impossible to know what you want. You talk about going, then you try to tell me you're in heaven.'

'I only want what I'm getting,' he said morosely, 'what I'm able to get. If there's anything bigger, it'll come along without me wanting it.'

'I suppose you want me to throw my life out of true before it comes to you? A little human sacrifice never goes amiss, especially when it's someone who's just taken ages to win a great personal battle. It makes it so much more satisfying.'

'I hate sarcasm. It's the worst disease I know.' The stare in his grey eyes had emptied them. He seemed far away from her, beyond the house, in a seclusion private to himself, a step back and above any patch or person of the world.

'Explain something to me,' she said.

'What?'

'Anything. Whatever you like. Just explain something.'

He thought her mood had marvellously changed. 'What, though?'

'Whatever you like. Think something up, and explain it.'

'What are you talking about?'

'I'm not being subtle or sarcastic. Just explain something about yourself.'

'You're trying to get it out of me with a knife, so I can't.'

'I didn't think you could. Can't you explain anything?'

'No, not yet. I don't see why I should, even if I could. Explanations don't automatically solve things. They don't always make life better, either.'

'Ah, now we're getting at the truth,' she said. 'You don't talk at all. All you can do is deny, deny, deny.'

'All you can do is destroy.'

'But you know, you're such a bloody letdown.' The hackles of destruction were out, all the goodness he had brought between them gone bitter in her in an inspired unguarded unjustifiable moment. 'You act as if you died at the age of five,' she said, 'and have been living ever since on what's left. You're soft. You can't take it. You can start it, but you can't take it. All you can do is mystify and bluster.'

He sprang to the bed and crashed his hand against her pale strained face: 'What are you going on and on for?' he exclaimed. 'Let it drop, can't you? All I asked was if ever you got fed-up with this one-eyed village.'

She fell sideways from the pillows, the bedside telephone spilling onto the floor. 'You stupid fool' – wrenched out by sobs of rage, words spinning at him like wheels of fire: 'If you want to do that you can get back to your housing estate or slum. I suppose they love it there.' This final end to a quarrel had never been imposed on her before. She felt a shame that stunned her, a rage spilling against him and herself. How Keith would laugh if he knew of this – but wasn't that why she had left a man with such a mind? But her face burned more from the blows, and tears forced themselves through, until the effort of fighting them turned shame to anger.

He stood at the window: black frost glazed the snow, covered ground; he hated it. Before, it had been comforting, an ally to his love, a balm to life. It now held the world's evil under whitened hoods and claws and clamped all things down that he wanted to spin out slowly from himself by way of explanation to Pat. By which time the snow and frost would have melted away.

She set the telephone back on its stand. It rang at the same instant, incising the four walls with urgent noise, and she spoke into it as if no quarrel had happened, perfectly ready for her work. He walked down the stairs.

8

WORK SERVED the same purpose as
snow and frost – to cover up scabs and interior minefields,
muffle the galleries of his mind leading to caved-in girders and
smashed hydraulic props. The air was keen, snow heavy on
the spade, granite and marble at deeper layers that he didn't
work at, but attacked. Frozen seams from previous hard
weathers called on the dynamite of his total swinging
strength to prise them free from the flagstoned path by the
side of the house. He went deep into his mind, but syphoned-
off energy prevented him getting anywhere near the end or
bottom of it.

She'd put on her overcoat, gloves, hat, picked up her bag
and gone out, climbing across snow towards the village, passing the school where, already and in such weather, children
were gathering. Phrases came to him, but the sounds contra-
dicted each other and kept his lips firm together, and she'd
gone off without a word, face set hard, like his own heart and
face, like the ice-snow he was trying to crack on either side of
the drainpipe. He didn't know what had sparked all of it off.
It seemed as if her sort of love was meant to eat each other

up, exactly the sort he was trying to escape. People should adjust themselves to the external world, not to each other, a diffuse connection with the whole world rather than the icy inbite of destruction. There is a natural tenderness in everybody which should make it possible for man and wife – or woman and man – to take care of each other, and ignore the fastenings of overstrung emotion which strangle at both of them.

Till midday he cleared snow from around the house, scraped walls and steps, shook it from fences. Standing on the floor of the shallow loft, he opened a skylight and freed a good part of the sloping roof, right down to its blue slates, by wielding a long brush and shovel. He hauled up an aluminium ladder and fixed it from the skylight. Within the radius of his burning mind and arms he worked to push snowridges down towards the eaves, over and off, a spluttering impact as it hit the ground.

A whole flank cleared, he straddled the roof to begin the other. The low sky, absolutely without feeling or sense, a forlorn William Posters at his wits' end and taking a breather, stood by his elbow and above his head, dumb, omnipresent, and never-pouncing.

Arms and chest sweated under his jacket, but he pushed strenuously at the snow. The thaw might not come for weeks, and his irritation at this was expressed by a slow, patient thoroughness in his task of uncovering the house. He swung the ladder over and fixed it to the ridge, made his way down almost to the eaves, scooping snow even out of the drainpipe tops.

A few beams of midday sun came through. On earth again, he shovelled snow from the lane, until the house and its outskirts was an island of brick, slate, paths and fences in an ocean of snow-covered wolds, an isolated clear speck of winter-liberated country. He inspected his work, walked around the cottage on solid ground, stamping his boots as if still neces-

sary to knock snow off them. Cold air penetrated now that he
was still, stood smoking a cigarette, wondering when Pat
would be back. Possibly there was no point in waiting, but it
wasn't in him any more to run away. The fighting had only
just begun and he hoped that both of them would be worthy
of what they could end up becoming to each other. Two more
calls had come in before she left, so a whole day would pass in
helping some bawling pink blob of a kid into this arctic-
orientated world.

He put on his coat and ploughed a way through to the
village pub. Five lanes met at Carnford, sloped in at various
points along the sinewy mile-long street. Much of the road
had been cleared, though no bread would come from Louth
that day.

He shook his way into the saloon bar, and the landlord was
talking about it to the only other customer. 'They'll have to
manage on biscuits and cakes then,' he laughed. 'I saw a fine
stock of them in the shop just now.'

Frank reached for his pint and the cold tusk of it going
down was something he'd craved during the snow-heaving.
He sat by the electric fire, more for company than warmth, a
solitary two-bar heater glowing from the depths of an ancient
fireplace. The other drinker caught his eye: 'I expect it'll last
a while.'

Frank didn't mind talking: 'I've cleared my lot. Been on it
all morning.'

'I'd never shift mine,' the man said. 'My kids are too idle.
Strong, but bone idle. They wouldn't lift a spade, not them.
I've got seven of 'em, all grown up. If I said: "What about
taking a spade to it?" as I did this morning, they say, as they
did this morning: "If we want to do that sort of thing we can
go to work. I suppose you'll be sending us to work soon?
Nothing would surprise me." So we have to keep ourselves as
best we can. It's not easy, it ain't. It's not, either. My name's
Handley, Albert Handley. I live at the Burrow. Turn left by

106

the next pub and it's up the hill a bit. You're living at Nurse Shipley's, aren't you?'

Frank couldn't be sure till he saw her again. He took the measure of Albert Handley during a few gulps and common-places. He was a tall, spruce-looking man with short dark greying hair, the sort you could comb without a mirror. He seemed about forty, had brown eyes, a reddish face, and a small dark moustache. There was something intelligent, con-siderate and ruthless about his face, as if he'd left the army as an NCO not long enough ago to have regained the easy-going appearance of a working man of the world who hadn't done much work because he thought himself a bit above it. He didn't seem like a farm-labourer, nor a farmer, nor even one of those men from the council houses who took the bus for Scunthorpe steelworks every morning. It was hard to say what he did though from what he said, he did nothing – hard to get to know such a man until you got to know him.

'How did you land up in this place, then?'

'Came to see Nurse Shipley, and stayed,' Frank told him. 'Have a pint on me.'

'I'll do that. Like the old village?'

Frank stood at the bar with him, pushed two empty jars towards the beer pumps. The landlord filled them. 'I'm fond of a bit of isolation. Lived in a city all my life.'

He chuckled. 'You'll get it here. Health to you.'

'Cheerio.'

'I'm a Leicester man. Was on the coast in the war, artillery. Met a girl from this village. Married her. Worse move I ever made. Still, mustn't grumble, as the parson says. Ever since then I've never had the bus fare to get back to Leicester. With a wife and seven kids every shilling gets snatched away. Perhaps I like it though, I don't know. What's your trade?'

'Machine operator, when I do it. I gave it up a few months

107

ago and came here to think things over. I read a lot, which stops me from thinking, so maybe I don't want to think after all – yet.' Half the pint slid into his throat.

Handley was also a fair drinker: 'You read a lot, do you? You don't look that sort.'

'Thanks,' Frank said. 'I wish I could meet somebody subtle for a change' – though aware of him being someone with whom small talk couldn't get you hung drawn and quartered. Handley laughed: 'I used to read a good bit in the old days: Marx, Conan Doyle, Michael Arlen, Lenin. Not that I get much time for it now, old chuff, what with writing my letters, and painting.'

'Painter and decorator, are you? Have another?'

Handley's brown eyes looked steadily: 'Are you rich?'

'No,' Frank told him.

'I didn't think so. Honour among thieves. Have one on me. It's my turn. I don't paint houses, I paint pictures.'

'Pictures?' Frank snapped into his new pint.

'I have to live. You've never heard of Albert Handley's Lincolnshire primitives? Neither has anybody else, above twenty miles away. But stay around a bit, and I'll show you something before the day's out. Get that drink finished, and we can walk up to the Burrow for a bit of exercise.'

'I'd like to,' Frank said. 'I haven't met anybody before who does paintings. Not that I need exercise after the clearing out I did this morning.' He bought two quarts of brown, and they were ready to go.

The sky was darkening, as if evening couldn't wait before closing in. An icy wind licked over the wolds, fit to prise open the village street, all doors clamped against it, smoke caught by it, scooped up slowly from every chimney. 'I've spent many an hour analysing winds according to what part of the body they seem most hell-bent on,' Handley said as they walked along. 'Up here they've all got characters, the winds – which is more than I can say for the people. Sometimes

108

there's a leg wind that paralyses the kneecaps, pulls you over by the ankles like a starvo-loony mixing you up with the N A B bloke. Now and again a wind will get at your breath – a chest wind, the most dangerous of all. Or there'll be a head wind, which makes the temples ache and the eyes smart. They just concentrate on one place, even in a gale. I've known a wind just go for the shoulders or the small of the back – leaves you groaning for three days with rheumatism or lumbago as if you've been conned into a job on the new motorway. A wind can give you a stomach ache as well, or it can get at the heart or liver. One consolation is that it never goes for two things at one time, but one is enough to floor you in most cases.'

The top of the snow had turned crisp, and boots cracked into it as they made their way through the shallower drifts. The sunken lane leading up to the Burrow had a three-foot depth to plough through, the only marks on it made by Handley on his way down. Even wild life shunned it on such a day.

'The worst of living in the country,' he said, 'is that it's not fit to live in.'

Frank was breathless. 'I still like it.'

'You're not used to it, that's why. Now and again I have a dull ache all over the left side of my chest as if my heart is going to seize-up, and stop all life in me. I lie down and try to sleep, but it's worse. I can't paint when it's on. If I dig in the garden I sweat. It lasts days, and when I wake up without it one morning I feel as if a fifty ton stone's been lifted from my head. The pain's terrible. It eats me up while it lasts but the local quack doesn't know what it is. Nobody does. I always say it's the wind – a special sort that just goes for that side of me. Why try to explain everything?'

The lane turned sharply, snow not too deep, so that a foot of it seemed like normal walking. 'If you want your bus fare,' Frank said, 'I'll lend it you. It can't be much to Leicester.'

'What the hell would I do in Leicester? Shoot roof rabbits?'

Back from the next bend stood a large three-storeyed plain-fronted brick cottage. 'There's the happy homestead,' Albert said. 'Fifteen shillings a week is what I shell out for it, and that's all it's worth, believe me. There are four buckets under the attic roof for when it rains, so thank God it's snowing. We're dreading the thaw. In winter it's an igloo; in summer a cullender upside down.'

Within fences was a large garden: coal sheds and chicken coops next to the house: bike shelter, rabbit-hutches and wooden porch. It seemed a bargain to him. Two sacks served as doormats, iced waterbutts on either side. Some kids had scrawled in chalk: 'Sticky bombs for sale.' They kicked snow off before getting out of the deadly wind that Albert had been too busy talking about to notice what part of him it was getting at.

The hallway was bare except for a framed portrait of the Queen on one wall, and one of Albert's larger pictures on the other. There were no mats or carpets on the wooden stairway, and it wasn't much warmer in than out. A sea-like clatter of spoons and pots sounded from somewhere.

'The family's having something to eat. Let me show you this painting.' Frank stood too close, stepped a few paces back, until he bumped into the Queen's head on the wall facing. 'Turn it round if it bothers you,' Albert said. 'I just keep her there because it looks good if somebody comes to see my paintings. They never used to buy any before I put that up. Then they thought I was a fine chap who should be helped. One of my best brainwaves.'

Frank got a good view, and nothing else bothered him. It was an epic combination of browns, greens, mauves and purple-blues, a massive background landscape as if meaning to depict the whole breadth of Lincolnshire. Against this was the vague grain of a brown cross, almost merging into it, and

110

on the cross was the shadow of a man, his head not, as usual, hung in the hello death position, but somehow upheld and looking inland, over a violent shift of darkly coloured and merging symbols in the foreground. His outspread arms were drawn back over the wood and tied there. Hanging beneath the crosstrees was a row of small dead animals that looked in no way out of place. 'They're rabbits,' Albert explained. 'I call this picture "Christ the Lincolnshire Poacher".'

Frank was transfixed. The totality of it reached a long way into his heart, touched a dark and not disagreeable world familiar to his senses and memory. It wasn't so much the dramatic content, startling and effective though it was, as the colours and juxtapositions of shapes that weren't relevant to the main theme, showing with terrible perfection a clash of personality punished by crucifixion. They were the colours he felt hidden between his everworking heart and disjointed soul, a coagulate of visual mechanism located somewhere behind the eyes. He had studied Gray's *Anatomy* in Pat's library over many weeks, but his idea of the body and its components retained the primitive impressionism of child-hood. The plates, as clear and marvellous as coloured dia-grams of the four-stroke engine, stood no chance against the eternal fixtures of his earthed imagination.

'Someone from Grantham offered me forty pounds for it last week, but I asked fifty – what with the time it took, and materials I had to find. I think he'll be back. Not that I'm worried. I could use the money, but I wouldn't like to see it go either. I like it myself, and that means it might be good.'

'It's really got something,' Frank said. 'I can understand it, you know, but I can't say much about it.'

'Ah, well, that's saying a lot in itself. I take small ones to Skegness in the summer, sell 'em for a few pounds on the front, but it's hard. Every month or two I raffle one in the village, send my kids out with books of tickets at a shilling a throw. I clear twenty quid on a system like that. Then the

111

odd few people come and buy one now and again. They must be scattered all over the county by now. I used to think it a funny thing, me being a painter, but I got over that long ago. I don't know what sort you'd call me, a sort of primitive surrealistic realist I suppose – which means keck-all, but sounds like something. I just go on painting though, because I can't do much else. I started during the war, saw some reproductions of modern stuff in a big book, bought an ordinary box of waterpaints and some cartridge paper. An officer saw me one day and encouraged me, got me books, oils, canvas. Went out to Burma and got killed. He said I had talent, but also I'd got idleness, and that made it better.'

They went up to Albert's studio, opened the beer. 'I didn't know there was somebody like you in the village.'

'I keep low,' Albert said. 'I'm busy and harassed most of the time, and can't be bothered with people.' The room was bitterly cold, the floor carpeted with newspapers which Frank felt like kneeling down to read, as if one might contain the message of his life. He'd never been in an artist's studio, looked at the vast square table scattered with utensils and bric-a-brac, all kinds of pictures leaning against it and the four walls. Some canvases were primed, other finished, but most were still raw, wounds of thought split and laid open among odours of turps and damp dust. 'I haven't been in for a couple of days, that's why it's so cold. I might get back to it tomorrow, but I'm like a bloody motor car – can't start in such weather. Maybe the wife's got a bit of dinner, so bring the bottles.'

They walked along the corridor and down by the shaking banister. Two children, pinch-faced and happy, lay on the bare floor playing Monopoly. 'It's time you went to school,' Albert said. 'Don't think you can stay away just because of a bit of snow. The vicar told me you played truant from Bible class last Sunday. If you don't keep it up we won't get another parcel at Christmas. See that you go.'

Via a bare parlour they entered a kitchen. A fire burned at the range, and down the middle of the room was a table flanked by wooden forms. Under the window was a huge pram, in which a baby played with blocks and rattles. A twelve-year-old girl with short straight hair and a face like her father's was reading a book at the table, and an eighteen-year-old sister was washing up at the sink. Frank fixed his eyes on her. She was fair-haired with a sulky, thin face that didn't altogether match her fine bust and mature hips well held by shirt and skirt. Her feet in carpet slippers, legs without stockings, she glanced at him with large blue eyes, a slight sneer on her lips.

Albert's wife sat at the table, a white-skinned, large-boned middle-aged blonde. 'Hello, Ina,' he said, 'this is Frank. He's the man staying at Nurse Shipley's.' The girl by the sink, and the mother, looked again. 'I brought him up for something to eat.'

A wireless-eye glowed green from the top of a low-lying pot-cupboard, one of its connections faulty. It kept coming on, staying for half a minute, then cracking out softly again in the middle of some BBC parlour game that would have sounded like the apotheosis of boredom had anyone been listening to it. 'There's something left,' she said, 'if you'll wait while it warms. It's rabbit stew as usual.'

'There wasn't any post,' Albert informed her. 'I would have got through. He's a bit soft, the postman we've got now. In the last big freeze-up the postman made a sledge. Never missed a day – till he died of pneumonia. Still, they say it'll be in either late tonight, or in the morning. Mandy can go down at six.'

The girl by the sink said: 'She can't. She does enough for this house as it is.'

'We can't exist without letters,' her mother said, 'you know that. We haven't paid the grocer yet for that wine. Nor have we settled the newsagent.'

113

'I didn't drink the wine,' Mandy said. 'You two did. I didn't read the papers either. You light the fire with them before I get up.'

'You should get up before midday then,' her mother said mildly.

'Tell me what for, and I will.'

'They'll have to wait for their money,' Albert said. 'They won't get blood out of a stone. Anyway, I'll write a few more letters after I've eaten. Mandy can hand them in when she goes down.'

'I'm not going down,' Mandy said, coming to the table and looking at Frank as if seeing him for the first time. 'I told you already.'

'I'll knock you about one of these days,' Albert said.

'Drop dead. Take an overdose.'

'You rotten little sybarite,' he called. 'Get out of my way.'

'You're not saying much,' she said to Frank, ignoring her father.

'I'm thinking though,' he answered.

'I suppose he's one of your pub mates,' she sneered. 'That wireless is driving me potty' – and went out of the room. Ina laid dishes: 'Mrs Warlingham came today for that painting you promised, of her house and orchard she said. I told her you were still working on it.'

'She'll be lucky if she sees that,' Albert said.

'She paid you for it.'

'Half. I'll do it when it thaws. Otherwise I might just as well give her a piece of white board.' He reached for the bread

'That's not a bad idea. As long as I frame it. It's been done before.'

Frank opened the beer. 'Got any glasses?' Ina brought three – one for herself. 'Are you any good at writing letters?' Albert asked.

'Only love letters,' Frank said. 'Why?'

'Well, I'm a great writer of begging letters, a born begging-

114

letter writer. To edge-up my income (such as it is) I turn out a few every week. You'd be surprised at the results. With an old typewriter, a copy of Who's Who, a few stamps and a bit of imagination, quite a bit trickles in. Where's that rough draft I knocked off this morning, Ina?' She passed him a sheet of paper from the shelf: 'It needs polishing yet.'

'Listen to this, though, it'll make your blood run cold. "Dear Sir, As you know from my last communication I have seven children on the point of starvation, and so far you have done nothing to help me alleviate their condition. At least, I myself had the goodness to write to you and describe their plight. I have had many vicissitudes in my life. Once a successful coal merchant, I went bankrupt when rationing stopped, had to leave the semi-demi mock-tudor pebble-dash detached I was buying on a mortgage and come to this rural slum. My car is rotting at the end of the lane, and I haven't had a smoke for a week. Apart from that, as aforesaid, my seven children are undergoing hardship in spite of the socialist benefits from this left-wing conservative government." A remark like that usually puts on an extra five pounds. You've no idea what pig-rats they are.'

'One day he'll come to see you,' Ina said.

'No he won't. They never do. They hate poverty even more than they like money.'

'But we aren't desperately poor.'

'Not much. The longer I live the more I know I'm poor. If he told me to get a job I'd throw a fit.' He turned to Frank: 'I'm a full-time painter and a part-time epileptic. But I'm so good at begging letters that I posted one to myself once by mistake. It broke my heart, spoilt my day, and I was putting a ten bob note in an envelope before I realized my mistake. My eldest son's going into the church. I can't think of a better trade for a lad of mine. He's at university already, thanks to a scholarship he was bright enough to get. He's glad to be away from home because he doesn't like my begging letters. I can't think why: he never gets one. He calls them "charitable appeals", the craven bloody hypocrite. Goes white as death when I talk about "begging letters" in front of his friends. They don't get them, either, though I've toyed with the idea more than once, and he knows it as well. What can you do when you're a painter? You can't go out to work. Work is a killer, occupational disease number one for a bloke like me. If I do a stroke it puts me on national assistance for a year.' He smoothed at his moustache, giving the same impression of sulkiness that had been on Mandy's face, indicating dangerous temper in such a grown man.

Frank stood: 'I've got to empty some beer. Where is it?'

'You'd better use the one upstairs,' Albert said. 'You'd sink without trace in the one outside. The door next to my studio. Show him up, Ina.'

'Don't bother, I can't get lost.'

He went through the hall – children still playing – and up the stairs. How could anyone live in a house so bleak? Snow beaded the windows, worried the chimneys with discordant yappings as the lifting wind hit them. It was a larger house than it looked, emphasizing the power of its protection as he reached the first floor.

He opened a door by Albert's studio, presumably the wrong one. When his eyes focused he saw a bald-headed thin-lipped man, illuminated by a table lamp in a room of drawn blinds, sitting at a transmitter-receiver with earphones on and fingers at a morse-key. The man, wearing a good suit, was sweating, shivering as if in the first stages of malaria. He turned a panic-stricken look on Frank's intrusion, then swivelled from the radio with a gun in his hand. 'Get out!' he screamed. 'Get out!' an unforgettable picture.

Frank slammed the door, went in the next before giving himself time to parry the surprise of his first incursion. It was a whitewashed room, open to milky daylight of the outside snow. Nearly the whole space was taken by a low table, over

116

which was spread a vast taped-together ordnance survey map. Two youths were leaning across from opposite sides, moving different coloured symbols across the co-ordinates. One, wearing a black leather jacket and a ban-the-bomb badge, looked up and said: 'I'm Adam. This is my brother, Richard. Do you want a game? We're practising civil war on England's green and pleasant land.'

'No thanks, I'm looking for the lavatory.'

'It's always more interesting when a third nation intervenes. Have a shot at it.'

'Another time. Not now. Thanks.'

'Across the hall,' Richard said.

He shut the door quietly, stood by the dim landing. What a way to kill time. It's like Ludo, or Snakes-and-ladders. And who was that bloke at the wireless? A notice posted on the back of the lavatory door advised him to now wash his hands, but one of the kids had pencilled underneath: 'All right, so where's the sink?' Another remark said: 'But pull the chain first.' I suppose that bloke must have been a lodger, though I don't know why he turned a gun on me, when I'm on his side. Not that he was to know. It was so authentic it didn't look real.

He pulled the chain and went outside, collided with the girl he'd seen at the sink downstairs – Mandy – felt her breasts and arms against him. 'Sorry,' he said, to step aside.

She took his hand: 'Don't be. Come in here.'

'Where?'

'In here, quick.' Her hand turned the door knob, and he followed. It was a clean whitewashed room with a single unmade bed, a chair and chest of drawers, magazine pictures of musclemen and Tommy Steele on one of the walls. An ashtray of cigarette ends lay on the chair, and the room smelled as if she had smoked in it most of the day.

'Quick,' she said, 'please' her arms around him, lips fastened thickly over his. He responded, and after a few minutes lay with her on the bed, his blood stiff and beating against her thighs, one hand gripping her long blonde hair. Would anyone come in? Was he safe in this madhouse? But he was ready, and didn't want to rush at it like a man who thinks he can't do it, or someone who doesn't think anything at all. On the other hand he didn't want his good luck to push off before he could get set. Her clothes were up and open, arms around him as he spread over her. Kissing her eyes, he felt tears on them, which may have been proof of an un-containable passion, or of some bleak snowbound despair, for her hands fell from his back, and she lay still, breathing softly. He was in no condition to ponder on her state of mind, exploded into her as if someone had pushed him violently from behind, and at this unmistakable impact her arms gripped him again.

After a few kisses she said: 'Now get up.' The encounter had been so rare and dreamlike that he obeyed like a zombie. 'Thanks,' she said.

'I should be the one to say that.' He stood, while she stayed on the bed, tear marks still at her eyes. 'Now give me some money,' she said. He took out his wallet: three pound notes, and some change in his pocket. He put all of it on the chair. His knees shook, as if all strength had gone at one blow. 'It's too much,' she said. 'I only want a token.'

'Enjoy it,' he told her. 'I did.'

'Don't tell daddy,' she smiled. 'Please go down now.'

'It's hard to tear myself away.'

'Please go.'

He walked to the stairhead, looked at his watch, and saw he hadn't been with her more than ten minutes. What sort of a family is this? In the hall he stopped again by Albert's picture of 'Christ the Lincolnshire Poacher'. He'd lost the romantic imaginative clarity of an hour ago, and the land-scape colours were sombre and meaningless, the figure of the hanging man desperate with the ages he'd been up there.

Rabbits turned to foxes, biting at wood, hanging on with filed teeth, as if after such great efforts they were going to climb and run at the man's head, finish him off. Frank lit a cigarette, trying to fix himself somewhere on the picture, draw its totality right into him, meet it halfway at least. The face held, looked as if wanting a drink from the vague line of sea behind, aching to eat what landscape nine-tenths surrounded it, taste both before rabbits or foxes got there first. It wanted the world pushing into its mouth, to digest it and shit it out. Yet no one was there to do it, or understand that it needed to be done, and he was hardly in a position to bend down and do it himself, scoop up earth and sea to cure his own agony.

Frank saw the picture as painted on the surface of a common house-brick, one pictorial from thousands plain that made an enormous wall he had to breach or climb. Maybe that man flexed on the cross isn't Christ, but none other than my old friend William Posters, not dead yet, but surely dying, hanging as a warning for all to see. Bill Posters will be prosecuted, persecuted, gut-smashed, blinded, crucified: all those pictures of the cross and the bloke skewered on it stuck up at street corners with the common caption blazoned beneath. What was behind it? A wracked, hot-spring, wide-throwing black sea perhaps, God's all-spewing bile slung into it like a dye-pill and churning it crazy. You'd think so from this picture. It can't be a calm sea. No seas are calm except on postcards. It might look flat, but just peel back the top skin and look below, and that will be another matter. Or maybe there's land behind, land you can walk across in a straight line to your life's end and not get to the finish of, only rivers to swim, never a sea to reach. Or maybe one day I'll be looking along a rocky, storm-coast: spray bursting by the bottom cliffs, mushrooming up as if mermaids were planting sticks of dynamite all over the place and blowing white water sky-high into the air, the full dull burst of breaking water battering my ears time and time again, never subsiding into flatness even though I button my coat against it, light a fag and walk off inland with my head down thinking.

Someone tapped his elbow: 'We wondered where you'd got to.' Albert wore a cap, as if against the cold in the hall.

'I was caught in your picture. I can't get away from it.'

'Take it, then, I don't need to have it up there. I'll make you a present of it.'

'It's all right. I don't need to take it. Thanks, though. I can't take a man's work like that. It should belong to everybody, if at all.'

'Ina's got the tea on. Come down and have a jamjar before you go.' He looked at the picture himself, then turned from it. 'It's strange, but I've always wanted to be sickly and neurotic, yet can't because I'm so strong and tough. I've been out on the bitterest nights for rabbits and pheasants, chased by the toughest keepers in the land, but got back none the worse for it. It's bloody weird. Maybe I've got a super-duper built-in death-wish – which is why I gave my wife seven kids. I don't know, but I suppose there's some reason why I'm a painter. I'd like to explain it, being wedged out here in the wilds for a lifetime, and getting the whole lot of us by as best I can while I do my painting.'

His brown eyes glittered, feverish with the night behind them that, in his talent, struggle, and world-ignorance, he was trying to illuminate. 'Come on down, and we'll get that tea.'

9

KEITH WAS so disturbed after a sleepless night that he missed a left-fork in the interlacing roadwork of north London, got himself shunted towards Cambridge instead of the Letchworth-Peterborough axis. This latter would have aimed his Sports-Triumph straight at the heart of Lincolnshire and the dead-end village in which Pat had incarcerated herself in a futile act of self-abnegation. Misery and injured pride improved his vocabulary while doing little for his sense of direction: that's how Pat would have put it, sarcastic at the beginning and the end. Match that to a high moral tone and you have an untenable relationship as far as man and wife are concerned.

He'd set out early, in spite of blackening rain. Carruthers had been difficult about three days off from the office, saying that the new Watkins table-sauce account was in urgent need of smart treatment for the next T V series which, he added, is worth a lot to the firm. But Keith was just as likely to come up with an incontrovertible dead-set image racing along the open road, as he was locked in the super modern office block above High Holborn. So Carruthers had no option but to drop his hidden persuader technique on someone already a master of it – a prize copywriter who earned every penny of his three thousand a year.

Hearing all the arguments, his psychoanalyst also disapproved. 'If you succeed, I'll be pleased and surprised. But the chances are that you'll fail, which will put you back two years' – as if advising a tubercular Sisyphus not to push his great stone once more up the mountain when the gods had ordained it.

But Keith had decided to isolate himself from all advice since Kevin called on his way through London and said Pat had a man in to share her bright little cottage. A high moral tone had always been her line, and now she wasn't only having an affair but had let Kevin go up and live in the same rotten nest. He at least had always kept that part of his life separate from what he termed his 'permanent domestic cage'.

He filled the car with a homely stench of French cigarettes – which made him feel somehow safe. The wipers cleared his vision, swilled rain and dust against the outside screen. A youth and rucksack at the next hilltop held up a thumb and smiled, as if the thumb were injured and he were putting a good face on it. But Keith pointed to the right, as if turning off too soon to bother stopping. He felt guilty again, but couldn't stand fifty miles of chattering, having to think of that bloody image, as well as plan his gambits for when he bumped into Pat. Not that there'd be much room for manoeuvre. It's plain as all hell, getting Kevin up there while she's living with another man. I'm not against it, oh no, she can do what she likes for all I care, but not in front of my son, understand? Not in front of my son, for God's sake. Kevin hadn't even disliked the chap, which shows how successful she was at, well, corrupting him – there's no other word for it.

He'd intended stopping the car to consult the R A C book

and find a way towards Peterborough, but whenever a layby was signalled his hands wouldn't react to the offer of it, and he held a steady sixty along the present road. I'll stop now, he kept saying, and draw in – but it was impossible. As long as I'm going north: he consoled himself for the strange state of his will, as if to stop would end his life, make him call off his expedition, fall asleep over the wheel, burst into tears, turn round, begin to doubt himself all over again. He pressed on the accelerator, nearly hit a grass verge at the next bend, then slowed to fifty on the straight because he had frightened himself.

Crossing London he'd licked through Highgate, and Muswell Hill – the place he was born and lived at most of his life. It hadn't altered, he saw, detouring along the avenue and stopping by his childhood house. The extrovert Keith loathed it, while the introvert tended a secret passion for the hidden depths and darknesses of it. He recalled those ideal days before the war, the long never-ending boyhood peace of them. Later he rebelled against all that house and suburb stood for, had even joined the Labour Party at one time. Who hadn't rebelled? Rebellion was the anaesthetic of youth, and that was the only way to get through it for some people; though if someone would kindly point out the anaesthetic for middle-age he'd be bloody glad.

Cambridge showed on the roadsigns: there was no point in turning off now, so he stopped for a legstretch and petrol. He wanted four gallons, watched the big hand of the meter slowly register, fascinated by its unclogged movement, an unattainable harmony that men got from machines but not themselves. A pity, but then, maybe they just sent machines ahead as an advance guard, and one day they'd catch up with the way machines worked now. Take this car: care for it, feed it with oil and fuel, drive it lovingly, and it would give good use and service for years. Why couldn't a man be like that? Because he can't. He's more mysterious, superstitious, clumsy, despondent, clever. There's too much we don't understand about the light and darknesses of his insides. Isolate a specimen, do everything right both flesh and mental, and what happens? He dies one day from something you can't trace. Not a hope. Even I'm like that, one time poet and now a mechanic of the wormy depths in the service of advertising, an instigator of conspicuous consumption which, as we all know, breeds spiritual cancer. But that's my job, so what the hell? I'm not one of those who paid cash for his house.

One time he travelled around in a Jag, but they were getting too common, so he preferred the distinction of anonymity in a souped-up sports. In any case he'd soon be a shade too old for a Jag. Maybe after forty he'd change to a Mini, just to be on the safe side. He walked impatiently along the pumps, his appearance that of a well-dressed young middle-aging man, fairly tall, with fair wavy hair and the troubled aspect of someone whom smallpox had thought to attack but changed its mind at the last minute, merely branding him as a person who had gone through the mill in some indefinable manner. He had a high forehead, lined to match, and hazel eyes that looked out from a man-created hell, imploring as they looked, not at those they turned on, but begging the furnace within to make them less imploring. Such eyes resented what the mirror of his soul had turned them into, without questioning the soul itself. His small mouth, the sort that didn't seem inclined to open often, would only say something if his soul in agony screamed at him to protest.

Working at the hidden springs of other peoples' slothfulness, he had no time (or perhaps, after all, no desire) to turn these perceptions on himself. This he left to a psychiatrist who hadn't till now made a good job of it. In spite of everything the expression of suffering was taken as sensitivity – which blended so well with his well-shaped chin and intelligent forehead that he not only inspired confidence in those he worked for, but was considered by women to be good-looking.

The sun shone, driving through Trumpington, up past Fitzbilly's and Pembroke. The sun had shone on it too during his three years reading English after the troopship crawl from Burma in forty-eight. Cambridge hadn't altered. The students weren't quite the sort he would have mixed with then, and might make good salesmen at Harrods, he thought, observing a scarved knot of them on the street. After leaving the Labour Club he had prayed many days in King's chapel, entranced by the stained-glass windows, meditating on their pictures of Christ and the Virgin. Even in the bursting cold of midwinter he would behold them for hours, scribbling fervent impressions in his leatherbound notebook, nose red but scarf well drawn. After Burma he considered this extreme change good for his soul, and remembered Cambridge as part of a rich and varied life. While others were roistering and masturbating, he had revelled in the mellow, satisfying depths of tradition and scholarship.

Foregoing coffee, he got out with his memories as fast as he could, on the road to Ely. Twice in this short burst of the rainy day he'd stumbled on places that brought back disturbing echoes, made off from each with relief, and guilt at having strayed into them against his will. Life, he had known for a long time, was something of a battle between his objective and subjective worlds, and neither treatment nor willpower could keep it level. If he looked out of the window one fine day and saw cleansing sunlight on opposite roof-slates, a voice within told him that all would be black rain before he got into his car for work. But if by then the sky was still clear and warm, he wouldn't revel in it and bless his luck, but would see it as a sign of impaired reason, as another point scored by the interior subjective bully of himself. It won continually, by the bell and on points, but for once he felt the victor, saw his daylight swoop on Pat and her boy friend as a rational blow in a scheme to coax her back to the comfortable

125

fold of his bijou gem and get some love and order once more into their lives.

But could he do it? He had his doubts on this, as on everything, as each corpuscle of his blood must have had as it entered his heart full of doubt, and left it with the same feeling. Yet blood moved just the same, flowed through and kept him alive. Doubts, in the end, looking back on things, didn't matter. It was what you did that mattered, and what he did in this case seemed already halfway done. Confronting her, he would have to sell the product before she would buy – to put it in crude and workaday terms. His ability to probe the pseudo-masochistic impulses of the human soul, and lay them out as alluring symbols of aquisitiveness or greed, ought to help in an expedition such as this. He smiled at the thought. Christ, what haven't I sold in my time? Persuaded people to buy? The bonfires of conspicuous consumption had lit up the housing estates, flames dead already, dustbins emptied, ash cleared away. The world is a furnace, a boiler house, wheels within dark satanic wheels moaning above the backs of the H P-paying multitude. It would be nice if the reality were so stark and clear. Yet he liked to dwell upon simplicities, no matter how exaggerated. Simplicity was oil on the wheels of his chronometer heart, reaching even the poetic cogs of them, the last hope of the divided man who could never really put humpty-dumpty together again.

He had always regarded himself as something of a poet, more so after he had stopped writing, on leaving Cambridge. Not only did his self-respect need this reassuring memory, but skill at his job proved some truth in it. At his desk, blinds drawn, 'DO NOT DISTURB' hung on the door (not locked in case someone should need to on urgent matters), he sat with only a desk lamp shining on pen and paper, a dictionary and thesaurus to each hand while he struggled in the jungles of myth and nightmare, an unacknowledged legislator who, with others, ruled the world. He wrestled for days over a single phrase, surfacing with it in the end like a drowning man who had been pulled under more than three times, a cracker motto in his teeth that in a few weeks would be dazzling around millions of peak-hour television screens. He found his work profoundly satisfying, in spite of snide articles against his trade that popped up now and again in the toffee-nosed weeklies. Work kept him above the brimstone lake of final despair, and made him forget the pain of living without Pat. In the last year he had not suffered unbearably, it was true, but Kevin's revelation that she was living with another man had filled him with a doomlike blackness. This was understandable, in spite of the bull and treaty of legal separation. Yet he thought the blackness should not have been so thick, nor the doom so heavy. It was the way that Kevin, in all innocence, had told it to him, for in spite of his eleven years he hadn't really understood the full strength of what was going on. But if this was the case how could the force of Keith's righteous anger be caused by his son's corruption? He was given to honest and penetrating analysis, so long as it was in the interests of self-preservation, yet he was afraid to admit (half sensed and so shied back from) that he was jealous of Kevin being an approving witness of his mother's new happiness. Kevin actually seemed to like the bloody man, which meant that Keith in time was going to lose his son as well (no matter what the law said) – or his son's respect, which was even worse.

He swallowed all of it, the whole bloody lot, blinded by a diffused jealousy, afraid to drive too fast over the straight flat road. The one solution was for her to come back, so that Kevin could be at home, and the wheels of a blissful domestic interaction fall into place once more.

He began to feel dead beat on the tiresome crawl along the back end of Norfolk. Veering across the flat roads and frozen landscapes of English Holland, cutting the afternoon mist of the Wash only a few miles beyond the desolation of his right-hand side, the country was coated with frost, turned pink and blue by the sun, penetrated in all directions by the thin spires of village churches. In spite of his determination to hate the trip, he found this part inspiring, surrounding him with a beauty never expected, a soft glaze of green frost blending with mist and sky at every point that the car nose turned to. Cold, impersonal, natural beauty always mellowed him with optimism, burnished him with hope.

Fatigue grew easy on his back, and he imagined returning to London this long way with Pat, especially to show her such mysterious and favoured landscape, watch her face as she enjoyed it with him. Maybe they could get a cottage here, use it for long week-ends, and holidays with Kevin when he came from school. They could go to the desolate marsh beaches and swim in the high tide of the gulf, a map of which on a café wall showed intriguing names: Thief Sand, Roaring Middle, Blue Back, Mare Tail, Herring Hill, Inner Gat, The Scalp, Black Buoy Sand, Westmark Knock, Wrangle Flat – names to fascinate schoolboys, some perhaps that he could use in advertisements for a new brand of salt. Along the straight but minor road beyond Boston the Fen drains were grey with ice, and house roofs looked as if they had been patched with snow after a hailstorm or cyclone. The land was darker: ice and snow had been the last of his expectations.

Eyes ached at the constant road. A pain needled his back, gnawed at his ankles after the gear and acceleration work getting out of London and the long haul up. There's no one more determined, he grinned, than the man who thinks he might fail. He would stay up here for days, if necessary, no matter how much it would upset Carruthers.

IO

ALL THE REST of that day it was her intention to pack him off, but he was out when she returned, and in the lighted solitude there was time to calm herself, to realize that such action against a man she loved would be a defeat for her as much as for him.

But he went to the stair-cupboard and drew out his rucksack: 'All right. You don't need to tell me. I'm off.'

'Going away only proves you haven't the guts to face what you've done.'

He threw the rucksack down, a pair of shoes still in one hand. 'I have,' he cried. 'But have you? That's why I'm off. If I was in your place I'd never want to see my face again.'

'What's the point in saying that? Leaving won't do much good either, though do it if you really want to.'

The lines on his face stood out. In the last few months his features had lost flesh, due to walking, exertion in the garden, the gathering in of fuel, and various repairs to the house. When she mentioned it he said that's what came from being in love, and living a new sort of life. At this moment his face was cast between the two big decisions. One of them she did not want him to make, but wouldn't say so even though her life seemed to depend on it. She saw the sky full of menace, crossed by long-tailed rockets that exploded on meeting, that threatened to descend and burn her life back into a solitude she could no longer face.

'I don't want to go,' he said. 'You don't even need to think of it. If I talk about what I've done I'll smash my head against that wall. But if I don't talk about it, I have to go away. You know what I mean? Yet you can't know, can you, unless I talk, talk, talk? I've never been much of a talker at such times. A thing like this is sure to stop me talking, and this is the time when you've got to. But I love you though, and that's true. If only I could talk, instead of eating myself up.'

I could talk to Nancy, he thought, and I can talk to other people ten to the dozen; I was fluent in the factory right enough, which caused all the trouble, but it was easier than this. He wanted to drag himself out by the roots, expose them for her, suffer. But it was impossible. She didn't think their quarrel deserved it from him in any case. They should simply give in and end it all, pull out before the burns went deep, walk to opposite ends of the house, get caught up by a different and superficial topic. She herself was already surfacing, but the blows had left greater marks on Frank, though it now seemed wrong that they should have done so.

He walked over: 'Stand up, Pat.' She looked into a face from which no elaboration could be expected until the tension had worn off and so unblocked his heart, by which time they would be happy perhaps, and explanations would seem irrelevant.

Her face was level, faintly smiling. They stared at each other, and when they could no longer bear to, his arms were pressing her to him, as if she had been the one to think of running away.

She couldn't imagine where Frank had gone. Where was there to go in such a place? She'd finished her rounds, lay her

130

bag on the dining-room table, took off her coat and hat after a hard day. They had all been hard, lately. Maybe it was winter grinding its way like a juggernaut and presenting her with too many sick. Snow still scattered over the lanes had thinned and turned to a stonier grip of ice.

Fields were darkening, houses and cottages with yellow eyes shining in the sharp dip of land. She plugged in the kettle, opened a newspaper. The light oppressed her, seemed to curtail her sight rather than clarify the small print. Feeling tired – it must be that – she put on her glasses. But still she could not read, uneasy that Frank wasn't in, surprised at it also, and smiling at how completely she lived with him.

The kettle shook her from drowsiness by a shrill cockcrow which she fled to stop. With Frank in the house there were two people to involve in her wishes, so no one could call her practical any more. She bent over a stack of logs by the hearth, to lay some on the coal. Practical people lived alone, had the run of their narrow earth. If they had any life in them they burned to death all by themselves. So it was either him or herself, and no one could tell who it would be. This was equilibrium perhaps, and maybe that was love. Balance, aid, interdependence, passion at the end burning these first three away like a sparkler, ever descending, ever decreasing, until the hand jumped and only the shock remained.

·He had power over her, and she wasn't used to it. He didn't exude or revel in it, probably didn't even know it was there, but its truth was proved by the fact that he had struck her and was still living in the house. That blow had taken her power, upset the balance, destroyed her independence. She saw it in simple terms: either it was true or, if she was exaggerating, her character was flawed. Even to think such denigration pointed to how much her self-reliance had cracked, compared to the days when, in London, she controlled her house, child, and husband. Memory let her down again, showing how Frank, on the day of his arrival, had

131

helped to clear out a larder stamped with chaos, the mark of a woman anything but ruthlessly efficient and self-contained. So the rot, she thought, had started before his appearance. But when, when, when? The inner fires of agony blazed just as painfully with a person you loved as they did with someone you hated. They also burned when you lived alone, facts which proved you were alive and could feel how much there was to be thankful for.

Getting up to close the kitchen door and stop a slow draught eating into her legs, she heard a car coming down the lane, a deceleration as if for a final drift into the village. It pulled up outside, wheels crunching the glass of frozen snow. She wondered who could be wanting her. It didn't have the weight of Dr Abel's stationwagon, or a police car. Her last thought, before the iron knocker flapped like a gun, was thank God something had come to snap away her useless self-questioning mood.

A figure stood outside: 'Hello, Pat. Aren't you going to ask me in?' The voice penetrated her memory, a tranquil afternoon blown away by a cold wind nosing around. Neither of them knew how to make the next move. He immediately puts me into the same old role of deciding for us both. 'All right,' she said, 'come in.'

Light dazzled him. Such unwelcoming words had, secretly, been one of his expectations. 'Sit down,' she said. 'It's nice of you to come and see me, though I don't see why you thought it necessary.' Such irony made him doubt his own reasons. By nature optimistic, he was easily discouraged. The greater his effort to wring success from impulse and optimism the more likely was he to back down at the first snub. When the great fire blazed, the drop of water frightened – though not for long, because optimism would eventually frog-march him back to his obligations.

He smiled, glad that whoever she was living with was not at home. 'I've been meaning to visit you for a long time. Out of curiosity, let's say. You seem to have a nice little place. How does work go?'

She was short of answers, except for blunt truth: 'All right. I bring babies into the world. Old people go out of it more comfortably than you'd imagine. I'm more use in a place like this. I feel a real person now.'

'Meaning that I'm not?'

'I only mean what I say. I've spent two years unravelling myself from that black knot we got into, so it's no use trying to put meaning into things I didn't even say. If you've satisfied your curiosity you can go.' She was aware of speaking too quickly, of saying too much. But Frank could walk in any minute and she wanted her visitor out of it.

'I didn't come to stay. Merely to have a talk. In any case this isn't a special trip to see you. I've taken three or four days off, and I'm just driving around the country. Quite without thinking, I found myself in Boston. Thought I'd call on you.'

'You could have telephoned. Kevin has the number. Enquiries would have given it to you. As you can see though, I'm well. I have a house. I'm working.'

'I think I could say the same.' He recalled that the main consolation in being married to her had been the knowledge that domestic peace would mean a living death – and who wanted that?

'You could,' she said, 'but I'm not interested in it. You're the one who came to see me. I still can't think why. Did you expect a better welcome than this?' His opening gambits were being thrown back on him. No, he hadn't hoped it would be easy, but she seemed more icy and bitter than he ever remembered. He'd give a lot to meet a woman who wasn't as neurotic as they bloody-well come. 'I suppose Kevin told you that I don't live alone any more?' she added.

'He did. He gave me the idea you were living very informally, breakfast in bed and all that.'

She laughed. 'What a way to put it! Though I suppose there's no other way if you think it worth mentioning at all.' He was bewildered, but hid it, had intended reaching this point only after, say, a couple of hours' pleasant enough reminiscence. With a good memory and clear brain available for such occasions he'd planned it on the way up – but without anticipating the possible moves that would operate against him. The image of Pat in those few and far-off hours of peace between the great storms had been unclear, unrealistic, an ideal face of his own creation based on the best of her nature. He planned, but when the test came he only reacted. In the car, planted somewhere above his rear mirror, her face had smiled, but it was unlike the flesh-and-blood Pat before him now, tired from work, face lined, altered, but alert and full of energy at the opposing force of him.

The world, she found, was a different colour every day, and now the spectrum, usually sombre in winter, had swung to purple. The clock ticked, someone walked heavily by outside, and for one moment she thought the steps would stop at the door and Frank would enter. Keith waited for her to say something, while all she wanted was to see him walk out, hear him drive off and vanish; but she knew how hard it was to discourage him unless she stood up and told him directly to go, and if she did this it would only confirm in him that there was even more reason to stay. His tenacity scared her, and she wished Frank would come back.

'Kevin sounded interested,' he said at last, 'affected, I might say.'

'I should hope so. He's intelligent, and fully aware of what goes on.'

'But he's only eleven. It's up to us to give him the protection he needs. I give it to him, at any rate.'

'Hasn't it occurred to you, after all these years, that you and I have different standards?'

'But we have the same son. We ought to have some common policy for his upbringing.'

'Perhaps,' she retorted, 'but whose? Yours or mine?'

'Both. Maybe we can talk about it.' He felt the initiative on his side. 'I didn't come here specially for that, though. I simply took off, on impulse, and ended up here. I wanted to see *you*. There must be a meaning to something like that.'

'Oh no there mustn't. You're just craving after the past.' This stupid, irrelevant, chance-meeting (which was what he made it out to be) had too much importance because of a unifying fatigue, and even this much in common she did not like. It coloured and thickened the atmosphere, made her doubt herself when she should have been decisive and brusque enough to send him away at once.

He lit a cigarette – the same blue packet Wasn't it still chic in his job to buy a case? 'We had a rough time,' he said, 'when we were together. Too rough for either of us. It was perfectly natural that we split up. But it's more than two years since those battles.'

There was a pause, in which he felt foolish that no one was talking, and until she felt the pity of so much wasted time: 'I'd forgotten about it. Even when I remember, it doesn't mean anything.'

'Maybe it's as well,' he said, encouraged. 'Instead of taking up where we left off, perhaps we can start even from beyond nothing. It's not Kevin's future that matters, but you and I. Things would simplify if we lived together again. It would solve all our problems.'

'You were always so concerned to solve problems. That's what made half of them. When you pull out you see that there aren't any. At least, you do after a while.'

'I don't understand that,' he said.

'That's honest, anyway.'

'I love you, have ever since we separated, even when we

135

were together. I still don't know why you left. We could have survived that storm.'

'And gone into others,' she said.

'And weathered those also. That's what life is. One big storm after another. You go on and on, but you can't let yourself sink under them.'

'At one time *you* were the one to sink. Have you forgotten? You see it all in a rosy light now, but I've got a sharper memory. These so-called domestic storms eat the middle out of you. They were a way of destroying you, taking up your life when you'd got no job to do. You went off to the office each day no matter what happened, but I was left at home in that dead, miserable house. You thought I should be happy in it, imagined I was unhappy because I wanted to be, because I was born like that, because I had nothing else to do. But nobody is born like that. People are made by themselves and other people. You wanted me to work for some charity or other in my spare time, something which would leave me free for you but still not get at the core of what was eating me. And now you have the nerve to ask me to go back to the same thing. You can keep your image of a storm and a ship for a new brand of tobacco, but I'm on my own feet now, and you'll never know how much it cost me to get her. And as for going back, I'm not that sort of person.'

He heard her out: 'Suppose we forget all that? I still don't see why there can't be some advantage in us living together again. You can do the same useful job: there's plenty of need for you in North Kensington. I know we'll be more tolerable to each other after all this time apart. It will have been good for both of us.'

Every word scraped against the carefully-built edifice of her self-esteem. 'I know,' she said, 'every disaster is a blessing if you're spineless and lack imagination. But you underestimate me. I could never live with you again.'

He lost patience in a passionate way that he thought might appeal to her by its intensity. 'Pat, why are you so bloody cold towards me? We have a son, remember?'

Everything he said seemed out of context, unconnected, yet from it she tried to disentangle the threats he was making in his subtle faint-hearted way. 'I don't even loathe you,' she said. 'It's not that. I just dislike you at times when you cross my memory. Seeing you doesn't make things any better.'

He was encouraged by the mounting force of her attacks, though they hadn't yet attained that pristine viciousness of the final days before their break-up. Still, he hoped that at last he might be getting somewhere. 'Even to say that means that I affect you.'

'I don't see any use in your wanting to recreate the holy family with me at the middle of it. The family is all right for the man perhaps, but it's no use for the woman. I refuse to be tied up in that way. Don't think my life's easy up here, either. It's harder than it ever was, but funnily enough, I like it. I actually like it, because I'm more myself than I ever was, and I don't care how many times I say it.'

'Even with your boy friend living here?'

'That has nothing to do with you.'

'Hasn't it? But why can't you still have this life, but with me in London? Come back, and I swear we can make a go of it. I'm not the same person as before, and you aren't the same, either. We've grown out of all that frightful quarrelling that puts you off so much. It puts me off as well, but we'll be able to manage with each other now.'

'Would you be prepared to give up your job and everything else in London, and come to live with me here?'

'I can't, you know that.'

'So neither can I,' she said.

'Why not? There's no real argument against it.'

'Not to you. To me there are dozens. Also I'm in love. Do you think I could live with someone without being in love?

137

That shows how little you know me. Do you think it was because I was lonely and needed a companion?'

It stopped him too sharply, and he recognized it as being the end. His fatigue had changed to a pallor she had never seen before in him, a whiteness at the side of the mouth, a flexing of hard veins at his temples. She couldn't believe that her blow had been so desperate, nor that he could simulate such pain. 'I see,' he said, 'and this is the person you were in bed with when Kevin went into your room one morning, having innocently made breakfast for you both?'

'Why make so much fuss of that? Kevin knew us well enough by then.'

'It won't happen again.' He smiled, in spite of his loud words. She was near to tears, iron control needed to dam them back: 'You must have been playing with that piece of blackmail all the way up. Not that I didn't suspect. I only hoped you'd never have the vileness to use it.'

'Do you think I'm a complete fool?' he cried, standing up. 'I mean what I say. That's *real* life, that you pride yourself on leading. The real life! These are the real facts of life. Simple and hard. What you think is real life is the fool's paradise that you've made for yourself up here. It never solves anything, to cut yourself off.'

'Real life isn't that,' she said, 'it isn't what the world says it is, but what you feel to be inside yourself.' He was harder, more direct than years ago. He didn't display miles of innuendo any more before coming to the point – in order to make the storm more violent and bitter when it burst. His skill and patience had gone, and the result was ugly to her. She didn't know how to deal with it.

'You left me,' he stated, 'and you abandoned Kevin, so he's in my care. He's only been seeing you in the holidays because I allowed him to.'

'You mean I take him off your hands while you go off to Majorca or wherever it is with some typist or other.' She raised her voice: 'And stop talking like a judge. You've no right to judge me, in spite of your blackmail.'

'I don't want to. But Kevin won't come here again. You can keep your facts of life away from him.'

They hadn't heard Frank come in. He stood at the open door: 'What facts of life? What's all this?'

II

EVEN BEFORE opening the door Frank knew who it was. His reasons were vague, but he didn't question his instinct. Two cars outside made it seem like a bloody roadhouse. He heard voices within but not what they were saying, Pat's tone quiet and insistent though edged with hysteria, the man's gruffer, loud, but with an odd shrill phrase chopping it – as if they'd been arguing for a long time and not yet convinced each other.

His instinct told him it was time to go, walk off, never look back, be a hundred miles away before midnight. The husband had returned, the game was up, and the rules said blow town. All's fair in love and war. But love that equals war ain't love. Running away was all right for a lark: it left everybody happy because things had fallen out as they should. But times had altered, and he happened to be in love, so there was nothing to do but turn that key and push that door.

They were facing each other across the table, tea things still on it. His unexpected entrance froze them. They looked like a brother and sister who had been talking about him. Keith's hands rested on the table, by his cigarettes, lighter, and cold cup. Hers were on her lap, out of sight. She knew some introduction must be made, but gave Frank time to take stock of what blind emotions were knocking about the room. Her normal reserve of control had been drained, left her pale, her life now at the mercy of the bare features of her face.

She hoped Keith would not leave and drive away. That was all she wanted a few minutes ago, but if he went now he would never let her see Kevin again. It was so possible that she felt faint from the effort of holding down her blind misery.

Keith forced himself to glance at Frank. Having lost himself in plans and hopes, pre-occupied to the utter depth of his life, pleading to the exclusion of all else, he hadn't foreseen this sudden appearance. Having failed, he wanted to go, but a new factor stood by the door as if it would never move or say anything, as if all of them were waiting for a bombardment to end before returning to normal life. Time passed. To Frank it seemed short because he was the first to speak: 'Why did you come up to see Pat, then?'

'A chance visit,' Keith said, easily.

Frank, deciding not to sit down, felt that Keith was no stranger, since Pat had told so much about him. He was often angry that he could still take so much of her, while he had kept Nancy out of it. 'It must have been important to bring you all this way. There's a sharp frost tonight. It'll need careful driving.'

Keith looked at this strong-faced broad-shouldered man still in top coat and scarf, the sort of working-class chap who, once out of housing estate and factory, lost his callouses and the final trace of discontent. He'd seen such types some time after the war at Cambridge, inmates of various colleges able to believe their intelligence but not their change of life – even in their second or third year. He looked younger than both of them at this moment, which gave Keith an undeserved feeling of superiority – somewhat mauled though by the fact that Frank had been the first to ask questions. Keith didn't like that at all, and he liked even less the fact that he had answered that question.

Frank waited for him to stand up: it was always for the husband to make the first move, or try to, though the rules were shaky these days because not only had he come into the house when he should plainly have fled, but he had already spoken to the husband in a way that seemed unlikely to start a fight. He was a traveller in a strange country, and he liked travelling. 'I'll make some more tea,' Pat said, 'if there's any talking to be done. There's no drink in the house.' Frank followed her into the kitchen to wash his hands: 'What's he come up for, then?' – the tap flowing loudly against the bowl.

She looked at him: 'I don't know. I honestly don't know.'

He stood with wet hands, regretting a question that only disturbed her. 'Has he been upsetting you?'

'Well, I was surprised to see him. I've had a difficult day, in any case.' That didn't explain her general air of bewilderment and shock. Hard days often left her in a good mood. He remembered she was menstruating, which certainly didn't help. People always choose the right time to visit those they don't like but pretend to love, he thought. 'If he did upset you I'd flatten him.'

She put down the teapot, face rigid, eyes burning with the force of her words: 'If there's any of that, there'll never be anything between us again. I'll be finished with you. I won't have any of that in this house. This is for me to settle.'

'All right.' But he knew something had been said, and that she was holding it to herself, too bloody tight and haughty to put the half-weight of it onto his back. 'I'll be subtle. Iron won't melt in my mouth.'

Both men looked equally at home. Keith picked up the evening paper, scanning the front page. Pat came in with the tea. 'Are you looking for a job?' Frank asked, sitting down.

142

'I have one,' Keith said. 'What about you?'

'I'm living on my savings.'

'Whose savings?'

'Mine. Do you want to look at my hands?'

'Not particularly. It wouldn't prove anything.'

'It would if you held yours up as well.'

Keith put the paper away. 'If this is the way you compete for your lady love it won't get you far.'

'It won't get me as far as London, and that's a fact. It ain't necessary for me to compete, in any case.'

'You think not?' Keith retorted. 'You'd be a lucky young man if it weren't. And the woman would be unlucky, wouldn't she, Pat?'

'She wouldn't think much about it,' Frank said, 'unless she lived in the Dark Ages.'

'We're in them now,' Pat said, pouring the tea, 'so perhaps she would.' She put bread and butter out, and biscuits. Frank ate, but Keith couldn't. Pat only wanted tea, feeling parched and feverish at the throat. A petrol stove burned in one corner, but Keith was chilled, unable to trace the moves that had landed him in this wintry unlucky cottage.

'Do you mind if we talk alone?' Keith asked.

'I do,' Frank said. 'I'm staying. But say what you like. Don't mind me. I live here.' He waited, curious and interested in this new kind of situation that at the moment made him forget his natural disadvantage of worldliness.

'After all,' Pat said, 'we did have a long time before he came.' Keith did not like him. In the old days, if any man looked at Pat otherwise than by accident, he imagined that man in bed with her, and immediately loathed him. Now he was in the same room with a man who was not only her lover, but had flaunted the fact in his son's eyes as well. He had no real claim on her, but saw Frank as an under-educated throw-out of a workman who had treacherously planted himself like a rank weed in the fair field of his hopes and affec-

143

tions. He and his type fell by the million under the sway of his sub-Freudian scythes, spent their sweaty wages before displays of deep and tricky symbols. No doubt Pat had told him of their past troubles, revealed secrets. There was an air as if they'd been living together for longer than they had. Present lack of speech didn't faze them. They were undisturbed by each other's weariness at the end of the day. Maybe she'd been truthful in saying she was in love. The idea appalled him. He knew they wanted him to go, be alone and console each other, but he would stay to the bitter end of what his own perversity had dragged him into. Yet at the same time he wanted so badly to leave, fly down those icebound lanes to Boston and the south, back to the warmth, light, and civilization of London. He could not get up and make an exit that would satisfy the pride that had suddenly become apparent in front of another man. 'I came to ask Pat if she would live with me again.'

'I don't see what else you could have come for,' Frank said.

Keith remembered the advice of his analyst, that speech was always less harmful than silence, often a definite advantage. 'I object to Kevin being up here when another man was in the house.'

Frank laughed: 'It's better for him to see a man here than not. Gives him a sense of security. It's even healthy for him. I'd like my wife to take up with another man, in case the kids grew up kinky. You never know.'

'I have different views,' Keith said. 'I happen to be still in love with my wife. I object to my son witnessing the life she leads with someone who isn't his father.' Frank thought that was the way people only talked in books and on the BBC. He was amazed to confront it in real life.

'There's nothing wrong with what he sees here,' Pat said. 'You're just turning it into something unwholesome.'

'I don't see the point of this,' Frank told him, almost gently.

144

'Pat stays with me. There's no need to bring Kevin into it.'

'You think not?' Keith said. 'You obviously haven't the power even to begin to understand my point of view, though it's simple enough.'

'We're different people, you and I,' Frank smiled, 'brought up in different ways. Is that what you mean?'

'You're saying it. I'm not.'

'You bet I am, when you can't come out with it straight. If I was in your shoes I'd pull out without any fuss.'

The tone was falling below standards that Keith had been moulded to respect and live up to. This man knew no rules, had an undisciplined uneducated mind, and was actually trying to tell him what to do, to give advice, insults which he had no way of countering. 'I'm sure Kevin would be better going to France or Austria for his holidays. If I were in his place I'd have had Lincolnshire by now. I'd want a change.'

'You mean that if we were divorced,' Pat said, a smile which made her lips seem thinner, 'and I was married again – all respectably – there'd be no objection to Kevin coming up here?'

Keith also smiled: 'Don't you know that we're living in an age of conformity?'

'Why try to soften it?' she said. 'Frank won't mind.' They all still sat, and she saw this as a help towards no real quarrel breaking out.

'I'll take anything from a cunning bastard,' Frank said, 'except action. Let's make it plain: you want Pat to choose between me and Kevin; and you think that if you can blackmail her into choosing Kevin, then I'll just quietly sling my hook and leave you on the field? How long does it take to put you off? Do we have to make a declaration of solidarity, or something?' He understood Pat's diffidence about provoking a row, but he saw there was nothing to be gained by listening. Keith might have the whip-hand but he couldn't have it all in tea-party manners.

145

'I don't see why we can't settle it in a civilized manner,' Keith said.

'I suppose by civilized you mean your way? There's nothing to settle. It's no use using your subtleties here. It won't work. You're not persuading anybody to buy Daz or vote Tory, so don't come it.'

Keith laughed. 'It's no use trying that line with me. I'm completely apolitical. I dropped all the political stuff years ago. I'm simply asking you to choose,' he turned to Pat.

'How can I?'

Frank sensed her tears, as close as when, weeks ago, they had quarrelled and he had struck her. The recall of it doubled his rage and bitterness. He felt as if standing on a shellbacked insect getting bigger under his feet, felt himself blacking out towards another strange light dominated by the smooth face, fish-eyes and polished shoes of the person whose opposing spirit wanted to crush and strangle his own: 'Listen, you bastard, you've got no right to come up here and spoil what doesn't belong to you, to wreck and ruin to your own sweet tune. Your cock crow's hoarse and false, mate, full of maggots, you miseducated boatfaced bastard eating food and wearing clothes you never earned or advertised on the telly. You speak calm but you boil like an empty kettle, the moon in your mouth and the sun up your arse. You're starry-eyed and cloudy at the brain except when it comes to doing the sort of job that will keep you like it forever. The world's top heavy with you and your sort who wank people's brains off every night with telly advertisements that make them happy at carrying slugs like you on their backs, but I'd like to see you do a real day's work, if you could, if anybody'd be crazy enough to set you on.'

Keith pulled back his chair and stood up, a hand at his forehead as if he had been hit with a sledgehammer and was wondering where the blood poured from. 'I had a commission in the army,' he said, his voice dry and shocked, 'and put people like you into detention.'

An almost soundless blow sent him against the wall, bent double as if to look at some intricate design on the carpet that he remembered seeing years ago in Heal's. Frank kicked him, a hand cracking on flesh, and the purple, spark-fanged floor on the sway and loose burst at Keith like a piece of ice over the eye-face, an engulfing polar cap. The chair cracked. Keith reacted, taller than Frank, heavily built, fist bursting, a whale-head driving across the light, packed with flintheads and darkness.

Pat cried out at the black sky: feeling the rotten, festering sores of the everyday world a thousand times enlarged bursting over her again, the love and peace, isolation and work made into a disease that she only wanted to shun. In a few hours it had happened, the impossible, unexpected, un-wanted, all out of nothing, for no reason, taking away two years of dignity and usefulness. 'Frank,' she cried, 'don't.'

He was unconcerned whether it was the end or not, in some ways hoped it was, considered himself in the way of it since leaving home, wife, and factory, splitting his life's tree with the axe of temperament and bloody-mindedness. The table roared, skidded before it could slice his spine, met the wall. He flung himself at the rushing figure, shoulder against chest and threw it stolidly back, drove his fist at an uprising forearm as if to break bone.

A voice telling him that this was no way to argue, a sur-render to barbarity, was stifled as a stab in the back from a world he had recently met. He hated this world because it let him down at such a time, didn't tell him how to avoid a punch-up nor how to survive it. With flooding eyes and face awash, a waterfall came crashing from the roof. His fist swung into a blind, wet, unkillable face that slid away, then wielded its own granite response.

There was no stopping or facing each other except by

attack. Frank wasn't conscious of thought, or even of seeing Keith's upright body helpless against the wall before the violence of his opponent left him a shell unable to dwell on how he had come to begin this spiritual carnage. The room was a lighted cave, purple corners, greying walls, blue floor underfoot seen from scarlet eyes that alone had strength left to know what had been done.

Keith fell, groped and spread. The house was silent but for a clock ticking from the kitchen. Frank felt isolated, pinned into the darkening hemisphere of his pain, used, shamed, unnoticed, an animal at large in the frightening wilderness of himself. No one else was conscious in the house – he was the shell who conquers, winner of desperate wars in which despair is the only winner because it takes everything and loses you to yourself.

He sat on the floor, leaning at the wall in the smashed room, knees drawn up and smoking a cigarette, wondering why he hadn't left when he saw the car and realized who was in the house. He had shunned the unwritten rules, the birthright, the tradition, and now the wage packet was proffered to be filled with his blood and life for repayment. Retreats are always wise, for if you retreat often and skilfully enough you may find that one of them has become an advance if you are quick to exploit it at the turning moment.

He was conscious of the room's true shape, geometry around chaos. How had it started? He didn't know, except that it was stupid and unnecessary and that he alone had done it. A sickness of hunger swelled in his stomach, but he couldn't break the barriers of misery to get up. Pat had gone, he knew, left some time during the fight. He didn't even wonder where.

Through the kitchen and out of the back door iced air gripped his throbbing head like a great hand, pressed more pain into it, a compress of cold sky. The big moon had been thrown up from the black net of bare tree-branches that stayed outspread waiting to catch it again should it fall back. Luminous, yellow and fire-bright, the blue-night sky held it, pale in the middle then darkening outwards. There were millions of stars. A car started at the front of the house, engine opening with a roar, charging down the lane, gear changes happening quicker than he could count. The garden was empty. Let her go. What else could she do? What else could he do, either, come to that?

He held fainting onto the rim of the sink, the grey narrowing cylinder of unconsciousness passing over, slowly receding. The roads were iced and dangerous. Why had she done this when all he'd wanted was to protect her, keep her from the insults of that mad bastard in there? There was some reason in it, but the only thing she could do was take-off into the black night of narrow lanes, the steep sleeve-hills of this winter land that burned the heart out of you with its ice and frost.

A cock crowed – shaking frost from its comb no doubt. He didn't know what hour of the night it was. Shutters had fallen over the sun and moon, and he couldn't break out of this timeless cottage. What had these last months been except a womb? Having taken off from trouble island he'd dived deep into what seemed like peace. Why did I do such a stupid thing? Not that I've been aware of it till now. Yet if it had been happiness, where was Pat? Gone, in spite of her so-called love, run away at the first sound of pain and responsibility, ultimately frightened at the back of her fine face and behind her strong front against life. He remembered her cry: 'Frank, don't!' when the fight had started. Why hadn't she shouted: 'Keith, don't'?

With a bowl of water he walked into the flaying light of the living-room. Keith slept on the floor, grey and cold, his face grazed, eyes blue, bunched mouth dark with blood. Yet his sleep was gentle, like a recuperation from some great struggle that had lasted all his life, and which would only

149

land him back into it when he woke up. He seemed more of a man, lying in such a sleep, stronger, more in control of his ultimate safety. Frank had intended reviving him with the water, letting a chute of it fall over him, but thought he deserved better than that, ought to be left alone in his prostrate dignity.

There was no point in staying. He was the bomb in the house with the slow-smoking fuse. Bill Posters was in paradise compared to this. To be prosecuted and persecuted, dogged and hunted is to be wanted at any rate. He hoped Pat would come back soon, but knew she wouldn't. The fires were played out, purple ashes cold, black waves chopping at the mast. His packing-in from family and job now seemed light-headed, a lark, a jaunt, a cowardly truant meant to be skedaddled back from if the novelty grew stale. But now that a second break was on him, the first one seemed real enough, pushing the old life one stage further back into the past.

He pulled the table to its usual position, set chairs in old places, closed doors, straightened pictures and mats. Order, order, order, there was no such thing as order in the land of the heart. The neat house and the bombed-out heart hid the truth from each other, a devastating fact. Restoration was quick and complete, the only incongruity being Keith. Why not leave it all as it was at the beginning? He set his mouth in a grin when all he wanted was to smash his head at the wall and finish off the live expanding stone in his chest.

He worked his fists under Keith's armpits, fastened his grip and dragged him towards the stairs. Every muscle in his body strained, as if, at each step, they would burst and leave him dead and helpless. He had never been more consciously afraid, for there seemed an element of death present in the effort to get him up towards the bedroom. In spite of Keith's weight it was an effort he knew could be easily mastered at other times, for his strength had grown since leaving the factory.

Time drew a circle round him, moved with him step by

step but refused to be measured. The spending of his total strength couldn't slacken for a counterfeit second. Unless he spent his agony in this way he wouldn't be able to leave. Any strength remaining would weaken him, make him sit down and think things over until it was too late – until she came back, or Keith regained his consciousness of life. There must be nothing left. He would take nothing from that house. At the blackest and most desperate part of his midnight she had gone, seen him as light headed and fickle, fighting for no reason, reverting to the animal of what she thought was his past – in spite of the knowledge and intelligence she knew he firmly had. It showed how little she had ever understood and therefore loved him. It was impossible not to leave, even in the middle of the deepest love he'd known, for that's how she wanted it, for her own good, for the good of Kevin, maybe most of all for the good of her husband – though she probably wasn't to know it yet.

The emptiness was breaking him. The dragging of this stone uphill was snapping the cord of his senses, tearing into his living strength like grapeshot. Maybe if she would come back. Maybe. Things didn't happen that way. It was impossible. And if that door swung open now, the end would be the same. It had to be. He would leave. He would save her for herself and the others. She had gone out for that, expected it of him, a test that she maybe hardly knew about, to see what sort of a man he finally was. The idea was awful but he knew it to be true, the one action that could atone for having started the fight, and the only one that could prove to her how much in love he was.

No more steps behind his heels, he moved along flat boards, tapping them and searching, hardly able to believe it. Where should he take him? Onto Pat's bed? He'd already given it up to that extent, to think of it only as hers. But that would be too final and complete. Kevin's door was open, so he pulled him in, a painful and steely emptiness dragging a loaded man towards the camp bed under the uncurtained window. One war was over and he could afford to pause, match the utter silence outside against the new battleground of his breathing. He listened to the desolation of silence, deepening in himself. The stone exploded. He couldn't remember this as a man before, ice breaking on midnight seas, the floes of dead passion crumbling inside him. He lay Keith, still senseless, on his son's camp bed.

Frank was breaking apart, a snap and creak of mooring-sinews, heart, stomach, brain, liver, body and mind separating, ripped out of him and filling the darkness. For a moment he felt battered, helpless, shorn of life; on the other hand he was like someone just born who needed the first and final knock to get him breathing. Answering this thought, he tapped himself on the head, and groaned at the bruise-fire that jumped around his temples.

Keith moved, but didn't open his eyes or wake up. Fetching a pile of blankets from the cupboard, Frank spread them over him. He'd made up his mind to go, and remembered it suddenly. The pain was greater than his bruises. It would be wrong to hope that further thought might alter his decision. He was bigger than that. He walked without thinking to the door, went downstairs for his things. In a few minutes he was out of the house.

Part Two

12

THOUGH BORN and bred in Hampstead, Myra was built for the country, George said. He'd once written a poem implying that while she might be no fit subject for Baudelaire or Boucher she was all that he wanted her to be: strong, passionate, and a lover of woods and gardens. As the last wheel of the barrow was dragged up the final step, her ironic grunt would have ruffled his peace of mind if he'd been home to hear it. He'd merely stated what he wanted her to be, and being in love she'd moulded herself to that off-beat image. Well-built and tall, she had small breasts and full hips, and arms that had grown strong and tanned in adjusting herself to George's ideal, while George himself, over their years in the house, spent more and more time in his study and less and less in the garden. She wore glasses, kept her hair short because whenever it grew long she looked too much part of the trees and landscape, a duller person than she thought she was, mistress of lawns and lettuce plots behind the six-roomed Georgian house.

In many ways Myra wished she had become a lover of the country, for maybe then the country would have grown to love her. But neither was it intolerable, which showed how George had been mistaken in at least one of his adjectives, for if she'd any passion left she'd be out of this green horseshoe of lawns and shrubs.

The false adjective told more of George than a score of right ones. Though his character was less flawed than most, he didn't show much of himself, which meant that more than six years had passed before she finally knew him, thereby proving the advantage of the strong silent type: marriage lasted longer, for one couldn't possibly lose interest until all secrets had been opened.

On first meeting he was quiet, shy, and big-built, a young man with short black hair and brown eyes, pipe smoking, comfortable, twenty-nine years old, working with a survey group somewhere in Kent. On Friday night the Soho pub was crowded. Myra stood well back from the bar, able to see only the glittering wall of bottles rising in the distance. She'd spent a day in the art galleries, and now wanted to see crowds and real faces. Drawings and paintings had shown little humanity, though they had, as usual, opened various aspects of her inner self – only to close them again the minute she stepped outside. She was fascinated by other people's visions, the colourful abstractions of singular rare beings called artists – until her perceptions were swamped by a sensation of drunkenness that didn't take away the ability to walk straight.

Having few friends at the L S E, she loved the comforting sight of people whose purpose in life was different from her own. Street lights and coffee smells, shouts and stars – she left them on impulse and went into the pub. This well-built man was talking in loud fluent French to another drinker. She looked, unaware that in observing him it might be said she was trying to pick him up. Faces fascinated her, so that she wondered whether she shouldn't have gone to St Martins instead of the L S E. On the street she'd look at a face –

belonging to a man or woman, it didn't matter as long as they were beautiful or interesting – and only realize she was staring when someone smiled and asked her to come and have a drink. She thought that, having what she considered a rather plain face, her stares would be taken as unimportant until she realized that looking at someone might make her face softer and more appealing than before she stared.

George looked drunk, his eyes lit, but his French sounded so perfect that she thought he might be French, though anglicized to the perfection of good clothes looking shabby, a button missing from his mackintosh, shoes needing polish, and a pipe that wouldn't light for more than two puffs. His face became rock calm when listening to the other man's replies, and she saw what it would be like when out of a pub and sober, found it interesting because it was profound and kind, a low forehead all the more attractive in an obviously intelligent man. Talking about books, the words Proust, Huysmans, Apollinaire bounced softly above smoke and noise.

The barrow of dead leaves, held from cold wind by the weight of a fork, was hauled to a mound already smouldering. George hinted that she clear the lawns and paths so that they looked once more part of the smartest house in the village. She'd intended doing it next week, after writing her lectures for the W E A, but George, thinking her unresponsive, sulked at last night's supper, a polite sulk which meant gruff replies to any question concerning the house. Not a word was said about the lawns, as the hours between supper and bedtime plodded on, both reading on either side of the dead television screen, and the reason for his silence came to her. She looked up at eleven o'clock and said: 'I think I'll get rid of the leaves tomorrow. Burn them.'

'All right,' he said, as if it didn't matter whether they were cleared or not – yet the petulance drained from his voice. She

157

imagined this to be the perfect marriage: intuitive, calm, diplomatic. If only I didn't know all his thoughts and wishes, and he didn't sense mine. There's little left at this stage, though it was the same after two years, so I've no reason to brood on it at six. He didn't even glance from his book, and her irritation was squashed by the fact that she'd hardly looked up from hers, either.

He'd noticed her staring at him, back in that far-off Soho pub, a young tall brunette with rounded cheeks, and glasses that hid the full glamour of her eyes unless or until you went to bed with her and she took them off. Maybe they stayed on even then. Her face was pale from too much walking, his red and flushed from striding fields with notebook and theodolite. She looked – and after six years she hadn't stopped looking for some sort of answer in him. Perhaps one came only when you didn't need to look. To look was to doubt, and answers were given only to those who trusted. But no, she'd gone through that phase years ago, and found it as false as any other. Permutations and subtleties were mere mechanics that explained nothing – though immersion in them was often a satisfying anodyne to stop you cutting your throat, or to enable you to do so.

Lifting another half-pint, he'd called: 'Mazel tov!'

The phrase startled, by its appropriateness when addressed to her, but coming from him the greeting lost its authentic blade-ending, that last syllable sharpened on whetstone that chopped you down the spiritual middle to make sure the good luck entered. 'Why not have a drink?'

'I have one.'

'I wasn't going to say anything' – he stepped closer – 'in case I reminded you of a brother you hadn't seen for five years.'

'You don't. But where do you get the "mazel tov"?'

'I buy it at Christmas, plenty of white berries. You kiss under it.' He kissed her: 'Mazel tov!'

158

'That's mistletoe,' she smiled. 'Mazel tov's Yiddish. I'm Jewish, so I thought you were.'

'Don't be literal. One of my pole-carriers uses it. He's a Cockney.'

'What are you?' she said.

'A surveyor. A bore. A technician mapping out the new age in Kentish swamps. I like being a surveyor, but don't ask me why. People fall into two tables: they either ask me that, or they say they've never met a surveyor before.'

'I'm in the second table,' she said, then ordered another brown ale. Half an hour later she was drunk, and George said: 'Will you marry me?'

'Yes,' she answered.

He had a room in Pembridge Square, and their taxi swayed between traffic along Oxford Street. The feast of talk that had possessed them in the pub lapsed before the wide curves of a traffic roundabout. Sobered, George leaned across, one hand behind her head, and his mouth pressing skilfully onto her lips. She saw other cars swinging towards them across the blue-black tarmac, giant sparks sliding into the central fire of their passion. They began from a distance, gathered speed while growing bigger as if guided by phosphorescent glow-lamps overhead and coming for the big smash, upshoot of fire and metal. His kiss grew hard, and she closed her eyes to fill in the bones of it.

She felt sick, so they got out on Moscow Road, soothed by a cool wind blowing in the darkness, hovering lamps, cats at dustbins outside grocery shops, milk bottles piled in crates. He put an arm around her. 'You need a meal. I have food at my place. Tins, anyway. Some biscotte. Tea. You'll feel better.' At nineteen this was adventure, far from that Hampstead monstrosity in which her family lived, double fronted, double garaged, double cream cream in the double sized fridge, a double lounge and double everything house that meant half a life she'd rather stay out of half the night than sit and argue with her mother who thought she should have left school at seventeen and learned hairdressing. Her parents were fine: as long as they left her alone, she loved them very much.

They walked into the outstretched arms of Pembridge Square, swaying a little towards its massive houses. The night filled her with a sense of freedom, gave her a visionary light-bodied walk, in the middle of the road, alone, her satchel of books and make-up swinging loose – until the noise of an onrushing car threw her breathless onto the pavement. George laughed, and took her arm. 'Will you still marry me?'

The stairs were steep, wide, dimly lit. Drudging around Soho all evening had drained her energy, and she ascended slowly. Halfway up she touched his arm and answered: 'Yes.'

I hadn't said yes to anyone before, and I don't know why I said yes then. Once in his room we didn't wait to eat. He told me later how surprised he was at the speed at which I undressed. I knelt on the bed and looked at him, loving my nakedness and not really concerned about his as I took off my blouse and brassiere. It was quick, and didn't add up to the sort of passion he wanted, but he was too excited to notice. He was drawn out too quickly by my split mixture of coldness and blinding rage, of wanting to be loved all the way by a man I had fallen in love with but who was for all that a stranger.

In a way he was still a stranger. She found that the only time he was free with speech was when using a foreign language, talking in French or Italian to some waiter or fisherman during a holiday. Myra's shyness never approached the dimensions of spiritual deformity it sometimes attained in George. She was protected by a more intelligent face from which comment was not always expected, though in which it was always assumed to exist.

The thunderbolt of soberness hit them so hard that they couldn't stay in the room either to eat or sleep. They walked

160

– traversing the lit-up arc of north-west London, hardly talking, between decaying houses towards Edgware Road and Swiss Cottage, as if to escape the ghosts of that unexpected lovemaking. Myra had been exhilarated, though not satisfied, by the straight-rutted contact with another person, as if they had put each other to a certain use through lack of patience or knowledge. She felt fine, full of energy, feverish, yet aware of the cosmic distance that had separated their feelings, good only in that it had sharpened the carnal matching of their bodies. She had expected a softening of the spirit, a drawing closer as this hard aloofness vanished with the years, but it had stayed in that same pristine state of pure contact – moon-love and nothing else.

Like natures were no good, she thought, tipping the barrow and scooping the last leaves out with her hands, raking them into a heap. If silence and shyness ever broke they would have become different people in each other's sight and fled apart. A lack of reserve would be fatal. Reserve is what we depended on each other for – to bolster it up in ourselves, to protect George from himself and me from myself. We each are afraid of ourselves, not each other, and won't ever get close until our separate fears are done with. One like nature holds the other in check, the sparks of mutual domination being all that remain.

They drank coffee and ate sandwiches near Hampstead tube station, walked towards the Heath. George knew it well, a short-cut from the Ponds to West Heath Road, a slow madcap around the heights of London. They found a place in the undergrowth, hidden from all lights. Myra felt no coldness, nor blinding rage either. The orgasm went into every limb, diminishing its impact at the vital centre of herself.

Beech, plane, oak and maple, the last dead twigs and branches were gathered from around the house and brought to the top bank for burning. She smiled at thinking so far

161

back, paused between sweeps of her rake and realized how much they had nevertheless changed since that first evening. If he hadn't changed so much – from untidy, generous and shy, to neat, maniacal and tight – she wouldn't be hounding the garden offal of winter for the first big conflagration of the year. At that first 'mazel tov' she would have consoled herself by the folk adage that still waters run deep if she hadn't seen this as an advantage in a man. But from running deep the banks had almost joined, due to limestone and chalk deposits. His lack of speech when sober had led him to choose a wife after half an hour's drunken talk. Through lack of experience she had accepted a husband in the same space of time. In the old days a girl was matched and married off by a broker, sold and traded like a slave, and in thinking she had done the opposite she had only done worse, because from what she knew of George she might as well have been taken to the canopy never having seen him at all. She drew herself back: that's not quite true; we did live together a while before marrying. And when they did – a quiet splicing at St Pancras town hall when the red flag still flew – George had chosen a house in the first spasm of looking, though she had to admit that as a surveyor he had made a better job of this than in his choice of a wife.

For George, the house was a dream come true, worked and toiled for since driving along the village street in his battered sports car six years ago. Realism was on his side. He'd seen it first in November, with no blue light and sun of summer to blind him into love for it. A square, neat, two storeyed Georgian structure, it stood in cold and drizzle, gardens empty, garage falling to pieces. The quiet sort, he was an optimist in material things, saw the garden cleared and the lawn laid, garage, woodsheds, toolhuts and wash house all hammered, relatched and painted; bricks repointed, windows cleaned, the front door gleaming black with a polished brass knocker, the back gate opening to a path that, running through the yard, would lead char or tradesmen to the kitchen door.

George had set himself and others to work on it. A thousand borrowed from his mother made the down payment, the last money in her account, but with George's cash a flat had been converted above the garage and she had lived there until she died two years ago, glad to leave the semi-detached in S.E. 98, become a member of the Women's Institute, the Old Folks Club, and be among friends and family for the rest of her life.

Myra went to make coffee. Mrs Harrod was vacuuming upstairs, but would be down when she heard the cups rattling. After coffee a laundry list must be made, then Myra would go to the village store. Notes for her next lecture needed re-thinking, and there were letters to write, as well as minutes of the last W I meeting to type. Doing nothing was even more of a full time job than a full time job, though it was easier than when George's mother lay in bed above the garage. It had been difficult to fulfil his dream of a perfect house, and still apply principles of family love and solidarity by emptying his mother's slops.

Another help in their long haul up was Myra's own money, five hundred a year from her father who wanted to stun the government out of death duty they'd scoop from his thriving shoe factory when and if he died. The indestructible old man sat in the big chair when he came to see them and grinned at the nestlike order his son-in-law had created with such hard-earned money – that he'd hoped he'd have the panache to spend like a man.

Myra's mother hadn't taken to George at first because his religion wasn't the same as theirs – though neither family had much – not to mention a difference in race which her mother was too polite to mention except everyday for six months when she wanted Myra to change her mind and marry one of their own sort. But Myra didn't succumb, knew

163

exactly what she couldn't help doing beneath that rounded face, smile and glasses. Under it, as under a calm moon of autumn, the sea moved. She went home often at the beginning, and each time, after arguments on love and loyalty and family, came away wounded but in one piece, bringing typewriter, gramophone or books. By the time she went to the registry office, standing in the large room with George and repeating all the pointless formulae, she felt a wild exuberant sea pressing to burst out and overwhelm her with laughter and gladness. Her face was on fire, her knees seemed about to commit the first and final act of treachery. She felt alone, a pillar of stone in the middle of a violent lake. George did not exist. No one was there but herself, and the faint influx of these tedious words that she must have been repeating: 'I do,' but the affirmation bashing against her shouted: 'I survived. I survived. I'm in one piece and free.'

It was freedom only because it was different. Finding a house and fixing it up hid the fact that underneath they were two wounded people who had met one morning after an inconclusive and agonizing battle. They had come together by the planned move of a psychotic God. 'Mazel tov.'

Coffee boiled, was poured out and blancoed by milk. Mrs Harrod, a grey-haired old woman with a lined face and cat-sly eyes, sat opposite. Her husband, working in a motorway repair gang, had been spun off his feet by a passing car five years ago, so neatly clipped that hardly a mark was visible when his mates lifted him out of hoar frost by the road and humped him to the tool hut. From this accident Mrs Harrod bought a doll-cottage, and voted Conservative instead of ignoring election days. Good fortune coming out of so much black could only be an act of God, so she went to church on Sunday and was even spoken to by other property owners of the village. But she had to live, so worked every morning for Myra. She was neither clever, neat, intelligent nor industrious, but drudged around and did the jobs that Myra could never face – though they sometimes appealed to Myra more than the gardening that had fallen to her lot. She'd thought of letting Mrs Harrod go, and paying a man to garden with what she cost, but George wouldn't like it, because Mrs Harrod was the sort of anachronistic rural institution that appealed to him in spite of his progressive brand of politics. And Myra was also fond of her. Mrs Harrod was the only person of the village whom she felt close to. Considering all the stillbirths, deaths, accidents and animal woundings that had gone on around her, Mrs Harrod seemed to have lived her life in the red. There was no one in the parish she didn't know about. The most obscure family in the council houses up the hill, or the remotest keeper's cottage set at the far corner of some copse and miles from the nearest lane were as simple illuminated books set out for the autodidact. She created a village of two faces for Myra, one of the Women's Institute singing 'Jerusalem' in this pleasant arcadian valley; and another of ferocious sexual Luddites liable to turn without thought and set axe or penis at the nearest body. The two blended and Myra saw it as part of her own life, though whether the village accepted her as quickly as she had accepted someone from it to do her housework was impossible to say.

Outside her activity with the Old Folks and the W I she felt the depths and working of Mrs Harrod's life close to her own which had not so far flashed and shuddered to all kinds of unjust visitations from chance. The recounted tales had the same edgy bitterness and gallows humour of certain Yiddish storytellers, whose poor of the Polish and Russian towns in the last century became finally real to her. The empty flat above the garage, though draughty in winter, was luxury compared to Mrs Harrod's cottage at Preston Bottoms. It had bathroom, gas and electric light, while the Bottoms had washbowl, fireplace, oil lamps and earth closet, and a long walk to the lane for every drop and swallow of water. Mrs Harrod never compared the blatant inconvenience of one to the normal equipment of the other, but Myra let her do a weekly wash in the huge white Axiomatic standing under the kitchen window. The spin drier made it light to carry back, saved her living among stalactites of steaming clothes during days when the fields were black with rain.

The sun dipped its beam through the kitchen window. 'Have a biscuit, Mrs Harrod.'

'Thank you. I do like these tinned biscuits. They're old-fashioned. Better made. Not like them one and tuppence, penny off packets. I used to cook my own when John was alive. He'd come in from his work and eat as many as a dozen before charging off to play darts at the Legion.' Myra remembered the last general election. She and George pinned a Labour poster on their gate, and one day, walking towards Preston, she saw a picture of the Tory candidate grinning in the window of Mrs Harrod's hovel. Here was she, mistress of a detached Georgian residence squat in its own grounds, with garage, outhouses and flat, off main village street and in quick reach of town (as it might say in the *Observer* if ever they decided to sell it for five thousand more than they'd spent on it) and there was Mrs Harrod stuck in a lopsided cottage, ready for the council to condemn it out of hand, so that by another malevolent crack of fate's bullcosh she'd end up in the workhouse, though still carried ga-ga to the polls in some spinster's car who'd guide her shuddering hand into a cross by the right Tory name. Myra smiled, though thanked God for the voting Labour masses that still seemed to inhabit the north: cloth-capped, hardworking, generous and bruto, or that was the impression she got from reading a book (or was it books?) called *Hurry on Jim* by Kingsley Wain that started by someone with eighteen pints and fifteen whiskies in him falling downstairs on his way to the top.

George had considered using the garage flat as a study, a snug retreat where he could have books and drawing board,

166

wireless and map table, a bed even – as if, Myra thought, to get away completely, wanting to leave me but not quite able to. His idea of marriage was to come home, eat, and read a book, thinking that enough communion passed between man and wife if they merely sat close and silent. He had great faith in his presence for generating love and affection. The miracle was that it sometimes worked, often enough for their marriage to be felt by Myra as pleasant, if not happy.

There were times when George drank himself into a three-day stupor. It came on him like a cold or illness, began when they went out to dinner or a party. He would drive home drunk – to prove he wasn't drunk – cool and slow, careful and safe. When Myra was in bed he would go on drinking, open a bottle of rotten steam (as he called it) and listen to Bach or Vivaldi until he fell asleep or senseless. The next day would be the same, and the day after, his private kind of necessary oblivion. She remembered him telling her how the electric spring of his life had tightened itself beyond bearing on many nights of his lonely youth. Sometimes at midnight, in a deliberate trance-like way, he would get into his car and drive around the empty, lit-up roads of London. He would go from Notting Hill to Kilburn and Cricklewood and Hampstead, swing back at full pelt through St John's Wood and Maida Vale to Kensington and Hammersmith, then via Shepherd's Bush to Pembridge Square, stopping for petrol and coffee on his mad figure-of-eight career. He played a game called 'Jump-the-lights' – seeing them on red a few hundred yards away, treading the accelerator as if it were a piece of sacred earth he wanted to get the feel of before going on a long journey. The reds glowed like blood-eyes in a great mirror, drawing him closer by the second, his eyes shining, half conscious, fixed by the hypnotic stare and defying them to make him stop – when he was already out of the zones of his own power to do so. He sped between, unscathed, always untouched, a sweaty smile of triumph and relief, a heart battering him back to consciousness.

Now he was a quiet, hard-working enjoyer of the settled life because his dream of the dream-house had come true. Lectures often took him as far away as Plymouth or Edinburgh. Calm authoritative George, she saw him as the young, heavying fuddy-duddy of thirty-five expounding on the geological structure of the Kentish Weald, and theorizing on its relationship to the economic life of today. He was considered brilliant, his knowledge overlapping into anthropological and all manner of social sciences. She loved him for this knowledge, could forgive all the nights spent reading and writing alone at the kitchen table, and hearing mad rain gunning the windows loud enough to drown any footsteps. She kept the house going, fires lit, bulbs in their sockets, stove, radio, gramophone, dishwasher, all machines in smooth running order, so that the house worked as soon as his hand touched the doorknob.

She saw him – drunk and happy after his lectures, arguing till daylight, a long fluent talker when he had something to say, a conversationalist all-admired. Books and papers overwhelmed his front-room study, and the thought of him taking over the garage flat might not be a bad one, except that he would then pass all his evenings there and rob her even of that much time with him.

Early on they had talked of turning the flat over to what children came along, for George's dream also included a pair of tow-headed Crispins crunching the gravel and grass, and high-jumping blue-eyed over the jungle-jim erected on the front lawn for all passing enviously to see. It had also been her picture, but she couldn't stand the thought of it now, for both pregnances had ended in miscarriage, the unexpected start of labour, and the bloody totality of George's dream pushing out too early and dead, bursting her asunder in a most awful pain and waste of the world's spirit. There was no

168

physical explanation for it. She should keep on trying, the doctor said, but to 'try' for such a thing was a spoliation of human dignity that believed in procreation before everything else. If at first you don't succeed, try try again – the spider image of Robert the Bruce – that Ouraboros of conventional response fitted only a fool without wit or patience, unable to wait, goaded by failure into accepting a maxim coined by the successful ashamed at the sight of other peoples' disasters.

So the house became a factory that produced good living: a day of work gave peace in the evening, and a fine table to pick and choose from. The larder was flexible in its offerings because Myra bottled, smoked, salted, pickled, baked and pre-packed; collected cook books and recipes from the *Observer* and *Sunday Times*, wrote cheques for magazines pandering to house and home, namely *Which? Where? How? When?* and *What?* – a super householder driven into the ground by it. Her ideal had once been to work in some newly re-linquished colony, teaching economics or social relations, helping to form a new nation from the top-heavy powergrid of exploitation, or rescue it from the threat of black dictator-ship. Love, getting married – it had occurred to her, but was to stay subservient to the main ideal. Even the dreamlike beginning of her affair with George didn't seem to threaten it, for one could live with a man, get married, have children even, and still axe out a career from the thousand circum-stances that tried to deflect one from it. But George's dream drew her in, engulfed hers because its bricks and slate reared up around her, a house to be worked on for months before the multiple lists of emendations were finally screwed up and burned one morning with the rest of his yesterday's rubbish.

Myra went to London, to shop, buy books, call at the house of her brother and sister-in-law, go around the galleries. These pleasurable expeditions took her off early in the morning and brought her back late at night, seemed to last long enough for her to face another month in her bucolic outhouse. She had

169

bought the framed drawings and pictures from her own pocket, wise purchases, easy in price, but transforming the white and empty walls. She received notices of new exhibitions, even an occasional invitation to a vernissage, but so far she hadn't gone to any of these openings, preferred seeing three or four shows at one outing. George had left this side of the decoration to her on the assumption that she had better taste, and she accepted, if only to have one aesthetic corner of their dream world to herself.

The house was supposed to run itself, yet where was the spare time? She still couldn't snap its iron grip and begin a life of writing and reading that George had promised when they first met. He had tried to get a man from the village to do part-time on the garden, someone at any rate who could hump the heavy work and cut Myra's time on it to half a day, but farms and gardens of the surrounding estates took all the labour, and George's ideal house was by no means set in an ideal countryside where people could help him maintain it.

Spring was breaking up the enveloping peace, and Myra couldn't say which would be a better life: something useless, sterile and exciting; or a writing, reading, constructive timepassing inside her own spiritual boundaries. In the long run, which was the best to have lived? The question was idle, a maggot that would kill you until you died, deny you either, push you into a limbo of both and nothing. You lived what you lived and couldn't change it by one act. Only an outside force over which you had no control – unexpected, huge, enthralling – could do that, and you wouldn't know it was happening because you'd be too busy fighting it.

Coffee finished, Mrs Harrod would clean out the livingroom. The sun's warmth drew back from the linoleum tabletop. It would rain later, so she'd better get that winter and spring rubbish burnt, smoke out the garden and maybe clear her thoughts. The deadness of life might blossom if she had

170

empty time. The soul developed and deepened in idleness, which was freedom. George would be the first to agree, because that was what he too had always wanted. Two incompatibles in quest of the same thing. She looked forward to firing the leaves, as if such action would release the held-in fire of her past existence into the wind.

13

PEOPLE IN the compartment sat dead to each other the whole four hours to London, refusing Frank's offer of fag-packet or batch of newspapers, and he thought what unsociable bastards. He supposed that in any other country somebody at least would have talked, said good morning, nice day, raining – but no, not here. And do you know, at the end it turned out they were all close friends going to a cricket match?

He found a room in Camden Town at three pounds a week, its walls distempered puke-green and kek-yellow, furnished with a gas-ring, bed, and a wardrobe so big he was surprised they hadn't let it out to a family at thirty bob a week. If they had he wouldn't have cracked his shins on it every time he tried to get into the room.

The stairs were washed every week by a disinfectant that smelled of sweat, soon overwhelmed by train-dust and smoke-soot from surrounding railways. There was no bathroom in the eight-roomed house, and the only lavatory for a score of people was a smashed pan stuck in a shed at the end of a postage-stamp garden. Coming to London certainly brought you down in the world. It was true of many people, for they couldn't have been born with such rancid unearthly pallors.

But the winter was almost over, a clean wind snapping along early-morning streets after fresh rain, letting him breathe a few minutes before the traffic roar opened its awful voice. People seemed to have been killed, pole-axed, driven to earth and sent pale at the blow. They looked as if they saw nothing but pavement and road, or advertisements ringing them: a silver jet-liner going through the heart spraying jelly-babies and electric shavers.

It was the first long time he'd spent in London, and he liked it so much he was a fortnight before starting work. He often walked eight hours through the streets and did not feel weak; but after three in the British Museum he almost fainted. The historical totality of the exhibits staggered him, and the precise old-maidish way in which so much insignificant stuff had been gathered together intimidated him as massive proof of his own unimportance. He almost wanted to set fire to it, blow it to bits, yet went on other days, fixed by Egyptian mummies and Samoan canoes, flint heads and spear tips – the preliminary skill and precision work that had, after thousands of years, landed him at his machine.

He bought a saucepan to boil eggs and make tea in – otherwise it was Lyons, fish and chips, or one-and-ten snacks at Mike's on the corner. He got work at a carpark in Soho, a safe enough place for a man who wanted neither past nor future. He guided cars in, drew them out, issued tickets and collected money, easy and mindless work, necessary at the moment because he also was mindless, caved-in and floating among dead buildings at the bottom of a smoky sea. With a spear in your metaphorical side the only thing you could do was move, move, move – even if only in circles, even if only on crutches. You could look at the traffic flowing around Cambridge Circus, bury yourself in Cyclorama or some museum –

as a man in the last extremities of toothache crawls under the bedclothes with a bottle of whisky – but sooner or later you have to get up and move again.

Anything to escape from this padded cell that he could only flop into blindfold, hugging the pick-up and sound-box of all he brought with him from Lincolnshire, still ripping at his psychic vitals. He gripped the splintered and tacky wood of the bed to stop himself taking a tube to the farthest out-post of the Northern Line and making a way to Lincolnshire, that county where his guts lay bleeding, and his love, still working perhaps, still alone maybe, waiting for him to come back and who knows, wanting to hear from him, a word, an address, an acknowledgement of agony, a promise to return tomorrow, soon, before long, something better than never. She sat alone, waiting. She loved him, wanted him to come back and love her, make love to her, show love, warmth, tenderness, care, make up for the promises he'd smashed like museum china, spread his spirit over the house. The bed frame deflected his beating fist, strong enough to outlast him. His mind swam through the fish-seas of doubt and reversal. He could never go back after doing so much the right thing in leaving when he did. There was no guarantee that she had given up her job and moved already to London with her husband, but at least she'd be able to see Kevin whenever she wanted. If she couldn't it wouldn't be his fault. For this big reason he couldn't go back; he had smashed promises by leaving, but would smash bigger ones by returning.

The rank walls, the damp spring darkness made a trap-cage baited with the rotten meat of all his life's impossibilities. They had got him, cornered him there in this room, while his Bill Posters' heart chewed on them, chewing itself, himself that he couldn't run from unless to Lincolnshire. Memories of her were burning ash-blue in the brain, wouldn't leave him alone. The voice of what he'd gone to bed with the night before had been calling him through the hours of sleep and

174

darkness – and it wakened him by six o'clock only to face it again, day after day.

He'd always wanted to live a while in London, enjoy himself and see things, but now that he was here the ashes were in his mouth, choking him. Out of the window, a great gaping hole torn to the north, was the open starbag of the heavens, and there was nothing to stop him fish-swimming through it except an outmoded feeling of pride and obstinacy.

Nine-thirty in the evening was too early to sleep, and too late for a trek to Soho, but he put on his coat and descended the narrow unlit stairs. A pram blocked one landing, he got round it and opened the front door. The orange-lit roar of Camden Road, and the cold heavy atmosphere of soot and iron filings surrounded him. It was invigorating, the one fact of London that shielded him from a final black fit. Even the museums smelled of it: if you were to bump into that mummy in the British Museum and accidentally crumple it up, the dust and plaster and death would reek of London pall, streets and petrol. On Sunday morning he would go out early, pick up an *Observer* and *Pictorial* at the tube station and ride down to Trafalgar Square to feed the pigeons, and the same throaty smell of tool sheds and locomotives dragged at his nostrils.

The pub was well enough packed for a midweek. He stood at the saloon bar feeling how out of place it would be to shout for a black-and-tan, unless he wanted a rough-house. Uncertain of its benefits, he felt more diffident about getting into one in London than if he was in Nottingham. The odds were too chancy, forces too foreign and remote. Yet he remembered one of his Nottingham mates who, unless he got blind drunk, spewed his guts up, and was knocked to the ground in unequal fight, didn't feel he'd had a good time – the sort of thing that now seemed a waste of life to Frank Dawley.

The pint tasted good, and he took a reasonable time over it.

175

A young man who sat at a nearby table with his girl friend was trying to light a cigarette. Every time he struck a match the girl blew it out, intent on revenge for something the young man seemed to have forgotten. He treated it as a joke for the first six matches, but eventually, once when he almost got his fag alight through a skilful cupping of hands and still her breath drove it out, he put down his box of matches, laid his cigarette on it, and landed her a sharp smack at the face. She burst into tears, and he comforted her, until she stopped crying and agreed to a Babycham.

All this stung his brain. Lincolnshire had been further away from Nottingham than London. He walked into the comforting lit-up dark, but after a hundred yards he hated it, and entered another pub as if the street had driven a nail into his back and pushed him through the door.

'What are you jumping into me for with such force?'

A pub was like a church, full of altars and incense, beer and biscuits, where you could either be with someone or alone. Frank eased the man out of his way: 'If you want a drink, say so.'

'I want nothing that belongs to you, but if you jump into me like that again, I'll swing this pick handle I've got under me coat, and there'll be no mistake about that.'

Frank stood at the bar: 'Drop dead. I tripped on the way in.'

The man hung at his elbow: 'Not at all, friend, not at all.'

Through the face he saw the snow-loam of Lincolnshire, the features that poached and wrote begging letters, the snow-tanned sun-lined phizzog of Albert Handley with the dark-brown eyes and short lips topped by a clipped moustache. The dawning came slowly, because Albert in his truculent joking had used a mock brogue. He also wore a new cap, a heavy good quality overcoat, buttondown shirt, tie, smart shoes and gloves. A long thin cigar hung from his mouth. He stank of prosperity, and a few whiskies: 'You're not dreaming, Frank. It's your old pal. I knew you a mile off, that square walk of yours, as if you'd hump through any door that wouldn't open. I'm only up this way tonight because I'm slumming. I got fed up with staying at the Metropole. Too posh for me, though I've only been there a week.'

'Two doubles,' Frank called. 'If this happened often I'd die from shock.'

'So would I. Let's down a few while we're at it: on me.'

'I'll pay my rounds,' Frank said. 'But what went on?'

Albert motioned him to a table. 'Let's sit down, then I'll tell you. It's something I'd always expected, but never knew would come. I often joked about it to Ina, to burn us up when there was no coal for the fire. It's so new to me I've hardly sorted it out myself yet.'

Frank wanted to ask him about Pat, to catch any fact or rumour of what took place after he'd left. 'You see,' Albert said, 'I was discovered as a painter, as the bastards say. Last week I lugged fifty prime canvasses and a roll of drawings to London for a show I'm going to have. That was after the owner of an art gallery here in London, the Arlington, had spent two days at the village getting photos of them, and another bloke had been taking down my life story for publicity. I got more money than I've had for all the paintings I've so far sold put together. I still can't believe it, Frank. I can't, my boy. It's bloody fantastic. If I took any real notice of it I'd be in chaos. Have another on me. You remember all them drinks I sponged off you in the village that snowy day?'

Frank downed another double. 'That still don't tell me how it all started.'

Albert grinned, swallowed. 'It was all your fault. You'll be surprised to hear it.'

'Go on, then.'

'You see, after you left, Pat Shipley's husband came up, to get her back.'

'Not after I left,' Frank said, 'while I was there.'

'Was it? Well, I never knew much of what went on in the village. But one morning I sent a lad of mine around the houses with a painting, and a book of raffle tickets at a bob a time. Everybody was dunning me, and I hadn't got a penny. I was desperate, always am when I come down to raffling a picture. So he calls at Nurse Shipley's, and who should come to the door but her husband. He's a fine man is Keith, a very good chap, quite a big advertising man here in London. Well, he asked who had done the picture, and to cut a short story shorter he comes up to the house and asks to see my other work. Then he goes back to the village and phones a telegram to a pal of his who owns the Arlington Gallery. This chap comes up after a couple of days, and the ball starts rolling.'

'This is the best thing I've ever heard about,' Frank said. 'When I saw that picture of "The Lincolnshire Poacher" I was crazy about it. Remember?'

Albert laughed. 'I offered it to you. You'd have been worth a good bit now if you'd gone off with it.'

'That doesn't worry me. That would have been robbery.'

'It's getting pride of place in the exhibition,' Albert said. 'That one knocked 'em all flat, so I'm glad you didn't take it.'

Frank came back with two doubles and two pints. 'Did Pat's husband stay long?'

'About ten days, I should say. He was well liked in the village. Bought four of my paintings even before the Arlington man came up. Not that he's my sort though. I can forgive a person anything, except when they buy one of my paintings.'

'You just paint to make enemies then,' Frank taunted. 'I'm glad I didn't take the one you offered.'

Albert laughed: 'So am I! I had a couple of reporters today at the hotel, and they kept asking me why I painted, so I got fed up and said: "If anybody asks me why I paint again

178

I'll punch his clock." Then I got my fists ready, expecting them to come for me, but they just wrote down what I said, thinking it was a gimmick, I suppose. But I happen to be serious. I've been painting for nearly twenty years, working all the time, going at it alone in between making a living and writing begging letters, not many people knowing that I even painted, and those that did wondering when I was going to get a job.' He sagged over his drink, head looking into it as if into the bulb of a flashlight. He swung to Frank, one eye closed, showing his teeth in a grin. 'Stop me, Frank. I still think I'm talking to reporters, or that fat get Teddy Greensleaves who owns the gallery.'

'All right, it's time,' the waiters and publican shouted. 'You've had your lot. Outside now.' Frank hated the way pubs closed in London. Customers were treated like dogs who'd been allowed to sup at the common trough. In Nottingham serving often continued twenty minutes after time, the pumps pulled surreptitiously, one eye on the towels and the other on the door for the coppers.

'Teddy Greensleaves is a strange chap,' Albert said. 'He tries to dazzle me with all his learning, and thinks I can't see him doing it. Talks about Oxford and rattles off the big art names, goes on theorizing about art till the cows come home – but they never do because it doesn't mean a thing. Lucky Dip I call him, because whatever you say he's always dipping into the sackbag of his mind to pull out a quotation from some book or other. I don't think he's got a mind of his own. He's consumptive in that way, a fat consumptive,' he affirmed, 'not a thin one. As long as Teddy sells my paintings, I should worry. Let me get back to the clean fields covered with cow shit.'

Frank shook him: 'Listen, Albert, I've got to know something.'

'Anything,' Albert said. 'Anything. Greensleaves said: "The hotel's on me. Where do you want to stay?" So I said:

179

"The Metropole" – which was the only one I'd heard on and cost ten pounds a night. He nearly dropped through the floor, but he kept his word. It's comfortable, central, but that's about all as can be said for it. I get paint all over the carpets. Had to smuggle it in. Wrapped canvas around me like corsets. Use the wardrobe for an easel. Not too boring like that.'

A waiter snatched their glasses. Frank pulled his back, still half filled with beer. 'You'd better get out,' the waiter said, 'or there'll be trouble.'

Frank finished his drink. 'I'd like to see it.'

'You will, mate,' the waiter said.

Albert woke up. 'Clear off,' he said. 'Get them glasses washed.' He winked, and slid a pound note across the table. The waiter took it and walked away.

'You've learned quick,' Frank said.

'It's easy when you've got money.'

'You won't have it long though, like that.'

'Plenty more where that came from. My wife and kids are swimming in it. I like to see people like that waiter crawl. They've got no backbone here in London. The other night in the hotel it was ten o'clock and I hadn't got a bean till the bank opened next morning. I was in my room reading the paper. I picked up the phone and said to the bloke at the desk: "Put two half crowns on a silver tray, and have it brought up to me here." I wanted to go out for a pint in one of them pubs up the Strand. So this waiter comes up and stands by my bed with the two half crowns on his tray. I pick one up and put it in my pocket. "The other one's for you," I say. "It goes on Mr Greensleaves's bill." And he says: "Thank you, sir," and humps off. I don't stand any fucking nonsense from this lot down here.'

'Tell me,' Frank said, 'where's Pat Shipley living?'

Albert opened his eyes. 'You don't know a thing, do you? Something funny happened at that house. She sold it, by the way, and got a good price for it. I would have bought it but it was too small for my mob. I'm buying the house we live in, remember? I'll have an extension built on, and a studio down the garden to keep me away from the sound of battle. All on private mortgage. The place is falling to pieces, but I'm soft-hearted.'

'What did happen?'

'She crashed in her car one night. Plenty of ice on the roads. It worn't bad. She was lucky. Broke her arm, got a few bruises and cuts. The car was a write-off though, but she got the insurance. Can't put a foot wrong that woman can't. She's back in London now with old Keith. I saw them the first night I was down, and they look happy enough. They've got a little house, in the Royal Borough of Kensington – Dogshit Borough, I call it. I've never seen so much dog shit on the pavements as down there. You've only got to step out of a taxi and splut! you're in it. Still, it's royal dog shit, so you just look happy and scrape it off on somebody's doorstep. But it's funny, when you go in that house it looks exactly the same as the one she had in Lincolnshire. She brought all her stuff down, but even so, it's bloody weird.'

They stood up. Albert swayed. The pub was dark except for light behind the bar. The waiter stood at the door: 'Good night, sir.'

Frank took his arm. 'I'll get you a taxi. We'd better cut through to Camden Road.' The council blocks had had most of their eyes knocked out for the night – a few yellow squares remaining, squat and baleful, as if kept in by the intermittent flush of traffic on the downhill road. It seemed darker, though the same lamps were lit, upturned orange troughs high in the air. Albert rallied: 'Greensleaves is going to throw a big party when my show comes on. Swill for everybody. I'll get him to drop you a card.'

'That's all right,' Frank said, his mind flying across the wastes of other things. I can't see her again, burned my boats and sunk 'em, blocked the river and collapsed the banks, blown up the bridges as well. Only swamp left. 'Good, then,' he said.

They walked as far as the canal, and no taxi passed. Albert leaned against the wall and looked over. 'It's not deep enough,' Frank said, thinking that he might go in first if it was. A train hobbled over the bridge. 'I've thought of that a few times since all this fuss began. But I'm pleased and happy that something's happening. I can't wait to get back home though and start work again. This fuss – I feel as if a great shovel comes out of the sky and scoops my willpower away. Then I want to drop under a train. I wouldn't live in London, not even for a pension.'

'I've seen the last of Pat,' Frank said.

'I reckon you have,' Albert agreed. 'So you ran out on her, did you?'

Through fire and dead soil, the pain unearthed itself out of his guts, tried to pull his eyes backward into the depths of his head, then to ram the back of his head into his eyes. Holding his face with both hands he spun into the middle of the road, roaring between the fire-lamps of traffic: 'Taxi! Taxi! Taxi! Taxi' I didn't run away from her. I jumped from the snow and ice of her life, and of mine. I was the odd man in, then the odd man out, the third man in a crowd, the trickster who is supposed to have no heart, who pulls the string and gets buried in the avalanche he makes. The only person she loved was her kid, and the one way she could go on loving him was by living with Keith, and I was dead right when I left her after she left me. The sky turned to water, froze, and slid under his feet.

'You can't stand up,' Albert said, 'and I'm the one that's drunk.'

'I can't take you in that state,' the taxi driver said.

Albert still held him. 'He doesn't want a taxi, I do.'

'Where?'

182

'Phone me,' Albert said, gripping him at the arm like iron. 'Do you promise?'

'Yes.'

'Metropole Hotel.'

'Who are you kidding?' the driver said.

'I've never felt less like kidding in my life. I don't work there either. If you don't want to take me though, I can walk. I'd rather walk than put *you* out, mate.'

'All right, all right, get in.'

Frank stood apart. 'I'll see you.'

'On the big night,' Albert smiled. 'Don't forget. Come and support me. I'll need it. Greensleaves said everybody'll be there, though I don't see how he's going to get forty-eight million people into that gallery.'

The taxi drove off gracefully, making speed along the shining road towards the tube station.

14

THE ARLINGTON was re-opening with Albert Handley's show. His work hung finely framed around the room, honoured in one of the smartest Bond Street galleries. It was difficult to see his paintings, for the huge, long, low-ceilinged hall was crammed with people who seemed to be holding them up by a collective gaze, meshing them to the wall with admiring words. A charming, high-haired woman stood by the door, Handley's face looking seriously up at her evening dress from a pile of handouts on the table containing his life story, list of exhibited works, and a few reproductions, including one of 'The Lincolnshire Poacher' in full colour. This celebrated picture at the far end was impossible to get at, except perhaps over the mass of elegant, poshly coiffeured heads. Cigarette smoke made her eyes sore, or maybe it was the lighting which wouldn't normally allow one to linger too long at any picture – brilliant and merciless, like the wit overheard when pushing towards some scrap of paint and canvas.

After all, it was a party, so she'd be lucky to see anything – or perhaps unlucky, since it wouldn't be fair to make judgements on a night given over to publicity rather than simple pleasure. Not that she'd be able to afford the Arlington prices, and was curious as to why or how an invitation had been sent to her. No doubt she was on the mailing list, having bought a couple of drawings in the days when prices weren't so fancy.

She took a glass of champagne, wondering how the waiter could manoeuvre so freely when she had been jammed five minutes in one place. She recognized living images from the Sunday papers and the rich sleek weeklies. A shadow-faced novelist from the north was saying to a famous American painter: 'When I have a cold I can only smoke cigars' – in a loud, bell-clear accent totally unlike any used in his books. The collective noise deadened all thought of speech. Her voice was normally soft, and toning it up would call for some force-ful inner assertion that she didn't feel inclined to use, shy of drawing notice to herself in case it should be unfavourable and so erode her long nurtured feeling of aesthetic superiority to these newspaper and television people, critics and middle-men, fashion-mouths and party-liners. Yet they impressed her as figures because they had the courage of their non-convic-tions, hired beliefs that they had grown to regard as their own, and which, to give them their due, they now put over with a certain amount of panache and literacy. Living in the country so long had given her a sense of detachment – which was something to be said for it – had taught her to appreciate the power and value of London's amenities, while occasional visits inclined her to despise them. On balance she took from it what she wanted, and was only contemptuous of what it tried to make her want.

Such a crush disturbed her. Also looking as if he didn't belong there a man made way, squeezed himself aside so that she could get through. Another bubble of conversation broke: 'My analyst said: "There's too much death in you." "I know," I told him, "but death is better than suicide." '

185

Glasses didn't stop smoke paining her eyes. Her body pressed by, and he held her arm, unable to give free way: 'Have you met Albert yet?'

'I've not long been here. I think it's impossible to meet anyone.'

'You've met me,' he smiled. 'I'm feeling a bit like a . . . spare man at a wedding. Greensleaves asked too many people. Come and see Albert though. He's an old pal of mine.' His middle-strong height cleaved between the backs of talking drinkers. He gripped her hand, turned to see if she were still the same person: 'There's plenty of booze, I will say that.'

She was intrigued at the thought of meeting the man responsible for 'The Lincolnshire Poacher' especially after the articles that had already garnished the fat Sundays. 'My name's Frank Dawley,' he said.

'I'm Myra' – and felt him press her hand in acknowledgement. He pushed one upright back too hard, a tall bald man in a lounge suit who stared furiously but said nothing. Frank wore a grey pinstriped two-piece, charcoal tie under a white collar, black high-sided shoes. He'd taken a day off from the car park, unworried as to whether he got the push or not, being flush for money from having saved much of his pay in the last few weeks. He was feeling the need to lift himself out of London, light off for the country, or drift over to France. A letter from his sister in Nottingham told that Nancy was living with someone else, a bachelor of the old days who had courted her even before Frank turned up, who had never married, whose mother had not long died, and who at last saw his chance. Another solid door of his past had locked – in which there couldn't be anything but a lasting good. 'What do you do?' Myra asked, as he paused to get a bearing on Albert.

'How do you mean?'

She felt foolish at having let out a direct and simple question. 'Are you a painter? Or a writer?'

186

'I work at a car park. An odd job until I find out what I want to do. How about you?'

'I live with my husband.'

'Is he here?' No, and he drew her through the crowd again, pleased because she had thought he might be a painter or writer. Well, he could be, but wasn't, not even a writer of letters because his separation from Pat was as final as if lightning had flashed between the ingrowing tree roots of them, split the sphere of the earth in two and set them spinning in different galaxies, finished forever, at distances that not even words could span.

Albert was answering questions against the wall, hating it, as if cornered by people whose belongings he'd filched, and who wanted to know, earnestly and sympathetically, why he'd done so foolish a thing – before they sent him to prison. Frank barged between: 'Meet Myra, an old friend of mine.'

Albert was glad to, red from champagne, eyes smarting and half closed as if he hadn't seen daylight for weeks. Myra was surprised at the open sensibility of his face, had expected something crude and northern after the write-ups. He was forty-two years old according to the catalogue, yet looked little more than a man of thirty who had already suffered the fires of life's iniquity and emerged with a broader, deeper comprehension of the fact that there was worse to come. She hoped his paintings mirrored such a face, fragmented it to the same depth and caught the enigma of his lips and eyes.

'I'm tired of meeting strangers,' he said, dismissing his court. 'I don't get on too well with them, especially this sort. If I'm to believe 'em, I've already sold the whole show out.'

'Too bad for me,' Myra said, 'though I don't think I could afford the pieces here, anyway.'

'Don't let that worry you,' he smiled. 'I was only joking. I probably haven't sold a thing. But I've got a few good pictures stowed away at my place in Lincolnshire, that you will be able to afford, so get my address from Frank. You can

187

always come up and pick one or two. I'll be only too glad to diddle old Greensleaves out of his whack.' Greensleaves may have heard this, Albert fearlessly nodding in his direction: 'I've told a lot of people that, and given them my address. I don't care who knows it, even if I am drunk. I'd tear this place apart if I thought it wasn't insured.'

'It wouldn't take much doing,' Frank cautioned, 'but there's no point in it.'

Myra was amused at his empty, touching arrogance. Yet it could explode. A troupe of Didikois called at the village last summer and one of the men whose eyes burned to the same pitch-emptiness as Albert's had been the ringleader to break up the pub after being refused a drink. 'I hate my pictures on these walls,' he said, unable to swing his arm towards any of them. 'The bastards have no right to put 'em up like that.'

'It'll help you to live,' Frank said sternly, 'and paint.'

'You think it will?' Albert cried savagely. 'I painted when I had nothing, don't forget. When I see a picture of mine on the wall, and look at it properly, I feel full of bullet holes, my guts showing, all of me stark naked, hanging there for everybody to poke their fingers at.' He took three drinks from a passing tray, handed one to Myra and Frank without a break in his talk. 'They don't know what to do. What few lights they've got go out when they look at one of my pictures. Ah! Don't think I'm saying they're good pictures. That's not the point. But I go cold when I see somebody looking at them, their eyes skimming over the outside top skin. They can't get through that little bit of surface and fly underneath. I never thought it would be like this. I'll be months getting over it.'

'You're drunk,' Frank said. 'It shouldn't upset you like that. Come out for a breath of air.' A beautiful, thin, middle-aged woman smiled before phrasing a question. Her dress was superb, rich, simple, subtle perfume penetrating even the cigarette smells and heat of people. A dull silver bracelet hung from her wrist, matched the neck-brooch. The dark, piled hair showed a pale, faintly lined forehead. She had a splendidly intelligent face, grey exposed eyes, a softly curving nose with slightly spread nostrils, and lips whose real shape could not be made out because of artfully applied lipstick.

'Not yet,' Albert answered, his eyes clearing. 'Somebody wants to ask me a question.'

'You're Mr Handley,' she said, pointing her folder.

'I think so. At the moment. I'm not always sure.'

'I've been looking at your paintings. They're absolutely wonderful. Quite original. A fine depth. How long have you been painting?'

'Ages,' he said, swaying.

'Ages?'

'Ages. Kiss me.'

'Hmmm?' Startled eyes. 'I'm Lady Ritmeester.'

'Kiss me again.'

'I haven't kissed you at all yet.'

'Albert' – Frank took his arm, firmly. 'Let's get him to a taxi, Myra.'

'My husband is here tonight,' Lady Ritmeester said, disturbed though not angry.

'You've looked at my paintings,' Albert went on, with a sad, lunatic persistence. 'That's like having been to bed with me. Go on, kiss me. We're in a crowd. Nobody'll see.'

She laughed. 'You *are* a strange man.'

'I'm a man, I suppose that makes me strange.'

She beamed. 'Witty, too.'

'Come on, Albert, let's get you back to the old Metropole.'

'I'm sure many other women would oblige you,' she said.

'But it's you I want.' He shook Frank's hand away and took her fingers. 'Lady Ritmeester?'

'Yes?'

'If I haven't got you, I haven't got anything.'

'How charming!'

189

He fell back into Frank's arms, eyes bloodshot, limbs twitching quickly again into cohesion and strength.

'A really charming person!' exclaimed Lady Ritmeester.

With Myra's help they walked him to a larger space near the door. An overcoat flashed by the cloakroom. Frank recognized him first. Two months had not blunted his eyes, though Keith's face was less sharp, a little grosser, smooth and more satisfied now that he'd been robbed of his suffering. His confident stance of lighting a cigarette had more imitation in its movement than unique feeling, and Frank recalled his face at the cottage aged by marks of agony in spite of himself. But now, he had lost even that. Something had happened. His wife had come back. He had got what he wanted, and had gone soft over it.

He called: 'What happened to Albert?'

'He drank too much. He's had a few hard days.' He noticed Keith looking at Myra. Who was she? Myra the darkish and married woman who'd come to the gallery on her own, wears glasses which give an attractive softening effect to her eyes. A smart dress showed the figure well: Frank liked to see tits on a woman, not too small, not too big, just so that they moved a bit when she walked.

Outside, photographers were waiting, cars drifting in with more and more people. Other traffic was being thrown towards Oxford Street. What shadow remained was filled with press cameramen fighting for position, to record this one-in-a-hundred shot of some stupefied-drunk painter celebrating what looked like an enormous piece of financial luck. Their readers would want to know all about that.

It was as if they'd walked into the focus of an electric storm, each flash freezing forever the limp form of Albert, held from the pavement, it seemed, by the startled angrily-set faces of Frank and Myra.

15

WITH ALBERT safely in bed at the
Metropole they walked back along the Strand. When Frank
left the gallery he'd felt savage and mysogynistic, but his
mood softened because the night was clear, a fresh breeze
lapping up from the river. It had rained, and lights were
mellow and far-spreading, traffic quieter. Myra felt free of her
normal life, walking with someone she didn't know, the
house forgotten in its dark owl-fold forty miles away.
Champagne had relaxed. Frank asked where she lived,
whether she had any children, if she had a job. He wanted
talk, but realized he was spoiling her mood, so they skirted
Trafalgar Square in silence. The fountains were two great
stationary flowers of light and colour, stamens of smoke trying to rise above the highest reach of spray, like Lady Ritmeester's orgiastic wig tinted against the sky. Reflected light
turned them blue, pink, gunmetal blue, snow blue, grey,
flown across by odd pigeons left among people still sauntering
around. A camera flashed near one of the lions: someone
stood between its paws. A policeman dragged him down. 'I
fed pigeons here the other day,' he said, 'but they didn't want

to eat. One of them was so fat that when it tried to walk away it fell over. I made a grab for it, meaning to tuck it under my coat, but it just managed to flutter up onto a lion's head. It was safe up there.'

A midnight train would soon draw Myra and her dreams out of Paddington, clattering its wheels back into the darkness. But not yet. Spring was felt more vividly and sweetly in the block-middle of the city than in the fields around her home. The air with which she would later embalm the deep mood of this rare evening was almost warm. It detached her from George and the house, made her feel closer to this young man by her side, as if he were responsible for it.

'Take my arm,' he said. Lulled by the noise of their own footsteps they walked towards Soho. 'We'll have something to eat. I know a Greek place, down in a cellar, used to be an old tube station. I sometimes go there after work, sit and read. It's more cheerful than my crumby room in Camden Town.'

An old deadbeat of Soho asked them for money and Frank dropped him a shilling. Smells from Wimpy bars chafed his hunger, yet he savoured it, in no hurry to eat. 'I'll buy you a drink.'

She tugged his arm: 'Let's walk. I live in the country, and like streets. I don't come often to Town.'

'If you don't like it, why do you live there?'

'I'm married to someone who does like it. We can't all choose what we want to do.'

'We can. If we don't it gets chosen for us. We end up doing what we want to do.'

'You believe that?'

'Yes.' Frank was sure of it, dead sure of all he said, because he was empty and without thought, desire or aim. He was walking with a woman, enjoying himself because of this, going off for a meal with the glittering impression of the party gnawed at by vague thoughts of work in the morning.

You could do exactly what your heart and soul wanted to do, if you had the courage and endurance to face the lifelessness it left in you. Emptiness was the terrible weapon fate bashed you with, but somehow you walked and worked through it, forgetting if you could the mechanics of those decisions that had landed you in the middle of a colourless psychic battlefield.

She liked his calm, quiet way of talking, and the comforting unimportant silences when he said nothing. At home with George such silences were only proof that they had little more to say to each other, a mutual reproach since both had never allowed the common areas of love to ignite and flare. Present silence was nothing to do with love, since they had only just drifted together for a few hours, though real love could come out of it. It gave her peace and rest, a sense of adventure without obligation, of easy loneliness that was only possible with a stranger. Everyone sensed the change of air and temperature, the renewed oxygen of night, and it was difficult to walk arm in arm along the pavement.

They went downstairs, sat at a rough wooden table without taking their coats off. The waiter brought two plates of rice, rained with a lava of exotic-chaotic meat sauce, a bottle of Cypriot wine, and chunks of saltless bread. It was a meal for the ravenous and she'd never felt so hungry, nor so unconnected with people and the world around – yet grateful for their continued presence, which she thought hardly deserved because she was doing so little in return. Smells of the meal and tobacco smoke in the tunnel-shaped cellar, the rough grapeyard taste of the wine, and this man called Frank busily eating in front of her, stopping now and again to rain salt on his food, had a sharp intimacy as if her senses had come back after years of nullity. It was no use searching for the cause. There'd be plenty of time for that when it had gone. The fact that it would go saddened her, as if a dagger were pressing into her side to end this good feeling in a

193

matter of seconds. Tears were scalding her eyes, then cool on her cheeks. His hand went out to her wrist. 'What's the matter?'

Her happiness was so real she wasn't even ashamed of her tears. 'Nothing.'

'Whatever it is don't think about it. It'll go away then. If it won't go away though, tell me what it is.'

She smiled. 'It was nothing, truly' – surprised that at her age, after an era buried in a country-and-domestic life with a normally loving husband she should be sentimental enough to think that an hour of happiness could go on forever. Still, maybe that hope, even if sentimental, was part of that happiness. She couldn't finish her meal.

They walked up Tottenham Court Road, plenty of time before her train left. Cinemas were spreading people over pedestrian crossings, lining them up for buses. 'I could spend years in London,' he said, 'and not get tired of it. I've lived most of my life in the Midlands.'

'I thought you had. You still have the accent. I was brought up in London – Hampstead.'

'You've got no accent at all.'

'I know. It's nondescript.'

'It sounds good to me. I like clear speech.'

'Do you have any friends in London?'

'Only Albert. He'll be back in Lincolnshire soon.'

'How did you come to meet him?'

'Lived in the same village. I was having an affair with a woman up there, until it blew up in my face.'

'What happened?'

He couldn't say that he'd left her so that she wouldn't be parted from her son, and that such an act of self-sacrifice was the hardest thing he'd ever done in his life. 'She loved her son,' he said, 'more than she loved me. We decided we'd had enough' – and having said that, he put an arm around her as they walked. 'You know the way it goes? Maybe you don't if

194

you're still living with your husband. Do you have many friends where you live?'

'Not really. I've been ten years in the village, but that's not enough.'

'I can imagine.'

'My old friends are scattered all over the place. My best friend is a girl who lives in Majorca. She's married to an American writer. We write about every three months. She's happy enough, as far as anybody can tell with someone who's married.'

'Why should anybody be happy when they're married?' he said. 'That's a load o' rammel. Even living together, it's not realistic to expect happiness. I used to think it was necessary, even possible, but as soon as two people start thinking about happiness then they're finished. If only one of them thinks about it, it blows up even quicker.'

'You wouldn't want them to think at all, then?'

'It's not that. But people are chewed up by a dog-rat inside them called passion. Cannibals eat each other, which is bad, but it's even worse to eat yourself. Don't think I haven't done it, or don't still. This passion is the wrong side of the moon. It poisons the liver. Everything is geared to making you eat yourself – the way this society works. Look around, talk to anybody about their job or life, switch on the wireless or telly, and it says: "Eat yourself. Go on, eat yourself – crunch-crunch." I feel it in here all right. My blood circles round and round, day after day, year after year, and where does it get you in the end? There ought to be some way of snapping out of this feeling except by cyanide or a knife in your back. It's time we discovered how to break it.'

'I suppose you want a war?'

'I used to wonder. Civil war, maybe. But even that's a bit too traditional, out of date. We need something new.'

'A new religion?' she smiled.

'That's all bitten out of me. You can't go back, not even to

195

look for a fresh direction. You've got to start from where your feet are planted. So don't mock me about religion.'

'I'm not mocking you. Show me how to break out of all this.'

'Maybe I will, but I can't tell you how. When you see the moon in a pond, like the three loons of Gotham, it's easier to reach it by sputnik than pull it in with a net, or swim out to it and freeze your fingers. As soon as you have patience you begin to go places. The only thing is, it takes longer. A year ago I didn't even know this. I'd give a lot to know what I'll know next year.'

'I'd give a lot to know where I'll be next year,' she said.

'You sound sad about it.'

'That's because I think I'll be in the same place as I am now.'

'You might as well put your head in the gas-oven if you think that.'

'That's a helpful suggestion.'

'It isn't easy to help anybody in that way.'

'Not if you can't help yourself. I don't need help, in any case.'

'We all need it. We've got to make it out of ourselves, out of each other, but in a new sort of way.' While living with Nancy and the kids he felt encircled by a high brick wall dozens of feet thick. This wall had gone down in a cloud of smoke, but another had formed, of equal height and thickness, though a little further out which anyway left him with more room in which to move, enough to haul out the answers she wanted. If he'd loved her it might have been impossible. 'People can act,' he said. 'They can do things. I came to London – which isn't much of an act, I admit, but things happen to me.'

'It's dull, living in the country,' she said, afraid of burning herself on the heat of his words. 'I suppose if you have children and lots of family nearby you don't notice it.'

196

'Don't you want any kids?'

'My husband does, but so far I haven't been able to have any.'

'Is that because you don't want any?'

'No, it isn't.'

'I've got two in Nottingham, which is a pity for them.'

'As you said, we end up doing what we want to do.'

'Now you're throwing my own words back at me.' On the next corner, along a length of recently demolished buildings, was a barrow of burning timber, ancient dry wood from gutted houses shaking its flames and sparks into clear sky. They stood by the fence watching it, his thoughts dimmed by the collective roar. It seemed as if mysteriously started, no one around its flanks, half-eaten beams a glowing geodetic pattern, smoke boiling darkly. If you can't light up the sky and make daylight for everybody to see in, he thought, burn it down. Darkness is a rotten castle for setting fire to.

They walked along Euston Road. 'Let's stay out all night,' he said. 'It's good to wander round a town like this.' His suggestion seemed crazy, until she remembered wanting to do such a thing before meeting George, but never able to because a girl alone might not be safe. 'My husband's at home,' she said, the final refuge. 'I have a train to catch.'

'I'll see you to the station.' She was tired, unable to walk all night even if she were free to. The shoes weren't right for it, and burns under her feet already promised blisters for tomorrow. Frank waved a taxi.

He said good-bye at Paddington. The train was crowded, but he found her a seat. 'What time will you get home?' he asked at the door of the compartment.

'About two.' People were looking over his shoulder for empty places. Neither was inclined to end the evening. The station had revived their nerves with its unexpected machine-noises, mysterious bangings, variously pitched lights, people going through barriers for last trains as if street-tentacles

197

would drag them back into a hostile city if they were missed. In the taxi, calm, purring, cocooned, they had accepted it as the end, but now the excitement had returned. Frank had walked along as with an acquaintance for whom he had little feeling, but imagining the memory of it from next week, saw clearly that it would turn out to be more than that. He wouldn't kiss her, or even shake her hand, for fear she'd be embarrassed by so many people, yet he felt the impulse to fix the evening as memorable in some way. Not that you had to fall in love with a woman before taking the first kiss. He even wanted to see her again. Maybe that's what railway stations did, and perhaps if she'd just nipped off in a taxi or dodged into the underground he'd have forgotten her in two minutes.

The train jolted under his feet. 'I expect we'll bump into each other again,' he said, for want of anything better, hating to say good-bye on trains. The evening had already lost its casual nature.

'Perhaps,' she answered, leaving it all to chance, empty also at the end of the evening. A deep-noted whistle, like the cry of a caged bird who realizes that its door is open but can't move, echoed around the station. 'See you,' he said, turned and walked leisurely to the door, dropped to the platform as the carriage moved. She settled in her seat, took a book from her handbag.

16

THREE DAILY papers fell through the letterbox. The two that he termed easy-to-read were left for Myra; the heavy, top-people newspaper he folded up and took to his job – wearing trilby hat, trench coat and heavy boots, for he was supervising a new agricultural survey on the bleak uplands of Bedfordshire.

Few people knew the land of England as well as George, or had a deeper feeling for it. There was little he hadn't hitch-hiked, biked, motored or walked over in what already seemed, at thirty-five, an immensely long life. He was alone, the complete man while making base lines out of far-off hills and woods, triangulation from church spires or the jutting shoulders of valley buffs. Derbyshire stone, Kentish chalk, Fenland sedge, each atmosphere felt different to his skin and lungs, bred way-out dialects, forced various dwellings on each landscape, was a geo-meteorology moulding the common psyche of its inhabitants. The subtleties of land and people were profoundly fascinating, and George was lord of all he surveyed when their composite reactions to land and air tied in with his knowledge and sympathy.

His sensitivity to the interdependence of land, animals and people was reflected in his calm and intelligent eyes, and in his now rather stolid features. As a young man his mind had been open and his brain limber, golden theories adorned and carried through – or rejected with a cry that there were more where that came from. Now he was at that middle-age when he tried to make ideas fit into harder traditional patterns – a style of personal and intellectual advancement in tune to the country he lived in. His visionary eyes did not seek harmony any more, but fixity into which people and the three elements slotted with neatness and safety. Any discrepancy, rather than point the way to philosophical adventure, was regarded as a mistake, a failure of logic, a miscasting of knowledge. He was building limits to defend his self-assured integrity against a greater awareness that middle-age threatened him with. These limits were also applied to Myra, who was an entirely different person. George had stayed very much the same since their marriage, his attitudes merely hardening, while Myra had changed as much as it was possible to while living with a man unable to recognize the fact that she was changing.

Yet he suspected some change between them in the last year, and if this feeling turned out to be correct something had to be done to keep them on the accustomed emotional lines. Blood ran deep but bloodiness ran deeper, he had once quipped about a couple they knew, who were unwilling to save their marriage by emotional compromise. In one of his rare moments of expatiation he said to Myra that such people were so shallow and spiritually null that any policy of give and take meant a living death to them. A vicious quarrel spelt life – while too many quarrels drove them apart. The great chisel-wedge of domestic realism eventually finished them off. For a marriage to survive needed stamina, intelligence, tolerance, a backbone of unique qualities that few people possessed. If peace were broken, how could one

work? Domestic battles were the most savage time-con-
sumers of any man's career.

Myra agreed. It was true. Everything he said was true. He
was full of staid, obvious, incontrovertibles, a parson in
reverse, a congregation preaching to one when at rare times
the speech-stops were out. Yet from his lips, words flayed the
empty air, certainly didn't cut into the parts of her consciousness deadened after six years married to him. Nothing
was wrong. They'd held back from quarrelling because it was
unreasonable to do so, immature, a waste of George's working time. But this wasn't it at all, she thought when on her
way back from town after her stroll with Frank. People in
love shouldn't be afraid to quarrel. People in love didn't
think about quarrelling: they just did or they didn't. If
you're in love what harm can it do? If you've never
quarrelled how can you go on living together? While persuading yourself that you love him, love him, the years roll
by between house and garden, velvet hands over your eyes
concealing the true reasons, so that the marks of these
multiple deceptions end up only on your mouth.

The meeting with Frank had lit fires in her mind, matched
them to the metallic light-clusters beyond the train window.
These far-off tinderous flames were pleasant to warm the
petrified limbs of the past by. There had been nothing
memorable attached to the walk – maybe that was why it
had been memorable. She hadn't even thought of her tasks
for tomorrow, the lecture on Roman remains in Buckinghamshire for the W E A to be prepared, a visit to Mrs
Wilkins to check entries for Friday's cake competition at the
W I. These pleasant enough jobs she often looked forward to,
and to have them vanish from her mind for five hours was
alarming – looking back on it.

George sometimes hinted that she gave too much time to
village work, meaning she'd neglected to do more typing for
his book of geographical essays which he hoped to finish this

year. It was more or less a collection of lectures given over the last decade, and the first draft lay in his study. The crucial workout lay ahead, that of excising, re-writing, polishing with the thesaurus, shaping each sentence for rhythm and texture and content – a harmoniousness finally gained by reading aloud. The slow sweet labour of getting it down in the first place was over, a matter of regret and relief, and in seeing the end of this work he recognized the trick that his achievement had played, that it had marked out the end of one phase of his life – a fact only occurring to him this morning as he turned off the alarm clock and left Myra asleep after her late night in town.

The house was silent, the smell of comfort everywhere, slightly damp odour of carpets, books and part central heating. In the unwakened house he alone was master, and his carpet slippers creaking the stairs seemed the only sound in the smokeless and recumbent village beyond the windows.

He shaved over the kitchen sink (memories of student and bedsitter days), the kettle squat on the electric stove. Myra, he told himself, was a marvellous wife to have kept such a perfect house for so long, which confirmed his feeling that one stage of their life should come to a finish with the final draft of his book. Myra had suggested the title: *New Aspects of Geography* by George Bassingfield, and he could feel and foresee the time when they would need a drastic change in their existence. In the last few months Myra had been weighed down by something that he had been too occupied to try and fathom. Driving to and from work he brooded on it, ended by inward raging when he got no answer whose authority he could have faith in. It showed his affection, and the strength of their marriage, that he had detected this prolonged mood in her and was trying to find its cause. But he must also unearth the reasons and do something about it. Best of all to do both, but one thing at a time.

The routine they had for so long enjoyed with a mellow almost sensual pleasure in this agreeable house had outlived both its usefulness and necessity. A change was coming, and when it was truly on them maybe what was bothering Myra would be revealed. It was a matter of patience, the interplay of acting and waiting, because one must first look to one's job, career, house, material necessities, and then search out the lesser plagues that burden the spirit.

He boiled an egg, made coffee and toast, a matter of minutes in such a kitchen. The perfection of it backed up his half-made decision: Dishmaster, Stovemaster, Wastemaster, Toastmaster, a circle of masters over which the mistress was master, an overpowering accumulation of labour-savers, to save your soul for what? You went to work in your Roadmaster, ate by Feedmaster, and died, no doubt, by Deathmaster. It was like that E.M. Forster story. He wanted to escape its paralyzing effect. Maybe Myra felt crushed by it as well, and that was her trouble. Surveyors were wanted in places like Ghana, Malaya, the Persian Gulf, Borneo, zones of rain and sun and steaming jungle, a beige dust-road running between granite rocks, a vast revolutionary switch from this idyllic piece of England, and his eyes would rove down advertisements, weighing salaries, prospects, tours of duty, allowances for living, home leave – reaching out for an atlas now and again to check a remote or altered placename. He saw this as a personal desire, and also as a solution to whatever subterranean difficulties were taking hold of Myra, and so of himself.

The idea of moving had started as a pastime, a dream, an exercise in transmigration of unequal physical comforts. The reality of it increased, shaded the outlines of an appealing picture and in spite of the English soil he mapped and trod on at present, it made him feel that a long time out would augment his love for it. He wouldn't dream of applying such an argument to Myra. The deepest love could only go so far, that is, to inanimate things such as earth and animals. To apply it to human beings, who were capable of reasoning could only degrade them, and he was the last person impious enough to attempt that. Life was like a Roman road: straight as a die, even when it went over the hills. It wasn't easy to construct this road, still less maintain it, but the surfacing went far enough down never to be washed away by time or storms. Most people made spidery trails through woods and wilderness, tracks that doubled back and tangled hopelessly in some morass: in real terms they fought like cat and dog, held on for as long as they could perhaps, then almost took pleasure in throwing down the barriers to let hate and chaos pour in. When the first passion vanished they moved to other beds and lovers.

Most of George and Myra's friends were either divorced or living apart, children scattered like so much ash over the eroded roads they had failed to build. So it had become almost a point of honour with George to keep his marriage going, as if it were a competition of which only he knew the rules, or even the existence of the game. Myra didn't know of it, but he had no fear of her ever going off with other men, betraying him in the worst way possible. Of course, if she said: 'Look, George, it's finished. I want to go. I'm in love with someone else,' he'd say: 'All right. If that's how things have worked out. It's good of you to be so straight about it,' then he'd understand. He would suffer, of course, but he was capable of that, and in any case it wouldn't be so bad as if she betrayed him while still living with him. There was only one way for the heart to move – honestly. Many people hadn't the strength of character for it, regarded honesty only as a valve to keep them safe from the worst of life's agonies, but George considered this to be false reasoning. To him the purpose of civilization was to make you aware of such agonies, to merge the undercurrents and the surface into one clear comprehensible mirror to life. To try and get behind such a mirror would mean wielding your fist to smash it, and that was the action of a madman.

He poured more coffee, and went to get the newspapers. He needn't leave the house for another hour, never liked to leave it at all unless Myra were up first. A house with no one awake in it during the day was like a dead beehive, generating an unnecessarily sinister ambience.

On one page a civil war loomed in Cyprus, on an other Algeria was blazing from end to end. He couldn't see the sense of it with so much new work to be done. Clipping open to the middle he saw a caption: THE LINCOLNSHIRE POACHER CELEBRATES, above a photograph of a man with alarmingly open eyes who looked as if he had mistakenly stumbled into a firing squad. On one side of him was a younger man trying to hold him up, and on the other arm was Myra.

Eyes half closed, as if too much light had stabbed into them, his heart beat against the dozen questions that were crushed to death in the door of his mind. A smile covered the idea of not believing it. Good plain Myra in her new dress was wearing the faintest smile, a cross between contempt and modesty that he had often seen on her face but not defined so clearly until the shock of seeing her in a newspaper deepened his perceptions more than he would ever have thought either necessary or possible.

She was looking down at this famous Lincolnshire painter, who had sagged from the liquid weight of his own success. The other young man (he and Myra were described as friends of the artist) had a rather stalwart appearance, as far as one could tell from such a picture, for the flash had caught him with a look of stolid disgust, as if, should Albert Handley really collapse, he would go over to the photographers and scatter them and their equipment up and down the space created by their lights. It was a visage made up of belligerence and sensibility, of intelligent spirit trying to push its

205

way into a strong yet troubled face not easy to forget.

Sitting at the table by the kitchen window, with the morning light streaming over his large hands on the newspaper, George leafed open the top-people journal and found a review of the painter's work though not, thank God, any mention of Myra. It was a perceptive though longwinded write-up. A certain flippancy was held against Albert Handley, but the reviewer balanced this by assuming that further development was sure to iron it out. Handley was compared to the unlettered primitive painters sometimes found in the nineteenth-century craftsmen's guilds in the north of England, men with minds of simple outline and sombre colour who had disciplined their exuberant souls into rough conventional scenes of workbench or churchyard, hovel or chimney stack, a comrade in voluminous apron wielding outsize calipers and hammer with a motto on unity and brotherhood underneath. This was Handley's tradition, the reviewer went on, but due to influences of the modern age, he had burst the bounds of these narrow limits and turned out something which was, after all, quite unique and original in that he had spanned both worlds. It was to be hoped that success would not ruin all this, and that he would respect his roots by leaving them as soon as possible and showing us the rest of the world coloured by his unique vision. The article ended by suggesting – tentatively – that perhaps Mr Handley's appearance marked the beginning of some new wave in the bloodless and disorientated world of contemporary English painting.

George was not impressed, would like to have known how Myra had got mixed up with him and the other fellow to the extent of being shown on the middle page of the worst gutter newspaper of them all. There was no real harm in it, of course, no harm at all – reaching for his pipe, jacket and briefcase. It made him see Myra in a light never wondered at before.

206

He settled himself in his car and drove along the village street, passing shop, vicarage, and row of crumbled cottages, nodding at the milk-girl rattling her bottles towards the policeman's door. He swung left at the mildewed war memorial. The river was still belly-swollen from last week's rain, flowing heavily into the lowest meadows on either side. With the window open, the air smelt fresh and moist, having already tasted the sap of green buds, the jewelled balances of morning dew. The countryside was soddened, sunny and peaceful, a mosaic of livid green and brown. There was no evil in this part of England. Woods closed into the road, primroses matted along its banks. Even the low purring of his engine in top gear couldn't hold back the languid harmonics of the birds. The other day he had heard the first cuckoo, a sound which gave him great pleasure. It would be a shame to leave this, find work in a harsher, hotter country at cross purposes to what his spirit really needed.

17

WHILE ALBERT was down at the gents Teddy Greensleaves slipped Frank a bundle of fivers. Frank promptly slipped them back. 'What was that for?'

'Keeping an eye on Albert. You've done nothing else in the last fortnight.'

'I don't need paying for it,' he said, in no way insulted at the offer.

'You haven't been to work, I notice. You have to live.'

'I've got enough to live on.'

'All the more reason for taking it,' Teddy laughed. 'If you had nothing you could be proud and refuse. People get kicks out of that. But go on, take it, Frank. We've got to keep Albert in one piece, see that he gets back to a long stretch of work in Lincolnshire.'

Frank took it: 'I'd better give you a receipt so that it'll come off your tax.'

'We'll settle that in the office,' Teddy said. Big Teddy wasn't only rolling in it – it was rolling in him. Every time he had an attack of asthma Frank expected great bundles of money to shoot out. He didn't dislike him, for Teddy was generous, outspoken, intellectual and rich, and who could ask for pleasanter company in which to learn about this sort of world? Albert came back: 'You haven't ordered yet? I'm starving.'

'We waited for you,' Teddy said.

'I've had no breakfast. I wouldn't mind if you'd ordered for me.'

Teddy guarded him like a prize dog. 'How did I know what you'd want, Albert?'

'If you'd ordered me the same as what you're having I wouldn't have gone far wrong.' Teddy picked up the menu and signalled the waiter, who floated over like a female dancer from Azerbaijan. 'What would you like, then?'

The menu was so big it seemed like a fireguard in front of Albert's face. 'I think I'll start with a little bit of pâté, go on to a Dover sole, and try a pepper steak. Maybe end up with crêpes Suzette – order it now because it takes them ages. How about you, Frank?' He slid the menu over. Frank wanted cannelloni and chicken Portuguaise, then cheese. Teddy ordered, and arranged for the wine. When he came he picked off the cork like a true connoisseur, sniffed it judiciously, as if at one time it had been up somebody's arse. He nodded to the waiter: 'It's all right.'

'Yes, sir.'

'I was reading my reviews again today,' Albert said, 'and the critics are so patronizing I could slay the bastards.'

'They were good reviews though,' Teddy said gently. 'You've sold every picture in the exhibition. They're clamouring for more.'

'I know. But if there's one thing I hate more than a bad review, it's a good review. As for those who show superlative understanding of my whole artistic project and endeavour, unquote, I hate them most of all, and would stand them up against a wall and shoot them down like dogs if ever I got the chance. They're my real enemies. They're all dogs

209

sniffing at the same wall. They turn my guts, I'm not joking. You'd think I'd just come out of the jungle, the way they talk.'

'They're only human,' Teddy said. 'They're eating out of your hand at the moment, but don't think it will stay like that, because it won't.'

'Don't worry, if I keep on getting good reviews I'll hang myself.'

'It's the space that counts,' Teddy said, breaking his roll and spreading it with butter. 'As long as you get the space, I'll be happy.'

'That's all that matters. I realize that. I reckon six feet of space would make you even happier.' The soft lighting of the midday restaurant pitched them into irritating candle-shadow in which nothing could be seen with real clarity. 'Do you remember,' he went on, 'how you gave me lessons on what to say when I was interviewed? He was dead clever, Frank, was old Teddy-bear. Whatever they asked me, I was never to answer with a direct yes or no. That would be playing into their hands. If they ask if you've stopped beating your wife just go into a long spiel on the rights of women, such as I only go for her when she slings a sizzling flat-iron at my mug and scores a bull's-eye. Teddy gave me two hours of his valuable time on that technique. I took it to heart, and talked so much with never a yes or no that I was bloody-well incoherent and the reporters had to bodge up their articles.'

'Don't sulk,' Teddy said. 'They'd have bodged them up anyway. You should be happy now.'

'You should,' Albert said. 'You've made as much money as I have, just about. Let's climb out of our trenches and slam each other, you mudstained bugger.'

'I don't know what you mean,' Teddy said. 'Let's eat first, at any rate.' Frank knew that this went on whenever they met, with sometimes such a mask of despair and loathing on

Albert's face that he wondered why he bothered to stay in London. The experience of it was eating into his soul. Yet he wouldn't hear of leaving until the last day of his exhibition. 'Why?' Frank had asked. 'You must have some good reason.' 'I want to keep my eye on Greensleaves.' 'Come off it. He's honest enough.' 'All right, I'll tell you. I want to get myself known to as many people as I can before I go back, because I don't want to come down again for another two years, not at all if I can help it. I want people to come up and see me in Lincolnshire and buy paintings off me there. The less I sell to Greensleaves the better. I've got myself fixed up with an accountant and a lawyer as well – to help me with the tax bullies, and contracts.'

'I'm fed-up with all this newspaper runaround,' he said. 'They even had Frank's picture on that first-night spree, not to mention that woman he got acquainted with. I expect her husband blacked her eye when he saw it next morning.'

'The meat's raw in these cannelloni. I didn't worry myself,' Frank said. 'She's not the sort to marry a man like that. I hated seeing myself in the papers though.'

Teddy said he didn't think there was any harm in it. 'I've got some blow-ups back at the office, which I forgot to give you. A souvenir of the big opening.' He refilled their glasses, topped up his own. 'I had some good mail this morning, Albert. They want some of your work at the Museum of Graphic Art in New York. Then there were a couple of feelers from Zurich. Of course I'll put them off: "Mr Handley is far from prolific, but I shall be glad to see your representative when next in London in order to discuss terms should any of Mr Handley's work become available in the meantime." Something like that. One must be cool, or they'd never forgive us later. A publisher phoned me as well, wanted to do a book of reproductions. I told him it was too early to think about it yet, and to phone me back in a couple of years. A letter also came for you, Frank.'

He was busy with his food. It surprised him how much people managed to talk during a meal, while his own mouth was too full to say much. A slow rhythm of death-jazz drifted through the restaurant, and Albert, thinking it interfered with his argument, told the waiter to can it. The music flowed away, and off. He took the letter with a plain thanks, puzzled as to whom it could be from. While Teddy and Albert discussed prospects and figures, made plans, he opened the letter and found it was from Myra, simply to say she'd be coming to London a week next Thursday to have a real look at Albert's work, so maybe he could meet her at Paddington, the seven minutes past ten train, if, that is, he was still in London and hadn't already taken off for other places, in which case he wouldn't be reading this letter anyway.

Teddy stopped talking, to point out a couple of famous actors. 'What am I supposed to do?' Albert said. 'Lick their boots or fall on my back? I'd rather see them on the stage, for a real thrill, to see if they're really any good. The thing about famous people is that they just aren't interesting.'

It was impossible to say why Teddy baulked at certain moments and not at others, but Albert's outrageous remarks weighed on him when he thought the actors may have heard them too. In the first week or so Teddy would simply blush pyjama-pink and lift up a hand to hide the giggles. But it wasn't funny any more. It had certainly ceased to be funny. 'You'll have to learn to behave yourself.'

Frank looked on, for after so long it bored him. Perhaps that's what Myra had sensed when she thought he might already have left. Where can you go to in this country? Bristol? Dover? Liverpool? Nowhere was where he was, because it was the same place she had left him in.

'You think I can't behave myself with the people I find in your sort of world?' Albert raged. 'They're either queers, frauds, playboys, or brainless public school sacks of blood living off newspapers and advertising.'

'My sort of world is now your world,' Teddy smiled, face reddening. There wasn't enough truth in this to subdue Albert: 'You'd never get half a foot in my world, not in a hundred years, mate. With all your lights and glitter you couldn't come anywhere near it. I might be eating the food of your world, but that's about all. It doesn't even taste all that good. My only reaction to your sort of world, when you throw it at me like you did with the party, is to get drunk, have a black out so that in record time I don't see it, I just don't see it, hear it, or smell it.' Albert had regained some of his youth. His sharp saturnine Norse face had given a Latin self-assurance to his eyes, a gesturing manner that comes of thinking you have a good reason for being alive. Before his success it had only occasionally flashed, but now it was part of him.

'I'm not asking for thanks, Albert. But your steak's getting chilled.'

'I know, but all this meat-eating makes me feel like Eric-the-bleeding-Bloodaxe. I'm not being too personal, Teddy, but there's got to be people like you in the world, otherwise how could I show my paintings?'

'Not to mention sell them. You put it in a very charming way,' Teddy said, temper smoothed, half smiling. Albert jumped up, smashing knife and fork on his plate: *'Will you stop patronizing me, you overfed fuck-monk?'*

A wave of distress passed through Teddy. He also stood, his great body shaking. 'I'm not patronizing you,' he cried, almost weeping. 'That's the only way I can talk.'

Frank looked up at them: 'If you don't drop dead I'll kill you. I've had my fill of this. I'll go back to the jungle if this goes on.'

A waiter drifted close. 'Anything else, gentlemen?'

'Not at the moment,' Teddy said, still glaring into Albert's demonic eyes.

213

'The manager would appreciate it then,' the waiter said, 'if you two gentlemen would stop quarrelling.'

They sat, unable to say who had broken off the staring match. Albert cheered up over his crepe Suzette. 'You see,' Teddy said to him, 'you're a fairly rich man, so you may as well begin to accept the responsibility of it.'

'I know,' he said. 'I'm going to do everything I can to see that I end up in the gutter. It'll be cleaner than this place. Sure, I can slosh down this stuff and smoke a fat cigar that stinks like arse-shit, drink from a skull-cup till I'm as bricked as a wall, but a mutton stew and a Woodbine would keep me just as happy, has done this last twenty years, hasn't it, Frank?'

'True,' he muttered, thinking of Myra and wondering why she had bothered to write, glad that she had. He remembered, on his way back from the station, a nagging agreeable need to see her again, and next day, the first time ever, he deliberately stopped himself hoping for it, cut off his wish at the roots and went on working as Albert's bodyguard. The letter had reopened all that, showed him the river again, the broad curving descending flood of the arterial river on whose bank he stood. Bodies, houses, trees were carried forcefully down it in the grey unearthly light of dawn, everything flowing away in the silence, the bleak scene composed of a single indefinable mood. He had often seen the river in his dreams, water clipping his feet and wanting him to be sucked in and swept away – as if he hadn't been in it all his life.

'I'll have no liver left by the time I get back,' Albert said cheerfully.

Teddy poured more coffee, drew on his cigar. 'Grow another in your rural retreat. It sounds idyllic, the way you talk about it.'

'It is,' Frank put in. 'I lived in the same place for a while.'

'You aren't going back there?' Teddy asked him.

'I'm not. Don't ask me where I am going though. Maybe

214

I'll get a job in some factory around London. Settle down, sort of.'

'Why do that? I can find use for you. At a better wage, I should think.'

'We'll see,' Frank said.

'I think you'll end up back in Nottingham,' Albert said.

'I might if I was born in Timbuctou.'

'He's got a wife and two kids up there.'

'I had. She's in with somebody else now.'

'It's shocking,' Teddy winked.

'You could always get her back,' Albert suggested.

'That's all finished. Nobody wants anybody back.'

'You people from the north,' Teddy said, 'make everything sound so final and full of fate.'

'They're exactly like people in the south,' Frank said. 'You see the gut-ache written on their faces just the same. The difference about London though is the underground. Have you ever been in it at rush-hour, Teddy?'

'Not in thirty years,' he admitted, 'and it wasn't such a rush-hour then – or so I understand.'

'I stood near a phone box once watching 'em come down the steps. I just looked at their faces. First, I thought they were dead people going into corned-beef tins. Then I saw that underneath these death-masks was a joy, a happiness that they'd accepted even though they felt wicked about it: this tragic face was put on to hide it, but it didn't kid me. They were going back into the tripes of the earth like worms, into these tapeworms that scoot around in the real guts of London. That's what they lived for every day. In their offices or shops they keep looking at the clock, thinking it's because they want to knock off, but it's only to get back for half an hour into these tripes, to be worms for a bit inside Great Mother Tripe. I wouldn't like to get caught down there if the four-minute warning went.'

'You're pessimistic,' Teddy nodded. 'Life is hard for anyone, but there's no need to make a virtue of it. I spent years keeping my head above water.'

'Yes,' Albert butted in, 'and when you climbed out everybody was surprised to see how fat you were.'

'They didn't have time,' Teddy said, pleased at such after-dinner wit. 'I bought them all up.'

'They must have had their backs to you.'

'Perhaps,' Teddy said, flushed by the meal.

'The trouble with you,' Albert said, mustering all his London venom, 'is that in that masculine great frame of yours there's a spiteful little bitch doing its bi-sexual nut.'

Teddy took it well: 'I'm learning quite a bit from you, certainly. Have another cigar. You still haven't explained why you're so pessimistic, Frank. You're always dark-browed and quiet.'

'You've no right to ask questions like that,' he said.

'Are we bringing human rights into it already? I thought we were just talking?'

Frank lit his cigar. 'Nobody has the right to ask me why I am how I'm not. The only questions I'll answer are those I've already asked myself and been able to answer. Those will be the ones I've spent my life answering – or trying to. Since coming to London I've not been getting very far.'

'I'm with you there,' Albert said. 'It's a dust bowl. All your time goes on drinking to keep alive. Any more wine in that bottle?'

Teddy slid it over: 'I get all my answers from other people. It's the best I can do, but I'm satisfied.'

'You have to be,' Handley said.

'I don't know where mine come from,' Frank said. 'So I suppose they come from myself.'

'The best thing is just to go on living, and doing the best sort of work you can,' Albert reflected. 'Pessimism is everybody's right, as long as they earn it.'

'You've got to break through that sort of thing

though,' Frank said, 'unless you want to die young – or be dead in everything after a certain age, which is the same thing. That's why I left home and lit off. Pessimism is an idleness inside you, a spiritual deadness, if you like. It's a load on your back that you've got to throw off.'

'Pessimism,' Teddy said, 'is a creative force for an artist. It puts spirit into his work. If he knows how to channel it properly it becomes genius.'

'Well, I'm not an artist,' Frank said. 'Not that I believe you. If I did I wouldn't want to read a book or look at a picture again.'

'You'd be starved of culture if you didn't,' Teddy laughed.

'That would be the fault of people like you, then.'

Teddy called the waiter. 'Why are you so quarrelsome, Frank? I suspect too much food does this to people, don't you, Albert? Your brains can addle from rich food.'

'Why don't you lay off?' Albert said. 'Keep your nail file out of him. I've seen you do this to people before, and I don't like it.'

Frank felt as if his head were about to shatter. He had wit enough to counter Teddy's low-powered stabs, but not the patience to tolerate Albert coming to his defence. 'It's time I was on my way,' he said, standing up. 'All the best of luck to you two money-faced bastards. I don't think any harm will ever come to you.'

'Don't go,' Teddy called. 'We were only talking. Come on, Frank, sit down.'

Albert caught him up at the door. 'For God's sake don't take things like that. Teddy's all right. He's a good sort, you know that.' He held his arm, to draw him back.

'If you don't let go of me,' Frank said, 'I'll kick you into the floor.' He went outside, and walked in the warm, humid sun down Greek Street.

18

DAYS DRIFTED through warm and open
weather, city air softened by spring, wind flapping between streets, getting a lift on the backs of red buses then
jumping off to charge around the next corner at oncoming
cars. He didn't see Handley or Greensleaves again. Neither
did he go back to work at the car park. For the moment,
maybe for good, he had finished with all that. He still had
money from saved wages, even from the sold car in Nottingham. Living on a few pounds a week he discovered in himself
a talent for thrift which at one time he would have squashed
with ridicule but now regarded as the equipment necessary
for survival. He felt a healthy leanness, existed within a
thinner casing of flesh which gave a more direct and brittle
contact with the world.

His life-long habit of getting up at six wouldn't leave him,
and he sat by the window, reading until eight o'clock, pages
punctuated by some black train shouldering a rapid pock-
thumping way through the cutting. The window rattled and
pages turned in its noise. He washed on the landing, where a
bathroom and lavatory had been built into one of the single

rooms, then sat in his shirtsleeves, ignoring the still sharp air
of morning. He boiled tea, and drank the pot out. The room
had lost its grimness, for he had adapted himself to London
standards of isolation, discomfort and independence. He
offered to paint the room white if the landlord paid for the
paint. When this was agreed to, he borrowed brushes,
pushed the furniture into one half of the room and covered it
with newspaper – halfway one day, all white the next. It
looked clean, felt more comfortable, a haven after climbing
the gloomy stairs.

Not working, and seeing no one, increased his perceptions
and sensibility, such moods in the past coming on only in
illness or the half-fever of a bad cold. His ability to connect
with these moods now, when the fever did not exist, provided a springboard for numerous other comparisons. It was
as if he'd worn glasses all his life and suddenly thought to
clean them: his sight seemed sharper, thoughts quicker.

Many of his days were spent in Highgate library. He went
through books that he couldn't take out, took books out that
he couldn't read there. He was able to extract the kernel of a
book, having read much and quickly while at Pat's. A history of Europe was absorbed by examining the list of contents
– joining and cementing what he already knew, concentrat-
ing on English social history of the nineteenth century to find
some explanation for the world he had grown up in. He
learned botany and anatomy by diagrams, geography by
reading and comparing maps, reinforcing and drawing together the scattered islands of his past knowledge which, he
discovered, were more numerous than he'd imagined. It was
a game for the uneducated: books of reproductions tied up
what he had seen in the galleries.

Large areas of a jigsaw were forming. The encyclopaedia,
dictionary, atlas, were three dormer windows high enough to
embrace new views. Fiction was the depth gauge, plumb-line
and echometer fathoming his deepest needs and feelings.

Knowledge for its own sake was bare-faced and domineering, but each title of a novel was the top winch of a fairy-tale well whose storyline of chain and bucket let you down with varying degrees of speed into the waters of illumination. Knowledge confirmed the structure of the outside world, while a novel prised open previously unknown regions within yourself. Conrad, Melville, Stendhal – the giants. In war novels, detective novels, shit novels, you put a scarf over your eyes before going into their unconvincing straightjackets; in the others, one had to take this scarf off before reading the first word. He wondered why he had not been born with this understanding, why nearly thirty years had gone by before touching the possibility of it. How many people had it in them, but never saw it?

He fought free of a narrow sort of life and began to wonder what he had let himself in for – though it didn't destroy his patience with this new existence. Calmness is death, he knew, but at the moment he enjoyed it, took advantage of the unlimited days to see if any meaning would come out of his life. To solve the enigma of anyone else's would only be possible after the unfettering of his own spirit.

Walking one day he recalled some words from *Moby Dick*: 'And if ever the world is to be again flooded, like the Netherlands, to kill off its rats, then the eternal whale will still survive....' In the Old Testament there is a story, (he remembered it from school, being full of memories in the sunny desert of London), of two armies face to face, one far larger than the other, a host as it is called. During the night God sent rats into the tents of the biggest army and they ruined it by chewing the leather of their shield straps. Rats are unacknowledged legislators that rule the world. They started the Black Death that wiped out half Europe in the Middle Ages. The Tartars, besieging a Crimean city, catapulted a bubonic corpse over its walls, so that plague as well as famine broke its obstinacy. Out of that town, the plague-scythe cut down Europe as if it were a single head of corn. A man's body is a battlefield of rat and anti-rat – the rat to kill, and the other to keep him human. Every man has his rat, his own brown rat sitting like an alter ego on his shoulder, dodging inside when storms flash and adversity baffles the air to stoke the inner chaos that such sights cause.

The legend of the rats had been a long time forming, a legend which for some reason exuded the heavy smell of a sagebush growing in sand. In some far-off time people didn't like the rats. They threatened to destroy the real souls in them, so the Pied Piper came and drew the rats away. But the people refused him the bread they had promised as his fee, called him a trickster. So the Pied Piper sent back the rats, but charmed away the peoples' children to inherit the innocence their parents had known before the rats came. The truth was that the parents couldn't live without the rats, wanted them back, took them to their bosoms and became one with them.

The Pied Piper was hunted for his never-ending hostility to the rats. The rats were a disease of society and also of the soul, and society, being imperfect, enabled them to survive. The rats were the carriers of this disease. They perpetuated it. The Pied Piper wanted to take this disease of society away. When people, used by those who desired power and not just to live, wanted the rats to stay with them they turned the Pied Piper into Bill Posters and hunted him forever as they had formerly, in their innocence, hunted the rats.

The rats, of course, became invisible: there weren't any to be seen. But they were continually breeding, ardently proliferating their rodent species in the various underworlds of oblivion. They dwelt far below the surface even of a child's dilatory mind, quick, cruel, whiskered and ordured noses exploring dark caverns and nibbling the energized vapours of cloaca that kept them alive. They lived in the rat-filled banks and hollows of ashtips and streams, feet planted, heads turned in momentary awareness against the outside world, on the forced refuse, the hopes, the gangrenous wrecks of peoples' lives, a thousand seams below. It was an evil impossible to fathom, excavate, analyse: the depths were too packed, putrescent, liquid, unrecognizable, a mud-death of suffocation, cone-roads descending. Such depths were wardened by rats, the only true history impossible to classify by seam or layer. One fell into it by turning on the gas-tap. One walked away from it – by walking away, or by the body taking you off if the spirit wanted you to stay by the world-wide rat-pit of rat-darkness which is body-death and soul-death.

Frank desired neither, fought both, wanted body-life and soul-life, to steer a narrow course on the narrowing tight-rope across the top of the world's circus tent, balanced safe above the rat pits spreading below, the world-width of black mud surrounded on every far distance by dim faces of spectators in thrall to the rats laughing and waiting for his fall.

He hoped there was no question of falling. He would not fall, hoped his limbs, blood and bones would hold him back. But it was necessary to fight in order to keep the same dignity and independence he had known in his more stable, traditional, less knowing existence where the rats had been less likely to get at him.

He forgot about the future. Living alone, it didn't exist. He hadn't talked to anyone for days, and thought he never wanted to again.

Wearing jacket, trousers and jersey shirt, and a pair of boots he'd splashed ten guineas on, he went to meet Myra at Paddington, her letter still in his pocket. He picked her out from the barrier as she stepped off the train dressed in a light brown coat and carrying a shopping basket. He had forgotten what she looked like and was afraid of not recognizing

222

her. 'I didn't expect to see you,' she said, handing in her ticket.

'It's a good beginning,' he joked, remembering his impression of her as someone cold and half awake, while thinking that you don't know what a house is like to live in until you've made a fire in it. They walked to the cafeteria. He was surprised that they didn't feel like strangers to each other as he stood in line for coffee and buns. She recalled writing her letter out in the garden one sunny day, sitting on the steps and trying to stop the wind flicking her pages. She'd wanted to be among streets and traffic, away from the so-called peace which was noisy enough to drown the real feelings in her. But silence wasn't finding it so easy to hold them down any more, and in becoming real again she hoped she wasn't making Frank too responsible for something that couldn't yet be seen as either good or bad. The few paintings glimpsed at Albert's party, the crush of people, the meal and walk with Frank, were important because she was inclined to overrate them. She shouldn't have written the letter, but had no power to resist it.

She asked how Albert was. 'I don't know,' he said. 'I haven't seen him for a while. Nor have I been to the gallery. I packed all that in.'

'You did seem a bit out of place there. What happened?'

'We were having some dinner, the day Teddy handed me your letter, and the talk went on and on, so vicious and useless that I couldn't stand it. It was starting to pull me in. When you feel that something's played itself out, you've just got to go.'

He seemed more real now that he was free from a world that had no genuine use for him. Some re-humanizing process had occurred in the time elapsed. The other night had been an artifact in which they were not quite being themselves. It seemed clearer now, with the reality of traffic roaring outside and a train journey behind her. There was so

223

little emotion between them that it couldn't possibly be false. Sun softened into the room and she felt drawn to his rather large hands resting by the cup, eating, pushing the plate away. 'I suppose you saw our photo in the newspaper?'

They talked in a clatter of metal trays. 'I did. But I hoped you hadn't, by some miracle. What did your husband say?'

'Not much, though he didn't like it. I said it was all chance and coincidence, that I happened to be there when the painter needed help.' It hadn't been easy, for George must have brooded on it all day, pacing it out in the fields, encasing it from hedge to fence to looping footpath. His high standards would tell him to ignore it, but they let him down as the endless belt of daytime wore on. By evening he was incensed, and only her calm talking smoothed things out for the hours that followed. It was a unique experience at her age, and in this so far quiet marriage. Why had such an innocent photo pitched him from accepted order and unthinking peace to a life of suspicion – that he hid very well but that she now felt in him all the time? It was mysterious to her. Could a man hold that stupid photograph responsible for portents which must always have been with him? The answer came now that she was sitting with Frank.

'My plan for today,' she said, to prove that thoughts of George did not worry her, 'is to visit my sister-in-law, then go to the gallery and see Albert's pictures. It closes soon, doesn't it?'

'You ought to go today. It's worth seeing. I hope his next show is as well.'

'What makes you unsure about it? You don't envy him, do you?'

He put down his cup. 'I used to, when I first met him in Lincolnshire and saw his paintings. I envied him then, if that's the right word. But now I don't. He gets into blind rages, attacking the art dealers, critics, and other painters' work. That's the sort of thing that'll ruin him unless he goes

back to Lincolnshire for ten years and sees nobody, like before. I'm not saying all those people aren't worth attacking,
but the best way you can do it is by ignoring their existence
– I should think. Teddy doesn't really want him to go back
to Lincolnshire, keeps trying to get him to go to Italy or
Greece for a year or two. There's nothing wrong with that,
but Albert has to make his own way there, not go under
Teddy's auspices. The less people he has looking after him,
the more he'll be able to look after himself again. Then he'll
be all right.'

'What about you, though?'

He laughed, cigarette smoke rolling across at her. 'Me?
Whatever happens I'll be all right – as long as something
happens.' She'd never thought of it that way. 'That's the
only way I *can* look at it,' he said.

'You're lucky, then.'

'I know. Every time I take a breath, or eat some bread and
cheese I say to myself: "You lucky bastard!" I was born
lucky in that way.' He told her the skeletal facts about
himself. 'Up to last autumn I was buried in three feet of cold
soil unable to move except for my arms and breath. Now my
feet are free, at least.'

He belonged nowhere, she reflected, but he had belonged
somewhere so solidly once that it would take him years to
find some natural way of life again. He was the sort of man
who could not turn back. His face was a mask of animation
and strength, grey piercing eyes, highish cheeks, firm jaw
and the sort of mouth that bends easily into anger – a man of
character shifting between two coastlines of existence. His
senses seemed out of tune with the rowdy and continuous
traffic-flow along Euston Road where they now walked, and
his face had a natural serenity whose only violence might be
to protect that serenity from the forces of history. She found
it impossible to guess where it would lead him; and difficult
to imagine from where he had set out. To try and deflect him

225

from his wilful half-conscious drifting would be an under-hand way of helping herself, for his limbo was only notice-able in that it seemed to give more purpose to her own life, while she didn't yet know what that purpose might serve.

They took a bus to the Embankment, walked up the steps and on to Hungerford Bridge. 'This is my favourite view,' he said, leaning on the parapet. 'I often come here, look at the river for hours, watch it change colour as the sky alters. I kid myself I'm looking at London because I can see up the river to St Paul's.' He reached down, closing a hand over her fingers so that she had no thought of drawing away. 'The river's moving, going somewhere.'

'Which is more than we are,' she said, seeing it swirling along, dark and grey.

'I want to stay here a while,' he teased, pressing her hand, feeling like one of those young lovers often walking this way. A train moved slowly out of Charing Cross, shook the bridge under their feet, a noise of steel and thunder that stopped her replying. 'If I travel,' he said, 'it's got to be out of England. There's no place for me on this right little tight little island.'

'Where, though?'

'I'd go to the moon if I could. I want to go over the water, onto a continent. The sky eats into my brain here.'

'You're running away from yourself.'

'I know. If that's the only way to find yourself, then you'll sooner or later run into what you're running away from, even if you don't know what it is. You'll recognize it when you hit it – or it hits you.' She smiled: he talked as if he'd just discovered the abstract and, like Columbus blundering into America, wanted to pull the whole world over into it. 'Maybe you won't like it when you meet it,' she said.

'It's a case of surviving, not liking.' They walked off the

bridge, through the tube station hall and up Villiers Street. 'If I decide to take off,' he said, 'why don't you come with me?'

His question flew into her heart like a piece of sharpened stone. She stopped walking, as if it would compromise her to answer while her feet still moved: 'Are you afraid of doing things on your own?'

He laughed. 'Maybe two can be saved for the price of one! I just think it's better with somebody else, and I thought you might have an idea of lighting off as well.'

'I hadn't,' she lied, which she knew came too quickly for him to believe it. They had a shepherd's-pie meal in a pub off Leicester Square, sitting away from the businessmen's crush at the counter. 'If you'd like to go to the gallery,' he said, 'I'll meet you somewhere later.'

She wanted to stay with him. 'I don't think so. I'll go another time perhaps.'

'When I've gone away?'

'I didn't mean that. Why do I have to explain myself step by step?'

'Because you want to. Have another glass of red plonk. I'll get more beer for myself' – the waitress saw him wave.

'Beer and wine don't mix,' she smiled.

'Anything mixes. Get me a quart of each in the same bowl and I'll drink 'em. In fact I'm almost beginning to feel like it.'

'The very idea makes me sick.'

'Add a cup of whisky if you like. Let's drink to a long life – wherever it is.'

'That's innocent enough,' she said. 'Perhaps I should go to the Arlington after all.'

'What about your sister-in-law?'

'Yes, I must go there.'

'I'll wait for you. Meet you later.'

'Come up with me. She lives in Hampstead.'

227

'Isn't it risky? They'll twig something. It'll get back to your husband.'

'It might, but I don't mind.'

'Are you sure?' he asked, wondering whether she liked him more than she hated her husband. 'Let's go then.'

The underground shuffled them north. She sat by his side, unspeaking, as if she had made a decision and to open her mouth might turn her from it. Leaving home this morning was an event beyond the far rim of the earth, and as usual in London she felt, with handbag and shopping basket, without a bed to go back to that night. It was alarming and exhilarating, a sort of soul-drift in a desert of streets where she felt no responsibility for the nomad state of her psychic life. At the moment only Frank was real, and the rattle of the carriage going under Belsize Park.

It was a two-floored house in a row of forty-year-olds, comfortable red-brick set on a slope with superb views towards Highgate. The front door was painted yellow, with a mosaic of different coloured heavily-leaded glass – pulling away when Myra tipped the bell.

Frank was introduced to Pamela, a tall buxom young woman wearing corduroy slacks and a green jumper. She looked at him with a half smile, as if surprised that Myra could ever have met a man apart from her husband.

With so much house he was surprised they sat in the kitchen, big as it was. Two small children played at a box of toys, a boy and girl who seemed rather subdued. He winked and tried to catch their eyes, but it was some time before they smiled.

'Are you going to see mother?' Pam asked. Myra said she wouldn't have time today, but might well call on them next time. 'They won't like it,' Pam told her, 'when they know you haven't been to see them.'

'I have a show to see at the Arlington,' Myra said, 'a new painter from Lincolnshire.'

'I read about him,' Pam said, filling the kettle to make them some tea. 'His work sounds marvellous, and I'd love to see it too, but I always have too much on with the sprogs' – meaning the children, Frank gathered. She must have been cleaning up when they came, because a heap of *Observers* and *Woman's Owns* still lay by the draining board. Or maybe she'd been reading, because he noticed some sort of manual called: *How to Deal with the Outstanding Child*, lying near the sugar dish.

They drank tea, and talked, and he was happy to see Myra so animated over news of family and old friends, and the chit-chat of what was on in town. He put in his comments now and again, but couldn't feel himself part of the main thread because he was so much a stranger. He couldn't tell whether Pam looked at him so openly out of curiosity, or whether she was giving him the eye. He smiled, to find out, and got a smile back, none the wiser. When Myra went to the bath-room she asked if he'd known her long.

'A couple of years,' he lied, and when she asked him what he did for a living he said he was a writer, though it didn't pay enough to keep an illiterate in postage stamps.

'Oh, and what do you write?'

'Stories,' he said. 'No luck yet though. I'm off to France in a couple of weeks. Bum around a bit. I can't stand England.'

'I've always wanted to leave it,' she said, 'teach in some exotic place like Persia or India. But there's no hope of that, I'm afraid.'

'You could teach in England,' he said.

'Perhaps I will when the sprogs are older.'

He felt sorry for her. 'Don't you think there's something wrong with the sort of world we live in?'

'I'd never thought of it,' she answered. 'It is difficult, that's true. But I suppose it's up to us as individuals, really.'

'No,' he said, 'not really. It's about time we got past all that, grew up, you might say.' Myra came back, only catch-

229

ing the last sentence. It was a rich house, as far as Frank could see, must be run on about forty pounds a week from Pam's photographer husband. Yet there was a squalor about it that he had always imagined such money could eliminate, an educated squalor, admitted, a stench of untidy intellect that didn't appeal to him. Myra had told him that Pam had a degree from Cambridge, in English, and he had been naïve enough to expect an impeccable house. Even the tea was weak.

By the time he left he had both children on his knees asking him to come again, and he saw how blind and irrevocable had been his own action in leaving his children.

Pam also asked him to call again, though gave a firm pressurized sort of handshake that could have meant good-bye for good.

They walked to a bus stop in Highgate. 'I can't go back on the underground,' he said. 'Let's go overland to my place for a drink. The house looks squalid, but the room's clean. Do you know Camden Town?'

'I wandered around it in my student days.'

'What were you studying?'

'I read economics, and got a first.'

'What are you doing then, being a wife? Maybe you get a kick out of wasting yourself.'

'I'm not wasting anything. I'm living.'

'It's not enough. You've got to do something with it.' His words disturbed her after the visit to Pam's. He knew it, and she wondered why he kept on when a more sensitive and considerate person would have let her fall back into pleasant sloth.

They sat on the top deck, descending into the smoke and view, and she told him about her work in the village so that it sounded worthwhile and even important, until she caught a note of justification in her voice, and stopped. 'I suppose London is full of women like Pam,' he said. 'Places like

Hampstead and Highgate. I've seen 'em around, dragged down by snotty and petulent kids, and wasting their educated lives out of inertia. I guess it's the fault of this country though, as much as them. They could do useful work, but there's just no need of it. It's a rare world.'

'What are you going to do about it?' she asked, and he had no answer. She took his arm when they left the bus. 'If I hadn't met Albert in Lincolnshire I wouldn't have met you in London,' he said.

'Does it seem so important, to trace it back like that?'

'It's fate,' he said. 'By politics I'm a socialist, but I believe in fate.'

She laughed: 'You want it both ways.'

'At the moment it's got me both ways. I was wondering what moves I went through to meet you.' They came to a road of dilapidated early Victorian houses. One or two had been fixed up, cleaned and painted, adorned with shiny brass knockers and fancy numbers, cars outside like metal watch-dogs. They walked to the far end, through a gang of playing children.

Stepping out of the sun Frank went up the stairs first, refusing to comment on how much of a dump it was because maybe she was thinking the same. Which was true. He certainly had no right to rail against Pam's house. She wondered whether it would be possible to sit down when she reached his room – until the door opened. 'I painted it out,' he explained. 'It was so bad even I couldn't stand it. Take this chair. The others are clean, but only this one's safe. I'll sit on the bed.' The walls were bare, like a top-floor cell, oblong and simple, a few books on a table, a suit behind the door, two pairs of shoes showing under the made bed. How lucky he was to be so free, she thought, no more belongings – material or spiritual – than could fit in a suitcase. He looked at her: 'If ever you want to make a decision, just say yes, whatever it is.'

231

'I wasn't thinking of anything.'

'That's impossible. You've always got something on your mind. I'm good at thinking on nothing, though it's getting less easy. I'm thinking plenty at the moment.'

'Such as what?' It was a dangerous question, as if she had said yes to something by making it.

'The same as before. I think we ought to go away.'

'Don't let's talk about it.'

He lit a cigarette and passed it to her. 'Do you think I'm blind and stupid? It's got to be talked about. I've never seen a woman so much at the end of her tether. You're like a sea being drained. The first time you meet somebody you get to know as much as you're ever likely to, even if all the pennies don't drop for a while. Something's been eating you alive for a long time.'

'Going away with you won't stop it.'

'If that won't, nothing will.'

'It sounds like boasting. You don't know what you're saying.'

'I do.'

'You don't know what you'd be doing.'

'All you need do is say yes.' She wanted to say it, to overwhelm him with it, but it just couldn't be so easy for him, or her. The house and room and the street outside were silent except for their own voices. No traffic sounded and the children had run off to fresh pastures of brick and pavement. The afternoon had reached its deep middle, a silent and stale sheet on the bed of the day, a blue sky at the square window, an emptiness all around them and through it in which no feelings could be hidden. 'Where do you think you'd go?'

'Off this island, then I'd tell you where.'

'I'm using the singular, not the plural. What would you do?'

'Why do you make a question out of everything?'

'Because I want to know.'

232

'Look,' he said, 'call it a holiday; call it the end of the world. What more do you want? I don't care whether the sun's shining or not. I don't expect to sprout wings and be a bloody angel. I just want us to crash this rotten barrier. I want to look at my life from the outside. My life and this big island are meshed up and I've got to separate them. I'm caught in a press, and I want to struggle out of it. Maybe then I'll fight my way back in, but then it'll be different.'

She listened in amazement: 'What does all this have to do with me?'

He sat, hands pressing against his head. 'Nothing, if you feel nothing when I say it. I thought you might.'

'Why did you choose me?' she said in a low voice.

'Who can say who chose who? I want you to come.' She trembled, drawn easily to her feet.

'No,' she cried, pushing him away. 'I want to come. I want to come more than you want me to, but the answer's no. It's got to be. I can't do it.'

She was weeping with a bitterness he'd never heard before, but he held her loosely, though knowing that she needed no support with such salt tears. 'Myra, don't cry. We're all right.'

'I'm a happy woman,' she wept. 'Leave me alone.' It would end well, he felt, so it would, but he could only hold her, his arms around and face close, eyes open blankly at the vacant window beyond her shoulders.

They stood, and he smiled at the window, the blank space. A pressure from her arms forced him away so that she could kiss him. Then she softened against him, limp and exhausted, her body shaking.

Her eyes were closed, and he lay by her side. The kisses she gave froze him. They felt so remote, so far away and detached that they came out of a dream he had nothing to do with, a form of revenge against what he hoped would not turn out to be himself. He stroked her hair and kissed her

233

closed eyes. He wondered if she were asleep, as a lethargy matched to the blue window seemed to creep over her, attuned to the soft folds of her body, under the coat that she hadn't thought to take off. A train rumbled, and behind the silence there was traffic along the main road.

19

HE BROUGHT IN food from a Greek
shop down the road – fruit, olives, bread, sausage, wine
and halva. They were like people mildly drunk, never mentioning plans or hopes, who understood each other perfectly.
'Will it matter, me staying here?' she asked the first night.
They talked with the light off, but the curtains open, a faint
moaning noise entering on sodium reflections and the softened beams of passing cars.

'Nobody asks questions in this place.'

'I didn't come out with luggage,' she laughed, 'but I came
out with money. We could have gone to a hotel.' She had
only a handbag and an empty basket – nothing to spend any
sort of night with, except a night like this. 'To me,' she said,
'the only sort of love I feel is when it seems as if I know
nothing, when I'm so inflamed and infatuated that I think
I'm a teenager and have never met a man before, as if there's
no past behind me except the non-sexual golden age of child-
hood that can't be divided into years. Everything to do with
the world draws away from me, except the man I'm with. I
forget everything else.'

He turned from the wall, wondering how many lovers she'd had, to talk like that. Several columns of shillings were stacked on the table, waiting to feed the gas fire whose bars glowed under the opposite shelf. 'The only sort of love for me is when it feels as if I know a lot – and when it doesn't matter whether I know anything at all. Love's not much more than a holiday in life. I think everything should be put in its place. The most important thing is work – to do something that means something. When two people meet who want to live together they should spend a fortnight in bed. There should be special hotels where you hand in your clothes, and then they lock you in, and slide your meals under the door every so often, so that when you come out you'll know all about each other and won't let it obsess you – for a while anyway. In my ideal society all advertisements would be ripped off the streets, and instead there'd be well-placed neon signs in red saying: 'Work! Work! Work!' Maybe now and again there'd be a little one going on and off saying: 'Fuck! Fuck! Fuck' – which I don't suppose would be necessary, though it'd get people on the hop a bit more.'

She laughed: 'What would they have to believe in?'

'Aren't work and fucking enough? Both of them excite me equally – though maybe that's because I haven't done any work for a few weeks, and have only just made love.' He stood up and poured wine, his broad-shouldered nakedness looming in the half light. She lay on her side, the room even dimmer as she was not wearing her glasses. Speech and darkness were healing. In spite of the black passion of his desires, her body seemed to belong to her again, was beginning to reinstate itself as part of her mind and thought.

She slept with an arm over his body, accustomed now to the Lysol smell of the room, the faint reek from the blankets, odours of tobacco-smoke and food, sour wine on their lips, the taste of their bodies. They didn't sleep well, and Frank was up by the first chorus of traffic. She hadn't opened her eyes, but he held a cup of tea near her face: 'Myra, get this. You'll sleep after it.' On seeing her awake, George's first act had been to kiss her, a formal passionless greeting that meant nothing after the first year.

Frank was crouching over the gas ring to boil more water, as if she weren't there. They slept till midday, a cold wind banging at the window to get them up.

She didn't leave the house for four days, fastened into the sensual timelessness of its warm room. She said: 'I suppose this idyll must be brought to a close some time. I want to see daylight again. I think I can take it now.' He had already been out, stood by the table unloading provisions. Blue sky and daylight filled the room, an open window letting in the chill air. 'You don't seem interested.'

'The only way I can be,' he said, 'is if you go back to your house, and finish with everything there. I'll go with you. Then we can take off somewhere.'

'Are you sure you want that?'

He held her: 'Myra, if this is the end, let's begin something. I know it's time we did.'

'I'll do it,' she said. 'But come with me then.'

They ate at a good restaurant in Soho. 'It's so perfect,' she said, 'I hope it isn't a last supper.'

'It won't be. Everything's settled, except for the details. Where do you want to go first?'

'I'd like to see my friend in Majorca. She's always inviting me down.'

'That's in Spain, isn't it? We can call on Franco as well, with a bomb. It's about time somebody got him.'

'I'd like to see my friend first,' she smiled.

'We could take in some propaganda, anyway. Teddy Greensleaves was telling me about somebody he knew who took a great trunk of it in his Jaguar. He didn't get searched, and handed it over in Barcelona, where his contacts had been fixed up.'

237

'It must be strange,' she said to him, 'how much your life's changed in this last year. I wish mine had.'

It will, he thought. It will. 'I've swum out of something but I've not swum into anything else. It's impossible to in England, if you're true to yourself, unless the whole way of life changes through some political switch. I'm nowhere yet. Albert thought his life had changed, but he'll be sound enough to see that it hasn't once he hits Lincolnshire again.'

'Are you sure you want to leave England?'

'Yes,' he said coolly. 'I'm finished with it. That fat staggering pigeon safe on a lion's head, and the lion is made of stone: that's how I see it. One blow from a catapult and its fat corn spills out. It's not what people are that matters; its what they want to become.'

'Perhaps you only want to go for a while,' she said.

'I won't know till I get there.'

'Get where?'

He still did not know, and felt foolish at having to admit he didn't by an empty sounding 'Ah' – which he had heard snap from so many fatuous mouths in restaurants and bars he'd gone into with Albert. It's catching, he thought, so that's one good reason I've got to scat.

It took George little time to realize that, after six years of comfortable marriage, Myra wasn't coming back, unless to collect her belongings. He knew he was in for one of those fatal hammerblows that he had comfortably chuckled over when dealt out to one of his friends. She hadn't been run over, obviously, or met with any accident: such a sound reason would at least make her absence less humiliating. His waking moments showed him another glimpse of the newspaper photo which undoubtedly held some clue as to what was in store for him. That night was ominous in that she had told so little about it, whereas before that she'd described her runs to town in such detail that he'd found it impossible not

238

to show boredom – almost irritation if he had papers to go over.

His mood swung between indifference, and a resentful bitterness. At times of indifference he nevertheless told Mrs Harrod that Myra had gone to her sister's in Somerset. In moments of despair he told himself that they had needed a rest from each other for a long time, and that Myra had merely gone to stay in some coastal place until her peace of mind came back. Then she would return – by which time he would be accustomed to living on his own.

In the long hours of evening he put the final touches to his book, working in the deep unscarred silence of the house. The same quiet had existed when Myra was there, but then he believed she had purposely created it so that he could work in peace. He now realized it was a part of the house and of himself, a silence which battened onto his spirit and robbed him of the will to work. He preferred the silence of two people to that of himself alone.

It was unjust and thoughtless of her not to let him know. It was downright bloody cruel, in fact. A letter saying she had gone off for good would have been better than this uncertainty. The saying that no news was good news didn't work between man and wife. No news could only mean indifference, and there was nothing good about that. The world hadn't shattered in colourful explosion, but it was breaking under his feet, even in this silence, ice in a slow thaw. Without Myra his occupation of the house seemed temporary by the third day, a place he'd moved into for a few weeks while somewhere else was got ready. He worked at the kitchen table, instead of in his commodious study, and if the kitchen had been big enough he would have slept there as well, concentrated himself into a single room as in the days before he met Myra.

He could, of course, go to London and look for her. But where? The only lead was the photo, flashed outside the

Arlington Gallery. He could call on her parents, or a few friends, but sensed these to be useless. If Myra had gone to such places she would have phoned him already out of boredom. He didn't want to move outside the axis of work and home.

On the fourth day he went up to Town, a desultory visit, calling at Stanford's to buy survey plans, then looking through the bookshops on Charing Cross Road. He reconnoitred the Arlington Gallery, but saw nothing of Myra. He was back in the village by six, vanguard of the rush hour spreading north out of London. The air smelled of evening when he came out of the garage, sun glowing lampwise down the green slightly inclining land of the valley. It would linger there, slipping gently from heavy cloud to dun-coloured fields and silver trees. He'd take a walk later, after tea, along one of the quiet lanes towards the woods that would darken first. He felt more tired than after a normal day – irritable, ragged, fundamentally disturbed – hoped a stroll would clear his body of lung-destroying air. Walking to the door, he caught the pungent sweetness of fresh-scythed grass – coming to him as if pulled out of the hard grip of winter's teeth, though spring was far enough on into the year.

This switched him into the gear of a good mood, and he looked forward to the long solitary evening to follow his walk. Where Myra was he did not know, and he was beginning not to care.

The door gave even before he turned the key. Taking off his coat in the hall he heard talking from upstairs, and the sound of music playing softly on the bedroom transistor.

'Myra!' he called, in the same voice he would use after a satisfying day at work. It was the only way he could tolerate the giant spider latched with all claws inside his chest.

The music stopped. He went into the lounge, sat with legs stretched out, trying to read a newspaper as if she still had not returned. He was too sick to move, at the thought of her bringing back the man she had presumably stayed with.

'I've come to say good-bye,' she said, 'and get my things.'

He didn't look at her: 'Sit down.'

'I'd better not. We want to catch the last bus back to the station.'

'You can phone for a taxi.' He was robbing her of a dead-line, a time she clung to as the unalterable mark of departure. 'Sit down,' he repeated.

'I've told you, I'm in a hurry.' He stood quickly, took her by the shoulders and pushed her into a chair. It was an unknown violence and she smiled slightly, a sardonic expression to conceal her first and sudden hatred of him. 'I've something to tell you before you finally make up your mind.'

'Everything's set. It's no use, George.'

'Perhaps not, but while your boy friend is getting your things downstairs I want to say that I'm giving up the house. A while ago I applied for a job as surveyor with a company that's looking for oil in Tripolitania. I've known for a long time that you weren't happy with the humdrum life here, and I've been wanting a change, as well as to do something useful in a country that needs help and patience and know-ledge. I thought all this would appeal to you, and as far as I'm concerned, if you want to change your mind, then I'll be glad. In six weeks we'll have sold this place and be out there. I got confirmation of the appointment this morning.'

To the one left behind the world becomes unreal, timeless, dead. The air itself alters, an alien covering of roof and sky that only action can throw off. He held himself tight at the centre, showing a calm almost lethargic exterior – that sharpened to hopelessness and a damaging inability to say anything else.

She stood up. 'I can't stay with you. I wish you luck in your new job.' Frank waited in the hall, trunk and suitcase by the stair rail. Myra was surprised that what she wanted to take fitted into so little, which gave her the feeling of really leaving.

There was no shaking of hands when she introduced them. George could not force his eyes onto Frank, and this, more than Myra's going away, caused a painful rage to burn in him. Frank found it a strange and sterile experience, enmeshed in such a polite but deadly ritual. 'Let's sit down and have a drink,' George said.

In the living-room he poured generous portions of whisky, emptying the last of the bottle into his own glass. Equal to his rage was the desire to know something about Frank, which also made him ashamed because the only way of finding out was to talk, to be calm and amiable at a time when it was not possible.

Frank accepted the drink, knowing that if he made any remark at all on the present situation, a man with a face as bunched and putty-coloured as George's would go berserk, smash the house from top to bottom – which would be a shame since he had to go on living in it after they had gone. He would also maybe smash anyone who got in his way, so Frank was ready, watching for any move that might lead to this. 'It's good whisky,' he said. 'I needed that' – and even this was too near the mark, as George's face took on a subtle but new shade of choler.

'I'm glad you did,' George said. 'It's not easy for any of us.'

'It isn't,' Frank said.

George could not talk. Why do people go away? he wondered. Because they are going to die and so hope to escape their fate; because out of impatience they can't wait to know their fate and future. Even the gypsy in them can't tell them that, unless they move. Movement is like gunpowder – needs a flame to set it off. People move because they haven't started to live to the fullest extent of their basic personality. Those who are always on the move have no personality.

'The trunk's labelled,' Myra said. 'I'd like the railway to pick it up tomorrow.' She sat down again, unable to stand, and dreading every second. George wished she had come alone. Not that he would have stopped her, but he would have spoken more freely. It was a vile blow to deal, to stand this other person in front of him when there was so much to say that he had never been able to say before.

'We must make that bus,' Frank said.

George had an idea, to do something that would open them all to the sky, and end everything in the only way possible. 'I'll drive you to the station. You can take your trunk then, at the same time.'

'Don't trouble,' Myra said.

'I can be back in forty minutes.'

'No,' she said. Frank had his coat on, the case by him. 'You've been at work all day.'

He couldn't insist. 'I was in Town, looking for you.'

'I'm sorry, George.'

His grey eyes smouldered lifelessly: 'Go on, then. Get out.'

They left him standing, looking into the tall drawn curtains that opened onto the back garden where she had worked so often, and with the mindless pleasure one often finds in a false role. Fresh cool air snapped at them. It was dark, with only a solitary lamp lit along the deserted street.

George was unable to believe that nothing else could be done. Clarity of mind existed, it seemed, but only at the restricted middle of the most complex labyrinth. He felt it, but had no way of reaching it. Life had always seemed a straight road, and he hadn't even been foxed by a simple dead-end or caught in a false cul-de-sac. Instead, he was now trapped in an unsurveyable maze of footpaths darkened by tall hedges. Such a labyrinth was extreme torment for a mind that could exist only on order and calm, which wanted everything measured and shaped, reduced to a beautiful de-

243

sign and set down on paper. The last few days had drawn him into the labyrinth, like a doomed fly fixed in helplessness until the spider-god came out for him. Or maybe he had been going towards it all his life, slowly and more deliberately than he'd known. Tonight there were a thousand routes open all around him, but none indicating with more certainty than any other either a track to the middle, or an exit to the outside world.

He got up, to follow them out.

Though it was a long walk to the bus stop, the heavy case didn't bother Frank. But the size was awkward, and now and again it slammed against his leg. 'Thank God that's over,' he said, to bring Myra out of the dark silence by his side.

'I can't believe it,' she said. 'At last. It's happened. You don't know what it means.'

'We can set off in a few days, when you've got your passport renewed.'

The departure hadn't been as bad as she'd imagined. She knew they'd both been dreading it, but now, as Frank said, it was over, and she couldn't think of anything except the freedom and emptiness ahead. A few lights glowed from cottage windows, but the two shops were shut, and the pub hadn't yet taken on its dim spark of evening life. Now and again a loud television set penetrated door and curtains. The street had no pavement, and they walked well into the road, away from the overhanging thatch. The bus and train would make a relaxing journey back to town.

He changed the suitcase to his outward side, not feeling much like speech – a silence which spread out the road to a greater length than when they'd walked it that afternoon. It was always longer travelling in the dark than by day. As a youth he'd often set off on the bike with friends, for the Peak District after a night at the pictures, and the journey seemed fifty times harder than in sunlight or even day-rain.

But now it gave time to let thoughts run through, a good moment for it because in a few days they'd be on the water, an end dropped like a dead fish into the sea, and a beginning drawn up like a corpse for resuscitation. In this unreal evening he had the feeling of already slipping out from the bank of an old life, not too much noise as he hit the water on a quiet stretch of this interior coast, and striking across the solitude of an unknown sea. For what? To go where? Getting out of your mother's womb you were already there. Maybe you were even there at the first shot of your father's prick. Life was wide, and maybe death was the only place where you could think about it. Or maybe life was death, and life was the only place where you could cogitate. If it was though, where was life? Life is in my eyes and my own two feet, and nothing more. Travelling across such water made for a cold journey, in spite of sun and daylight interspersing night and the presence of accompanying fishes. Dawns were cold and bitter, and only the first hours of darkness comfortable – like now, walking with Myra.

He switched the case over to the inside. 'There won't be long to wait,' she said. Lights prowled a long way behind, somewhere on the road, like lions let out of a cage, skirting across the far flank of the eye as Frank half turned in changing the case over. A car engine snarled, as if some mad bastard was hell bent for his favourite country pub. He moved out of the way, giving him room to pass, Myra almost into the doors of the cottages.

The dimly lit bus shelter was a hundred yards away, no one else there. A lamp flickered on and off. The car seemed close, revved-up to choking point, but he didn't turn round to see the make of it. Myra gripped his arm, as if she knew what would happen when it was too late.

It struck him, spun him against a garden hedge, a spade at his back and a thousand knives all going for his eyes at the same time. He heard a scream, then a tremendous shudder-

245

ing smash as the car went out of control and hit the solid perpendicular wall of the church. He was falling through the red and black, the vast acreage of intestines in a vat as wide as the world and in which there was no stopping as black beat red and closed over him.

Part Three

20

THE ISLAND LAY like a death-mask,
the tip of its black chin flashing a lighted pimple in
dubious welcome to the ship that had steamed south all
night from Barcelona. A few peasants and soldiers making
the passage on deck watched the distended visage of the
island coming out of its cavern of darkness. A soldier
shivered in the November wind, spat some of his bodily
warmth into the calm and indigo water, then raised his eyes
to the first streak of light and turned to finish rolling his
blanket. Another soldier drew off an enormous slice of bread
with a razor-sharp clasp knife and sat down to eat it dry. The
only noise was a heavy breathing of engines and the slop of
parting water at the bows.

Frank buttoned his overcoat. On the night train from Paris
a few dozen French soldiers had been singing and bawling up
and down the corridors. They barged into compartments
looking for seats to rest their tired and fuddled heads, and
Frank had to ease one out who wanted solace on Myra's lap.
Frank gave up his seat so that she could make use of both.
He had gone outside and smoked, talked as best he could to a

dark-faced youth from a mining town in the Nord. The soldier pointed with staring exhausted eyes in the direction of the train: 'Algeria! Algeria! Algeria!' – his mock English pronunciation not quite matching the rhythm of their separate travels.

The moon showed its continents, like an X-ray plate held up to a lightbulb. He took bread and sausage from his pocket and began to eat, uncorked a bottle of cognac which he offered to the soldiers. Each took a sip in silence, as if afraid to speak before the day came, then handed it back. Frank was emerging from the débris and suffering of a prolonged battle. The nightmare of recovery left scars in, wiped scars out, scars cone-deep that almost robbed him of the desire for life – while his skin healed and gave back the possibility of it without consulting him. George had been killed, the pulp of him indistinguishable from the lip-twisted mass of his car. Myra had been unharmed in her body – the only good to come out of the 'accident'. He could understand why George had done it, but not why he had missed, and killed himself alone. If he were determined to die he should have taken all three with him. By some failure of split-second reasoning he had bungled the job, robbed of his surveyor's precision when he really needed it for the first and last time.

The ship never lifted the level of its silent advance, while stars and moon pushed back the limits of a cloudless sky. Myra was sleeping down in the ship. In spite of everything, and the past miscarriages, the child hung on in her body, grew and prospered beyond the danger point. And beyond that point she had decided to come with Frank, on balance to discard regret and bitterness and apathy, and to trust herself with him. It was a shade too close to be called a decision, but his persuasion worked and they were together. For how long was up to him, and up to her, as if the opening of her eyes every morning took place on the heels of a renewed consultation that would become less and less necessary, he hoped, as time went on and distances increased.

She was exhausted after their stay in Paris, and the days in Barcelona. It was hardly the time for travel, with the kid already kicking, but if you waited until it was time for anything at all you'd never shift one foot. The sound of George's death wouldn't leave her, a noise as if he'd tried to rend the night apart in order to see through it and beyond to a vivid daylight in which everything was clear and conspicuous – something ordered specially for him but which existed for no one at all, ever. Perhaps by trying to breach the night he'd hoped to find some reason as to why she was going away with Frank. There had to be something outside the immediate mad act of revenge and murder. His death hadn't returned her love to the memory of him – if that was what he posthumously wanted.

They hadn't been able to talk about it while in England, but their senses opened on the trains in France, even on the upchucking storm-hauled boat across from Dover. Frank had a greater respect for George than if they had simply caught the bus that night and forgotten all about him. The injury, scars, and weeks of pain seemed unconnected with him, as if they'd been dealt by a dislodged boulder or a fall of lightning.

A passenger came out of the first-class lounge and stood by the rail, a tall young American of indeterminate age, well-wrapped in a grey overcoat and several folds of woollen scarf. Narrow blue jeans came down to the top of his cheap Spanish shoes. He had short, grizzled, greying hair and a rugged sort of pug-dog face that made him look like a ramrod Napoleon getting his first look at desolate St Helena. Frank had helped him carry his trunk aboard the night before, been cautioned as he took one end of it: 'Steady up the gangway, pal. It's full of books.'

'Don't worry,' Frank said. 'I shan't crease myself.'

251

'My name's Shelley Jones,' he said. 'What's yours?'

Frank called out a good morning: was he going to live on that island? 'Hell, no,' Shelley responded, cigarette held over the water. 'I'll stay a few days in Palma, then maybe get me a cab out to that monastery where Chopin shacked-up with George Sand. Then I'll hump the hell out of it – to Morocco or some place. What are you doing then, in little old fascist Spain?'

'I'm just waiting for the sun to shoot up.' He turned to the empty sea and, seeing that a new tint had been born, stared hard to observe the exact birth of the next colour. He saw shades of dark green on the mountainslope that had jumped there while he watched the sea; and going back to the sea, other colours had spread themselves meantime on the horizon. 'I'm travelling,' Frank said, passing the brandy. 'Drifting for a few months.'

'As long as your wife likes it. What's your work, if you don't mind my discourtesy?'

'I'm in a factory, but I'm taking time off.'

Careful to wipe the spout, Shelley returned the bottle: 'I thought you weren't the usual kind of Limey. I even told myself you were a working man.' People were still sleeping on deck, huddled in blankets or overcoats against the sharpening wind. An old woman in black leaned against the saloon, eyes open in a wide stare as if she didn't hear the clink of spoons and coffee cups inside. 'Even an American recognizes me as a worker!' Frank laughed. 'There's hope for me yet.'

Scorn didn't put Shelley off: 'I suppose in 1936 someone like you would have been in this country helping the Republic.'

'If I'd had enough food in my belly to get here I might. There ain't anything like that, in these days. As soon as we get enough bread and cheese in us we have to start looking for a soul. It's a waste of time though.'

'What do you want to look for?'

'A world to build, maybe.'

'Fine, pal. But you got to pull a few down first.'

'I don't mind starting that way.'

'I almost know,' Shelley said, 'what the sailors of Odysseus must have felt, seeing an island for the first time, that had no soul because they hadn't yet poured out their libations on its beaches. They carried their souls in wine-jars, and that was three thousand years ago.'

'Cut the Homer,' Frank said, 'and tell me about yourself.'

Shelley had a gentle way of speech, for he liked to be ironic without giving offence. 'That's hard. History at Chicago. Then work on Madison Avenue. But I gave that up, though I was careful to save out of my fifteen thousand a year – to do a lot of travelling around. Sure, Frank, I've been around, but we won't talk about that. I have a girl in Barcelona who I love-up and leave every few months – which brings me out to this neck of the woods. One day I think the poor girl won't be here because she's involved with the C N T – the good old C N T – getting their stuff printed and handed out.'

'I thought that mob wasn't operating any more,' Frank said.

He smiled. 'Well, you can never stop anybody. Look at the French, they've half a million soldiers in Algeria, and the shindig going on there is no big celebration for any man at all.'

'You've been there?'

'Ask me where I've never been,' Shelley said, a jocular brush-off. 'I go quietly. Pussyfoot. Back in the silent watches of my room – wherever it happens to be – I open my case and play patience, shuffle a lot of little books from one hand to the other, fan them out, and choose a passport. Soft-shoe-shuffling from hot spot to hot spot, after a few lessons in Cuba. In Spanish, you understand?'

253

'If you're not a nark,' Frank grinned, 'how do you know that I'm not?'

'If you aren't forthcoming, Frank, you cease to operate. Get me?'

'As long as you get yourself, that's all that matters.' The water was like ink, ship turning in it. A light still flipped its beams from the outermost rock. More people were on deck, and an English voice brayed: 'I say, what a fabulous colour the water is!' His wife agreed, in a similar bray. Frank reached for the cognac, and told Shelley to drink until he no longer felt the cold. A heavy ball of blood on the horizon. Stars gave final signals. The beige houses of a fishing village passed between sphinx-cliffs. But the sea here wouldn't accept warmth or colour from the sun, clung to its sombre cold. The wind bit now, and people kept back into the superstructure, feet shaken by the stubborn jolts of a donkey engine.

Frank went down the narrow companionway, out of the nagging wind. Myra was about to get her case from the cabin, but a Spanish woman lifted it for her. Frank took it, appreciating her help. 'Do you want some coffee?'

'Not till we land.'

'Sleep O.K.?'

'Very well. It was so calm.'

'Let's go on deck then. We'll dock soon, and you ought to see the view first.' She said good-bye to the Spanish woman, to kisses, laughter, and delicate touches of her stomach. Frank went up with her case.

The ship was turning, bows sliding along the eastern hills whose summits slumped above a bank of blue cloud, rounded the headland and carried them into Palma Bay. 'I'll be staying at the Fonda España,' Shelley said. His face had lost the open truculence of early morning, a stern gaze was still fixed on the island. 'Call me some time and we'll have a drink.'

254

'Let's have one now,' Frank said. 'There's some left.' As though the hills had pushed towards them an unwanted cloud, the ship ran into a roll of mist, and instead of an all-flanking view of city and waterfront, the boat's fog signal sent its blunted death-hoot over the bay. Shelley grinned, then grimaced, hands for once out of his pockets and pressed together on the rail as if praying. They drank until brown and yellow houses appeared near the shore.

The ship was snapped up by the grey-jawed breakwater, moved slowly towards the towered and pinnacled cathedral shooting up above the ramparts. Grey, jagged mountains to the left were like the fossilized end of some prehistoric eruption. The wind had died, vanished, leaving warmth and sunlight over the seaport and island. 'I hope the kid in there can feel this sight,' Frank said, holding her hand.

'There'll be a lot more beauty yet,' she said.

'Naples and Genoa,' Shelley called. 'Or New York. New York takes some beating.' Rowing boats moved out of the ship's track like shoals of small-fry confused at the descending presence of a bigger fish whose food they did not happen to be. Frank tossed the empty drink-bottle into green water, then moved their luggage to where sailors were erecting block-and-tackle for lowering the gangway. On one side of the bay were bright and fashionable suburbs; on the other were cranes and warehouses. The ship edged along, almost at a stop. The excitement of people on the quay, and those on the ship about to land, spanned the narrowing channel like electric current breaking down a condenser. Beneath his brandied and buoyant spirits Frank felt layers of tiredness clamouring for rest. He'd been up all night, unable to sleep, his brain matched to the racing engines of the ship.

The train traversed a plain of red-earthed field clouded with almond and carob trees. After half an hour a rocky terrain of olives lifted them into long tunnels, in which everyone stopped talking to wait for the sun to re-flood the wooden-benched carriages. The earthquake rifting across Myra's life left her incapable of focusing herself on the matter within and the world in front of her eyes. Under the sudden warmth her senses rebelled, became sharp. The last months of up-heaval couldn't be put down to nothing. Things happened for a purpose. Frank's eyes were fixed more often out of the window than on her, which she didn't mind, but which told her there was no certainty of her continuing to live with him. She had felt at peace with George, but some turbulence in Frank was buried too deep to put her at ease. Maybe to have his baby was the best and most logical solution, enough proof of love for him ever to want. Romance, as Frank had said, is finished. And maybe he was right. Life is difficult enough without that agony piled on top as well. Love is cosmic, real love coming when you spurn the need for it. Love then released goes out to everyone else. But not on its own. One must see that it did.

She shivered. Fresh air had the scent of lemons and oranges, and a subtle odour of snow from the high face of a far-off mountain. It was the sort of air that made Frank feel hungry and ready for love, both at the same time. Myra no longer wondered why her friend had stayed so long out of England. The sea lay in a corner of the horizon, pale blue and calm, slightly darker than the descending light-grey of the mountain-sides.

Frank sat in shirt sleeves to feel the new air closer to him. The train swayed downhill with such speed that at one point Myra felt afraid it would shoot over some stony bank and kill them all. Then she smiled at the fact that fear and life were reappearing. 'Are you glad we came?' he asked, thinking the landscape impressed her. The train slowed along the contour line, turned into the bowl of the valley through lush plants, trees and high cane, over the narrow bridge of a stream.

256

'I am,' she answered with a smile.

Joanna was on the platform, a tall woman wearing fashionable expatriate clothes. Myra had told him that she and her husband lived abroad because they were poor, and Frank now saw that there must be more than one sort of poverty. Her welcome was genuine, in that few people passed by or called on them in the winter months. Long hair swung down her back, and she had a tanned, almost swarthy face, a prominent nose, wide lips and almond eyes. Frank was introduced. She kissed Myra: 'I was sorry to hear it all,' she said. 'Not that I ever liked George. But I know you'll soon forget' – a look at her stomach and another smile.

Frank carried the cases down the steps and into the little plaza, where a taxi was waiting. 'Larry thought he'd put in an hour's work, so he couldn't run me down in the car.' They went two miles along the valley, and away from the sea, through farms, gardens and orange groves. Joanna's husband was an American writer, a short thin auburn man with grey darting eyes, and features as sharp as his wife's were generous. From six every morning till one he shut himself in a whitewashed room at the back of the house, bars at the window because a donkey had stabled there before they bought the property.

Frank and Myra had a room under gnarled wooden beams. The bed was mahogany and Spanish, a matrimonial bed hugely placed on the uneven floor. There was a wardrobe, a chair, chest of drawers and a straw mat of island make. Window and wooden shutters opened down the valley, over the smoky autumnal air of citrus trees, a trundling stream with deep banks winding between gardens and tile-roofed houses. Across the valley were the precipitous olive green slopes of the mountain range down which their train had roamed.

Myra sat on the bed: 'We made it.'

'Didn't you think we would?' He was unpacking the case.

'I was too absorbed in travelling. I'm relieved we're here, though. Maybe I can find myself again.'

'You mean it's an anti-climax? I never want to be myself again. I'm hoping that's impossible.'

'Perhaps you came out of England to avoid it?'

'This place is exactly how I imagined it,' he said, 'with such weather. It's not warm, but it's sunny. This room is fine. This bed, the window, the beams, the crooked floor. There's something heavy and good about it, a sort of dignity, untouched by machines or traffic. It'll be O.K. for a while, but only for a rest. It's not real life – for me.'

She took the dark ribbon from her hair, ran it through her fingers. If she and George had had similar tastes, she and Frank certainly didn't meet in their opinions. It took time to discover such things, but how much less than it had about George! Did that mean she was wiser now, or was Frank a far simpler man? Joanna called out that coffee was ready, and they walked down without speaking.

They sat on the terrace to a breakfast of fresh rolls and cuts from a solid block of ham that Joanna had stopped the taxi to buy, coming back from town. Larry was reticent in his enquiries about their journey. Frank asked how long they'd lived there. 'Eight years,' Larry said, 'and it's not a day too long, for me. I never speak for Joanna, but I know she feels the same.' He was puzzled when Frank didn't readily agree that exile and solitude were wonderful. But Frank felt an uncertainty about everything while travelling, in which opinions could only be reactions – yet true enough when they managed to escape him.

Joanna smiled, touched her husband's arm. 'It's wonderful living here. I couldn't go back to London or America, ever. I'm uneasy when I move off the island, as if I might die before I see it again.' She laughed, to prove her sentiments deep and genuine. Larry thought this unnecessary, too revealing perhaps, and grimaced – but so that she couldn't see it. Frank guessed they must have a rather submerged sort of relationship, a passionate couple fighting each other with torpedoes and submarines, deepsea mines and harbour netting, rather than with tanks and dive-bombers, clubs and boiling oil. They'll take a lifetime to kill each other, and call it love – which was one way of doing it. Such people were cheerful in front of others, and it was a happy breakfast out in the Majorcan sun, with hot rolls and coffee to push the dawn brandy into second place.

'The main reason for my being on this island,' Larry said, 'isn't only that I feel I've still got possession of my soul, but that it helps it to stay healthy as well. I can watch the seasons come and go. I can smell and see the real earth. I can see things growing on the trees. It's quiet enough for me to think. This is life to me.'

Myra was inside talking with Joanna, both recouping the gall and breadcrumbs of two married lives. 'I don't need to pamper my soul,' Frank said. 'If it doesn't like the life I lead it can lump it. This place would be death to me.'

'You're a different sort of person,' Larry said. 'I need a god to believe in, even if it's only a composite of these hills, trees, Joanna, this house. I write my stories and live my life in that framework. It's narrowing at times, but enriching as well. I envy the way you feel. You're the Uncomplicated Person.'

Frank took this as a compliment: 'I'm the empty man, the man without religion. All I believe in is houses and factories, food and power-stations, bridges and coalmines and death, turning millions of things out on a machine that people can use, people who also turn out millions of things that other people can use. It's no use harping back to poaching rights and cottage industries. We've got to forget all that and come to terms with cities and machines and moon landings. We're going to become new men, whether we like it or not, and I know I'm going to like it.'

259

'You mean mankind has to lose its soul?' Larry suggested.

'What soul? Still, if you want to put it like that, you can. All the space that's left by kicking out the soul is taken by a railway, a hammer, a whole landscape of industrial and material necessity. The soul is so big that you can get all these things in, and more. The bum-bailiffs march up to the soul and sling God out kicking and screaming. Then the real things of life move in, and that space that God inhabited (all his bloody mansions) is enormous. We can get so much in there.'

'Who's "we"?' Larry asked.

'People who think like me, and those who have it in their blood but don't yet know how to think. I had to step out of factories to realize this, though I've always felt it, and that's a fact.'

Larry's sallow face had turned pale. 'How can you live like that?'

'I've been living like it all my life,' Frank told him, lighting a brown-papered Spanish cigarette. He tapped his heart: 'It's rich enough inside, in here. It's getting richer, the more I live and know.'

It was a long, convivial day. They drank a bottle of Cinzano before lunch. Frank hauled up buckets of icy water from the well to go with it. Even in the sun cold air lingered from the dawn and they sat with jerseys on, talking right up to the confines of an exhausted midnight – when he followed Myra up to bed.

In spite of the cold she was drifting into sleep, too tired to wait for Frank and a possible exchange of views on the day. Sleep was revolving far away, between two flying storms of snow and sand. Her heavy weight drifted her down, away from the sway of trains, the purring of last night's boat, the incessant talk and the smell of cold oranges. She was beyond the clash of tree branches outside the window, her body sinking and settling, eyes forced shut into a dark world that was empty except for a spark of light that never went out, an illuminated distant life-dot recognized as the stirring inside her.

They could either rent a furnished house in Majorca, and arrange for Myra to have the baby here, or go somewhere else and not bother too much about where the baby was born. They sat in a café, looking out at the muddy square while they discussed it. Rain had been falling ten days without stop. In such a monsoon the house was small for the four of them. The continual thumping of Larry's typewriter made it seem as if they were still on a ship. The noise penetrated Frank's reading and drove him to walk along lanes and mule-tracks whether it rained or not. The mountains were swathed in cloths of rain, cloud-shirts, mist boiling up the valleys, clinging by grey fingernails to escarpments and treetops. Larry said it was usual weather for the time of the year. 'December and January are better,' he said, 'but February and March get lousy again.'

Frank was in favour of moving. So was Myra. They set out on a boat to the mainland, wet decks and cold ironwork steaming through drizzle. Blue domes of Valencia did not shine in the distance. Harbour lights and quays stretched before the boat which edged towards tie-up, still a thrilling part of any journey for Frank. Beyond the customs sheds an orange tram passed on its way into the city.

They stood on the open deck rather than queue to get off, Myra in no condition to be pitched among bundles and boxes on a swaying gangway. Once on the quayside Frank walked into the hold of the ship and pulled out his trunk.

The road was straight and flat through dingy suburbs, their taxi dodging trams, swinging around cars and bicycles. Larry had given them addresses of cheap pensions in all the southern towns. Rain clouds hung over the city. Having once started on a journey Frank wanted to get it over as soon as possible. If Frank had been George, thought Myra, they would have stayed a few days in Valencia at such a time instead of rushing on without any thought. In fact George wouldn't even have started the journey, and she couldn't finally decide what she wanted most. Maybe they'd miss the train, then they'd have to stay for a while. Frank didn't even know where the journey would end, but wherever it was, he felt a need to reach it.

With ten minutes to go he booked the trunk and bought tickets. The only place for Myra to sit was a small emergency seat near the door. The train moved almost as soon as their luggage was in, pulling away between tall buildings and wide boulevards out of the middle city. The first night they met he had seen her off on a train from Paddington – into blackness and never to be met again, lights, noise and smells different from this lit-up uneasy move together into the Spanish south. 'Another four hundred miles, and we'll be in Granada,' he said.

'I'd like to know where we're really going,' she said. 'I like travelling at the moment, and wouldn't mind if we never stopped, but where are we going right now?'

'We'll go to Tangier,' he said, eyes fixed on row after row of orange trees flickering by, content again at the feel of a train under him. 'I've always wanted to go to Africa!'

'Don't think I'm worrying,' she said, 'but where am I going to have the baby?' The train ran into sun, clear sky over flat fertile land spreading to mountain peaks. He took the brandy from the travelling basket: 'Tangier's a big town. Have it there.'

'But no further,' she said. 'I don't want to have him in a tent in the desert.' They laughed. She leaned against the window and managed to sleep. He stood guard so that ticket collectors or people opening and closing the nearby door shouldn't disturb her. He wondered, now that it was too late, whether they shouldn't have stayed in Valencia.

Myra had bought a guidebook, and he read it in calmer

moments, opened the map and followed station names, mountain ranges, rivers. The train slowed between weed-grown walls in a suburb of flat-roofed houses: Alicante, stayed half an hour by the large harbour, that called for another swig of brandy. He found comfortable seats for them. For some reason he had picked up Spanish quicker than Myra, wielded it fluently at stations and cafés.

The train passed along the sea edge, a blue gradient of mountains lifting from each cape on either side of the city. There were many ships in the harbour, and bathing huts along grey beach like sentry boxes put there to keep back encroaching surf. They turned inland, date palms and orange trees almost brushing the windows. Train wheels were thumping south-east – another eight hours for Granada – taking them over arid plains and within clear sight of grandiose mountains to the north, and villages propped on isolated hills, a huddle of poor houses baked in summer and frozen in winter, desolate and destitute. It was hot in the carriage, sun shining strongly through windowglass. Myra sat in her blouse, head now and again resting on her bare arms. Frank took off his jacket, walked through the carriage to bring water for Myra, and beer for himself.

Hardly anyone was speaking, and the whine of the diesel engine drowned the voices of those who were. The carriage was wrapped in the afternoon silence of the outside landscape. It was perfectly still and not a word could come from it. It lacked meaning, took on a death-like quality. The wheels were circular hammers beating on the tracks. Such a time brought momentary boredom with life, and memories came in speed and secrecy to dam up and strengthen the crumbling walls of courage. Frank stared at the beige land, not seeing it, but seeing himself.

The journey was enlivened when the train came to a bridge over a ravine. The driver stopped before it, uncertain whether it was possible to get his loaded train across. Frank looked along the track. Workmen on the upper banks of the ravine stood aside, waiting for the train to make up its mind.

'We'll be here all day,' he said to Myra. 'You should see that bridge.' Planks formed a parapet only along part of its length, while tree-poles buttressed and reinforced its shaky girders. Frank thought he saw it sway, but knew that this was imagination, mirage, fatigue. The train inched forward, lurched, a hundred heads poking out to gauge its progress. Frank felt scared. The train stood full on the bridge, not a word spoken, only a grinding of wheels, a creak of structure.

They were over. 'I hope there aren't any more like that.'

Myra laughed. 'I knew it would be all right.' She had had this feeling, that all things would be all right, ever since leaving George, but as the afternoon spun itself slowly out it seemed that the magic weave was falling away, that the train was taking her to a stage beyond both George and Frank, not out of Frank's love so much as into her own self where life would be lonelier and yet more solid, frightening, exhilarating and independent. The baby lulled her, and the journey went on and on.

Plains on either side seemed without limit, as if they were going into the hinterland of a newly born and endless continent. Sunlight spread yellow wings through sparse cloud, turning the arid countryside into a blood-irrigated desert. Mile after mile without house or horse. They cat-napped through the dusk, Frank wondering whether he hadn't, at last, encountered those vast and endless spaces dreamed about with such love and longing. He'd given up everything to find this, to find Myra, to find a new brain and absence of mind by drifting anchorless or, rather, attached to the built-in anchor of himself. But these weren't the spaces, nor these the feelings. Wherever he was going, he was some way from it yet.

264

When he opened his eyes and looked through the window the sun was sometimes on one side, sometimes on the other, but always lower down towards the horizon, until nothing could be seen and the world was confined to a train whose wheels were spinning towards Granada.

21

THEY WALKED the streets of Granada under a clear, cold, sun-blue sky, spiritually unable to leave. 'I feel I've been here before,' she said. 'But I never have. Not in this life, anyway. George didn't approve of the régime to let us come this far south. These smells of oranges and flowers, and snow in the air. It's strange.'

He didn't know what she meant; it was new to him, but rich in its newness. 'The Jews and Moors lived here at one time.'

'Maybe it was that,' she said. 'It's such a strong feeling. It exists right inside me.'

'It could be that,' he said. 'I could believe in that.' Such new impressions overwhelmed him still, but he was strengthened by them, no longer disorientated. Having no time to think of himself, resolution grew firmer because decisions that moved him from one place to another were less hard to make. They walked in the garden of the Generalife, between the shadows of gigantic cypresses. 'I was with George so long,' she said, talking through the sound of spraying water, 'that I forgot I was Jewish. But it's been coming back to me since I met you, for some reason. And this place has given it to me strongest of all.'

'Where did your grandparents come from, then?'

'From Bessarabia. I think that's in Russia now.'

'Arabia,' he smiled, 'it doesn't seem much different, does it? We're in a bit of Arabia now. When the Jews left here they went to North Africa and Turkey. Maybe some ended up in Bessarabia.'

'Why not?' she said.

'Myra of Bessarabia,' he said, taking her hand. 'I never thought we'd be in Granada.'

Her eyes filled with tears. 'What is it, love? Tell me what it is?' A group of Germans armed with guidebooks, plans, cameras and measuring tapes trod gutterally past, pinkfaced and coatless, stepping over hosepipes with exaggerated care. 'I'm afraid,' she said, 'and I don't know why.'

He embraced her by a tall tailored hedge: 'I'm full of love for you. Everything will be all right. The baby will come, and we'll be happy with it.'

'It's not even that,' she said. 'It's not that at all. It's more than that.'

'You'll be all right. Don't cry.'

But Myra felt a desolation of the soul, was a young girl again thinking of beautiful things, locked in an ancient world passed on to her from an exclusive state that only women can inhabit, and that men catch (if ever) in rare moments when they are happy. It was a sensation carried from one woman to another by some dying goddess who never quite died. To Myra it became a self-induced ivy-dream of queens and princesses in whom the beauty of physical mating was admitted to become the finality and further beginning of childbirth. It was a world they kept unjealously because of a divine right that seemed to flower in the alleyways and upper streets of the Albaicin. A parapet had guided her eyes directly across at the blood-coloured towers of the

Alhambra buttressed by great snowbanks of the Sierra Nevada – where it also flowered. This desolation went through a procession of images towards something it could never quite reach, a dream containing all the animal realities of the earth. She saw in other women her perfect counterparts infused with the orgiastic motions of which childbirth was the last great cry and connected to the delicate inborn tendernesses in herself. She felt the force of living and was glad to be alive, a positive sensation for the first time which had nothing to do with Frank. The time was close when she could live in as complete a way as she would ever know, for this was the end of her life so far, the phosphorescent deadness that would give place to a new and unique person. It pointed the rebirth towards a life that would be hers only.

He looked out at the white midnight roofs of Granada, steam-breath clouding the glass which he rubbed clear. The city was sleeping at last, and smelled of snow. Noise still came from the hotel kitchen, Andaluz voices subdued and rapid, the clash of plates, a door banging as he got in bed and tried to sleep. He wanted to show her eyes beautiful landscapes, feed her heart with more tenderness and pity than it already possessed, fill her body with more sensations than it had ever known. But this was turning against himself. It was impossible because the end had been reached, not the end of love, but the beginning of something else in which the sort of love he had always known about and felt as fully as anyone was to be discarded as a fraud and a trick, the stone tied around a corpse to make it sink. To cut it loose would enable a man and woman to live in equality, with regard and respect for each other's purpose in the world. Mutual destruction had to cease.

Copulating cats roared like lions in the night. Myra was sleeping, curled in her nightdress. At dawn an inquisitorial roll of bells came loud and dissonant over luminous rooftops. In the street a ripped poster waved like a frantic hand. Leaves fell thick as copper snow over an autumn square. He had lived through a hundred seasons in one year. Hump-backed clouds looked like disappointed pilgrims returning from some mountain shrine, glad to be back over streets and houses. If you like a city, he thought, it protects you; if you don't like it, it drives you away. I like this one, but still I'm going. He did not know what he would be doing a week from now. He did not remember what he dreamed last night. If he did not want to wake up, the dream had been good; if he had been glad to wake up, it had been a nightmare. He was uncertain about it.

A fine rain fell as the train pulled along the ascending valley. Olive trees gridded the hillsides. Wet towns and villages in the distance were like wooden uneven nailheads hammered into the earth. The train was crowded and smoky, full of luggage, food hampers, people in black and grey, silent children. A man came in out of the rain, from one station, wearing dressing-gown and slippers, smoking a cigar and carrying two suitcases, alighting at a town twenty miles further on.

'I like Spain,' Frank said. 'I like the people. They don't seem to let things bother them.'

'I felt that ever since I stepped over the border.'

'I really think I'll feel at home wherever I am,' he said.

'As long as you're moving, on wheels,' she joked. In the afternoon the train was descending, into clearer sky and sunlight. Ronda showed through a gap in the mountains, a far-off patch of towers and houses perched beyond the immediate circle of hills like an imagined dream in a saint's vision. Then it was cut from view, and the rugged scenery reminded Myra of the engravings in an edition of Byron resting in the glass case among George's books. She wondered whether she'd ever see them again, the first real question since setting out. She saw the titles, and the rich binding, the house, then the village, the edge of tall corn clipped near its summer roots, a brief run of pictures left to flower in her at a later time. How far would the thread that held her stretch before it snapped, while the new thread thickened into a rope?

Tunnels took them into gorges – romantic for those that passed by in trains but not for people who lived roundabout, he thought. Barren limestone slopes sent swollen streams curving from tightly-packed villages built in impossible hill positions. Why had it been Frank? she wondered, who had come into her life only a few months ago like a man with pick and mattock and hewn her out of it so savagely? Perhaps it was all so futile and unnecessary, and she'd have been better off staying where she was: the unlanced lake, calm and stagnant under an English sky.

She looked forward to getting off the train. Beyond the window by a bleak-looking stream, a sinewy weather-beaten woman stood outside a house, pegging sheets onto a clothes-line, steadying them from the wind to watch the slow progress of the train. Her life must be hard and lonely, Myra thought, but less so than my own which never stops moving. Bent low in the saddle a man on horseback raced half a mile and beat them to the next bridge, then stood grinning, hat in hand, before sauntering back to his red-roofed and isolated house.

Rolling hills and flat marshland drew them to the sea. Cattle browsed at sky-reflecting pools, between cork and carob trees. Across the bay lay the enormous slouching rock of Gibraltar. 'We'll get over the straits tomorrow,' Frank said.

'Tangier will have to be our last stop.' She leaned back, pale, all life drained out. 'I can't go any farther.'

'You won't,' he said, concerned at the deathlike marks of fatigue, and wondering now why he had brought her so far.

'I love you,' she said, 'but we must stop in Tangier.'

270

'It's nothing to do with love,' he said gently. 'We'll find a house there, and you can rest for three or four months.'

'I'm so tired,' she said, no complaint but a fact that wrenched his heart. At the hotel their room had a map of damp marks down the wall, and stank of fumigation powder, so he argued bluntly with the receptionist and made him find them another. Myra bathed, then ate soup, omelette oranges. She was asleep before he left the room. Her dark hair, grown long in travelling, fell over the pillow away from her cool exhausted face. He touched her forehead. She didn't hear the door close.

He walked over the bridge, a cold breeze swelling in from the sea. Across the few miles of water Gibraltar lay like a long bank of burning coal. He ate at Arturo's (recommended by Larry), then sat outside a harbour café to drink coffee and smoke at a bitter full-tasting cigar.

He too was exhausted, in all things nearing the rock-bottom of his heart, touching the extremities, as if the end of some journey within himself was in sight. He had reached the limit of his concern for Myra. He loved, had no fear of that, but as a man and a human being, not as an adventurer, and so all inner directions were spent – or those were that he chose to consider. Whatever occurred within himself, in the rich mineral coal lump of his brain, he would always, being a strong character, decide what was going to happen to him.

Sitting on the harbour front was like being at the world's edge, and the only way he could move was on, across the world. To understand people, go into the desert, and do not come out until you understand yourself. Not to know this meant that the inner journey was suspended, and that could never be, though you kept it in its place by a richer surface life, so that it helped, not dragged you down as it had so far done. Thirty years had taught him nothing except that life was good but limited (the innerlife anyway that the society he'd been brought up in told him existed) – limited in every-

271

thing, depth, space, decision, strength. The soul was a load of bollocks; the heart was a useful depth gauge in the machine shops of social life; the mind was good for thinking, building, helping; the hands were right for making and doing. He felt at the forward point of the world. Death was nothing to write home about, to dwell on, think of. The shell went through you, the tank trundled over you, the hydrogen bomb flashed you up, old age put you to sleep – as long as you were *doing* something when any of this happened, lifting, helping, firing a gun.

The only fear and cowardice in life was idleness, inactivity – either sitting still or doing work that nobody wanted or would benefit from. Hell wasn't other people; it was the inability to work, to act, to do. Hell was having nothing to live for, a pit he'd steered away from without realizing how close he had been to it. Heart and soul, they were fetters that the new man of the world took to a blacksmith and had chopped away. The new man of the world must work and live as if he weren't going to be alive the next day. This would make him more careful and tender to others, not less.

It was a new way to live, and even now, he was trying it, the first kick-off started the day he left the Nottingham world of moribund William Posters. Let's face it. I've got no love left in me – not of the kind I should have. It's being burned out of everyone else as well, by the oxyacetylene glare of tube-light and telly-fire. We must love more people than just each other. The old idea of love is sliding away from the fingertips of the new man, like a thousand-coloured ferry boat heading for the open sea.

They steamed in late morning through a zone of green water towards mid-channel blue. Land seemed to be all around, cloud obscuring the mouth of the Mediterranean, and the mouth of the Atlantic, mixing Gibraltar with African peaks above Ceuta and Tetuan. Huge liners and tankers drifted by as if hardly moving, then vanished or were mere dots when Frank looked again from the saloon window. They headed by the white houses of Tarifa, hugging the Spanish shore, with Cape Trafalgar dim and shifty in the distance. The Moroccan side was rocky and sheer, a sandy beach now and again visible as if someone had dropped a white handkerchief from the mountaintop above. It was peaceful at sea, the tilt and gentle pitch of the boat resting both of them after the night's deep sleep.

They went under the archway up the cobbled street, into the narrow lane of the Moorish town. The porter led them to the hotel off the Socco Chico. They entered by a small door from a side street and ascended the washed steps. Myra found it good to talk to the French proprietress after so long in Spain, felt civilized again with the edge on Frank's Spanish which now sounded as rough and uncouth as north of England dialect. The woman was interested in Myra's pregnancy, which meant a five-minute chat every time they went in or out.

The hotel was a second-floor flat, which seemed to go along the whole length of the street, making it little more than an endless corridor of small rooms. At first there were so many women's voices coming from them that Frank wondered if they hadn't stumbled into a brothel, but since he heard no sounds of men he had to conclude differently – though in Tangier you could never be sure. In the next room was a Frenchwoman with two small dogs, and often through the paper-thin walls came the sound of clanking bowls and swilling water, great lip-smacking kisses, and the sliding of the dogs' paws on the tiled floor.

Their room was the largest in the hotel, the bed a rough frame nailed together, with bedding neatly and skilfully laid on top. There were two old basket chairs, and a small table for books, cigarettes, matches, tangerines and make-up. A sink in one corner had no plug, and one had to keep the

273

faucet pressed to get water – as on a ship. Frank shaped a plug out of a cork, rather, he said, than give up washing. There were two huge coat pegs on the blue wall, and a small piece of Moroccan artisanry for matting on the floor. A single window looked onto a dim alley-street, so that even in daytime they needed the light on. The hotel was on its last legs, and so was more expensive than many others.

They lay at night listening to Moorish music that came from café radios and permeated the whole building, Frank feeling as if he were in the chill-middle of Arabia. Myra warmed him, her belly a stove, kisses still tasting of spice from Moslem food eaten on their day's wanderings through the winding alleyways of the medina, or of mint and sugar from the innumerable glasses of tea drunk before coming to bed. Frank had bought a spirit stove and cooked-up his own brand of Arab tea at night and morning. They lived in the room a fortnight, and revelled in the refurbishing powers of retreat, a calm hideout in a medieval walled town.

They were strangers there and knew no one, walked up the steep Rue des Siaghines and into the flower filled market at the top that smelled of mimosa and cloves. They went on into the new town, along the boulevards and among modern blocks of flats, then got a bus through the suburb of the Dradeb. They climbed up to a point overlooking the straits, with Spain a definite coast only thirteen miles away. A mule track led along the clifftops to Cape Spartel, the shoulder of Africa where Hercules was said to have shaped millstones in his solitary wave-bashed cave. The track climbed above the sea, up then down, from one headland to another, a violent Atlantic wind spitting at the prominent arbutus-horn of Africa. Jebel Kebir was forested, and they turned up into its shelter, a subtle mixture of juniper and eucalyptus smells, laurel and cedar and pine, a moving sky that drew their eyes during rest, as if up there a blacksmith were reshaping clouds that a storm had raged out from its own belly, the wind moving leaves and branches in an inspired concord of smells and shapes.

They made love under the trees ('He should find his way out without too much bother when the time comes,' Frank joked on the way back), gently going into her, as if savouring it because a farewell was imminent. Flames from all her limbs leapt to the middle of her as if to greet the guest that slid so ceremoniously in, an unexpected climax far in front of his own. They hadn't come to her so easily of late, Myra believing that the enlarging animal processes of pregnancy held them back, compensating by the almost visionary light it threw on what was happening to her. Frank lived on the extremity of this influence, the man whom she loved and who, in his own way, looked after her well, out of his own sort of love. But during this mechanism of change he was the person closest to her, and what she dreaded most was the emerging fact that he would soon be removed from this intimate nearness. In calmer moments she realized that this was bound to happen when a child was born, a thought which toned off the sharper edges of her vision. Yet an uneasiness lingered through her dreams, dreams which, since pregnant, she could never remember.

The green hills of Tangier in winter were drenched and heavy. On walking back skyscraper blocks appeared white and pink between olive groves. It was enchanting and new, a fitting scenery in which to change gear and come back to life. Myra puzzled him by her unwillingness or inability to show more of what was going on in her own mind. She drifted uncomplaining, almost happily, enjoying new sights, physical love, the sensual effects of food and travel. He could put it down to pregnancy, but he knew better, wondered instead whether she didn't resent all that had happened to her since they met, blame him for some unwanted foreign upheaval that his appearance had caused. A sharp pride prevented him

275

asking anything, and he thought maybe she hardly knew herself yet.

At the Place de France a rainstorm burst on them, a leaden throwdown of water that seemed to be trying to stamp all animal life back into the asphalt. The gutters burst, over-flowed, and water drove in sheets along the roadway, traffic fighting against it and hardly able to see, trees by the French consulate buckling before the wind. They sat in a café till the storm was spent, watching through the windows, the air heavy with smoke and coffee steam. He ordered brandy, and tea for Myra. 'We just made it. What an end to the day.'

'It's only four o'clock.'

'Tired?'

'A bit. I feel good after our walk. I like Tangier, which is just as well, I suppose.'

'It is, since we'll be here for a while.' Yet he hoped not, thought not, but finally couldn't say. It was hard, if not impossible to stop moving when movement was the only thing that at the moment seemed to be keeping him alive.

22

IN YOUTH SHELLEY had been tender
at the lungs, and though that passing phase seemed only
to have made him tougher in the end than the average
person, he still paid them the homage of maximum protection. Thin and raddled after a week in the whorehouses of
Palma, he followed his luggage down the gangplank, his grey
overcoat well-buttoned against the damaging wet winds of a
Catalonian winter. He looked forward to pouring himself a
shot of hot cognac in one of the wilder bars of Barcelona,
sliding it in to his favourite toast of 'Hemingway, I hate
you'

His luggage would stay in the consigna until he found a
hotel. Fatigue focused his eyes on the fading labels of his
oldest trunk. Since pressing the ejector seat of his job on
Madison Avenue he had travelled to many places, and a
flaking discoloured label could bring back to him the smell of
many a hotel hall from those early days, humidity and
mothballs and the fruity reek of an Amazonian forest as he
opened the window and wondered once more why the hell
he'd stopped in this particular place, parrot-cries and dilapi-

dated streets mouldering into the vast area of shimmering river. Craving the impossible, an ambitious decadent shaped and fired by the fevers of desk-dreams, he took a long time to re-cross the boundary into reality. He'd envisaged a heaven somewhere, a small collapsing corporate state in a back corner of South America whose economy was on the crash – that razor's edge of heaven between a fabulous exchange rate for dollar-tourists, and a revolutionary upheaval from within – a matter of a few weeks perhaps in which the local currency stood at a thousand pesos to the dollar, with full board at the Grand Hotel Esplendido for ten cents, and the having of some worthy bourgeois beauty for as little as five. He'd never found it, quite, and the search died hard.

He'd wandered around the first two years, an exponent of positive negativism in his desire to forget the past and create his future by recording it as a travel book. These were his own phrases, wicked, sardonic and empty. Not empty, he thought. Emptiness is when you're full of something that can't be put to use, or that you cannot define. That's not me. It was, but not now. The mud and destitution of La Paz, and a proletarian riot in which a police baton had smashed onto his head, had been the blinding light of his Damascus that made him 'the man at the door with the gun'. He looked old before his time, but with a freshness and naïvety that suggested he might not be able to take advantage of it. He travelled over frontiers, forbidden pamphlets in the false bottom of his trunk when moving legally; panniers of dynamite filched from the copper mines of the Andes when crossing by unfenced jungle towards some hide-out of co-revolutionaries never expecting him but always glad of his loot delivered after enormous risks that they would never take.

South America was a big place, but not, eventually, big enough. Cuba came and went. His favourite books were those works on guerilla warfare, by Mao Tse Tung, Ngoyen Giap, and Che Guevara – authors who for him had taken

278

their places in world literature even before Shakespeare and Tolstoy. Shelley lived by the principles of guerilla warfare. The enduring Maxim of Sun Tzu: 'Uproar in the East, strike in the West' was the basis of exercises which combined intellect and imagination whenever there was time to kill before catching boat or train. Walking the streets he staged uprisings in that particular town; on the train he laid ambushes in the passing terrain; pacing the beach he planned clandestine landings. 'Life is war, but guerilla war, not the old artificial war that the world's lived with up to now. One of the deepest instints of Man is to conquer by stealth, to create an uproar at one point while striking with deadly effect at another.' His one unalterable dream was to see Madison Avenue and its thousand commerces erupt into smoke and flame.

A wall of noise roared by his face like cold sandpaper: trams and buses, taxis and handwheeled carts. After a journey of brandy and sweat and sleeplessness, his legs were moving once more, a surge of life backing into him. Barcelona was noisy, good to get to in the early morning. He'd rather go a roundabout way to a city simply to reach it in the morning. To arrive in the afternoon was a corroding experience: twilight savaged you like an octopus in slow motion, made you wish you were anywhere else but on earth. It was all right once darkness fell, for Man had lights to show as proof of his victory over the dark.

A coastal sun brewed warmth between wet clouds. Shelley smoked a cigarette, walked with his portable typewriter on one hand, and a straw travelling-basket on the other. Even the taxi drivers and hotel touts clammering at the dock hadn't broken his good temper:
> 'Barcelona, here I come,
> Right back where I started from. . . .'

and he'd find a hotel along the Boqueria, sleep until lunch time, and look up Maricarmen in the afternoon.

279

At the Columbus Statue he turned up the maindrag of the Rambla. None of the hotels along the Boqueria had vacant rooms, which was strange at this time of the year. At the fourth hotel, up steps and along a corridor, he stopped at the counter: 'Buenos dias! Hay habitacion para dos o tres dias?'

The duena said she had a room vacant, and asked if he'd be needing meals. Shelley told her he would be eating out, as he was a tourist and wanted to see the sights. Two men were by his side. One pulled a huge steel-and-Technicolor badge from his pocket and said he'd like to see his passport. Shelley gave it to the man, who walked away with it to the other end of the hall, leaving his friend on guard in case anyone tried to run. When they didn't ask where he'd come from Shelley realized they'd followed him from the dock, a couple of detectives in hats and gaberdines who might have stepped out of some Hollywood B picture if they hadn't been so underfed.

Shelley acted on the principle that caution was unnecessary in a fascist country. Where the guilty were taken with the innocent everyone was guilty and it was up to you to bluff your way out of it if caught. The man came back and asked if he had any other means of identification. Shelley gave him an old carte de séjour which he had collected in the south of France.

He played the tourist: it's no use getting annoyed. They want to check up. That's their job. Maybe they're looking for anarchists, bomb-throwers whose activities are just as likely to endanger tourists like me as anyone else. He was told to come to the police station, and to bring his typewriter and travelling bag.

They walked through the streets. When stunned by the baton in La Paz he had thought, on waking up in a nearby café: 'Shall I phone the US consulate, and complain?' No, he told himself, and later felt that to be the most important

280

decision of his life. They assured him it wouldn't take more than a few minutes. Shelley talked like a rubberneck, though his good Spanish betrayed him, asked in which direction was the cathedral and the Tibidabo, said that Barcelona was a fine city and that there was none so fine in South America – glad that his passport had recently been changed and that other evidence of Spanish visits wasn't on the present one.

The police station was a barracks, armed guards at the entrance. They climbed two flights of stairs and walked along a corridor, uniformed and plainclothes men inside little offices smoking, talking, or hovering over typewriters. With so many stairs and corridors he saw that a criminal would have a tough time trying to get out. They went into an office. Shelley was asked to sit down, which he did willingly, feeling tireder than ever. They took his passport and French identity card, and left him there alone.

It was a small room, with a coloured portrait of General Franco on one wall, and a plan of Barcelona opposite. The only desk held a typewriter, blotting pad, trough of pens and some paperclips. Glued to another wall were photographs of criminals whom they had not yet succeeded in capturing.

Shelley, engrossed in the city plan, was trying to bring a complex of street battles into one unified action. A convent had been sacked and fortified, thoroughfares blocked and certain houses sandbagged, but no central command had yet been set up, though underground leaders were at last moving in because, according to news from the rest of Spain, the revolt had a chance of becoming decisive. He was itching for a pencil with which to make squares and circles on the map.

The detectives came back with an elderly white-haired man wearing wire-rimmed spectacles, a kindly person who looked like a philosophic cobbler caught in the wrong job. He said that Shelley's passport was forged. Shelley replied that it was issued in London, and properly visaed by the Spanish consul in Gibraltar, so how could it be? The elderly man lifted his

typewriter from the floor and asked him to open it. Shelley
did so, and was about to show him how it worked, when the
old man nodded thoughtfully and told him to close it.

'Why are you in Spain?' asked a detective.

'Because I like the country. I like the people.'

'You sound like a communist.'

'I'm a tourist. There are lots of art treasures here.'

'But why did you come on a forged passport?'

He said they should check with the American consulate,
finding it unfair to mention this, but impossible not to because it would be the reaction of the ordinary American
traveller. The old man said the passport was obviously forged
because the stamp wasn't pressed far enough into the photograph.

'Have you any money?' the detective asked. Shelley
reached for his back pocket, but the detective said that he
didn't want to see it. He asked where he got his income.
Shelley said he had money invested on Wall Street, which
impressed them. 'I have share certificates on me to prove it,'
he said, but the detective wasn't interested in them, either,
asked instead to see the contents of his travelling basket.
Shelley took out a bottle of wine and a bottle of brandy. He
offered them a drink, which was refused. There was a Blue
Guide to Spain, a book of poetry, and a bundle of decom-
posing sandwiches. 'Put it back,' the old man said.

All three went out of the room, this time leaving a man on
guard at the door. Shelley went back to the plan of Barcelona. The insurrectionary forces tended to concentrate west of
the maindrag, fortifying the lanes between there and the
Rond San Antonio. Some streets to the east were also in their
possession, and workers from the northern suburbs were
moving in. But Government troops were gathering under the
hill of Montjuich and preparing to clear the city centre.
Which was fine, because workers from the factories of Sans
were already filtering behind the hill of Montjuich for an

attack in the rear as soon as the army made a move. 'Uproar in the East, strike in the West.' It couldn't fail. Badalona and other suburbs were mobilizing their workers. The uprising in Madrid had failed, but Valencia was in insurrectionist hands. Street names were being changed, and paving stones put back. Workers' representatives were talking to the sailors at Cartagena. Malaga had gone completely over to the rebels, and was already being strafed by American Sabre-jets. Russia had protested, and Chinese technicians had started flying in from Peking. . . .

They'd been gone half an hour, and it seemed that the man at the door kept observing Shelley for any sign of nervousness or guilt. 'Kafka, I love you,' he thought, taking several drinks at the bottle of brandy and thinking that if they didn't come back soon he'd be either dead drunk or asleep.

In the meantime the guns had opened up from Montjuich, and soldiers of the loyal garrison were coming down the hill with flamethrowers. Agitators were talking to them through loudspeakers, and one had already gone over to them. A woman with a red bandera had blown another to pieces with a handgrenade and a whole street was burning.

Bad news came, that Valencia had surrendered. The sailors at Cartagena had scuttled their ships. Malaga alone remained, and the whole fascist spite had been turned (as usual) against it. Shelley wondered whether there were a map of Spain in the desk on which to plan a guerilla campaign in the mountains, so that the insurgents could withdraw and carry on resistance from there.

'It's a beautiful city, Barcelona,' one of the plainclothes men remarked pleasantly, handing him his passport. He apologized for having detained him, but said that many people were going around with forged papers. Shelley smiled, understood that he had his work to do. The policeman thought he should be more angry than he was, so apologized again, and this time Shelley didn't look too pleased, a gruff response that blew away all suspicion from the policeman's narrow and infantile mind.

The policeman took him back to the street. They shook hands, and he pointed the direction to his hotel. Shelley walked in the sunshine, feeling no malice towards any man or being, as he called a taxi and ordered it to the docks, where he would get out his luggage and head for Tangier. To contact Maricarmen would put her in danger as well. He'd shuttle through Valencia and Granada without delay in case any other autonomous Gestapo unit pulled him in for no reason and decided this time to keep him. He was puzzled and disturbed. Why should they arrest me? I'm guilty, after all. These bastards usually get the wrong ones, though. It's not cricket, as that swish piece from London said when I laid her in Malaga.

A week later he was in Tangier, at a café in the Place de France thinking about his next excursion south. A date had been fixed, lorry and supplies assembling, but he wanted another head and pair of hands. A face came in from the rain which he knew, and he called out the name that belonged to it.

A shock passed through Frank because the voice that called his name out loud was only half recognized by memory. Shelley set a briefcase down on their table, stood tall beside it, wrapped in the same long overcoat and cumbrous grey scarf. Frank knew him, in spite of the crew-cut and heavily-rimmed glasses that made him look like so many other Americans. 'And what the hell are you doing in this god-forsaken Bidonville?' Shelley asked.

'If you'll sit down and have a drink, I might tell you.' There were handshakes: 'I got swacked on your brandy, remember?' Shelley said, and called the waiter, who seemed to know him well, and came over immediately from another table. He ordered two double cognacs and more tea for Myra.

284

'We ended up here,' Frank said. 'After Granada it was the end of the line. We've got to hole up for a few months.'

'It's a good place,' Shelley said with a high-powered laugh, 'but it's not the end of the line. I know a few places after this, and I don't mean Casablanca.'

'What about your girl-friend in Barcelona?' Myra asked. 'Is she here too?'

'Hell, no. She works up there, and I do my work down here. Now and again we have a date. I had to pull out quick.'

'What sort of work?' Frank asked. Shelley leaned back with a music-hall avuncular look from such contemporary shoulders. 'Just wouldn't you like to know? Oh boy, just wouldn't you?'

'Maybe I would at that,' Frank said.

Shelley asked where they were staying. Frank told him: 'But we can't bed in that fleapit for ever. We're looking for a house or flat.'

'Since independence you can pick up apartments cheap. But a furnished place isn't so easy.' The rain eased off, settled to a steady civilized downpour. Traffic livened the dusk, and beggars held out their hands again. Vendors toted hats, flowers, peanuts, purses, wooden puppets. The café lighting served as blinds, rain and dusk neutralizing everything. Myra felt out of time and place, Shelley telling of a flat he knew with four rooms, kitchen, bath and maid's bathroom not far from the Boulevard Pasteur. 'Belongs to a Frenchman who tears off six months of every year in Marseilles. I know the agent, a lawyer. Lets for around thirty thousand.'

'That's about five quid a week,' Frank said. 'We could manage that.'

Shelley took a large diary from his briefcase: 'Meet me here, nine-thirty, tomorrow morning?'

'All right,' Frank said. 'Why do you need such a big diary

285

in a place like this? Are you in business, or something?'

'How you bug me, Frank! Sure I'm a business man, but don't ask me what I sell. It's too specialized.'

'Forget it,' Frank said. 'And if you can't forget it, drop dead. I don't mind if you run a brothel.'

'Tell me he's broadminded, Myra,' Shelley said, beckoning for another tray of drinks.

The agent took them through a palatial entrance and up on a fine lift, four floors high in a modern block to show off the central heating and garbage disposal point. Myra had stayed in bed, so Frank was to decide. The furniture was ornate and heavy, but sparse enough not to be intimidating. Windows looked over the town towards Tetuan. Frank went back to the lawyer's office with Shelley, signed the six-month contract and paid two months of it. They'd move in that afternoon, and Shelley suggested that since it was only ten maybe they could have breakfast and talk.

Frank agreed. The way he said 'talk' made it sound mysterious, but that was Shelley's way. Cutting up through the streets Frank said the only thing wrong with Tangier was the number of beggars, to which Shelley replied that though they were poor they might be happier than he imagined.

'Whoever gave you the idea that the poor can be happy?' Frank retorted, not sure how serious Shelley was being.

'Who is happy then? The rich?'

'Nobody's happy,' Frank said. 'There's no such thing as happiness except when you are doing work for yourself that at the same time is helping other people.'

'You don't want much,' Shelley laughed, 'except the Millenium maybe.' They turned a corner and went into a teashop-patisserie.

Shelley ordered coffee and croissants: 'It's no use giving money to beggars. They get to know you and hound you to death. It does no good. Things have to get worse before they

286

get better. If all these people didn't like being poor they'd get up and change it.'

'Who are you preaching to?' Frank demanded. 'They might want help in getting started. And what are we doing except sitting here and spreading the butter on thick?' Shelley slapped him on the shoulder with a conspiratorial laugh: 'One thing at a time, Frank.'

'What thing?' Frank wanted to know.

'Maybe I'll tell you,' Shelley said, 'though there's a catch in it, unless you want to pull out now and not listen further. You're all right to help, and you're the sort of man we want on this job.'

'I'm listening,' Frank said. 'Let me know what I might want to pull out of, first.'

'Can you drive? You have a licence? I didn't ask you that. I want to know whether you can make with the clutch on rough roads and open ground. I take it you've been in the army, that you can fire a gun, read a map, throw a bomb? Don't get excited. All I asked was can you drive? Sure, sure, you've got all the right answers, except that your sweet wife is pregnant and waiting for a new little Frank to pop out in beautiful Tangier. Stop telling me, man.'

'Belt up, and get on with it, you clever bastard, and spill those fags. I forgot to get some this morning. Black Spanish ones, not those Yank coffin nails.' Shelley's hand shook slightly at the light, as if imitating shell-shock he might one day get, his laugh grating Frank's nerves, then telling how he'd been drumming around Morocco and Algeria a year or so, and that he'd done all manner of work, not for money, you get me? For principles, though he'd taken some beigebacks now and again for stamp money to supplement his ill-gotten savings from Mad Avenue, New York City.

Frank was learning nothing from this insane spiel, didn't like jokes or smokescreens. Shelley asked if he was partial to the violent life and Frank said he could manage it if it came his way, or if he walked into it.

'Or drove into it?' Shelley supposed he'd heard of the war of independence in Algeria, and Frank said he'd supposed right, but what was he getting at? 'The fact,' Shelley went on, 'that the FLN are losing. They're desperate for certain things, and that means everything: rifles, shells, men, printed matter – such as maps and guerilla manuals in Arabic printed you-know-where. I'm going down in a fort-night, and want a co-driver to play a banjo by my side, strum that wheel when I'm knocked up from the shakes of the rocky trail. It'll take a few days to reach that rendezvous point (the way I have to frigging well go) and most of the time the humps are far from smooth.'

Frank felt himself getting the shakes, too. Shelley wanted to know if the job was accepted and Frank said yes after a bare minute of packed thought that he'd sort out when it was too late to back down from – not that he could imagine wanting to, all change being good as long as you never for a second thought it might be bad. And wasn't this something he'd wanted all his life but considered to be nothing more than an impossible vision? To get out of his spiralled airtight shell and carry violence to the enemy camp instead of letting it run amok and cause destruction in his own? His anguish had been in abeyance during the year of life-change, but on drifting into Africa the bare bones of his own construction had sharpened again, surfaced.

Shelley said that no frontiers were marked where they would go. The real border between Morocco and Algeria was sealed by the Monice line, a great electrified fence running from the sea to the desert edge that not even a gnat could flutter over without getting its stones scorched. Apart from that there were six million mines patterned around, everyone counted by the FLN! So they'd set off in a lorry loaded with crates of guns and ammunition, bales of printed matter, to a point south of this mined and electrified frontier in the wilderness of Adam and the Holy Bible where they'd wait for a truck to reach them from the other side, then switch loads and head back north. The half dozen recruits they'd take would stay there, be lifted into the Khabylie or Monts des Ksour as reinforcements to carry on the good fight.

Frank asked why he'd been chosen when Tangier was full of bums and loafers only too glad of a few thousand francs. 'Let's say it's for old times' sake,' Shelley said, 'in honour of brandy on the Majorcan boat – and because a bum would be no good on this kind of job.'

'Aren't there enough Moroccans jumping for a chance?'

'Sure. Except that they want to stay in Algeria. The others, well, I shan't say they can't be trusted, but there are good markets even inside Morocco for gear like this. Ever heard of dissident tribesmen? The Rif mountains? Abd el Krim? Untimely cravings for autonomy waiting to be sup-plied with guns by Hi-jackings Incorporated? It's just that those (no names, what?) who shell this stuff out want it to get there for the purpose intended. I'm an old hand at it. And they trust me to find the right assistants.'

'You mean it's dangerous?'

'If it isn't you won't go?'

'I like to know things.'

'Do you see any shell-holes in me, any craters in my skull?'

Frank asked when they started, and Shelley, never having imagined it would be so easy to inveigle him into the job, mentioned a big garage on the outskirts of town. 'At seven a.m. on the 18th – which leaves you two weeks to set up a little love nest in the Frenchman's apartment and get Myra a good servant to wait on her while you're away. I know a fatima who's out of a job, a jolly, middle-aged, veiled woman who won't let Myra lift a finger.'

Frank did not know how to tell her. A few days after

289

moving into the new flat he said he was going on a motor trip with Shelley, to deliver some stuff to a friend of his who lived in a Kasbah beyond the Atlas Mountains. It would be interesting to see the country down there, so they'd be taking off in ten days, and be away that length of time. He'd like her to come with them, but didn't see that it'd be all that wise, with less than a couple of months to go before the baby was expected.

'It's a good chance of seeing the country,' she said, 'but try not to be away too long.'

The flat was large, airy and sedate, scrupulously respectable, a place he'd never lived in before. The standard was similar to the house of Myra and George, almost the sort of place they would have chosen if they'd come out here together. He grinned at the sight of it, wouldn't have known what to think if he hadn't been going away so soon and if it hadn't, after all, been in a foreign country.

'Ten days,' he said, 'and no longer. Miriam will look after you. I'll give her a bonus so's she can buy stuff for her family.'

Shelley called one morning and took him to a bookshop near the Fez market. Rain pummelled the town, as if the Atlantic were filtering through its gutters. Ships' hooters sounded from the mist-blocked straits. 'This is bad for the roads,' Shelley said in the taxi, 'but as long as we can get over the Big Atlas in one piece we'll be O.K.'

Frank looked at the titles while Shelley went through to the back. The only books in English were dirty books, and when Frank opened one which set off with a bang on the first page, a tight-trousered Moroccan youth in dark glasses tapped his elbow and beckoned him to the back room.

A man sat at a table, facing Shelley. He was well-built, yet his face seemed frail, with open and delicate features, spectacles and receding grey hair. There was a notice board on one wall, a map of Africa on another, with Tangier a flea-dot on the very edge. 'I'll speak English,' the man said – as if he could have spoken Swahili just as well, 'for the benefit of our friend' – meaning Frank. 'All I want to know, because Mr Jones has vouched for you and I take his opinion sincerely, is whether you want the money paid to you in Tangier, or on a bank in Gibraltar.'

Frank couldn't speak. 'I'm sorry,' the man said, 'but I absolutely refuse to pay you in dollars.'

He held his rage back: 'I don't want money for this work.'

'The last person who said that turned out to be a spy.'

Shelley stood up angrily: 'I didn't bring the spy along. Look, Frank, don't play hard to get. The reality is always a little sordid. Just go along with it. It's a hell of a lot smoother that way.'

Frank understood, not being without his rock-bottom sense of realism, saying that if a condition of his being allowed to go was to accept money, then he preferred payment when he came back. It wasn't his habit to get paid until after the work was done. 'They don't do that where I come from.'

'You're not there any more,' Shelley said.

'Part of me is, or I wouldn't be doing this job. I'm not in it for kicks and I'm not out for money. We can talk about that when we get back, otherwise I don't go.' They discussed it now, in French, and then in Arabic when they thought Frank was getting the gist of it. He wasn't, stayed out front looking at the books until Shelley came to say that stalemate had been broken by their giving in. Frank was surprised that an issue had been made of it at all. 'That's how they are,' Shelley said. 'Everybody has to learn.'

Frank spent an hour in the American library, went in for a few minutes out of the rain. He picked up a volume of Arab stories and read one, about how a stream had reached the edge of the desert and was in danger of being sucked away completely by the sand. The stream knew that its destiny was to cross the desert but it didn't know how. A voice said that the wind got across safely enough, so why couldn't a river? 'Let yourself be absorbed by the wind, and the wind will get you across.' But the river didn't want to lose its individuality. 'You won't lose it,' said the voice, 'because the wind will absorb all your moisture, carry you over the desert, let you fall like rain, and then you'll be a river once more.' 'But I shall be a different river,' said the river. 'You'll be different after any experience,' argued the voice, 'and that is all to the good. But if you stay here trying uselessly to get across you'll end up as a salty quagmire. If you let the wind carry you over the desert you'll then know what your true identity is.'

Frank liked the tale, wondered why he'd had to come as far as Tangier for the accident of reading it. Going south, he'd see the desert, but not roam far into it. The slow days were beating down his spirit, and he wanted to set off, though at the same time aching at the thought of having to leave Myra at such a point in their lives.

He woke at four o'clock, more disturbed than he'd imagined, birds of prey and an insomniac beast worrying him all night. He had coffee and bread in the kitchen to a low murmur of sleepless people out of the Emsallah district on one side, and a roistering noise from a couple of cabaret places on the other. A boat-hooter sounded in the port, a low, dreadful gut-mover indicating a funnel and row of lights about to set off for another land, which caught at his stomach like an ancestral voice, tugged at his journeyman legs. But it's not so bad, he thought, because I'm moving as well, in another direction, but moving just the same. It's harder for those said good-bye to, for Myra whose got to stay among all the indications of what our life's been like. I only want to live properly with her; to work hard by the day, until life is so absorbing that it jets by. Yet his return was only ten days away, and there was no use trying to wring three months of sentiment out of it.

He did not know how to say good-bye. He stood in the dark bedroom. He had never said good-bye to anyone he was in love with. The thought of leaving her turned him to salt, to ice. He stood there, her face hardly visible, trying to tell himself he wasn't in love with her, that to be so would mean a defeat for all he had lately surmised and stood for. But he was leaving too much, felt as if about to drop from the last grip of the lifesaving rope end. He blamed such thoughts on the morning, when the brain was clear and ruthless, showing in true light one's bravery and apprehension.

She felt his presence by the bed. 'Are you going?'

He waited a moment: 'I don't have to. Nobody's dragging me. If only they were.'

'You're saying this for my sake,' she said, opening her eyes. 'I'll see you quite soon.'

'I'm a fool,' he said. 'I don't want to leave you both.'

She sat up. 'I know. But don't make it too difficult. I know how much you want to go.'

'I love you,' he said. 'My roots are in you.' You did love me, she thought. You're incapable of love. You've wanted to be free of it for so long that now you've made it, you've won. 'Just take care,' she said, 'that's all.'

'I'm running guns to the Algerians,' he said.

'I know. I'm glad. But Miriam already told me.' She hoped that Shelley knew there was no danger in taking him from her at such a time.

'If we can burst that frontier we'll be O.K. I'll be careful. I'm cool enough' – feeling at last that there was no limit to what he could do. 'I've come full circle, going off on a thing like this. I feel as if I left the factory only yesterday, got paid up, clocked-out, and took a plane down. There's a natural connection between that work and what I'm going to do. My muscles feel it, and my head as well. It's not much perhaps, but it means everything to me. I used to dream of being able to *do something*, but I'm not doing anything. I see that now.

I'm just being myself. I've learned to be myself. I want to prove it finally though. Then I'll come back. You'll be all right. I know you'll look after yourself.'

'I've got Miriam and a few friends. You make it sound more final now. Do you think you won't come back?'

'No. I'll come back. This is just dawn talk.' But the tears bled out of her. Desolation would rend her bones and close her eyes, but there was no one to tell, Frank least of all. He roared her name, unfragmented syllables thrown out by his exploding heart. He felt it emptying, knelt by the bed, his hand under the clothes, smoothing her breasts, her enlarging belly. 'He'll be there when you come back,' she said, her throat hardening into firmness, 'but not if you come back too late.'

'I've got so much to look forward to. That sort of thing used to frighten me, but not now. It'll be an easy trip. Shelley's been there before, and swears it's a piece of cake. It's just the fact of leaving you for any time at all that creases me.'

It was cruel and weird, this voluntary wilful parting. He kissed her and left, casually, as if coming back in ten minutes with fresh bread for their breakfast.

She lay still, the door slamming through her, feeling that he'd never open it again. If he weren't back in two weeks she would take a plane to London, go to the house in Buckinghamshire and wait for her baby which, by time scheme but not physical possibility of touch, could have been George's. After that, she would carve out her own life as Frank was carving out his, in action and not love. If he survived his crossing of the desert he would know where to find her. In that sense they belonged to each other and she would always wait for him.

The blue light of dawn clawed at her belly. She had a baby, and love must die. The universe was taking it back. Where the claws of love had rested the flesh was rotten. Frank knows this, and is acting it out in the only way possible, by leaving me. Will God allow the world to be proletarianized in this way? He's emptied me of love, but I feel better than I've ever felt in my life. To live out a great emptiness is to fulfil yourself completely. I can't put into words what has happened.

23

A WET ATLANTIC wind lurched in from the chopping sea, and all the clouds, ragged and green, looked as if they'd decided to come south and make a party of it. 'One big downpour,' Shelley said, 'and every dip of the road between here and the desert will be a lake. In which case we won't get through this side of a month.' He decided on the coast road, rather than risk the mountains beyond Tetuan. Egrets stared into pools by the open roadside, their reflections like question marks upside down. 'If you hadn't looked so much like a working man, our friend at the book-shop wouldn't have smelled two rats. Especially when you wouldn't take his gelt,' he went on, continuing an earlier argument.

An anaemic forest spread out from the road. 'He can stuff his gelt where it belongs,' Frank said. 'What do I want money for? I don't care if my job isn't pensionable.'

The word HIELO was written plain and big along the side of their covered lorry. Ice it is, Frank thought, but bugger-all whisky to go with it. He'd brought nothing except two cartons of cigarettes and some money, and couldn't imagine a more perfect way to depart. Shelley was at the wheel, and Frank took the spare seat, a closed map on his knee. Four Moslems lay on bales and boxes behind, smoked and talked, well-built, thuggish men of about forty wearing khaki trousers and battledress under blanket-like burnouses. Another six would flag them at a crossroads beyond Fez.

A squad of police manned a roadblock at the next junction, a zone of short steel spikes laid out like a carpet. 'You'd better make with the Arabic, or we'll have to use those guns on these bastards.'

Shelley pulled in: 'Keep quiet.'

Frank saw himself back in Tangier by midday, either laughing about their misadventure in Myra's arms, or cursing his luck behind bars, with Myra trudging up to the Kasbah jail with a billy-can of rice and mutton, kif-fags and tea.

The Moroccans in the back were motioned outside, not a word said, rifle spouts and law-faces moving around the lorry. Shelley's hand stretched from the cab. The officer looked at his papers, saluted as if a bee had flown out from them and stung him, and waved them on. The Moroccans climbed back, and Shelley manoeuvred the lorry through a gap in the spikes.

'What was on those papers?' Frank asked as they turned up into the olive-grown hills. 'Khrushchev's signature?'

'The Prophet himself signed it,' Shelley laughed, 'then Mao Tse Tung. Don't think we're the only lorry on Route Twenty-One. Not that there are many. As always, the north fares better, because you can always find ships to put stuff down along that coast. You'd be shocked if you knew how many Englishmen were making a fortune on that run, with their little ships from Gibraltar. Trust the Limeys with their little ships.'

In the afternoon, under a lead-coloured sky, the lorry roared its guts beyond Meknès and up into the Middle Atlas.

Snow soon piled on either side of the road, curving and twisting to seven thousand feet. 'This is nothing,' Shelley said – though no one complained, 'you'll be crying out for water in a few days and having your nuts scorched off.'

'I'd have brought a keg of brandy if I'd known,' Frank said. 'You mean to say they're fighting a desperate civil war over there for country like this? Don't blow your top, commissar. I'm making a joke. I know it's rich country for all that. The Yorkshire Moors are rich, as well, snowed-up or not. Still, the desert is healthy, for hermits and scorpions. At least I could have brought my skis though, if I'd known about this.'

Peaks and rolling flanks were bolsters of snow, a vast rumpled skybed that someone had left in a hurry. The sight and smell of snow when they pulled-up for a legstretch made him almost lightheaded. Moroccan shepherds huddled their flocks into rough shelters. Frank was salaamed when he gave one a cigarette. A knife wind scraped along the drifts, dusted the road that had been cleared by ploughs a few days before. A bus, its top piled with bales and suitcases, passed at a speed even Shelley shook his head at. Veiled women and Old Testament faces of impassive men gazed from inside.

The snow made Frank feel spiritually clean. He'd never seen so much of it, nor been so high among mountains, nor so many miles from any churning sea. This last fact impressed him most, and he wondered whether the moon got this far inland. Certainly the sun did. A bleak thumbprint showed for a minute from a mountain shoulder. A Peugeot cruised by, a French family up from some holiday oasis, woman driving, crewcut head of a man leaning out with a ciné camera aimed at the sheepfold and forest of high cedars humped and laden with snow. Snow took the sense of density out of a forest, made it seem more accessible in that it widened the space between trunks. Larch trees and ilex patched the cedars, hard to pick out unless one had the trained eyes of Shelley. 'I expected a desert and I got Siberia,'

298

Frank said, glad of his cap, overcoat and heavy boots.

By nightfall they were over the Middle Atlas, and ready to bed down near Midelt. In spite of bitter cold the Moroccans slept in the lorry, guarding in turn the stuff they were moving south. A fire in the hotel yard huddled them in talk except for the blackest hour of the night. Frank and Shelley drank Pernod at the kerosene-lit bar inside. Frank asked why there was so much unemployment in Tangier and Morocco. It didn't puzzle him, yet he wanted to know.

'Since the French pulled out of Morocco the industry has collapsed. Also, a developing country needs a statistical system to measure its progress and potential, otherwise, it doesn't move. You can't do anything until you get one. When Tangier became part of Morocco, forty banks closed in one day. And when money stops circulating, the economy stops running – what little there was.'

'People can work, even without money,' Frank said, 'until things get properly organized. It's better than not working at all.'

Shelley smoked a pipe on long hours of driving, and lit up now. 'They'd work for food, if there was any to hand out. They're primitive enough for that. And they're good workers, in spite of what a Frenchman might tell you. But there's no surplus flour to pay them with – unless it's a handout from Uncle Sam.'

'Maybe it's a case of them having the wrong sort of government.'

'Some people in the big cities are trying to alter it, but it's hard. Most Moroccans are tribal and primitive – let's face it – and they don't want things to change.'

'It's the towns that matter,' Frank said. 'Sling me some more of that water. This stuff's punching holes in my stomach.'

'The Chinese Revolution began with the peasants. Same in Cuba and Vietnam. Algeria as well. You're old-fashioned, still harping on 1917. I don't have much faith, Frank, in the modern masses, as too many individuals are called. The only magnanimous action of modern times was a passive and unconscious one – that they allowed the hydrogen bomb to get cooked up. Which is where we come in. Guerilla wars are the only possible ones from now on.'

'You talk as if capitalism is finished,' Frank said. 'It's not that easy. I wish it was.'

Shelley laughed: the idealist with practical solutions. 'Capitalism is a luxury liner washed up on an island: the people already there swarm down to the shore and loot it, to rebuild their own boats with its help – almost from nothing.'

'Have you ever tried to make a nut and bolt?' Frank asked, fed-up with his flippant images.

'No, but I've known many people who *can* make them. They're a dime a dozen. I'm getting stoned. I've got to sleep. Allow me to flip off to my pad like a cross-eyed penguin.'

Through the rock-rock-rocky mountains and the pure-and-driven snow, balancing on bootlace roads with the smell of pine cones and nostril-burning frost to clear the head, Frank became as adept at such turnings as Shelley, as if they'd been on the trek for weeks. Stapled by front bend and backmirror hairpin, the new land blinded him to past or future. Trees hammered the sky over them like a circus tent in which only thoughts and sensations of the present could perform. In spite of plenty to eat and smoke and a shower last night at Midelt, he already felt as if he were living rough, a tramp with a purpose, sharpened by driving and fatigued by lack of past or future.

The country was cold (even at midday), stony, laced with iron trees, vast. The world is small until you come to the wilderness, he thought, then you see how big it is. Beyond the desert there was jungle, land still unexplored, unsurveyed, unconquered.

They followed a narrow river hemmed in by sheer rock, going under a tunnel at one place. The first palmtrees appeared, stuck like worn-out mops along the water-edge, thickening to a belt of green on either side. Luxuriant green snaked between barriers of red-coloured rocky pinnacles, the narrow wedge of a valley opening towards blue sky. Under high sedate palms grew orange, lemon, pomegranate trees, flourishing by the knife-glint of irrigation ditches cutting out from the main bountiful stream.

Seen from above it was a pattern of glass fragments, crystal strips scattered in green chaos, yet made orderly and precise by the water rations delivered to each plot or field. Nothing had come about by accident, only by labour and brain, time and patience, a battle for increase against the nearby desert – so marvelled at by Frank that he once misjudged the acute switch of a curve and almost shot the whole of them down towards it.

They stopped for a meal of cold beans and mutton, bread and mint tea. Filling watercans and loading them on the lorry, he tried to imagine what Myra might be doing at this moment, saw her dimly in the flat wearing her maternity dress reading and relaxing on the Frenchman's grand divan, abstracted and distant from him, as he was from her, certainly. He loved her like that, hoped to be back with her soon, to be there when the baby was born. He heard its cries already, brought to the nearby stream as an antidote to the desert.

West and south from the last village of their trip, dusk-clouds higher than the highest reddening escarpment were banked up tall and rugged with pink fire, as if part of a wall enclosing the whole world in whose middle he seemed to be standing. Transfixed, he stood alone, a clank of buckets and gabble of women at the well behind.

The light at dusk was of a half-clear quality that made him doubt the power of his eyes, rub them and wonder whether he needed glasses. But wind and dust was the breath of evening desert in midwinter. He expected to feel particles of snow against his skin but got grit and sand, differing temperatures striated one within the other. The sharp line of spectacularly jagged cloud seemed like real wall from this village of gardens and date groves, goat-bells and camel-grunts. They would head towards it at night, as if darkness were the only way to get through safely, no meaning left of its terror. They would come back that way, return under its mounds and hillocks – if it were still there.

Smoking, shuffling his boots on a boulder, he turned to see whether this same red wall surrounded everything. Since it rarely rained, why were such big clouds gathering? All he could see was a deeper fallen night, a corrugated ceiling to the spreading darkness, with land the same non-colour. He returned to his more livid views of the Hamada du Guir, but they had gone, red wall vanished – though perhaps only the deepening night concealed it. The nearness of the desert made him feel like a machine rather than a man, its capacity well-marked and he his own toolsetter for it. He walked back into the village, finding his way in darkness over stones and rubbish.

All number plates had been taken from the lorry, and they had given up their passports to the village agent. Frank felt glad as he handed his over, as if the last of all labels had been unpinned from his back, though remembering how impressed he had been on receiving it.

The road soon worsened, headlights bucking at rocks and sliding gravel. They drew back as if shaking a fist at the sky, then dipped. The lorry rocked, like a lifeboat in a storm disregarding what other boats flee from. Bringing his head forward from the seat Frank looked out at lights and dust, the occasional bush, desert rose, or rockhump sliding out of vision like an escaping footpad who had had second

302

thoughts. They moved slowly south in the bitter night cold of an empty three-thousand foot plateau, yet it seemed that the way was a strip of land only a few feet wide, and that they would pitch into nearby oblivion should the lorry, on one of its two-wheeled tilts, slip right over and roll, roll, roll.

'This is the safer route,' Shelley explained. 'We're by-passing a Moroccan post where the officer isn't so sympathetic to the Algerians, believe it or not. He'd hold us up a few hours, which would throw us into daylight and get us seen by one of the flying napalm wagons. So we'll go this way – because any rational man would think it's suicide. The French don't look much where we're going.'

'What about these lights?' Frank said. 'They've had me worried all the way from the village. We can be seen for miles. Or don't we bother about that sort of risk?'

'We're a long way from the border yet,' Shelley laughed. 'I'll clip them off when the time comes.'

Frank hung on when the sway took him unawares, thinking that a man could get seasick this way. But no one did. Ten of them were packed in behind, all smoking shit-fags, except Shelley who smoked his in a pipe, sucked away as if it were whisky in the bowl. Frank couldn't imagine what lay ahead in the way of landscape or human events. He was spinning out the rope of his life behind. It dragged along the ground, and only when it touched hard rock did it disturb him. In front was space, untouched spiritual and corporeal territory, darkness for a sharpening mind to enter and fill up on. Unable to consider the past, he tried feeding on the future, but shied back from it because nothing was there. Only idleness has a future. Work, fatigue, dust and grit imposed the prison-minutes of passing time on him. He had to think on the present, dwell on it with the great concentration that can only be employed by a man who has no future. 'These are the times when I'd like to read,' he said. 'At least you can see something in daytime.'

'Recite a piece of poetry, then,' Shelley laughed, 'or a passage from the Bible. Isn't that what the English do when they're in a tight spot? If we can't rub the boredom out of our lives we're no use as people.'

Frank smiled, in response to a grin he didn't see but knew had happened. Those clearcut platitudinous teeth of Shelley's will be the ruin of him, he thought, like the third match in the trenches. Three grins, and a mortar bomb's got them all.

By night and in secret they crept nearer to the border. 'It's no use looking for it on that map,' Shelley said, maintaining the air of uncertainty. 'According to mine we're in Algeria already, so take over while I hand out the medal ribbons, will you?'

Lights off, towards dawn they stuck in an unexpected pool of sand. 'You bloody night-owl,' Frank said. 'I thought you knew the way a bit better than this.'

'You can't stop mistakes. What sort of a holiday do you think gun-running is?'

'I always thought it was a man in a turban,' Frank said, 'picking off Beau Geste with a silver-handled blunderbuss and then getting signed up for Hollywood.'

Shelley rubbed his greying, close-cropped head. 'No, it's just getting jammed in a patch of lousy no-good sand when you're not expecting it, and at the most god-awful time.'

Everyone worked, with rakes, planks and shovels. Rubber burned from wheels uselessly spinning, and the futile grind of the motor seemed to broadcast its trouble across the blackness. Shelley tried again, but every attempt to get it out by engine-power dug the wheels further in. He raged at the unexpected: 'We'll have to race for that ravine now, to drop in safe before dawn.'

The fire they were playing with was beginning to burn

304

their fingers. Frank wanted to get at the wind and throttle it – in spite of the fact that, as Shelley said, it would obliterate their tracks. Its erratic moaning made him sweat. The sky was an owl's eye they were crawling around in. Stuck fast in the sand, the whole dawn world of the wilderness was hooting softly over them – until totally drowned by a raving lorry engine like a massive dum-dum drill dividing his life with the maximum pain and clumsiness.

Four planks were under the tyres, sand spaded clear. They were a team of horses and, all their goods scattered as if to start a market where one had never been before, the wheels gripped and climbed along the wood. Frank felt like cheering. The sand was grey grit, bone dry, and once off the planks they were in at again. The pool had turned into a lake, a morass of dust. This was the raw, real sweat of life, plagued by a burning cold wind and empty stomachs, tindermouths opening from the extreme backbone of life, trials and hazards before dawn where everything is impregnated with the total discouragement of universal past happenings. If the spirit can recognize this feeling and laugh at it, boot it down and go back to hope and work, then the book is closed and the trek without print or maps can begin.

Frank pushed, lifted, heaved with all his strength. He lay on his back shovelling sand from the oily stinking undergut of the lorry, with danger of it subsiding, pressing him down into suffocation and death. 'I've done some rum work in my time,' he said to the uncomprehending Moroccan working the same seam nearby, 'shifted all sorts o' rammel, but this lot takes the bleddy cake, mate.'

Shelley knelt by, a half-knowing glance at the overall situation. Frank was becoming an unknown man to him: the broadening of his accent back to a deeper Midland Limey made him intimidating, a stranger, lying there at his ferocious and vital work. But the mood passed when the lorry was clear again.

305

Frank lit a cigarette. While working he had forgotten the wind. Now it was back in his ears, functional at least in that it dried his sweat, stiffened the dishrags of his clothes. He saw himself in the oblong mirror of the lorry as he climbed in, conscious of his increasing strength. His short hair was grey from ash and sand, face pallid showing a wide grin with even teeth, arms apart as he heaved himself in, ready for the death-grip of whatever might get at him. But in his face and frame, subtlety was on the march, infiltrating, penetrating, ignoring his parapets, swarming into the desert of himself.

Dawn was breaking, free-associating ink spreading into daylight: black, blue, green and red. The land was uneven to the east, but still fairly level. Shelley drove, and the lorry went like a rhinoceros in panic. They held on, wishing long life to their bones. Some rocks were hit as if the lorry would split in two, send guns flying, bullets spitting and grenades coughing over humps and hollows. Was it like this on the moon? Even the grey dust in saucers of earth looked cosmic in the spreading light. Yesterday had no connection with this.

One case of rifles had been given out. 'If any point of doubtful return exists on the trip,' Shelley said, 'this is it.' French planes flew from airfields at Colomb Bechar, eighty miles east, and patrols operated now and again from Meridja. FLN scouts in the area would warn of any approaching danger. But nothing would be seen if all went as it normally did, quietly. The only people met would be those of the FLN waiting to come for the supplies.

24

'WE STAY HERE all day,' Shelley said when they reached the ravine, 'and tonight trundle fifteen dark miles east and hope to meet up with the boys coming to get the stuff.' It was easily said, and to move your finger a few inches here and there on an empty map. The ravine was a narrow cutting in a country of many similar concealments. They covered the lorry with cloths, sand and thornbush to make it invisible from the air, and from land unless someone stumbled right into the hiding place. 'If that happens,' Shelley grinned, 'he'll never see mom or pop again.'

Out of the twelve, six were continually deployed among clefts and boulders surrounding the ravine. Warning signals would not only bring the rest up to reinforce them, but a further system of ankle-trips set out by Shelley with great skill and patience ensured all twelve firing at once without any voice being heard – though this was elaborate precaution rather than seriously intended defence. However, Frank couldn't see how a more skilful ambush could have been set, a perfect trap in the middle of nowhere. It was a combination of guard and ambush, a magnetized web of defence known in the Chinese manual as the 'spider layout'. Of the two Brens, Frank manned one, and a Moroccan held the other. The rest had rifles and grenades.

Frank was flattened beside a rock, an enfiladed view of the plain matched to the Moroccans strung around to the right whom he knew to be there but could not see. The half conscious workings of his brain were muzzled by the uncannily sharp alertness with which his eyes registered the landscape they were to watch. He felt like a boat out in this grey and beige wilderness, rocky plateau in front, ravine behind. The sun burned, his ears still filled with the sound of the engine racing as, towards the last dawn, its tyres had spun to escape the rut they'd sunk into, as his own mind and body had formerly and likewise crazed him in the thousand useless revolutions of his own spirit. The land turned a dim red, then purple, the horizon shimmering, a line beyond which the remains of a man's soul might find final rest, or the ways and means of change that he had always deserved.

The last time he'd held a loaded Bren was on an army range eleven years ago, and not hoping to kill anyone. To wait was theatrical, because waiting meant thought, a continual monologue of destruction and fulfilment. I'm waiting in case the French show up, when I'd give a lot for it to be the British, because they are the ones I should be doing my nut against. Each to his own, and the rest will look after itself. If Kenya was still on I'd make my way there – or somewhere else if I get safe out of this. The past wouldn't come to him, and he didn't know whether to be glad or not. It seemed good that it wouldn't, that it skulked beyond some horizon he'd left behind. His grey eyes glazed the rocks and dips for signs of life. Nothing. Even William Posters blended with the landscape, ghost of the bleak steppe toting a gun, on a level of equality with those who would persecute and prosecute. He hadn't thought of him for months, in any case

– William Posters, that soul-anchor stuck in your craw, those dim jerking pictures flickering on the screen behind your eyes when closed, working bewildering renegade rebel magic on the sentimental layers of your caked heart asking for pity and understanding as he flitted, half butterfly, half oil-rag, between the changing shadows of the past. He had lost his cap, dismantled his face, outspanned his for ever nebulous cause, and walked over the bottomless cliff towards which you – Frank – had been leading him, not quite without knowing it, from the days of consciousness, whenever that was.

Bill Posters, thank God, had died at last in the ruins of Radford-Stalingrad. Frank had seen it, or pictured it as if he had: poor Bill sitting by the wall eating his bread, having given his persecutors the ten-minute slip, relaxed and rested at this small victory, smiling to himself at the peace, and at the good taste of bread, thinking so devoutly how good-looking was that gorgonzola moon above chimney pots he hadn't noticed weren't smoking any more. O Bill, you go off the boil for ten minutes, and the game is up! A crane starts working and smashes an ironball down against the wall he's leaning against (men on night-work because they can't clear this slumland quick enough) and William Posters is crushed to death under the slabs and bricks, beams and fireplaces. Undernourished and hunted, he never stood a chance. They found him dead after digging him out, and nobody recognized him as the William Posters whose legendary name had been on so many walls for a hundred years. So he died, unidentified. He hoped he'd died, but who could tell? Such unknown great men sometimes become ghosts and haunt you long enough for it to last the rest of your life. Unless of course you had a hand in their killing. That would be treachery, but what the hell – you not only had to live but you had to survive as well.

He spat the brandy taste out, a strange stillness, no man

309

visible. He was alone, facing a wind hundreds of miles across. It brought no panic, didn't frighten him. Bravery was something he'd never thought about, like so much else. Overcoming the pain of sun and thirst brought back memories that were sweetened by solitude. Three hours were three days, three months, three years, three decades. He no longer felt a new man. The old man who had gone through his tether and was about to become the new man, perhaps. That was more like it, the old man doing violence to himself and others without knowing it, but the new man knowing it, already committing violence against nature by wanting to overpower the wild stallion of nature that must be held down, gelded, hobbled, and put to use. He remembered the factory vividly, more so than the layout at home, than wife, kids, or furniture. The factory was a permanent set-up in the back rooms of his brain, the violence and rationality of machinery, its benevolence when kept full-tilt at its proper use.

The day would drag on – that was as far as he wanted to see ahead, teeth locked like the fixed bolt of his machinegun. A headache rolled vibrations of the parched wilderness through him, but a grid of clarity before his eyes drew in memories that his brain tried to reject because he hadn't been able to control them, none at all except the one that had landed him here. His heart beat like a flower bomb fixed in the culvert of his own life's iron road, waiting for some long predestined train or convoy to come along. His body lay upon the stillness, stones hot against his fingers.

He had lived most of his life on the assumption that whatever he wanted was unattainable. That bastard, William Posters, had to die, even if Frank had to snuff it with him, leap that cliff with his ten-ton immortal shadow still gripping his back. Posters was too English for this world. He laughed to himself, could afford to out here where it only bounced back in his face. That sponge-man who'd gobbled up his life and fantasy didn't mean a thing any more, that telly-rat and dope-peddler who hammered the nails into hands and brain to stop you moving, whispered that since something in life was unattainable you had to stop reaching for it, that it was better to rot among the slums and ruins of a played-out way of life, persecuted and prosecuted, flitting from wall to shadow whither your own demons pursued you in an ever narrowing maze with misery and failure at the middle. It was about time that crane-ball stunned him into the wickedest oblivion of all – oblivion deserved.

Even in his own pure dreams Frank had felt something in life he might never get, though mulling now in clear day-light, there'd been no reason why he shouldn't. He didn't know at all what it was. Maybe it wasn't attainable in this life (and that was that) but would form the unearned reward of lives coming after him. Perhaps that also was for the birds, for the desert hawk circling and cawing above. But if he led his life to the greatest extent of which he was capable and disregarded this premonition of dreams, then he would break beyond this horizon wall, sensed all his life, whether it was of brick or cloud or ultimately nothing at all.

His dreams and thoughts were ancient and similar: to dissect them would be like chucking a fag into the latrines and pissing it to bits; nothing gained. All he wanted to do was fire a single shot, finish off the shite-hawk or corpse-gosling that went on circling their hideaway.

He pressed a stone-edge onto a scorpion, and the insect's tail, animating like an aerial gone mad, hovered and twisted for the suicide stab. It came. Frank watched it turn grey, and the tiny ants patrolling for it. In half an hour exactly it had gone, his private desert clock wherein six of them made a three-hour guard period. William Posters, his body swinging over that cliff and down through space, wouldn't leave him alone, that snivelling muffle-capped man on the eternal run who'd never had a Bren at his shoulder, and whose fall was followed by the wide-winged bird swooping along the ravine for a quick look and to drop its napalm shit.

A plane flew over at midday, a Mystère jet playing west and south from Colomb Bechar. Frank was edging towards his second round of guard when the hollow, continual boom of its approach rolled like a barrel along the stony earth. When the noise leapt into the sky, he flattened. Shelley had told them there would be no danger. Only the slow ones mattered, and a battle was splintering around the Monts des Ksour, north-east of Colomb, so maybe they were chewing away up there. Head down, Frank felt the sound go over, stayed a half minute before latching himself to the Bren, his fingers on it before the Moroccan took his away and slid back to the ravine.

More sweat piled out than if he'd been walking, certainly not less than when shovelling sand from under the chassis of the stranded lorry. The sun was no longer overhead, and he waited for its decline so that they could move through the cold and more preferable night. Having controlled his body for so many hours between the sun and stones, in perfect stillness and silence, he felt that he had become harder, craftier, and more subtle as a soldier than any who might belong to a national and conscript army.

If only the long day would fall and break its back, get killed like that finished and shared-out scorpion. He poured water on the back of his hand and licked it off. He hadn't eaten, not even in the ravine, felt no hunger left in him. He fed on eighteen months of thought, chewed through and thrown aside like the rammel of sucked-out bones, like the oil-rag Bill Posters didn't get a smell of. But he was dead now, like the past. Bill Posters my vanishing brother, my colossus amigo turning to stone and sinking in quicksand, the multiple dream-deaths that a hero deserves; maybe caught by swarming napalm in the final barbaric ritual of Promethean fire, or edged out by old age after a lifetime of work and

312

wisdom. Who is to say, and who is to care? There was nothing left except the brown paper of himself filling up out of the fertile desert.

That shite-hawk spun into twins now. An aeroplane, birds, the sun – only the sky had life. The twelve men were dead until they got up and walked, moved, or fired a shot. In the ravine Shelley had sat huddled in a shallow cave, Arab music playing low on a transistor small as his hand, saying to Frank that this was always the worst day of the trip, when he felt cut off from mankind and needed proof that the world hadn't been obliterated. Frank smiled. He didn't need proof. If it had been obliterated he would have felt it without any proof.

'Not me,' Shelley said. 'I want to know when to get up and shout for joy.' He looked thin and tense, though no one could call him worried because he was incapable of it.

The sun was on its way down. Frank rubbed his eyes, scraped grit from the corners with his finger nail. Once in Tangier, after a night's booze-up with Shelley on straight red plonk, black specks had jumped before his eyes all next day, as if the midges of summer had taken over the winter air. At the worst it was like walking near a dead paperfire when the wind played on it – specks of all shapes that he actually believed were there and tried to brush away. Shelley laughed that it was his liver acting up because of too much wine.

At five o'clock he wondered if it wasn't happening again, this time the result of rough water heaved up from village wells on the way down. The weakening sun played against him, and he tried to press the dots away, but they hovered to the west, clear cut on the horizon. He didn't think his eyes could betray him at such a time. There were, after all, other men still on the earth. He jerked his foot, a thin piece of string reaching down into the ravine.

The specks had vanished. Shelley was by his side. 'You'll see them again. They may not hit this spot. I can't understand it. They're coming from Morocco, but they're bound to be French, one of their patrols sprung as a surprise. But why Morocco? There's the rub, Frank. Look, see them again?' The second Bren had been moved to form a more solid front, to perfect the spider. Shelley used his glasses. 'I make six.' Frank remembered the manual: if there are more, retreat. If there are less and you can win, attack. He wondered on the state of his gun – which had seemed all right when he'd taken it to pieces, but who could tell? 'If they pass a good distance on either side,' Shelley said, 'it's their lucky day.'

We're a web, Frank thought. He had said nothing while Shelley talked. Flies always come into a web, just as rats can never resist a trap, even when they can't see it, even in the middle of a plain like this when they could easily miss it. Noiselessly, almost without movement, Shelley was somewhere else. He checked the signal string around his ankle. His breath was shallow, forceless, as if he had no lungs and his windpipe opened on the empty air of the desert, a nothing-pump of sun-stroke and gut-ache. It would take them an hour to get here. From behind them a white light flickered once. If the plane had spotted us, he thought, they'll fan out and make a web of their own, a war of spiders. Still far off, they came in line, as if to cut across their front, in which case there'd be no contact. He steeled himself not to drink water. Gravel chafed his boots but he wouldn't move to empty them. Shelley was back: 'If we pull off this ambush, we retreat the way we came. There'll be no time to spare.'

'What about the lorry, the crates of stuff?'

'The others will come for it during the night. They know our stopping places. We've done all we can.'

'Or will have,' Frank said.

At dusk the six men came towards the high rocky flank of the ravine. Waiting: they were moving towards his gun like one end of a micrometer being wound in in slow motion, to meet the other end which was him. They were drawn by

314

thousandths of an inch, a boon speed to his precision patience. He eased in the trigger at a few hundred yards. They were ambling along as if ready for a night's camp and a meal, two of them laughing. They were well-spaced, called for a wider, chancier arc of fire than Frank would have thought ideal for an ambush now that they were face to face, but enfilading rifles enveloped the first and last man as they stumbled under the wall of bullets. The kick at his shoulder was the joy of life.

The gun worked: greased, set, and aimed, half a magazine blew out of its spout towards their feet. He was human in that he had acted without thought; inhuman in that he hadn't felt terror while waiting. They were eaten up, tossed into death. It all seemed so quick and thoughtless, silent and pantomimic under the canopy of noise that was terrifying after the long wait. The day seemed to have begun only now, and it was dusk.

One of Shelley's Moroccans was killed stone dead. There was no dust. It was too quick for confusion, a silent horror film you couldn't wind back, noise tacked on later when remembered. He was afraid of such first-time success. The Moroccans smashed open the air, hurling grenades as they moved over like panthers, approached firing into the bodies, taking less than no chances, as if they hadn't had their money's worth and wanted a full scale battle. A cold wind blew, shattering Frank's bones. He glanced at the scattered bodies, and lit a cigarette. He felt more empty than safe, more sure of himself than sorry for them, his feet riveted.

It was quiet before complete darkness, an anticlimax of boredom and irritation, everyone sullen, hating to speak. Shelley had collected the soldiers' papers: 'They've all got German names, except the officer. Maybe they were Alsatians. Maybe. The French are demoralized, but they're winning. It often happens. It breeds viciousness, and lack of

315

caution – but they've got too much stuff and too many men.'

Frank set up the Bren on a rock, trained it on the lorry: 'We'd better head south-east, then work north to Monts des Ksour. You said there was fighting there.'

Shelley took this suggestion as a joke, post-action madness he'd expected even from Frank, but which would quickly pass. He gave orders to unload the lorry: 'We leave the equipment here. There'll be quite a heap of it with the stuff they're bringing in from the dead. The Moroccans are heading east on foot to link up with the FLN tonight, who'll send a truck for this. We've got to make tracks for Tangier and report back. Our work's done for this trip.'

Frank felt anything but mad, saw Shelley as only wanting to skedaddle now from the consequences of his skill, and leave the dump of arms to take its chance with whoever might be first to reach the spot, soon to be clearly marked by weaving and hungry birds. 'We're fifteen miles short. The only sure way of getting this across is to drive it as soon as it's dark.'

'It's all taken care of. They know we're here.'

'We can't be sure of that,' Frank said. 'Whichever way we go, it's dangerous. That patrol came from where we didn't expect it. It's death to go back that way.'

'And death to push on.'

'So we push on. Get them boxes up. I'm delivering this stuff – and myself. They need anyone they can get.'

Shelley looked into the Bren, opening towards him, a grey fossilized toothless mouth that struck in neither east nor west but straight at unresisting points of the body. The Moroccans stopped work, understood, and waited. 'Listen, you lunatic bastard, if you want to go into Algeria, then hit the trail with them. I've been there before, and it's no Thanksgiving. I'm heading back for Tangier. There are other loads to be brought down.'

316

'Not to this place,' Frank said. 'Not after this ambush. I want that lorry, and I'm not going without the stuff. You're coming with me as well. I can't speak to these others – yet – unless you interpret.'

'Why are you doing this?' Shelley's eyes diminished, his face skeletal from sand and work, thirst and the unexpected situation they had dropped into.

'There aren't any more "whys" in my life,' Frank said calmly. He couldn't go back; every footfall or turn of the wheel made it more impossible. The bullets from the Bren had stitched a row of foolproof locks across the door of the past.

'It's crazy thinking; it's suicide. We're all finished unless we go back. The French have half a dozen patrols beamed on us. You're ignoring the rules, Frank. We'll end up like those poor bastards, with even less reason in it. It won't work.'

'It will,' he argued. 'If it doesn't, it will still work. That's how I think. If you do something, it works, whether you fail or not. In any case, you say we'll draw French patrols on us. Well, the Algerians in the Monts des Ksour are having a hard time according to the agent at the last village, so it's possible that what is sent against us might relieve them a bit. It's no more dangerous for us than for them. We're mobile. We've got good chances. This country's broken enough to hide us. We've got as good a chance of surviving as any others of the FLN. If the uproar is to the north, we're free and mobile and can strike from the south. I'm learning quick. We'll pick up others. We'll be the surprise party.'

'I still think it's suicide. It's a hard deal.' But he was changing his mind, wanting only the final nail in the argument.

'We'll get through. Hump that stuff and get everybody in, or I'll let fly so much lead that even the shite-hawks won't know where to find you.'

Out of the desert, into the desert. The loaded unlit truck

stumbled from the ravine without lights but going steadily in one direction. Frank felt that the desert was the only place where he would find something. People might say he'd had everything: job, wife, children. What more was there? He wanted to go into the desert to find out. What there was was the wanting to go into the desert. Only in the desert did one learn. He had learned all that there was to learn outside the desert. Something in him was going to be reconstituted, and he, by his own effort and actions, had put himself into the position to achieve it. His life had to be filled from the fountains of his own desert, the cruel ash of his own heart. The ovenwinds would send him grey.

The desert was the unknown that was being made known again. His empty soul was explaining itself, beginning to feel once more. He'd thought it could never have been filled. Now he knew it couldn't help being filled. There was too much to go into it. Each unexplored sand dune hid a regularly flashing light: living-dead-living-dead-living-dead. His mind had been empty for a purpose; its false fulness had created this emptiness in an act of creation.

A NOTE ABOUT THE AUTHOR

ALAN SILLITOE was born in 1928 in Nottingham, England, and grew up in the slums of that industrial city. The son of a laborer in a tannery, he left school at fourteen to work in a bicycle plant, then in a plywood mill, and later in another factory, as a capstan-lathe operator. He was called up just after the war and spent two years as an R.A.F. radio operator in Malaya. After his discharge, he married an American girl and lived for several years on Majorca, where he met and became friends with the poet Robert Graves. In a few short years, with the publication of six books of fiction and one of non-fiction, Mr. Sillitoe has come to be regarded as one of the most important British writers of the postwar decades. His first novel, SATURDAY NIGHT AND SUNDAY MORNING, *was awarded the Authors' Club prize for the best English first novel of 1958. His second book of fiction,* THE LONELINESS OF THE LONG-DISTANCE RUNNER, *won the coveted Hawthornden Prize in 1959. He has also written* THE GENERAL *(1961),* KEY TO THE DOOR *(1962),* THE RAGMAN'S DAUGHTER AND OTHER STORIES *(1964), and most recently* ROAD TO VOLGOGRAD *(1964).*

July 1965

A NOTE ON THE TYPE

JULIANA is a new Linotype face of
sixteenth-century Italian style, yet
entirely original, designed by S. L.
Hartz, an eminent Dutch typographer
and engraver.
This book is among the first to have
been printed in this type-face anywhere in the world.